The Lark and The Wren

Book I of
BARDIC VOICES

Baen Books From Mercedes Lackey

Bardic Voices: The Lark & The Wren
Knight of Ghosts and Shadows (with
 Ellen Guon)
Born to Run (with Larry Dixon)
Reap the Whirlwind (with C.J. Cherryh)

The Lark and The Wren

Book I of

MERCEDES LACKEY

This is a work of fiction. All the characters and events
portrayed in this book are fictional, and any resemblance
to real people or incidents is purely coincidental.

A Baen Books Original

Baen Publishing Enterprises
P.O. Box 1403
Riverdale, N.Y. 10471

Cover art by Darrell Sweet

Distributed by
SIMON & SCHUSTER
1230 Avenue of the Americas
New York, N.Y. 10020

Printed in the United States of America

***Dedicated to**
Ellen Guon;
writer, musician, and lady of quality
And to those who dream, then work to make
their dream a reality

The Lark and The Wren

Book I of
BARDIC VOICES

CHAPTER ONE

The attic cubicle was dark and stuffy, two conditions the tiny window under the eaves did little to alleviate. Rune reached up to the shelf over her pallet for her fiddle case, and froze with her hand less than an inch away. Her mother's nasal whine echoed up the stairs from the tavern sleeping rooms below.

"Rune? Rune!"

Rune sighed, and her hand dropped to her side. "Yes, Mother?" she called over her shoulder. She'd hoped to get a little practice in before the evening customers began to file in.

"Have you swept the tavern and scrubbed the tables?" When Stara said "the tavern," she meant the common room. The kitchen was not in Rune's purview. The cook, Annie, who was also the stableman's wife, reigned supreme there, and permitted no one within her little kingdom but herself and her aged helper, known only as Granny.

"No, Mother," Rune called down, resignedly. "I thought Maeve—"

"Maeve's doing the rooms. Get your behind down there. The sooner you get it over with, the sooner you can get on with that foolish scraping of yours." Then, as an afterthought, as Rune reached the top step, "And don't call me 'Mother.' "

"Yes M—Stara." Stifling another sigh, Rune plodded down the steep, dark attic stairs, hardly more than a ladder down the back wall. As she passed the open doors, she heard Maeve's tuneless humming and the slow scrape of a broom coming from the one on her right. From the bottom, she crossed the hall to the real stairs taking them two at a time down into the common room.

The shutters on the windows on two sides of the room had been flung wide to the brisk spring air; a light breeze slowly cleared out the last of the beer fumes. A half-worn broom leaned against the bar at the back of the room, where Maeve had undoubtedly left it when Stara ordered her upstairs. Rune took it; her first glance around had told her that nothing more had been accomplished except to open the shutters. The benches were still stacked atop the tables, and the latter pushed against the walls; the fireplace was still full of last night's ashes. Nothing had been cleaned or put into order, and the only sign that the tavern was opening for business was the open shutters. Probably because that was all anyone had thought to tell Maeve to do.

Rune went to the farthest corner of the room and started sweeping, digging the worn bristles of the broom firmly against the floorboards. The late Rose, wife of Innkeeper Jeoff, had called Maeve "an innocent." Annie said she was "a little simple."

What Stara called her was "a great lump."

Poor Maeve was all of those, Rune reflected. She lived in a world all her own, that was certain. She could—and did, if left to her own devices—stand in a window for hours, humming softly with no discernible tune, staring at nothing. But if you gave her clear orders, she would follow them to the exact letter. Told to sweep out a room, she would do so. That room, and no more, leaving a huge pile of dirt on the threshold. Told to wash the dishes, she would wash the dishes all right, but not the pots, nor the silverware, and she wouldn't rinse them afterwards. Of course, if anyone interrupted her in the middle of her task, she would drop what she was doing, follow the new instructions, and never return to the original job.

Still, without her help, Rune would have a lot more to do. She'd never have time to practice her fiddling.

Rune attacked the dirt of the floor with short, angry strokes, wishing she could sweep the troubles of her life out as easily. Not that life here was bad, precisely—

"Rune?" Stara called down the stairs. "Are you sweeping? I can't hear you."

"Yes M—Stara," Rune replied. The worn bristles were too soft to scrape the floor the way Maeve's broom was doing, but it was pointless to say anything about it.

So Stara didn't want to be called "Mother" anymore. Rune bit her lip in vexation. Did she really think that if Rune stopped referring to her as "Mother" people would forget their relationship?

Not here, Rune told herself sourly. *Not when my existence is such a pointed example of why good girls don't do That without wedding banns being posted.*

Even though Stara was from a village far from here—even though she wore the braids of a married woman and claimed that Rune's father had been a journeyman muleteer killed by bandits—most of the village guessed the real truth. That Stara was no lawfully wedded widow; that Rune was a bastard.

Stara had been a serving wench in the home of a master silversmith, and had let the blandishments of a peddler with a glib tongue and ready money lure her into his bed. The immediate result had been a silver locket and scarlet ribbons from his pack. The long-term result was a growing belly, and the loss of her place.

Stara lived on the charity of the Church for a time, but no longer than she had to. After Rune had been born, Stara had packed up her belongings and her meager savings, and set out on foot as far as her money would take her, hoping to find some place where her charm, her ability to wheedle, and her soft blond prettiness would win her sympathy, protection, and a new and better place.

Rune suspected that she had soon discovered—much to her shock— that while her looks, as always, won her the sympathy of the males of the households she sought employment with, she got no favor from the females. Certainly on the rare occasions when she talked to her daughter about those long-ago days, she had railed against the "jealous old bitches" who had turned her out again after they discovered what their spouses had hired.

And so would I have, Rune thought wryly, as the pile of dirt in front of her broom grew to the size of her closed fist. The girl Stara had been was all too likely to have a big belly again as soon as she'd wormed her way into the household. And this time, the result would have been sure to favor the looks of the master of the house. She had no credentials, no references—instead of applying properly to the women of the household, she went straight to the men. *Stupid, Mother. But then, you never have paid any attention to women when there were men around.*

But finally Stara had wound up here, at the "Hungry Bear." The innkeeper's wife, Rose, was of a credulous, generous and forgiving nature; Innkeeper Jeoff a pious Churchman, and charitable. That alone might not have earned her the place as the serving-maid in the tavern. But luck had been with her this time; their pot-boy had signed with the army and gone off to the city and there was no one in the village willing or able to take his place. Stara's arrival, even encumbered as she was, must have seemed like a gift from God, and they had needed her desperately enough to take her story at face value.

Although the villagers guessed most of the tale easily enough, they too were obliged to accept the false story (outwardly, at least), since Jeoff and Rose did. But Rune was never allowed to forget the truth. Stara threw it in Rune's face every time she was angry about anything— and the village children had lost no opportunity to imply she was a bastard for as long as she could remember.

They only said openly what their parents thought. Stara didn't seem to care, wearing low-cut blouses and kilted-up skirts when she went into the village on errands, flirting with the men and ignoring the sneers of the women. Back in the tavern, under Rose's eye, however, she had pulled the drawstrings of her blouses tight and let her skirts down, acting demure and briskly businesslike in all her dealings with males. Rune had more than once heard Rose defending her foundling to her friends among the villagers, telling Jeoff afterwards that they were just envious because of Stara's youth and attractiveness.

And that much was certainly true. The village women *were* jealous. Stara was enough to excite any woman's jealousy, other than a tolerant, easy-going lady like Rose, with her long, blond hair, her plump prettiness, her generous breasts and her willingness to display her charms to any eye that cared to look. Of course, none of this did any good at all for her reputation in the village, but Stara didn't seem to concern herself over trifles like what the villagers thought.

It was left to Rune to bear the brunt of her mother's reputation, to try to ignore the taunts and the veiled glances. Stara didn't care about that, either. So long as nothing touched or inconvenienced her directly, Stara was relatively content.

Only relatively, since Stara was not happy with her life as it was, and frequently voiced her complaints in long, after-hours monologues to her daughter, with little regard for whether or not Rune was going to suffer from loss of sleep the next day.

Last night had been one of those nights, and Rune yawned hugely as she swept.

Rune wasn't precisely certain what her mother wanted—besides a life of complete leisure. Just what Stara had done to reward such a life eluded Rune—but Stara seemed to feel quite strongly that she deserved it. And had gone on at aggrieved and shrill length about it last night. . . .

Rune yawned again, and swept the last of the night's trod-in dirt out into the road. It would, of course, find its way right back inside tonight; only in the great cities were the streets paved and kept clean. It was enough that the road through the village was graveled and graded, from one end to the other. It kept down the mud, and kept ruts to a minimum.

As well wish for Stara to become a pious churchgoer as to wish for a paved road. The second was likelier to occur than the first.

Rune propped the broom in a corner by the fireplace and emptied the ashes and clinkers into the ash-pit beneath the fireplace floor. Every few months the candle-maker came to collect them from the cellar; once a year the inn got a half-dozen bars of scented soap in exchange. A lot of the inn's supplies came from exchange; strawberries for manure, hay and straw for use of the donkey and pony, help for room and board and clothing.

There were four folk working under that exchange right now; of the six employees only two, Annie Cook and Tarn Hostler, received wages. The rest got only their rooms, two suits of clothing each year, and all they could eat. While Rune had been too young to be of much help, she'd had to share her mother's room, but now that she was pulling her share of her load, she had a room to herself. There wasn't a door, just a curtain, and there was no furniture but the pallet she slept on, but it was hers alone, and she was glad of the privacy. Not that Stara ever brought men up to her room—she wouldn't have dared; even the easy-going Rose would not have put up with that—but it was nice to be able to pull the curtain and pretend the outside world didn't exist.

Provided, of course, Stara didn't whine all night. There was no escaping that.

With the fireplace swept and logs laid ready to light, Rune fetched a pail of water, a bit of coarse brown soap, and a rag from the kitchen, with a nod to Granny, who sat in the corner peeling roots. Annie Cook was nowhere in sight; she was probably down in the cellar. From the brick ovens in the rear wall came a wave of heat and the mouth-watering smell of baking bread. Rune swallowed hard as her stomach growled. Breakfast had been a long time ago, and dinner too far away. She was always hungry these days, probably because she was growing like a sapling—the too-short cuffs of her shirt and breeches gave ample evidence of that.

If I hurry up, maybe I can get Granny to give me a bit of cheese and one of yesterday's loaf-ends before Annie makes them all into bread pudding.

With that impetus in mind, Rune quickly hauled the tables and benches away from the walls, got the benches down in place, and went to work on the tabletops, scouring with a will. Fortunately there weren't any bad stains this time; she got them done faster than she'd expected, and used the last of the soapy water to clean herself up before tossing the bucketful out the door.

But when she returned the bucket to the kitchen, Annie was back up from her journey below.

Her stomach growled audibly as she set the bucket down, and Annie looked up sharply, her round face red with the heat from the oven. "What?" she said, her hair coming loose from its pins and braids, and wisping damply about her head. "You can't be hungry *already*?"

Rune nodded mutely, and tried to look thin and pathetic.

She must have succeeded, for Annie shook her head, shrugged, and pointed her round chin towards the pile of ingredients awaiting her attention. "Two carrots, one loaf-end, and a piece of cheese, and get yerself out of here," the cook said firmly. "More than that can't be spared. And mind that piece is no bigger than your hand."

"Yes, Cook," Rune said meekly—and snatched her prizes before Annie changed her mind. But the cook just chuckled as she cut the cheese. "I should ha' known from yer breeches, darlin', yer into yer growth. Come back later if yer still hungry, an' I'll see if sommat got burnt too much fer the custom."

She thanked Annie with an awkward bob of her head, took her food out into the common room, and devoured it down to the last crumb, waiting all the while for another summons by her mother. But no call came, only the sound of Stara scolding Maeve, and Maeve's humming. Rune sighed with relief; Maeve never paid any attention to anything that wasn't a direct order. Let Stara wear her tongue out on the girl; the scolding would roll right off the poor thing's back—and maybe Stara would leave her own daughter alone, for once.

Rune stuffed that last bite of bread and cheese in her mouth and stole softly up the stairs. If she could just get past the sleeping rooms to get her fiddle—once she began practicing, Stara would probably leave her alone.

After all, she'd done her duty for the day. Sweeping and cleaning the common room was surely enough, especially after all the cleaning she'd done in the kitchen this morning. Sometimes she was afraid that her hands would stiffen from all the scrubbing she had to do. She massaged them with the lotion the farmers used on cow's udders, reckoning that would help, and it seemed to—but she still worried.

From the sound of things in the far room, Stara had decided to turn it out completely. She must have set Maeve to beating the straw tick; that monotonous thumping was definitely following the rhythm of Maeve's humming, and it was a safe enough task for even Maeve to manage. This time she got to her fiddle, and slipped down the stairs without being caught.

She settled herself into a bench in the corner of the room, out of direct line-of-sight of the stairs. It hadn't always been this hard to get her practice in. When Rose was alive, the afternoons had always been her own. Yes, and the evenings, too. As long as Rune helped, Rose had made it very clear that she was to be considered as full an employee as Stara—and Rose had counted entertainment as "helping."

Rose had forbidden Stara—or anyone else—to beat Rune, after the one time Rose had caught her mother taking a stick to her for some trifle.

Rune carefully undid the old clasps on the black leather-and-wood case. They were stiff with age, and hard to get open, but better too stiff than too loose. Rose had taken a special interest in Rune, for some reason. Maybe because Rose had no children of her own. But when Rose died of the cough last winter, everything changed.

At first it hadn't been bad, really; it made sense for Rune to take over some of Stara's duties, since Stara was doing what Rose had done. And work in the winter wasn't that difficult. Hardly anyone came in for midmeal, there were very few travelers to mess up the rooms, and people came for their beer and a bit of entertainment, but didn't stay late. There wasn't any dirt or mud to be tracked in, just melting snow, which soaked into the old worn floorboards fairly easily. Really, winter work was the lightest of the four seasons, and Rune had assumed that once the initial confusion following Rose's death resolved itself, Jeoff would hire someone else to help. Another boy, perhaps; a boy would be just as useful inside the inn as a girl, and stronger, too. There had even been a couple of boys passing through earlier this month on the way to the hiring fairs who'd looked likely. They'd put in a good day's work for their meal and corner by the fire—and they'd even asked Rune if she thought Jeoff would be interested in hiring them on permanently. But Jeoff always found some excuse not to take them on—and Rune kept losing a little more of her free time with every day that passed.

Now she not only found herself scrubbing and cleaning, she was serving in the common room at night, something she hadn't had to do since she was a good enough fiddler to have people ask her to play. That was one of the reasons the Hungry Bear was so popular; even when there weren't any traveling musicians passing through, people could always count on Rune to give 'em a tune to sing or dance to. Why, people sometimes came from as far away as the next village of Beeford because of her.

But now—she was allowed to play only when the crowds asked Jeoff for her music. If they forgot to ask, if there was no one willing to speak up—then she waited on them just like silly Maeve, while Stara presided in Rose's place over the beer barrels, and Jeoff tended, as always, to the cashbox.

Rune bit her lip, beginning to see a pattern in all this. There were more changes, and they were even more disturbing. There was no doubt in Rune's mind that her mother had set her sights on Jeoff. Aiming, no doubt, for matrimony.

When Rose was alive, Stara had kept herself quietly out of sight, her hair tightly braided and hidden under kerchiefs, wearing her blouse-strings pulled tight, her skirts covering her feet, and keeping her eyes down. Rune knew why, too—Stara flung it in her face often enough. Stara had one bastard; she was not minded to attract the master's eye, only to find herself in his bed and saddled with another bastard.

But since Jeoff put off his mourning bands, Stara had transformed from a drab little sparrow to a bird of a different feather entirely. She was rinsing her hair with herbs every night, to make it yellow as new-minted gold and smell sweet. She had laced the waist of her skirts tight, kilted them up to show ankles and even knees, and pulled her blouses low. And she was painting her face, when she thought no one could see her; red on the lips and cheeks, blackening her lashes with soot, trying to make herself look younger. Where she got the stuff, Rune had no idea. Possibly a peddler, though there hadn't been any with things like that through here since before winter.

Stara didn't like being reminded that she had a fourteen-year-old daughter, and she certainly didn't want Jeoff reminded of the fact. It helped that Rune looked nothing like her mother; Rune was tall, thin, with light brown, curly hair, and deep brown eyes. She could—and occasionally did—pass for a boy in the crowded common room. She was nothing at all like soft, round, doll-pretty Stara. Which was exactly as Stara wanted things, Rune was sure of it.

For there was a race on to see who'd snare Jeoff. Maeve was no competition; the girl was plain as well as simple—although it was a good thing she *was* plain, or she would have been fair game for any fellow bent on lifting a skirt. Rune wasn't interested—and half the time Jeoff absentmindedly called her "lad" anyway.

Stara's only competition would come from the village. There were a couple of young women down there in Westhaven of marriageable age, whose fathers saw nothing wrong with running a good, clean inn. Fathers who would not be averse to seeing their daughters settled in as the innkeeper's wife. None were as pretty as Stara—but they all had dowers, which she did not. And they *were* younger, with plenty of childbearing years ahead of them.

Much younger, some of them. One of the possible prospects was only sixteen. Not that much older than Stara's daughter. No wonder Stara wanted to be thought younger than she was.

Rune got out her fiddle and began tuning it. It was a little too cold to be playing outside—but Jeoff liked hearing the music, and once she started playing it was unlikely that Stara would order her to do something else.

The gift of the fiddle had been Rose's idea. She'd watched as Rune begged to play with traveling minstrels' instruments—and had begun to coax something like music out of them right away—she'd seen Rune trying to get a good tune out of a reed whistle, a blade of grass, and anything else that made a noise. Perhaps she had guessed what Rune might do with a musical instrument of her own. For whatever reason, when Rune was about six, a peddler had run off without paying, leaving behind a pack filled with trash he hadn't been able to sell. One of the few things in it worth anything was the fiddle, given immediately to Rune, which Rune had named "Lady Rose" in honor of her patron.

It had taken many months of squealing and scraping out in the stable where she wouldn't offend any ears but the animals' before she was able to play much. But by the time she was eight, minstrels were going out of their way to give her a lesson or two, or teach her a new song. By the time she was ten, she was a regular draw.

Rune was smart enough to remember what the common room had looked like on any day other than a market-day before she had started to play regularly—and she knew what it was like now. Rose's "investment" had paid off handsomely over the years—gaining in new business several times over the worth of the old fiddle.

But Stara—and there was no doubt in Rune's mind who was behind all the changes—evidently didn't see things that way, or thought that now that the extra custom was here, it would stay here. Rose could have told her differently, told her how it wasn't likely the Hungry Bear would hold anyone who didn't actually belong in Westhaven if there wasn't something beyond the beer to offer them. But Rose wasn't here, and Jeoff was not the kind to worry about tomorrow until it arrived.

On the other hand, although Stara was behind the changes, Jeoff was behind the cashbox. If Rune pointed out to him that he was losing money right now, that people weren't coming from outside the village bounds, and that those within the village weren't staying as long of an evening because she wasn't playing, well, maybe he'd put a stop to this, and hire on a good strong boy to do some of the work.

She thought again about going outside to practice, but the breeze coming in the window decided her against the idea. It was really too cold out there; her fingers would stiffen in no time.

She tuned the fiddle with care for its old strings; she wanted to replace them, but strings were hard to come by in this part of the world. If she was lucky, maybe a peddler would have a set. Until then, she'd just have to make sure she didn't snap one.

She closed her eyes for a moment, and let her fingers select the first couple of notes. The tune wandered a bit, before it settled on a jig, a good finger-warmer, and one of the earliest melodies she'd learned. "Heart for the Ladies," it was called, and folks around here usually called for it twice or three times a night when they were in the mood for dancing.

Rune closed her eyes again; she remembered the woman who had taught it to her as clearly as something that had happened yesterday.

Linnet had been her name, so she said; odd, how many of the traveling players had bird-names. Or maybe they just assumed bird-names when they started playing. Linnet had been one of a trio of traveling minstrels doing the Faire circuit, a mandolin player, herself on flute, and a drummer. Linnet was a tiny thing, always smiling, and ready with a kind word for a child. She had more hair than Rune had ever seen let down on a woman; she didn't wear it in a wife's braids, nor loose under a coif like a maid. The coppery-brown tresses were twined with flowers and piled in loose coils about her head when Rune first saw her, and later, it was tied in two long tails bound around with leather and thongs for traveling. When she let it down, it reached past her knees.

She had been as ready with her help as her smiles. When Rune brought out her fiddle, and attempted to follow their tunes silently, fingering but not bowing, she had taken the girl aside and played "Heart for the Ladies" over and over until Rune had gotten it in her head, then helped her to find the fingerings for it on the fiddle.

And then, the next day, when the trio had gone their way, Rune had practiced the piece for hours until she got it right. She'd waited until someone in the crowd that night saw her and called out, "Well, little Rune, and have ye got a new piece for us to hear?" the way some of them used to, half in earnest, half to tease her. This time, she'd answered "yes," and brought out her fiddle.

She'd surprised them all with the jig, so much so that they'd made her play it again and again—and then, several times more, so that they all could dance to it.

That night had brought her a pair of copper bits, the first time she'd been paid for her fiddling. It had been a heady moment, made all the headier by the first money she had ever owned.

She played the jig over twice more, until her fingers felt flexible and strong, ready for anything she might ask of them.

But what she asked of them next was the very latest piece she had learned, a slow, languorous love song. The lilting melody was the kind of song popular at weddings, but mostly not in the tavern.

A real fiddler had taught her this one; this and near two dozen more.

She smiled to think of him. Oh, he was a villainous-looking lad, with a patch over one eye, and all in gypsy-colors, half a brigand by his looks. But he had played like an angel, he had. And he'd stayed several days the first time he'd stopped at the Bear—because of the bad weather for traveling, so he'd said, and indeed, it had been raining heavily during all that time. But he'd had a horse—a pony, rather—a sturdy beast that was probably quite capable of taking him through rain and snow and anything else he might ask of it. It wasn't weather that had kept him, but his own will.

The rains pounded the area for a week, providing him ample excuse. So he stayed, and enlivened the tavern by night, bringing folks in from all over, despite the weather. And he'd schooled Rune by day.

Quite properly, despite her early fears as to his behavior. Fears—well, that wasn't quite true, it was half hope, actually, for despite his rascally appearance, or even because of it, she'd wondered if he'd pay court to her. . . .

She certainly knew at thirteen what went on between man and maid, male and female. She had taken some thought to it, though she wasn't certain what it was she wanted. The ballads were full of sweet courtings, wild ones, and no courtings at all—

But he was as correct with her as he had been bawdy with the men in the tavern the night before. He'd stopped her on her way to some trivial errand, as he was eating his luncheon in the otherwise empty common room.

"I hear you play the fiddle, young Rune," he'd said. She had nodded, suddenly shy, feeling as awkward as a young calf.

"Well?" he'd said then, a twinkle in the one eye not covered with a patch. "Are you going to go fetch it, or must I beg you?"

She had run to fetch it, and he'd begun her lesson, the first of four, and he had made her work, too. She worked as hard at her fiddling under his critical eye as she'd ever worked at any task in the tavern.

He saved the love songs until the last day—"A reward," he'd said, "for being a good student"—for they were the easiest of the lot.

If he'd introduced them at the beginning of the lessons, she might have suspected them of being a kind of overture. But he'd waited until the last day of his stay, when he'd already told her that he was leaving the following morning. So the songs came instead as a kind of gift from a friend, for a friend was what Raven had come to be. And she treasured them as completely as she would have treasured any material gift.

He'd returned over the winter, and again the next summer, and this winter again. That was when he had taught her this melody, "Fortune, My Foe." He should be coming through again, once the weather warmed. She was looking forward to seeing him again, and learning more things from him. Not just songs—though courting was not on her mind, either. There was so much she needed to learn, about music, about reading it and writing it. There were songs in her head, words as well as music, but she couldn't begin to get them out. She didn't know how to write the tunes down, and she didn't have enough reading and writing of words to get her own down properly so that another could read them. She had barely enough of writing to puzzle out bits of the Holy Book, just like every other child of the village, and there was no learned Scholar-Priest here to teach her more. There must be more . . . there must be a way to write music the way words were written, and there must be more words than she knew. She needed all of that, needed to learn it, and if anyone would know the way of such things, Raven would, she sensed it in her bones.

Raven was weeks away, though. And she would have to be patient and wait, as the Holy Book said women must be patient.

Even though she was almighty tired of being patient.

Oh, enough of such lazy tunes.

The trill of an early songbird woke another melody in her fingers, and that led to many more. All reels this time, and all learned from a rough-faced, bearded piper just a few weeks ago. He'd come to play for the wedding of some distant relations, and though he had not made any formal attempt at giving her lessons, when he watched her frowning and following his music silently, he'd played everything at least three times over until she smiled and nodded by way of a signal that she'd got the tune straight in her head.

He'd gone before nightfall, not staying—he couldn't have played at the tavern anyway; the pipes were *not* an instrument for indoors.

But this winter, after her fiddler had come and gone, there had been a harper who had stayed for nearly two weeks. He was a Guild Minstrel, and was taking a position at the court of the Sire. He was ahead of time, having come much faster than anyone would have ever expected because of a break in the weather, and had taken the opportunity to rest a bit before taking the last leg of the journey.

He was an old man, his hair half silver, and he had been very kind to her. He'd taught her many of the songs popular at the courts, and she had painstakingly adapted them for fiddle. He hadn't had much patience, but fortunately the melodies were all simple ones, easy to remember, and easy to follow.

But from those simple songs, her fingers slowed, and strayed into a series of laments, learned from another harpist, a real Gypsy, who would not come into the village at all. Rune had found her with her fellows, camped beyond the bridge as she had returned from an errand. Unaccountably, eerily, the girl had known who she was, and what instrument she played. It still gave Rune a chill to think of her, and wonder how it was the other musician had known all about her.

She'd stopped Rune as the girl lingered, watching the Gypsies with burning curiosity. "I am Nightingale. Bring your fiddle," she'd said abruptly, with no preamble. "I shall teach you songs such as you have never heard before."

With a thrill of awe and a little fear, Rune had obeyed. It had been uncanny then, and it was uncanny now. How had Nightingale known who she was, and what she did? No one in the village would have told her—surely.

And indeed, Nightingale had taught her music the like of which she had never heard before. The strange, compelling dance music was too complicated to learn in a single afternoon—but the laments stuck in her mind, and seemed to make her fingers move of their own accord. . . .

"Rune!"

She started, and opened her eyes. Stara had a mug in one hand, and most of the rest up on their pegs, above the beer barrels, and she had turned to stare at Rune with a strange, uneasy expression on her face. Rune got ready for a tongue-lashing; whenever Stara was unhappy or uneasy, she took it out on someone. And Maeve wasn't within reach right now.

"Haven't you practiced enough for one day?" Stara snapped crossly. "You give me the chills with that Gypsy howling. It sounds like lost souls, wailing for the dead."

Well, that was what it was supposed to sound like—

"—or cats in heat," Stara concluded, crudely. "Haven't you got anything better to do than to torture our ears with that?"

"I—" she began.

A cough interrupted her, and she glanced over at the door to the kitchen. Jeoff stood there, with a keg of the dark ale on one shoulder.

"We're going to be working in here for a while, Rune," he said. "I don't want to sound mean, but—that music bothers me. It's like you're calling something I'd rather not see."

Meaning he's feeling superstitious, Rune thought cynically.

"Don't you think Jib could use your help in the stables?" he said—but it sounded like an order.

"Yes, sir," she said, trying not to sound surly. *Just when I was really getting warmed up. It figures.* "I'll see to it, Master Jeoff."

But as she put her fiddle away, she couldn't help watching Jeoff and her mother out of the corner of her eye. There was something going on there, and it had nothing to do with the music.

It looked like Stara's ploys were working.

The only question was—where did that leave Rune?

CHAPTER TWO

With her fiddle safely stowed away, Rune made her reluctant way to the stable-yard—such as it was. This little road wasn't used by too many people, certainly not the kind of people who would be riding high-bred horses that required expensive stabling. When the Sire traveled, he took the roads patrolled and guarded by the Duke's Men. And when someone was sent to collect taxes and take the man-count, it was never anyone important, just a bailiff. This village never gave any trouble, always paid its taxes with a minimum of cheating, and in general was easy to administer to. There were robbers, occasionally, but when robbers cropped up, a quick foray into the woods by the local men usually took care of them. There were places said to be dangerous, because of magic or supernatural menaces, but the road bypassed them. People who traveled between here and Beeford were simple people, without much in the way of valuables.

So the stable was a bare place, nothing more than four walls and a roof, with a loft and a dirt floor. Half of it was the storage place for hay and straw—no grain; the inn pony and donkey were sturdy enough to live on thistles if they had to, hay and grass suited them very well. The other half had been partitioned into rough stalls. There was a paddock, where beasts could be turned loose if their owners couldn't afford stable-fees, or the inn beasts could be put if their stalls were needed for paying tenants. That had never happened in Rune's experience, though they had come near to it in Faire season. The loft stood over the half where hay was stored, and that was where Jib slept, hemmed in and protected by bales of hay, and generally fairly snug. Tarn Hostler, the stable-master, slept with his wife Annie Cook in her room next to the kitchen. In the winter, Jib slept next to the kitchen fire with Granny.

Rune hoped, as she took herself out the kitchen door, that Jib wouldn't try to court her again today. He was her best friend—in point of fact, he was her only friend—but he was the last person she wanted courting her.

She'd been trying to discourage him; teasing him, ignoring his clumsy attempts at gallantry, laughing at his compliments. She could understand why he had the silly idea that he was in love with her, and it had nothing to do with her looks or her desirability. There were two available women here at the Bear, for Jib was too lowly ever to be able to pay court to one of the village girls. And of the two of them, even a blind man would admit she was preferable to Maeve.

Jib was fine as a friend—but nothing more. For one thing, he was at least a year younger than Rune. For another—he just wasn't very bright. He didn't understand half of what she said to him, sometimes. He wasn't at all ambitious, either; when Rune asked him once what he wanted to be when he was a man, he'd looked at her as if she was crazed. He was perfectly happy being the stableboy, and didn't see any reason for that to change. He didn't want to leave the village or see anything of the outside world but the Faire at Beeford. The only wish he'd ever expressed to her was to become a local horse-trader, selling the locally bred, sturdy little ponies and cobs to bigger traders who would take them to the enormous City Faires. He didn't even want to take the horses there himself.

And—to be honest—when a girl dreamed of a lover, she didn't dream of a boy with coarse, black hair, buck teeth, ears like a pair of jug handles, a big round potato of a nose, and spots. Of course, he'd probably grow out of the spots, but the rest was there to stay.

All in all, she wished he'd decide to settle for Maeve. They'd probably suit one another very well as long as he told her exactly what to do. . . .

The yard was deserted, and Tarn Hostler was grooming the two beasts in the paddock, alone, but Rune heard straw rustling and knew where she'd find Jib. And sure enough, when she entered the stable, there he was, forking straw into a pair of stalls.

She grabbed a pitchfork and went to help him, filling the mangers with fresh hay, and rinsing and filling the water buckets at the paddock pump. The pony, Dumpling (brown and round as one of Cook's best dumplings), and the donkey, Stupid (which he was not), watched her with half-closed eyes as old Tarn gave them a carefully currycombing, brushing out clouds of winter hair. They knew the schedule as well as anyone. Bring back loads of wood for the ovens on Monday, haul food for the inn on Tuesday, wood again on Wednesday (but this time for the baker in the village), be hitched to the grindstone on Thursday, since the village had no water-mill, wood again on Friday for the woodcutter himself, odd jobs on Saturday, and be hitched to the wagon to take everyone to Church on Sunday. They'd done their duty for the day. Now they could laze about the yard and be groomed, then put in their stalls for the night, once Jib and Rune finished cleaning them.

"Hey, Rune," Jib said, after trying to get her attention by clearing his throat several times.

"You ought to see Annie about that cough you've got," she interrupted him. "It sounds really bad."

"My cough?" he replied, puzzled. "I don't have a cough."

"You've been hemming and hacking like a wheezy old man ever since I got out here," she replied sharply. "Of course you have a cough. You ought to take care of it. Get Annie to dose you. I'll tell her about it—"

"Uh, no, please," he said, looking alarmed, as well he might. Annie's doses were fearsome things that took the skin off a person's tongue and left a nasty, lingering taste in the back of the throat for days afterwards. "I'm fine, really I am, please, don't tell Annie I'm sick—"

He babbled on about how healthy he was for some time; Rune paid scant attention, simply pleased that she'd managed to elude whatever he'd planned to ask her. With that much nervousness showing, it had to be romantic in nature, at least by Jib's primitive standards of romance.

Which were at best, one step above Dumpling's.

She looked about for something else to distract him when he finally wound down, but fate took a hand for her—for his babble was interrupted by the sounds of hooves on the hard-packed dirt outside, and a strange voice.

They both ran to see who it was, just as they had when they were children, Rune reaching the stable door a little before Jib.

At first glance, the newcomer looked to be a peddler; his pony had two largish packs on its back, and he was covered from head to knee in a dust-colored cloak. But then he pulled the cloak off, and shook it, and Rune saw he was dressed in a linen shirt with knots of multi-colored ribbon on the sleeves, a bright blue vest, and fawn-colored breeches. Only one kind of traveler would dress like that, and her guess was confirmed when he pulled a lute in its case out of one of the packs.

He was very tall, taller than Rune, and lanky, with dust-colored hair, and wonderfully gentle brown eyes. The stable-master saw them both gawking from the shelter of the doorway, and waved them over abruptly.

They obeyed at once; Tarn told them to groom the minstrel's pony and put it in one of the prepared stalls, then come fetch the inn beasts when a third stall was ready. He himself took the stranger's packs, leading him into the inn as if he owned it.

Jib and Rune eyed each other over the empty pack-saddle. "Flip you for it," Rune said. Jib nodded wordlessly, and Rune bent down long enough to fetch a pebble from the dust at her feet. She spat on it, and tossed it into the air, calling out, "Wet!" as it fell.

It landed wet side up, and Jib shrugged philosophically.

She led the visitor's pony into one of the stalls, unsaddled him and hung his tack over the wall of his stall, and gave him a brisk grooming. He seemed to enjoy it, leaning into the strokes of the currycomb with an expression of bliss on his round little face.

When she had finished, Jib was still forking in hay for the new stall. She turned the pony loose in this temporary home, made sure that the door was secure (some ponies were wizards at finding ways to escape), and took herself back into the inn.

She was met at the inner door by her mother, who barred the way with her arm across the doorway. "His name is Master Heron and he's on his way to the Lycombe Faire," she said, as Rune fidgeted. "He promised Jeoff he'd play tonight, and that means that you serve."

"Yes, M—Stara," she replied, catching herself at the last minute before saying the forbidden word.

"Jeoff wants you to go down to the village and make the rounds of all the Guildsmen," Stara continued. "He wants you to tell them all that Master Heron will be entertaining tonight; from them it will spread to everyone else in Westhaven."

"Yes, Stara," Rune said, curbing her impatience.

"He has to be on his way first thing in the morning if he's going to make the Faire in time," Stara finished, dashing Rune's hopes for a lesson. "And you'd better be on your way now, if we're going to have the extra custom tonight."

Rune sighed, but said nothing more. If she got down to the village before the men went home to their suppers, they'd likely eat lightly or not at all, those who could afford to. Then they'd come here, and eat plates of salt-laden sausage rolls and sharp cheese while they listened to the minstrel, making themselves thirsty. They'd drink plenty of beer tonight to drown the salty sausages. Jeoff was probably already hauling up extra kegs and putting them behind the bar. It would be a good night for the inn.

And at least Rune would hear some new songs. If she was lucky, the minstrel would repeat them enough for her to learn one or two.

She turned and started down the path to the village, hoping to get back quickly enough not to miss anything.

The village of Westhaven was set back from the road, because there wasn't enough flat land for more than the inn right up beside it. Those who had business in Westhaven itself—not many—took the path up the valley to find the village. Rune usually enjoyed the walk, although it was a bit long, and a little frightening after the sun went down. But today, halfway between the inn and the first buildings of the village itself, she stopped; the path was blocked by two of Westhaven's girls, Joyse and Amanda, gossiping in the middle of the path and making no effort to move out of the way.

They knew she was coming; they could hardly miss her. But they pretended not to notice her, clutching baskets of early flowers and keeping their heads close together. Joyse, as blond as Stara, but thin, was the baker's daughter; Amanda, as round and brown as Dumpling, but without the pony's easy-going nature, was the offspring of one of the local farmers. Joyse, with her hair neatly confined under a pretty red scarf that matched her brand new kirtle, was betrothed already to another farmer's son. Amanda, in a blue dress that looked almost as new, but was already straining at the seams around her middle, was one of the contenders to replace Rose. From the way it looked, one or the other had been up to the inn, possibly to spy on Rune, Stara, or both. Rune had the feeling that Amanda would do just about anything to become the innkeeper's new wife, except surrendering her virginity before taking wedding vows.

Both girls looked down their noses at Rune as she approached slowly.

"Well, I wish *I* had time to play games in the hay and flirt with boys," Amanda said nastily. "Of course, some people have lots of time. Some people have all the time they want, not just to play games, but to pretend they're minstrels."

Joyse laughed shrilly, showing buckteeth, and looking uncannily like a skinny old mare whinnying.

"And *some* people are so lazy, they pretend to be working, when all they really do is stand around and make up stories because the truth is too dull," Rune said aloud, to a squirrel in one of the trees beside her. It chattered, as if it was responding to her. "And *some* people are so fat they block the path, so people with work to do can't travel it. And of course, *some* people are so bad-tempered that no one will have them for a wife, not even with a big dower."

Amanda squealed with rage, turning to face her directly, and Rune pretended to notice her for the first time. "Why Amanda, I didn't see you there. I thought it was a pony blocking the path."

Amanda's round face turned bright red, and her hands balled into fists beside her skirt. "You, little bastard-brat—were you talking about me?"

"Talking about you?" Rune shrugged, and pretended surprise. "Why would I bother? There's nothing at all interesting about you. I'd put

myself and that squirrel to sleep talking about you. Besides, you know
what Father Jacob says about gossiping. He says that women who spend
their time in idle gossip spend three hundred years in hell when they
die, with their lips sewn shut.'' She shuddered artistically. ''I'd never
want to end up like that.''

''I'll show *you* how you'll end up,'' Amanda hissed, taking a step
forward.

But Joyse grabbed her shoulder, bent to her ear, and whispered something fiercely to her, stopping her. Rune had a fairly good idea what the
general gist of the advice was, because the last time any of the Westhaven youngsters had tried to turn a confrontation with Rune into something
physical, it had ended with the girl getting her hair rubbed full of mud
while Rune sat on her back. Not even the boys wanted to risk a physical
fight with her; she was taller and stronger than most of them, and knew
some tricks of dirty fighting Tarn had taught both her and Jib (though
Jib never kept his head long enough to use them) that they didn't.

Rune took one deliberate step forward, then a second. Joyse whispered
something else, her eyes round with urgency, and Amanda backed up—
then turned, and the two of them flounced their way up the path. Rune
watched them go, seething inwardly, but refusing to show it.

She'd won—sort of. In most ways, though, it had been a draw. They
could continue to pick on her verbally, and she could do nothing, and
they all three knew it. Most of the time she couldn't even get her own
hits in when it was a verbal confrontation. It wasn't fair.

She waited a few more minutes for them to get far enough ahead of
her that she shouldn't have to encounter them again, then continued on
her way. Slower, this time, trying to get her temper to cool by listening
to the blackbirds singing their hearts out in the trees around her, trying
to win themselves mates.

There was this much satisfaction; at least this time she'd been able to
give as good as she got. And none of them would try to touch even Jib,
these days, not even in a group. Everyone knew she was Jib's protector.
She wasn't averse to using teeth and feet as well as fists when she was
cornered, either. They *had* to keep their abuse verbal.

One of these days I'm going to write a song about them, she thought
angrily. *About Amanda, Joyse, all of them. All of them pretending to be
so much better than me . . . but Amanda steals her mother's egg-money,
and Joyse only got Thom because her father promised to help his father
cheat on his taxes. And they don't know I know about it. That'd serve
them right, to go to a Faire and hear some strange minstrel singing a
song mocking them.*

Not a one of them ever missed a chance to tell her that she was scum. It would be nice to watch their faces as someone told *them* exactly what they were. And why not? When Raven came, maybe she could get him to help her with that song. With his help, surely it would be picked up by other singers.

Savoring that sweet thought, she picked up her pace a little. The first stop was going to be the chandler's shop.

Maybe with luck she'd get through this without having any more little "encounters."

After the chandler, she left her message at the tannery and the baker's, wishing she could stay longer and savor the wonderful aromas there. The baker said nothing about her little encounter with his daughter; she hadn't really expected that he would. If he knew about it, he'd likely just chalk it up to the "bastard-brat's" bad breeding. But since Rune had gotten the better of that exchange, and in fact had not said a single thing that—taken literally—could be called an insult, she doubted either girl would even mention it to a parent.

In fact, she thought, as she crossed the lane to the smithy, she'd handled it rather well. She'd simply said that some people were fat, were gossips, and couldn't get a husband because they had such terrible tempers. She'd only repeated what the Westhaven priest—shared with Beeford—had told all of them about the fate of gossiping women. She hadn't once said that either Amanda or Joyse were anything other than dull. And while that was an insult, it was hardly one that was anything other than laughable.

The smithy was full; Hob and his two older apprentices, hard at work on sharpening farm tools gone rusty after a winter's storage. They stopped work long enough to hear what she had to say; she spoke her piece quickly, for the forge was hot as a midsummer day, and plain took her breath away. All three men paid her little heed until they heard her news. Then they reacted with considerably more enthusiasm; it had been several weeks since the last real minstrel had been through, after all, and spring had brought with the new growth a predictable restlessness on everyone's part. Tonight's entertainment would give them a welcome outlet for some of that restlessness.

The next stop on Rune's mental list, as she passed behind the smithy and the blacksmith resumed his noisy work, was the carpenter—she'd take this shortcut behind the smithy, between it and its storage sheds, for the smithy and the carpenter's shop lay a little to one side of Westhaven proper, on the other side of the tiny village pond, out where their pounding wouldn't disturb anyone, and where, if the smithy caught fire, there'd be no danger of houses taking flame.

"Well, look what jest wandered inta town." The blacksmith's son Jon stepped out from the side of the shop, blocking her path.

She stopped; he grinned, showing a mouth with half the teeth missing, and rubbed his nose on the back of his hand, sniffing noisily. His manners hadn't improved over the winter. "You lookin' fer me, girl?" he drawled.

She didn't answer, and she didn't acknowledge him. Instead, she turned slowly, figuring that it would be better—much better—if she simply pretended to ignore him. He'd grown over the winter. Quite a bit, in fact. Suddenly, her feeling of superiority to the rest of the village youngsters began to evaporate.

As Hill and Warran, two of the farm boys, moved out from the other side of the blacksmith shop to block her escape, the last of her assumption of superiority vanished. They'd grown over the winter, too. All three of them were taller than she was, and Jon had huge muscles in his arms and shoulders that matched his father's. Becoming his father's apprentice on his fifteenth birthday had developed his body beyond anything she would have anticipated.

It hadn't done much for his mind, though. She whirled at a sound behind her, and saw that he had already moved several paces closer.

"What do you want, Jon?" she asked, trying to sound bored. "I'm busy. I'm supposed to be delivering messages from Master Jeoff. I left one with your *father*," she concluded pointedly.

"What's the matter?" he asked, scratching his behind with one sooty hand, and grinning still wider. "You in a big hurry t' get back t' yer lo-o-over?" He laughed. "What's Jib got, huh? Nothin', that's what."

So, now it was out in the open, instead of being sniggered about, hinted at. Someone had finally said to her face what everyone in Westhaven had been telling each other for a year.

"He's not my lover," she said as calmly as she could. "I don't have any *lover*."

"Then maybe it's time you got one," said Hill, snickering. "Little lovin' might do you some good, string bean. Teach you what a woman's for."

"Aww, Hill, she just means she ain't got a *real* lover," Jon said genially, flexing the muscles of his shoulders, presumably for her benefit. "She just means she wants one, eh?"

"I meant what I said," she told him defiantly.

"Ah, don't fool around, Rune. We know your Mam's been in ol'

Jeoff's bed since Rose died. An' we know 'bout you. Your Mam wasn't any more married than m' Dad's anvil.'' He advanced, and she backed up—into Hill's and Warran's hands. She suppressed a yelp as they grabbed her. "You got no call pretendin' that you're all goody-good.'' She struggled in the farm boys' hands; they simply tightened their grips.

She stopped fighting, holding very, very still, part of her mind planning every second of the next few minutes, the rest of her too scared to squeak. "Let me go," she said, slowly, clearly, and sounding amazingly calm even to herself.

"Yer Mam's a whore," Jon said, his grin turning cruel, as he reached out for her. "Yer Mam's a whore, an' yer a whore's daughter, an' if yer not a whore now, ye will be—"

He grabbed her breast, crushing it in his hand and hurting her, as he slammed his foul mouth down on hers, trying to force her lips open with his tongue.

She opened her mouth and let his tongue probe forward—and bit down on it, quick, and as hard as she could, tasting blood briefly.

At the same time, she slammed her knee up into his crotch.

As Jon screamed and fell away from her, she brought her heel down hard on Hill's instep, and slammed her head back against his teeth. That hurt, and she reckoned she'd cut her scalp a bit, but it surely hurt him worse.

Hill let out a hoarse cry and let go of her immediately, and bumbled into Warran. She pivoted as much as she could with Warran still holding onto her, and kicked Hill in the knee, toppling him; he went down, taking Warran with him. As Warran fell, she managed to pull free of the last boy's grip—and she pelted away as fast as her legs would carry her, never once looking back to see if she'd hurt them seriously or not.

She ran all the way out of the village, her side aching, her head hurting, half blinded with fright. No matter who might have been following her, she still had longer legs and better wind than any of them. When she slowed and finally paused, near where she'd been stopped by the girls earlier, she couldn't hear any pursuit.

That was when she started to shake.

She started to drop to her knees beside the path, then thought better of the idea. What if there was someone following? What if the boys recovered and decided to come after her?

But she had one place of shelter, one they wouldn't know about—one that was completely defensible.

She got off the path somehow, and fought her way through the brush some twenty or thirty feet into the forest. And there was her shelter, the biggest oak tree for miles around. She forced her shaking legs to carry her up the side of the forest giant, and into the huge fork, completely hidden from below by the new young leaves of lesser trees. There she curled up, and let her mind go blank, while she shook with reaction.

After a while, her heart stopped pounding in her ears, and she stopped feeling sick to her stomach. Mostly, anyway.

Her mind began to work again, if slowly.

She put her hand to the back of her head, but surprisingly, didn't come away with any blood on it, though she felt the hard lump of a rising goose egg back there. That, and a torn and dirty shirt were the worst she'd taken out of the encounter.

This time.

She chewed some young leaves to get the nasty taste of Jon out of her mouth, but she couldn't get the nasty feel of him out of her mind.

One thing was certain; her immunity had vanished with the snows of winter. The girls might leave her alone, but she was completely at the mercy of the boys, even in daylight. The girls might even have set their brothers on her; that would certainly fit Amanda and Joyse's personalities. And that this attack had taken place in daylight meant that they were not particularly worried about hiding their actions from their parents.

That meant their parents didn't care what they were doing to her. If anything happened to her, nothing would be done to punish her attackers. That had always been true—but the threat of attack had never included rape before.

The boys had said it all; her mother was a whore, she was the daughter of a whore, therefore she was a whore. No one would believe anything else. Anything that happened to her would be her own fault, brought on her own actions, or simply by being born of bad blood.

Not even the Priest would help, unless she took holy vows. And even then—he might not believe that she was an innocent, and he might refuse her the protection of the Church. She had nowhere to turn to for help, and no one to depend on but herself.

How long was it going to be before she was cornered by a gang she *couldn't* escape? It was only the purest luck, and the fact that they hadn't expected her to fight back, that had let her get away this time.

Next time she might not be so lucky.

Next time, they might win.

The realization made her start to shake all over again.

It felt like hours later that she managed to get herself under control, and climb down out of the tree—but when she made her way back to the inn, no one seemed to have missed her. At least, no one seemed to think she had taken an extraordinary amount of time to deliver her messages.

After much thought, she had decided to keep quiet about the attack; after all, what good would complaining about it do? None of this would have happened if the boys hadn't been sure they were safe from punishment. Jeoff wouldn't do anything to risk the anger of his customers, Stara and Annie Cook would be certain she'd brought it on herself, and Jib would only get himself into fights he couldn't hope to win. No one would care, at least, not enough to help protect her.

But she could protect herself, in clever ways. She could refuse to go into the village alone, or better still, she could send Jib to run errands for her, trading chore for chore. Even if it meant more of the kind of work that might stiffen her hands. . . .

Better that, than the little entertainments Jon and his friends had planned.

But she didn't have long to brood on her troubles, for despite the fact that she hadn't been able to deliver more than half her messages, word of the new minstrel had traveled all through the village, and the men and their wives were already beginning to take their places behind the rough wooden tables. There were three couples there already; the baker and his wife, and a couple of the nearer farmers and their spouses. The place would be full tonight, for certain.

She dashed upstairs to change her torn shirt for a clean, older one— a loose and baggy one that didn't show anything of her figure—making sure no one saw her to ask about what had happened to the first shirt.

She stripped off the shirt and frowned—more in anger now, than fear—at the bruises on her breast. She touched it gingerly; it was going to hurt more later than it did now, and it hurt bad enough now that she waited long enough to wrap her chest in a supporting and protecting— and concealing—band of cloth. She slipped the new shirt over her head, pledging herself that she'd find a way to make Jon hurt as much as he'd hurt her.

If he didn't already. She hoped, devoutly, that he did. He'd surely have a hard time explaining away his bitten and swollen tongue. She was quite sure she'd drawn blood, for there'd been blood on the back of her hand when she'd wiped it across her mouth. With any luck it would be so bad he'd have to drink his meals tonight and tomorrow. And she had a notion his privates ached more than her breast did right now.

The thought made her a little more cheerful.

She scraped her hair back and tied it into a severe knot at the nape of her neck. There had been no sign from any of the adults today that they thought the way the boys did, but she had no intention of finding out the hard way. When she made herself look like a boy this way, most of them actually forgot she was a girl. And she didn't want to start anything among the beer-happy men—she knew for a fact that she wouldn't be able to defend herself from a grown man. Stara was safe enough behind the bar, but she was going to be out in the open.

A few months ago, with Rose in charge, anyone bothering "the wenches" would have found himself getting a rap on the head or hand with a spoon—or invited to leave and not return, which could be quite a punishment in a village with only one inn. Rune hadn't ever thought that the situation might change—

Until this afternoon. That changed everything.

Now, she wasn't taking any chances.

For a moment she hesitated at the foot of the stairs, afraid to face the crowd, afraid that she might see knowing looks in their faces, afraid of what they might be thinking—

But Annie Cook seized her as soon as the red-faced woman spotted her, and shoved a tray of sausage rolls into her hands, not giving her a chance to think about anything else.

The young minstrel was in the common room, tuning his instrument, as she delivered the salty sausage rolls to the customers. He glanced up at her as she passed, and smiled, the setting sun coming in through the inn windows and touching his hair and face with a gentle golden light. It was a plain, friendly smile, unlike the leers of Jon and his companions, and it warmed a place within her that had been cold all afternoon.

The next time she passed, this time with a tray full of beer mugs, he stopped her, on the pretense of getting a mugful of beer himself.

"I understand you're a fiddler," he said, quietly, taking his time about choosing a mug. "Will you be playing tonight? Do you think you'd like to try a duet?"

If only I could— But Stara had given her direct orders. She shook her head, not trusting her voice.

"That's too bad," he answered, making it sound as if he really *was* disappointed that she wouldn't be fiddling. "I was hoping to hear you; well, let me know if I do anything new to you, all right? I'll make sure to try and repeat the new songs so you can pick them up."

Speechless now with gratitude, she nodded emphatically, and he took his mug and let her go.

As the evening passed—and the women left—the atmosphere in the room changed. Some of the men from the village, who a month ago would never have dreamed of taking liberties, were pinching and touching Maeve, their hands lingering on her arm or shoulder—or, when they thought no one was watching, her breasts. Maeve seemed oblivious as usual. And neither Jeoff nor Stara were doing anything about it. Now, more than ever, Rune was glad she'd made herself less of a target. As she'd hoped, some of the men, with several mugs of dark beer in them, were calling her "boy." As long as they thought her a boy, she'd probably be safe enough.

True to his promise, Master Heron watched her closely at the conclusion of every tune he played. If she nodded, she could be sure he'd play that song later in the evening, and as the crowd grew more intoxicated, he could repeat the songs a little more often. His hat, left at his feet, was quite full of copper by now. There was even a silver piece or two among the copper. Rune didn't know for certain what he was used to, but by the standards of Westhaven he was doing very well indeed.

Finally he pled the need to take a break, and as Rune brought him more beer and a bit of bread and cheese and an apple, the villagers gathered closer to ask him questions. She ran into the kitchen and out again, not wanting to miss a single word.

"Lad, you're the best these parts have heard in a long while. Are you a Guild Bard?" the mayor wanted to know.

Of course he'd ask that, Rune thought cynically. *It's always better if it comes from a Guildsman. As if the music cared who plays it!*

"No, that I'm not," he replied, easily. "Look you, Guildsmen always wear purple ribbon on their sleeves, purple and gold for Bards, purple and silver for Minstrels. I doubt you'd ever see a Guildsman through here, though; they're not for the likes of you and me. They play for no less than Sires, and sure they'll tell you so, quick enough!"

He said it so lightly that no one took offense, not even the mayor, who looked a bit disappointed, but not angered.

"No, now I'm just a rover, a Free Bard, seeing that everyone gets to hear a bit of a tune now and again," he continued. "Though after the Faire, I'll admit to you I've been asked to play for the Sire."

That put the mayor in a better humor. "So what's the difference, lad?" he asked genially. "Besides a bit of ribbon, that is."

"Ah, now that *is* the question," he replied, with his eyebrows raised as high as they could go. "And the answer to it is more than you might think. It's not enough to be able to play, d'ye see. The Bardic Guild seems to think that's only part of what a man needs to get into it. You've all heard of the great Midsummer Faire at Kingsford, right by Traen, have you not?''

All heads nodded; who hadn't heard of the King's Faire? It was the greatest Faire in the land, and one or two of the crowd, the mayor being chiefest, had actually been there once. So great a Faire it was, it couldn't be held inside the capital city of Traen, but had to be set up in its own, temporary city of tents, at Kingsford nearby. It lasted for six weeks, three weeks on either side of Midsummer's Day, with a High Holy Mass celebrated on the day itself, adding the Church's blessing to the proceedings.

"Well," Master Heron said, leaning back against the hearth, so that the firelight caught all the angles of his face, "it's like this. On the second week of Kingsford Midsummer Faire, the Guild comes and sets up a big tent, hard by the cathedral-tent. That's where they hold trials, and they go on for three days. Anyone who wants can sign up for the trials, but there aren't many that make it to the third day.''

"You didn't make it, then?" said Ralf, the candle-maker, insolently.

But Master Heron only laughed. "I never tried," he said, "I'm too great a coward to face an audience all of musicians!''

The others laughed with him, and Ralf had the grace to flush.

"So, here's what happens," the minstrel continued. "The first day, you sing and play your best instrument, and you can choose whatever song you wish. There's just one catch—as you play, the judges call out a kind of tune, jig, reel, lament—and you have to play that song in that style, and improvise on it. The second day, you sing and play your *second* instrument, but you have to choose from a list of songs *they* pick, then you drum for the next to play. And the third day, you go back to your first instrument, or on to your third, if you have one, and you play and sing a song you have made. And each day, the list of those that get to go on gets shorter by half." He laughed. "Do you see now why I hadn't the courage to try? 'Tis enough to rattle your nerves to pieces, just thinking on it!''

The mayor whistled, and shook his head as the crowd fell silent. "Well, that's a poser. And all that just to get in as an *apprentice*?''

"Aye," Master Heron replied. "When I was young enough, I didn't have the courage, and now—" he spread his hands. "Wouldn't I look foolish now, as an apprentice?''

The men nodded agreement, as Rune went back to the kitchen, aflame with ambition, but half-crushed as well. She could compose, all right— yes, and she played her fiddle well enough, and drummed too, and sang—

But he'd said quite distinctly that you had to have *two* instruments, or even a third, and be proficient on all of them.

Even if she could find someone with a lute or mandolin to sell, she could never afford it. She could never afford the lessons to learn to play it, either—and that was assuming she could find a teacher. And if she waited for minstrels to come along to teach her, the way she'd learned fiddle, she'd be an old woman of eighteen or twenty by the time she was ready to go to the Midsummer Faire and the trials.

Well, she *could* play the shepherd's flute, and even she could make one of those—

No. That was no kind of instrument for the trials before the Guild. These were people who played before princes and kings; they'd hardly be impressed by someone tootling simple shepherd's jigs on a two-octave pipe.

Then the mayor put the crowning touch on her ambitions, placing it out of the realm of "want" and into "need." For what he told the rest, told *her* that this was the way out of all her problems. Apprenticeship to the Guild would not only get her out of this village, out of danger, but it would place her in a position where no one would ever threaten her again.

"I heard that no one touches a Guild Bard or a Guild Minstrel, am I right, Master Heron?" he asked.

The minstrel nodded, though his face was in shadow now, and Rune couldn't read his expression. His voice held no inflection at all. "That's the truth, sir," he replied. "Only the Church has a right to bring them to trial, and if anyone harms a Guild musician, the Church will see to it that they're found and punished. I'm told that's because a good half of the Guild apprentices go into the Church eventually—and because musicians go everywhere, sometimes into dangerous situations."

No one could ever harm her again. She was so involved in her own thoughts that she hardly noticed when Master Heron resumed playing, and had to forcibly drag her attention back to the music.

There had to be a way to get that second instrument, to get to the trials. There *had* to be!

CHAPTER THREE

The customers stayed later than usual, and only left when Master Heron began pointedly to put his instrument away for travel. By the time the evening was over, Rune was exhausted, too tired to think very clearly, arms aching from all the heavy trays and pitchers she had carried all night, legs aching from the miles she'd traveled between kitchen and tables, bar and tables, and back again. From the look of him, Master Heron wasn't in much better shape. There were hundreds of things she wanted to ask him about getting into the Bardic Guild, but she knew from experience how *his* arms must feel after a night of non-stop playing, and how his tongue was tripping over the simplest of words if they weren't in a song.

So she left him alone as she carried the heaps of dirty plates and mugs into the kitchen again—and predictably, was recruited as dish-dryer and stacker, for Granny couldn't cope with putting the plates away. So she walked several more miles returning mugs to the bar and dishes to the cupboard. By the time she was able to leave the kitchen, he'd gone up to his room and his well-earned rest.

The common room was empty at last, fire dying, benches stacked atop tables, and both pushed against the walls, shutters closed and latched against the night. She didn't see her mother anywhere about, which in itself was predictable enough. Stara did not much care for kitchen and clean-up work, and never performed either if she had a way out of doing so. Rune expected to find Stara up in her own attic cubicle next to her daughter's.

But when Rune reached the top of the attic stairs, the moonlight shining through the attic window betrayed the fact that Stara's bed was empty.

Odd. But she'd probably gone to visit the privy before turning in. Rune stripped off her shirt and breeches, and slipped into an old, outworn shift of Rose's, cut down to make a night-shift just before Rose had taken sick, expecting to hear her mother coming up the stairs at any moment, and hoping this wasn't going to be another night of complaint.

But as Rune crawled under the coarse sheet of her pallet, she froze at the sound of murmuring voices in the hall outside Jeoff's rooms below.

One was certainly Jeoff. And the other, just as certainly, was her mother.

Suddenly Rune was wide-eyed; no longer the least bit sleepy.

She had only time to register shock before the closing door below cut off the last sound of whispers.

Stara—and Jeoff. There was no doubt in Rune's mind what was going on. Stara had been unable to get Jeoff to marry her by simply tempting him, but remaining just out of reach. So for some reason, tonight she had decided to give the man what he wanted to see if that would bring him before the altar.

She must be desperate, Rune thought, numbly. *She'd never have gone to him otherwise. She must think that if she lets him sleep with her, guilt will make him want to make an honest wife of her in the morning. Or else she thinks she can seduce him into marrying her, because she's such a fabulous lover. Or both.*

Whatever was going on in Stara's mind, there were a number of possible outcomes for this encounter, and they didn't auger well for Rune.

The worst threat was that her mother would slip and become pregnant. In all the time Rune had been paying any attention, Stara had never once calculated anything correctly if it involved numbers greater than three. That made a pregnancy horribly likely—if not this time, then the next.

Rune stared up blankly at the darkness of the roof above her. If Stara became pregnant, married or not, it would mean the end of Rune's free time. She'd have to take all of Stara's work as well as her own for months before the birth, and after—

And doubtless the added expense of a non-productive mouth to feed would convince Jeoff there was no money to hire any more help.

And Rune would have to help with the baby, when it came. As if she hadn't already more than enough to do! There would be no time for anything but work, dawn to dusk and past it. There would be no time to even practice her fiddling, much less learn new music, or work out songs of her own.

No time for herself at all . . . things were bad enough now, but with Stara pregnant, or caring for another child, they'd be infinitely worse.

Her eyes stung and she swallowed a lump in her throat as big as an egg. It wasn't fair! Stara had a perfectly good situation here, she didn't need to do this! She wasn't thinking—or rather, she wasn't thinking of anyone except herself. . . .

Rune turned on her side as despair threatened to smother her, choking her breath in her throat, like a hand about it. *At least I'll have a roof over my head,* she thought bleakly. *There's plenty that can't even say that. And food; I never go hungry around here.*

But that wasn't the worst possible situation. Supposing Stara's ploy didn't work? Suppose she couldn't get Jeoff to marry her—and got with child anyway? Jeoff probably wouldn't throw them out of his own accord, but there were plenty of people in the village who'd pressure him to do so, especially those with unmarried daughters. He was a member of the Church, a deacon, he had a reputation of his own to maintain; he could decide to lie, and say that Stara had been sleeping with the customers behind his back, so as to save that reputation. Then, out she'd go, told to leave the village and not return. Just like the last time she'd gotten herself with child.

Oh yes, and what would happen to Rune *then?*

She might well be tossed out with her mother—but likelier, far likelier, was that Jeoff would get rid of Stara, but keep her daughter. After all, the daughter was a proven hard worker, with nothing against her save that she was a light-skirt's daughter, and possibly a bastard herself.

That wasn't her fault, but it should give Rune all the more reason that she should be grateful for a place and someone willing to employ her.

And what would that mean, but the same result as if he married Stara?

Rune could predict the outcome of that, easily enough. She'd wind up doing all her work and Stara's too.

Eventually Jeoff would marry some girl from the village, like Amanda, who'd lord it over Rune and pile more work on her, and probably verbal abuse as well, if not physical abuse. It would depend on just how much Jeoff would be willing to indulge his wife, how much he'd support her against the "hired help."

And when the new wife got pregnant, there'd be all the work tending to *her* precious brat. Or rather, brats; there'd be one a year, sure as the spring coming, for that was the way the village girls conducted their lives. It was proper for a wife to do her duty by her husband, and make as many babies as possible.

No time for fiddling, then, for certain sure. No time for anything. At least Stara was old enough that there likely wouldn't be another child after the first. With a new, young wife, there'd be as many as she could spawn, with Rune playing nursemaid to all of them.

Unless Rune told them all that she wasn't having any of that, and went off on her own, to try her hand at making a living with her fiddle.

And for a moment, that seemed a tempting prospect, until cold reality intruded.

Oh, surely, she told herself cynically. *A fine living I'd make at it, too. I'm not as good as the worst of the minstrels who've been here—and surely they aren't as good as the Guild Musicians, or the folk who make the circuits of the great Faires. Which means, what? That I'd starve, most like.*

What would be better—or worse? Starvation, or the loss of music, of a life of her own? A dangerous life alone on the open road, living hand-to-mouth, or a life of endless drudgery?

She sniffed, and stifled a sob. There didn't seem to be much of a choice, no matter which way she turned—both lives were equally bleak.

And what about Stara herself? Stara was her mother; how much did Rune owe her?

If she did get with child, and Jeoff did throw her out, Stara would be in an even worse plight than Rune faced. She would be pregnant, out of work, nowhere to go, and no longer young enough to charm her way, however briefly, into someone's household.

For a moment, Rune suffered a pang of guilt and worry. *But no one forced her into Jeoff's bed,* she told herself after a moment. *No one told her to go chasing after her master, hoping for a wedding ring. She's the one that made the decision, to risk her future without even a* thought *for what might happen to me as well as her!*

That killed any feelings of guilt. If Stara got herself into trouble, it was *her* problem, and she could get herself right back out again. *Why should I suffer because my mother's a damn fool? She doesn't even want me to call her "Mother" any more.*

But that brought up still another possibility.

There was no doubt of it that Stara didn't like having a fourteen-year-old daughter; that she thought it made her look old. If she decided that Rune was a liability in her plan to capture Jeoff and become his wife, she might well do something to drive Rune away herself.

It wouldn't even be hard to find an excuse. All Stara would have to do would be to tell him that Rune was sleeping with Jib or any of the boys from the village—or, most likely of all, with the musicians that had been passing through. The villagers would be glad to believe such tales, and might even make up a few of their own.

And Jeoff was like any other man; he was fallible and flawed, and subject to making some irrational decisions. Even though he was en-joying himself with Stara—or perhaps, because he was enjoying himself with Stara—he would never tolerate openly loose morals on his premises on the part of anyone else.

While the large inns—so Rune had heard, from the female musicians—were tolerant of such things, Jeoff never had been. He could get away with forbidding prostitutes to use his inn because most of his custom was local. Larger inns couldn't afford such niceties, and in fact, larger inns often kept whores to supply their clients. But the folk needing rooms out here, off the main roads, most often traveled alone, or with a long-time partner. In a case like that, if the partner was a female, and the male of the pair said they were married, then they might as well have posted the banns, so Jeoff didn't enforce his rule. There was no inn nearer than Beeford, and that gave him something of a monopoly on trade. Those who needed Jeoff's rooms had no choice—and the locals would come to drink his beer whether or not he allowed loose women about.

In fact, Jeoff and Rose had been considered pillars of the community for their godly ways. That was part of what made Jeoff such a good marital prospect now.

And that was precisely what made it likely that he'd dismiss her at the first complaint of looseness, particularly if it came from her mother.

Maybe I just ought to turn whore, she thought with another stifled sob. *At least then I'd have something in the way of a trade. . . .*

Despite Jeoff's strictness, she wasn't entirely innocent of the ways of light-skirts. Some few of the travelers, men with gold and silver in their purses rather than copper and silver, had brought with them their own, brazen, hard-eyed women. And once or twice, other travelers in Faire season had met such a woman here, each departing in another direction after a single shared night. Jeoff had never turned these men away; they paid well, they often carried weapons or acted haughtily, and as if they were either dangerous or important. But he had served them himself, not permitting either Stara or Rune anywhere near them, and Rose had always worn a frown the entire time such women were under her roof.

Then there was the fellow who came through at Faire-time with his own tents and wagons, and a collection of freaks and "dancing maidens." His "maidens" were nothing of the sort, whatever his freaks were. There were always a lot of male visitors from the village to his tents after dark when the Faire closed. . . .

She turned on her back again, biting her lip in remembrance. That man—he'd made her feel so filthy, just by the way he acted, that she'd wanted to bathe every time she had to be anywhere near him. . . .

He'd hired Rune once, when his own musician took sick, having her play for the performances given during the day. Rose, innocent of what those performances were like, had judged she was unlikely to come to any harm during the daylight hours and had given her leave.

The dancers hadn't danced, much. Their costumes seemed to consist of skirts and bodices made entirely of layers and layers of veils. Their movement was minimal, and consisted of removing one veil after another, while wiggling in a kind of bored pantomime of desire to the drumbeats. It wasn't even particularly graceful.

Rune hadn't said anything to anyone; if Jeoff knew what was going on, he didn't bother to enlighten Rose, and Rune doubted anyone else would tell her. There wasn't any reason to; Rune sat behind a screen to play for the "dancers," and no one in the audience had any notion who the musician back there was. She'd needed the money rather badly, for strings and a new bow, the old one having cracked to the point that Rune was afraid to subject it to too much stress—and she'd given her word that she'd take the job, and felt as if she couldn't walk out on it once she'd agreed. But she'd been horribly uncomfortable, embarrassed beyond words, and feeling vaguely sickened by what she saw from her hiding place. She'd been glad when the regular musician recovered from his illness after two days and resumed his place.

It hadn't been the taking off of clothes that had bothered her, it was the way the women had done it. Even at thirteen, she'd known there was something wrong with what was going on.

The Church said displays like that, of a woman's body, were forbidden, and a sin. Rune had never quite reasoned out why that should be so—for the Holy Book said other things, entirely, about taking joy in the way of a man and a maid, and celebrating the body and the spirit. But the dancers certainly seemed to feel the same way as the Church— yet they kept dancing, as if they reveled in doing the forbidden. And the men who came to watch them gave Rune the same feeling. There was something slimy about it all, tawdry and cheap, like the way Jon had made her feel this afternoon.

The man who ran the show was horrible, able to make almost anything sound like an innuendo. He was *using* those women, using them with the same callousness that Kerd the Butcher displayed with the animals he slaughtered.

But they, in turn, were using their audience, promising something they wouldn't deliver, not without a further price attached. Promising something they probably *couldn't* give—promising gold, and delivering cheap gilded lead.

And the men in the audience were part of the conspiracy. *They* certainly didn't care about the women they ogled, or later bedded. They cared only for the moment's pleasure, sating themselves without regard for the women, using them as if they were soulless puppets. Things, not human beings.

No, she couldn't do that . . . couldn't reduce herself to a creature. There was something wrong about that. And not the Church's notion of right and wrong, either. No matter what happened, she could not put herself in the position of used and user. . . .

And yet, that's exactly the position that Stara put herself in. She was no different from any of those hard-eyed women who stayed only the night, from the "dancers" at the Faire. She had determined on a price for herself, and she was using Jeoff to get it, with never any thought of love or joy involved.

And Jeoff was most definitely using Stara, for he was taking advantage of her by demanding what he wanted without "paying" for it first, forcing Stara to put herself in the position of begging for that price.

It would be a different story if they had come together with care for one another.

Not that it mattered, in the end. Whatever came of this, it would probably spell trouble for Rune.

And with that comforting thought, exhaustion finally got the better of her, and she slept.

". . . and when I got out of the kitchen, he was already gone," she lamented to Jib, as they raked the area in front of the stable clean of droppings, and scattered water over the pounded dirt to keep the dust down. "I picked up a few songs from him, but he really was awfully good, and he knew more about the Bardic Guild than anyone I ever talked to before. There was so much I wanted to ask him about! I wish I hadn't had to work so hard—I could have gotten a lesson from him—"

"It don't seem fair to me," Jib said slowly. "I know Stara wasn't doin' anythin'. She was just foolin' around the common room, actin' like she was cleanin' mugs and whatall, but she weren't doin' nothin' but fill pitchers now an' again. Them mugs was still dirty when she was done. Cook was talkin' about it this mornin' t' Tarn."

"I shouldn't have had to play server," she complained bitterly, swinging the watering can back and forth to cover as much ground as possible. "They should've let me fiddle, like they used to. You can't have a whole evening of music with just one musician, not if you don't want him to wish he'd never walked in before the night's over. Master Heron was tired, really tired, by the time he was done. If they'd let me play, I could've let him take a good long break or two. And he *wanted* me to play, he said so, he wanted to know if I would play a duet with him. He could have helped me, taught me songs right—"

"Well, heckfire, Rune," Jib replied, sounding, for the first time in weeks, like her old friend instead of the odd, awkward stranger who wanted to court her. "I dunno what t' say. Seems t' me pretty rotten unfair. Ye know? Looks t' me like your Mam is gettin' what she wants, an' ol' Jeoff is gettin' what he wants, an' all you're gettin' is hind teat. Ev'body here is doin' all right but you, and ye're th' one pickin' up the slack."

Rune nodded unhappily, as they walked back to the stable to put the watering cans away under the shelves by the stable door. "Nobody ever asks me what I want," she said bitterly. "Anything that needs done, they throw on me, without ever asking if I've got the time. They all seem to think they can do whatever they want with me, because I'm not important. I'm just a girl, just Stara's brat, and I don't count. I'm whatever they want me to be, with no say in it."

And that includes Jon and his friends.

"Well, ye got a roof, an' plenty t' eat," Jib began, echoing her pessimistic thoughts of last night. "This ain't a bad life, really—"

"It's not enough," she continued, angry now. "I hate this place, and I hate most of the people in it! I don't *want* to be stuck here the rest of my life, in this little hole back of beyond, where everybody knows everything about everybody else, or they think they do. And they think that they're so good, God's keeping a special place in heaven for them! I can't get anywhere here, because no matter what I did, I'd never be good enough for *them* to even be civil to."

Jib's brow puckered, as if he had never once thought that someone might want something other than the life they now shared. That Rune would want the freedom to play her fiddle, he should have understood— she'd dinned it into his head often enough. But that she'd want to leave was probably incomprehensible. He certainly looked surprised—and puzzled—by her outburst. "Well," he said slowly. "What do you want, then?"

Rune flung her arms wide. "I want the world!" she cried extravagantly. "I want all of it! I want—I want kings and queens at my feet, I want wealth and power and—"

"Na, na, Rune," Jib interrupted, laughing at her in a conciliating tone. "That's not sensible, lass. Nobody can have that, outside of a tale. Leastwise, no musicker. What is it ye really want?"

"Well, if I have to be sensible . . ." She paused a moment, thought about what it was that was making her so unhappy. It wasn't the drudgery so much, as the loss of hope that there'd ever be anything else. And the confinement in a corner of the world where nothing ever happened, and nothing ever changed, and she'd always be looked down on and taken advantage of. "Jib, I want to get out of here. The people here think I'm scum, you know that. Even if the High King rode up here tomorrow and claimed me as his long-lost daughter, they'd look down their noses at me and say, 'Eh, well, and she's a bastard after all, like we thought.' "

Jib nodded agreement, and sighed. He leaned up against the doorpost of the stable and selected a straw to chew on from one of the bales stacked there.

"So?" he said, scratching his head, and squinting into the late afternoon sunlight. "If ye could go, how'd ye do it? Where'd ye go, then?"

"I'd want some money," she said, slowly. "Enough to buy another instrument, a guitar, or a lute, or even a mandolin. And enough to keep me fed and under shelter, and pay for the lessons I'd need. I couldn't do that here, it would have to be in a real city. Even if I had the money, and the instrument, I can't keep going on like I have been, begging for time to play, and making do with lessons snatched from other minstrels. I need to learn to read and write better, and read and write music, too."

"All right," Jib responded, pushing away from the doorpost. "Say you've got all that. What then?" He led the way towards the door on the other side of the stable-yard, where they both had chores awaiting them—her to clean the common room, him to scrub pots for the cook.

"Then—" She paused just outside the inn door and looked off down the road with longing. "Then—I'd go to the big Midsummer Faire at Kingsford. I'd march straight in there, and I'd sign right up for the trials for the Bardic Guild. And I'd win them, too, see if I wouldn't. I'd win a place in the Guild, and a Master, and then just see what I'd do!" She turned to Jib with such a fierce passion that he took an involuntary step back. "You said nobody had money and power and kings and queens at their feet outside of a tale? Well, the Guild Bards have all that! All that and more! And when I was a Guild Bard there'd be nobles come wanting me to serve them, begging me to serve them, right up to kings and even the High King himself! I could come riding back in here with a baggage train a half dozen horses long, and servants bowing to me and calling me 'My Lady,' and a laurel and a noble title of my own. And *then* these backwater blowhards would see—"

"Oh, would we now?" asked Kaylan Potter mockingly, behind her.

She whirled, already on the defensive. Kaylan and three of his friends lounged idly against the door to the common room. Kaylan and his friends were almost fully adult; journeymen, not 'prentices, tall and strong. They looked enough alike to be from the same family, and indeed, they were all distant cousins, rawboned, muscular and swarthy, in well-worn smocks and leather vests and breeches. She wondered, frantically, if she was in for another attempt like the one Jon and his friends had made. Her heart raced with sudden fear. Surely not right here, where she'd thought she was safe—

No. Her heart slowed, as the young men made no move towards her. No, they were older and smarter than Jon. They wouldn't risk their tavern-privileges by trying to force her on the doorstep in broadest daylight. Elsewhere, perhaps, they might have made some sort of move— but not here and now.

But they were not particularly amused at her description of them—by implication—nor her assessment of their parents and neighbors.

"We'd see, would we?" Kaylan repeated, looking down his snub nose at her. "And just what would we see? We'd see a braggart, foolish girl-child with her head full of foolish fancies getting her comeuppance, I'm thinking. We'd see a chit with a head too big for her hat learning just what a little fish she is. We'd see a brat who never was able to win even a village Faire fiddling contest learning what it means to brag and fall. That's what I think we'd be seeing, eh, lads?"

The other three nodded solemnly, superior smirks on their dark faces.

Her heart squeezed in her chest; she felt her face grow hot, then cold.

"Oh, aye," said Thom Beeson, his hair falling into his eyes as he nodded. "Aye that I'd say, seein' as the wee chit couldn't even win the Harvest Faire fiddlin' contest four years agone, and her only competition a couple of old men, a lad claimin' t' be a Guild 'prentice, and a toy-maker."

She gathered all her dignity about her and strode past them, into the tavern. There wasn't anyone in the common room but Maeve, who was sweeping the floor with a care that would have been meticulous in anyone but her. The four young men followed her inside and threw themselves down on a bench, their attitude betraying the fact that they figured they had her cowed. "Now, how about beer and a bit of bread and cheese for some hard workin' men, wench," said Kaylan carelessly. "You can be a first-rate servin' wench even if you're only a second-rate fiddler."

She held her temper so as not to provoke them, but it was a struggle. She wanted to hit them—she wanted to throw their damned beer in their smug faces. And she didn't dare do any of it. Thom was right, damn him. She *had* lost the Harvest Faire fiddling contest four years ago, and it had been the last contest their little village Faire had held. She'd never had another chance to compete. And they all remembered her failure. So did she; the remembrance was a bitter taste in her mouth as she filled their mugs from the tap and took them to the table.

She thudded the filled mugs down in front of them, so that they foamed over, and turned on her heel.

"So, what else were you going to show us, wench?" Kaylan asked lazily. "Is it true that you're takin' after your mother that way?"

Someone else had been spreading tales, it seemed. Already she was judged—

"Or are we gonna hear more boastin'?" Thom drawled. "Empty air don't mean a thing, wench. If ye could fiddle as well as ye can yarn, ye might be worth listenin' to."

She lost the tenuous hold she had on her temper.

She spun, let the words fly without thinking about the consequences. They had challenged her too far, in a way she couldn't shrug off.

"What am I going to show you?" she hissed, her hands crooked into claws, her heart near bursting. "I'll tell you! I'll do more than *show* you! I'll prove to you I'm the best fiddler these parts have ever seen, and too good for the likes of *you*! I'll go fiddle for—for—"

"For who, wench?" Thom laughed, snapping his fingers at her. "For the Sire?"

"For the Skull Hill Ghost!" she snarled without thinking. "I reckon he'd know a good fiddler when he heard one, even if a lout like you doesn't!"

Thom threw back his head and laughed. "From braggart t' liar in one breath!" he said derisively. "You? Fiddle for the Ghost? Ye'd never dare set foot on Skull Hill in daylight, much less by night! Why, ye never even step outside th' building oncet the sun goes down! I bet ye're so 'fraid of the dark, ye hide yer head under the covers so's th' goblins don' git ye!"

"Liar, liar," taunted Kaylan, wagging his finger at her. "Little girls shouldn't lie t' their betters. Little girls should know their place. Specially when they're old 'nuff t' be big girls." He grinned, insinuatingly. "Specially when there's big boys as can give 'em things, an' do nice things for 'em, if they've got the wit t' be nice back."

If she'd had any notion of backing down, those words put the idea right out of her head.

"I'll show you who's a liar!" she shouted, too angry to keep her voice down. "I'll show you who's the better around here! I'll go tonight! Right now! Then we'll see who's the coward and who isn't!"

She dashed for the stairs, and took them two at a time, grabbed her fiddle from the shelf, and pelted down the stairs again as fast as her feet could take her without breaking her neck. She burst into the common room to see Jeoff just entering from the kitchen, alerted by the shouting. He turned around to see her hitting the bottom landing with a *thud*.

"Rune!" he called, holding out a cautionary hand. "Rune, what's a-goin' on?"

"*You* tell him," she spat at Kaylan, as she headed out the door, fiddle in hand, at a fast, angry walk. "You started this, you bully—*you* tell him."

By then she was out the door, and the walk had become a run, and no one of Jeoff's girth was going to be able to catch up with her. She pelted down the dirt road as hard as she could run, her fiddle case bumping against her back where she'd slung it, her heart burning within her and driving her to run even faster, as if she could outdistance the cruel taunts.

At least her parting sally should get Kaylan and his friends into a situation they'd have a hard time explaining themselves out of. Jeoff wasn't going to like losing his help for the night.

She took the road away from the village, deeper into the forested hills, slowing to a walk once she was out of sight of the inn and it looked as if there wouldn't be any immediate pursuit.

By then, her side hurt and she was winded and sticky with sweat and road dust. And by the time she reached the place where the Old Road joined the new one, she'd had ample chance to cool down and think about just how stupid she'd been.

The Old Road represented a more direct path through the hills—but one that was never taken after dark. And, more often than not, local travelers avoided it even in daylight. Hence the overgrown condition of the Old Road, the grasses sprouting in the eroded ruts, the bushes creeping up onto it a little more every year. Even though the Old Road would save the weary traveler several miles, no one took it who had the slightest chance of being on it after the sun went down.

For there *was* a ghost that haunted the place, a vengeful, angry ghost; one that inhabited the Skull Hill Pass. It was no legend; it had been seen reliably by the few very fortunate souls who had managed to elude his grasp by fleeing his pursuit past the running water of the stream at the foot of the hill. The new road had been built fifty years ago, or so Rune had been told, after Father Donlin went up on the hill to exorcise the Ghost, and was found up there in the morning, stone cold dead, with a look of utter terror on his face.

That, in fact, was how most of the victims were found; and no one who ever went up there at night returned alive. Those few who had escaped death had been going down the hill when the sun set, having miscalculated or suffered some mishap on the road that had delayed them past the safe hour. There had been five victims besides the Father that Rune herself knew about, and stories spoke of dozens. . . .

No one knew how long the ghost had been there, nor why he haunted and killed. Granny Beeson, Thom's grandmother, and the oldest person in the village, said he'd been there as long as she remembered.

And now Rune was walking straight up the haunted hill, into the Ghost's power. Deliberately. Seeking the Ghost out, a spirit that had killed a holy priest, as if her music had a chance of appeasing it.

With more than enough time, as she climbed the uneven, root-ridged track, to regret her impulse.

She squinted through the trees at the setting sun; she reckoned by the angle that once she reached the top of the pass, she'd have a little more than half an hour to settle herself and wait for her—host. There seemed fewer birds on this track than the other, and they all seemed to be birds of ill-omen: ravens, corbies, blackbirds, black boat-tails.

She tried to think if any of the ghost's other victims had been female. Maybe he only went after men—

But, no. Granny Beeson had said that two of the dead had been lovers running off to get married against the girls' parental wishes, so the thing killed women too.

Stupid, stupid, stupid, she berated herself. *If I live through this, I am never going to let my temper get me into this kind of mess again. Not ever. I swear.*

But first, she was going to have to survive the rest of the night.

CHAPTER FOUR

As sunset neared, the few birds that had been about made themselves vanish into the brush, and Rune was left alone on Skull Hill without even a raven for company. It might have been her imagination, but the trees seemed a little starved up here, a strange, skeletal growth, with limbs like bony hands clawing the sky. It seemed colder up here as well—and the wind was certainly stronger, moaning softly through the trees in a way that sounded uncannily human, and doing nothing for her confidence level.

She looked around at the unpromising landscape and chose a rock, finding one with a little hollow. She spent some time pulling up some of the dry grass of last year's growth, giving the rock a kind of cushion to keep the cold away, and sat down to wait. As the crimson sun touched the top of Beacon Hill opposite her perch, and crept all-too-quickly behind it, she began to shiver, half with cold, and half with the fear she had no difficulty in admitting now that she was alone.

Of all the stupid things I've ever done, this was one of the stupidest.

It was not a particularly spectacular sunset; no clouds to catch and hold the sun's last rays. Just the red disk sinking towards and then behind the hill, the pale sky growing darker—deepening from blue to black, and all too soon; the stars coming out, brightest first, pinpoints of cold blue-white light.

The wind died to nothing just at sunset, then picked up again after the last stars appeared. Rune took out her fiddle with benumbed fingers, and tuned it by feel, then sat on her rock and fingered every tune she knew without actually playing, to keep her fingers limber. And still nothing happened.

She was tired, cold, and her fear was fading. Her bones began to ache with the cold. It would be so easy to pack up, creep down the hill, and return to the inn claiming that she'd fiddled for the Ghost and gotten away.

The idea was very tempting.

But—that would be a lie and a cheat. She swore she'd do this; she pledged her word, and even if the villagers thought her word was worthless, that didn't make it so. If she broke her word, if she lied about what she'd done, what would that make her? As worthless as the villagers claimed she was.

Besides, they probably wouldn't believe me anyway.

The moon appeared, its cold silver light flooding over the hills and making them look as if they'd been touched with frost. She marked time while it climbed, keeping her fingers warm by tucking them in her armpits, and taking out the fiddle now and again to make sure it was still in tune. There was a great deal more life around here than there had been in the daylight—unless her presence had frightened everything away until she stopped moving. Owls hooted off in the distance, and a few early crickets sang nearby. Frogs croaked in the stream below her as bats and a nighthawk swooped through the pass, looking for flying insects. And once, a great hare loped lazily down the road, pausing in surprise at the sight of her, and standing up on his haunches to take a better look, for all the world like a white stone garden statue of the kind the Sire had in his pleasure-garden.

At the sight of him, she lost the last of her fear. He was so quizzical, so comical—it was impossible to be afraid of a place that held an animal like this.

She chuckled at him, and he took fright at the sound, whirling on his hind feet and leaping into the underbrush in a breath.

She shook her head, relaxing a little in spite of the chill. There was no Ghost, most likely, and perhaps there never had been. Perhaps the "ghost" had been no more than a particularly resourceful bandit. Perhaps—

The moon touched the highest part of her arc, marking the hour as midnight, just as the thought occurred to her. And at that moment, absolute silence descended on the hill, as if everything within hearing had been frightened into frozen immobility.

The crickets stopped chirping altogether; the owl hoots cut off. Even the wind died, leaving the midnight air filled only with a stillness that made the ears ache as they sought after the vanished sounds.

Then the wind returned with a howl and a rush, blowing her shirt flat to her body, chilling her to the bone and turning the blood in her veins to ice. It moaned, like something in pain, something dying by inches.

Then it changed, and whipped around her, twisting her garments into confusion. It swirled around her, picking up dead leaves and pelting her with them, the center of a tiny, yet angry cyclone that was somehow more frightening than the pounding lightning of the worst thunderstorm.

It lashed her with her own hair, blinded her with dust. Then it whisked away to spin on the road in front of her, twisting the leaves in a miniature whirlwind less than ten paces from her.

Her skin crawled, as if there were something watching her from the center of the wind. Malignant; that was what it felt like. As if this wind was a living thing, and it hated every creature it saw. . . .

She shook her hair out of her eyes, hugged her arms to her body and shook with cold and the prickling premonition of danger. She couldn't take her eyes off the whirlwind and the swirling leaves caught in it. The leaves—it was so strange, she could see every vein of them—

A claw of ice ran down her spine, as she realized that she could see every vein of them—because they were glowing.

She'd seen foxfire—what country child hadn't—but this was different. Each leaf glowed a distinct and leprous shade of greenish-white. And they were drawing closer together into a column in the center of the whirlwind, forming a solid, slightly irregular shape, thicker at the bottom than at the top, with a kind of cowl-like formation at the very top.

Kind of? It *was* a cowl; the leaves had merged into a cowled and robed figure, like a monk. But the shape beneath the robe suggested nothing remotely human, and she knew with dread that she didn't want to see the face hidden within that cowl. . . . The wind swirled the apparition's robes as it had swirled the leaves, but disturbed it not at all.

Then, suddenly, the wind died; the last of the leaves drifted to pile around the apparition's feet . . . if it had feet, and not some other appendages. The cowl turned in Rune's direction, and there was a suggestion of glowing eyes within the shadows of the hood.

A voice, an icy, whispering voice, came out of the darkness from all around her; from everywhere, yet nowhere. It could have been born of her imagination, yet Rune knew the voice was the Ghost's, and that to run was to die. Instantly, but in terror that would make dying seem to last an eternity.

"Why have you come here, stupid child?" it murmured, as fear urged her to run anyway. "Why were you waiting here? For me? Foolish child, do you not know what I am? What I could do to you?"

At least it decided to talk to me first. . . .

Rune had to swallow twice before she could speak, and even then her voice cracked and squeaked with fear.

"I've come to fiddle for you—sir?" she said, gasping for breath between each word, trying to keep her teeth from chattering.

And it's a good thing I'm not here to sing. . . .

She held out Lady Rose and her bow. "Fiddle?" the Ghost breathed, as if it couldn't believe what it had heard. "You have come to *fiddle*? To play mortal music? For me?"

For the first time since it had appeared, Rune began to hope she might survive this encounter. At least she'd surprised this thing. "Uh—yes. Sir? I did."

The glow beneath the hood increased, she was not imagining it. And the voice strengthened. "Why, mortal child? Why did you come here to—fiddle for me?"

She toyed with the notion of telling it that she'd done so for some noble reason, because she felt sorry for it, or that she wanted to bring it some pleasure—

But she had the feeling that it would know if she lied to it. She also had the feeling that if she lied to it, it would not be amused.

And since her life depended on keeping it amused—

So she told it the truth.

"It was on a dare, sir," she stammered. "There's these boys in the town, and they told me I was a second-rater, and—I swore I'd come up here and fiddle for you, and let you judge if I was a second-rater or a wizard with m' bow."

The cowl moved slightly, as if the creature were cocking its head a little sideways. "And why would they call you second-rate?"

"Because—because they want me to be, sir," she blurted. "If I'm second-rate they can look down on me, an'—do what they want to me—"

For some reason, the longer she spoke, the easier it became to do so, to pour out all her anger, her fear, all the bottled emotions she couldn't have told anyone before this. The spirit stayed silent, attentive through all of it, keeping its attitude of listening with interest, even sympathy. This was, by far, the most even-handed hearing she'd had from anyone. It was even easy to speak of the attack Jon and his friends had made, tears of rage and outrage stinging her eyes as she did.

Finally, her anger ran out, and with it, the words. She spread her hands, bow in one, fiddle in the other. "So that's it, sir. That's why I'm here."

"You and I have something in common, I think." Did she really hear those barely whispered words, or only imagine them?

She certainly didn't imagine the next ones.

"So you have come to fiddle for me, to prove to these ignorant dirt-grubbers that you are their—equal." The Ghost laughed, a sound with no humor in it, the kind of laugh that called up empty wastelands and icy peaks. "Well, then, girl. Fiddle, then. And pray to that Sacrificed God of yours that you fiddle well, very well. If you please me, if you continue to entertain me until dawn, I shall let you live, a favor I have never granted any other, and that should prove you are not only their paltry equal, but their better. But I warn you—the moment my attention lags, little girl—you'll die like all the others, and you will join all the others in my own, private little Hell." It chuckled again, cruelly. "Or, you may choose to attempt to run away, to outrun me to the stream at the bottom of the hill. Please notice that I did say *attempt*. It is an *attempt* that others have made and failed."

She thought for a moment that she couldn't do it. Her hands shook too much; she couldn't remember anything—not a single song, not so much as a lullabye.

Running was no choice either; she knew that.

So she tucked her fiddle under her chin anyway, and set the bow on the strings. . . .

And played one single, trembling note. And that note somehow called forth another and another followed that, until she was playing a stream, a cascade of bright and lively melody—

And then she realized she was playing "Guard's Farewell," one of her early tunes, and since it was a slip-jig, it led naturally to "Jenny's Fancy," and that in its turn to "Summer Cider"—

By then she had her momentum, and the tunes continued to come, one after another, as easily and purely as if she were practicing all by herself. She even began to enjoy herself, a little; to relax at least, since the Ghost hadn't killed her yet. This might work. She just might survive the night.

The Ghost stood in that "listening" stance; she closed her eyes to concentrate better as she often did when practicing, letting the tunes bring back bright memories of warm summer days or nights by the fire as she had learned them. The memories invoked other tunes, and more memories, and the friendships shared with musicians who called themselves by the names of birds: Linnet, Heron, Nightingale, and Raven; Robin, Jay and Thrush. When only parts of tunes came, half-remembered bits of things other musicians had played that she hadn't quite caught, she made up the rest. She cobbled together children's game-rhymes into reels and jigs. She played cradle-songs, hymns, anything and everything she had ever heard or half-heard the melody to.

When she feared she was going to run dry, she played a random run, improvised on that, and turned it into a melody of her very own.

It happened with an ease that amazed her, somewhere in the back of her mind. She'd wanted to write songs, she'd had them living in the back of her mind for so long, and yet she'd never more than half-believed that she was going to get them to come out. It was a marvel, a wonder, and she would have liked to try the tune over a second and third time. But the Ghost was still waiting, and she dared not stop.

Hours passed, longer than she had ever played without stopping before. Gradually the non-stop playing began to take its toll, as she had known would happen. Her upper bow-arm ached, then cramped; then her fingering hand got a cramp along the outside edge. The spot below her chin in her collarbone felt as if she was driving a spike into her neck.

Then her fingering arm burned and cramped, and her back started to hurt, spreading agony down her spine into her legs. She fiddled with tears of pain in her eyes, while her fingers somehow produced rollicking dance music completely divorced from the reality of her aching limbs.

Her fingers were numb; she was grateful for that, for she was entirely certain that there were blisters forming on her fingertips under the calluses, and that if she ever stopped, she'd feel them.

Finally, she played "Fields of Barley," and knew a moment of complete panic as her mind went blank. There was nothing there to play. She'd played everything she knew, and she somehow had the feeling that the Ghost wouldn't be amused by repeating music.

And there was no sign of dawn. She was going to die after all.

But her fingers were wiser than she was, for they moved on their own, and from beneath them came the wild, sad, wailing notes of the laments that the Gypsy Nightingale had played for her. . . .

Now, for the first time, the Ghost stirred and spoke, and she opened her eyes in startlement.

"More—" it breathed. "More—"

Rune closed her eyes again, and played every note she remembered, and some she hadn't known she'd remembered. And the air warmed about her, losing its chill; her arms slowly grew lighter, the aches flowed out of them, until she felt as fresh as she'd been when first she started this. Free from pain, she gave herself up to the music, playing in a kind of trance in which there was nothing but the music.

At last she came as far as she could. There was no music left, her own, or anyone else's. She played the last sobbing notes of the Gypsy song Nightingale had told her was a lament for her own long-lost home, holding them out as long as she could.

But they flowed out and away, and finally, ended.

She opened her eyes.

The first rays of dawn lightened the horizon, bringing a flush of pink to the silver-blue sky. The stars had already faded in the east and were winking out overhead, and somewhere off in the distance, a cock crowed and a chorus of birdcalls drifted across the hills.

There was nothing standing before her now. The Ghost was gone— but he had left something behind.

Where he had stood, where there had once been a heap of leaves, there was now a pile of shining silver coins. More than enough to pay for that second instrument, the lessons for it, and part of her keep while she mastered it.

As she stared at the money in utter disbelief, a whisper came from around her, like a breath of the cool dawn wind coming up off the hills.

"Go, child. Take your reward, and go. And do not look back." A laugh, a kindly one this time. "You deserved gold, but you would never have convinced anyone you came by it honestly."

Then, nothing, but the bird song.

She put her fiddle away first, with hands that shook with exhaustion, but were otherwise unmarred, by blisters or any other sign of the abuse she'd heaped on them.

Then, and only then, did she gather up the coins, one at a time, each one of them proving to be solid, and as real as her own hand. One handful; then two—so many she finally had to tear off the tail of her shift for a makeshift pouch. Coins so old and worn they had no writing left, and only a vague suggestion of a face. Coins from places she'd never heard of. Coins with non-human faces on them, and coins minted by the Sire's own treasury. More money than she had ever seen in her life.

And all of it hers.

She stopped at the stream at the foot of the hill, the place that traditionally marked the spot where the Ghost's power ended. She couldn't help but stop; she was exhausted and exhilarated, and her legs wouldn't hold her anymore. She sank down beside the stream and splashed cold water in her face, feeling as if she would laugh, cry, or both in the next instant.

The money in a makeshift pouch cut from the tail of her shift weighed heavily at her belt, and lightly in her heart.

Freedom. That was what the Ghost had given her—and from its final words, she knew that the spirit had been well aware of the gift it had granted.

Go and don't look back. . . .

It had given her freedom, but only if she chose to grasp it—if she did go, and didn't look back, leaving everything behind. Her mother, Jib, the tavern . . .

Could she do that? It had taken a certain kind of courage to dare the Ghost, but it would take another, colder kind of emotion to abandon everything and everyone she'd always known. No matter what they had done to her, could she leave them for the unknown?

Her elation faded, leaving the weariness. She picked herself up and started for home, at a slower pace, sure only of her uncertainty.

Go—or stay? Each step asked the same question. And none of the echoes brought back an answer. The road was empty this time of the morning, with no one sharing it but her and the occasional squirrel. A cool, damp breeze brought the scent of fresh earth, and growing things from the forest on either hand. It was a shame to reach the edge of the village, and see where the hand of man had fallen heavily.

The inn, with its worn wooden siding and faded sign, seemed shabby and much, much smaller than it had been when she left yesterday. Dust from the road coated everything, and there wasn't even a bench outside for a weary traveler to sit on, nor a pump for watering himself and his beast. These were courtesies, yes, but they cost nothing and their absence bespoke a certain niggardliness of hospitality. She found herself eyeing her home with disfavor, if not dislike, and approached it with reluctance.

Prompted by a caution she didn't understand, she left the road and came up to the inn from the side, where she wouldn't be seen from the open door. She walked softly, making no noise, when she heard the vague mumble of voices from inside the common room through the still-shuttered windows.

She paused just outside the open door and still hidden from view, as the voices drifted out through the cracks in the shutters.

". . . her bed wasn't slept in," Stara said, and Rune wondered why she had never noticed the nasal, petulant whine in her mother's voice before. "But the fiddle's gone. I think she ran away, Jeoff. She didn't have the guts to admit she couldn't take the dare, and she ran away." Stara sounded both aggrieved and triumphant, as if she felt Rune had done this purely to make her mother miserable, and as if she felt she had been vindicated in some way.

Maybe she's been telling tales to Jeoff herself, the way I figured.

"Oh aye, that I'm sure of," Kaylan drawled with righteous self-importance. "Young Jon said she been a-flirtin' wi' him day agone, and she took it badly when he gave her the pass."

So that was how he explained it, she thought, seething with sudden anger despite her weariness. *But how did he explain his swollen tongue and bruised crotch? That I hit him when he wouldn't lay with me?*

"Anyways, she's been causin' trouble down to village, insultin' the girls and mockin' the boys. Think she got too big fer her hat and couldn't take it t' have her bluff called." Kaylan yawned hugely. "I think ye're well rid of her, Mistress Stara. Could be it was nobbut spring, but could be the girl's gone bad."

"I don't know—" Jeoff said uncertainly. "We need the help, and there's no denying it. If we can find her and get her back, maybe we ought to. A good hiding—"

I'd turn the stick on you, first! she thought angrily.

"Well, as to that," Kaylan said readily. "Me da's got a cousin down Reedben way with too many kids and too little land—happen that he could send ye the twins to help out. Likely ye're goin' to want the extra help, what with summer comin' on. Boy and girl, and 'bout twelve. Old 'nough to work, young 'nough not to cause no trouble."

"If they were willing to come for what Rune got," Jeoff said with eagerness and reluctance mixed. "Room, board and two suits 'f clothes in the year . . . haven't got much to spare, not even t' take a new wife, unless things get better."

Rune looked down at the bag of silver coins at her belt, hearing a note in Jeoff's voice she'd never noticed before. A note of complaint, and a tight-fisted whine similar to the one in Stara's voice. And as if she had been gifted with the Sight of things to come, she knew what would happen if she went into that doorway.

No one would ever believe that she had dared Skull Hill and its deadly Ghost, not even with this double-handful of coins to prove it. They'd think she'd found it, or—more likely—that she had stolen it. Jeoff would doubtless take it away from her, and possibly lock her in her room if suspicion ran high enough against her, at least until she could prove that she'd stolen nothing.

Then when no one complained of robbery, they would let her go, but she'd bet they still wouldn't return her hard-earned reward to her. They'd figure she had found a cache of coins along the Old Road, dug it up in the ruins in the Skull Hill Pass, or had found a newly dead victim of the Ghost and had robbed the dead.

And with that as justification, and because she was "just a child," Stara and Jeoff would take it all "to keep it safe for her."

That would surely be the last she would see of it, for Stara would see to it that it was "properly disposed of." She would probably spend a long night closeted with Jeoff, and when it was over, the money would be in *his* coffers. She'd promise it all to him as her "dower," if he agreed to marry her; and since there wasn't a girl in the village who could boast a double handful of silver as her dower, he'd probably agree like a lightning strike. Stara would tell herself, no doubt, that since this ensured Rune a home and a father, it was in her "best interest." Never mind that Rune would be no better off than before—still an unpaid drudge and still without the means to become a Guild Bard.

Jeoff would hide the money away wherever it was he kept the profits of the inn. Rune would *never* get her lessons, her second instrument. She would always be, at best, the local tavern-musician. She would still lack the respect of the locals, although Jeoff as her stepfather would provide some protection from the kind of things Jon had tried. She'd live and die here, never seeing anything but this little village and whoever happened to be passing through.

If she was very lucky, Jib might marry her. In fact, Jeoff would probably encourage that idea. It would mean that he would not have to part with any of the Ghost's silver for Rune's dower—assuming she could induce any of the local boys to the wedding altar—and he would then have Jib as an unpaid drudge forever, as well as Rune and her mother. He would do well all the way around.

She would still have the reputation of the tavern wench's bastard. She would still have trouble from the local girls and their mothers, if not the local boys. And there might come a time when beer or temper overcame someone's good sense—and she still might find herself fighting off a would-be rapist. There would be plenty of opportunities over the next few years for just that kind of "accident." And the boy could always pledge she'd lied or led him on, and who would the Sire's magistrate believe? Not Rune.

That was what was in store for her if she stayed. But if she followed the Ghost's advice, to go, and not look back—

What about Mother? part of her asked.

A colder part had the answer already. Stara could take care of herself. If she couldn't, that wasn't Rune's problem.

Besides, I've been standing here for the past few minutes listening to my own mother slash what little reputation I had to ragged ribbons. She's not exactly overflowing with maternal protection and love.

Her jaw clenched; her resolve hardened. No, Stara could damned well take care of herself. Rune wasn't about to help her.

But what about Jib?

That stopped her cold for a moment. Jib had been as much prey to the village youngsters as she had, and she'd protected him for a long time now. What would they do when they found out he didn't have that protection anymore?

How could she just leave him without a word?

She moved into the shelter of some bushes around the forested side of the inn, leaned up against a tree, and shut her eyes for a moment, trying to think.

He didn't need to worry about rape. No one was going to try and force him because his mother had the word of being a slut. His problems had always stemmed from the bigger, stronger boys seeing him as an easy target, someone they could beat up with impunity.

But the bigger, stronger boys had other things to occupy them now. They'd all either been apprenticed, or they'd taken their places in the fields with their farmer-fathers. They had very little time to go looking for mischief, and there'd be no excuse for them giving Jib a hiding if he'd been sent to the village on an errand.

Nor did Jib have to worry about the girls' wagging tongues. They didn't care one way or another about him—except, perhaps, as to whether or not he'd been tupping Rune. That might even earn him a little grudging admiration, if he refused to tell them, or denied it altogether. They'd be certain to think that he had, then.

Besides, one way or another, he was going to have to learn to fend for himself eventually. It might as well be now.

Sorry, Jib. You'll be all right.

She worked her way through the bushes, farther along the side of the inn, to stand below the eaves.

There was one way into her room that she hadn't bothered to take for years, not since she and Jib had gone swimming at night and hunting owls.

She looked up, peering through the leaves of the big oak that grew beside the inn, and saw that, sure enough, the shutters were open on the window to her room. Stara hadn't bothered to close them.

Very well, then. She'd make the truth out of part of the lie. Carefully, she put the fiddle down beside the trunk and pulled the pouch of coins from her belt, tucking it into her shirt. It was safer there than anywhere else while she climbed.

She jumped up and caught the lowest limb of the oak she'd been leaning against, pulling herself up onto it, and calling up an ache in her arms. It was a lot harder to climb the tree than she remembered—but not as hard as fiddling all night.

From that limb she found hand- and toe-holds up the trunk to the next branch. This one went all the way to her attic window, slanting above the roof and sometimes scraping against it when high winds blew.

She eased her way belly-down along the branch, with the pouch of silver resting against her stomach above her belt. She crept along it like a big cat, not wanting to sling herself underneath the way she had when she was a kid. It was easier to climb that way, but also easier to be seen. The branch was still strong enough to take her weight, though it groaned a little as she neared the roof.

When she got to the rooftop, she eased herself over, hanging onto the branch with both hands and arms, feeling with her toes for the window-sill. This part was easier now that she was older; it wasn't as far to reach.

It was a matter of minutes to pack her few belongings in a roll made from her bedding: shirts, breeches, a winter cloak that was a castoff from Rose, a single skirt, and a couple of bodices and vests. Some underclothing. A knife, a fork; a wooden dish and a mug. Two hats, both battered. Stockings, a pair of sandals, and a pair of shoes. Rosin for the bow, and a string of glass beads. An old hunting knife.

She hesitated about taking the bedding, but remembered all the work she'd done, and lost her hesitation. Jeoff owed her a couple of sheets and blankets at least, she figured, for all the work she'd done for him without pay.

Then she tossed the bundle into the brush where she'd left her fiddle, and eased herself down over the sill, catching the branch above and reversing her route to the ground.

Bedroll on her back, fiddle in her hand, and silver in her shirt, she headed down the road to Beeford and beyond, without a single glance behind her.

CHAPTER FIVE

Rune paused for a moment, at the top of what passed for a hill hereabouts, and looked down on the city of Nolton. She forgot her aching feet, and the dry road-dust tickle at the back of her throat no amount of water would ease. She had been anticipating something large, but she was taken a bit aback; she hadn't expected anything this big. The city spread across the green fields in a dull red-brown swath, up and down the river, and so far as she could see, there was no end to it. A trade-city, a city that had never been under attack, Nolton had no walls to keep anyone out. Nolton wanted all comers *inside,* spending their coin, making the city prosper.

The strategy must be working, for it surely looked prosperous. Houses of two and even three stories were common; in the center, there were buildings that towered a dizzying ten or eleven stories tall. The cathedral was one; it loomed over everything else, overshadowing the town as the Church overshadowed the lives of the townsfolk.

She had also been expecting noise, but not this far away from the city itself. But already there was no doubt that she heard sounds that could only come from Nolton; even at this distance, the city hummed, a kind of monotonous chant, in which the individual voices blended until there was no telling what were the parts that comprised it.

She had anticipated crowds; well, she'd gotten them in abundance. There had been some warning in the numbers of travelers for the past day and more on the road.

Although there were throngs of people, until today she hadn't been as apprehensive as she might have been. After all, the whole way here, she had made her way with her fiddle and her songs—

It hadn't been easy, drumming up the courage to approach that first innkeeper, trying to appear nonchalant and experienced at life on the road. She'd taken heart, at first, from the heavy belt of silver coins beneath her shirt. The Ghost had thought her worth listening to, and worth rewarding, for that matter. The memory gave her courage; courage to stride up to inns with all the assurance of the minstrels that had been her teachers, and present herself with an offer of entertainment in exchange for room and board.

It got a little easier with each approach, especially when the innkeepers stayed civil at the very least, and most were cordial even in their rejection.

Not that she had tried great inns; the inns where the Guildsmen and lesser nobles stayed. She didn't even try for the traders' inns, the kind where every traveler had at least a two-horse string. No, she had stuck to common enough inns, the sort simple peddlers and foot-travelers used. Inns like the one she had grown up in, where she figured she knew the custom and the kind of music they'd prefer. She'd been right, for they welcomed her; always, when they had no other musicians present, and sometimes even when they did, if the other musician was a local or indicated a willingness to share out the proceeds.

No one ever complained about her playing—although she dared not try her luck too far. She didn't want to run afoul of a Guild Minstrel, so she kept her ambitions modest, collected her pennies, and didn't trespass where she had any reason to doubt her welcome. There would be time enough to play for silver or even gold, later; time enough for the fine clothing and the handsome pony to ride. Time enough, when *she* was a Guild Bard. She didn't want to give *any* Guildsman reason to protest her admittance.

So for now, she pleased the peddlers, the farmers, and the herdsmen well enough. She took her dinner, her spot by the hearth-fire, and her bread and cheese in the morning with no complaint. She collected the occasional penny with a blessing and a special song for the giver. Every copper saved on this journey was one she could use to buy lessons and that precious instrument when she reached Nolton.

And when there was no dinner, no spot on the hearth—she slept in barns, in haystacks, or even up a tree—and she ate whatever she had husbanded from the last inn, or doled out a grudging coin or two for the cheapest possible meal, or a bit of bread or a turnip from a market-stall. Twice, when the inns failed her, she was able to avail herself of a travelers' shelter operated by the Church. For the price of a half loaf, she was able to get not only a pallet in a dormitory with other woman travelers, but a bath and two meals. Dinner was a bowl full of thick pease-porridge and a slice of oat bread, and breakfast was more of the bread, toasted this time, with a bit of butter and a trickle of honey. More copper, or silver, produced better food and accommodations, but she saw no reason to waste her coins.

The hidden price of this largess was that she also had to listen to sermons and scripture at both meals, and attend holy services before and after dinner and dawn prayers in the morning.

She had been left alone, other than that, though any females with a look of prosperity about them were singled out for special attentions. Those who were single, and well-dressed, but not Guild members, were urged to consider the novitiate—those who were married or in a trade were reminded that the Church favored those daughters who showed their faith in material ways.

Those two rest stops were enlightening, a bit amusing, and a bit disturbing. She had never quite realized the extent to which the Church's representatives worked to build and keep a hold on people. It was true that the Church did a great deal of good—but after years of living in an inn, Rune had a fair notion of how much things cost. Oat bread was the cheapest type there was; pease-porridge just as inexpensive. The Hungry Bear had never served either, except in the dead of winter when there were no customers at all and only the staff to feed. Granted, both meals at the hostel were well-made and food was given out unstintingly. But the labor involved was free; as was the labor involved in keeping the travelers' dormitory and bathhouse clean. That was provided by the nov- ices—the lower-class novices, or so Rune suspected; she doubted those of gentler birth would be asked to scrub and cook. The Church was probably not making enough just from the meals and the price of lodging to make the kind of profit a real inn would—but there was another factor involved here, the donations coaxed from the purses of the well-off. The Church got more than enough to make a tidy profit in "free-will offer- ings"—at least on the two occasions Rune observed. So the lodging was a pretense for extracting more donations. For all the prating about the poverty of the Church, for all that what she saw was as bare and sparse as the clergy claimed, the money had to be going somewhere.

She couldn't help wondering as she walked away that second morning; what happened to all that money?

Was there something beyond those stark, severe walls, in the places where the layman was not allowed to walk?

It was a good question, but one she didn't dwell on for long. She had her own agenda, and it had nothing to do with the Church's. She simply resolved to keep a wary eye on dealings that involved the clergy from here on. So long as they left her alone, she'd hold her peace about their profits.

Nolton had become her goal very soon after leaving the Hungry Bear, once she'd had a chance to talk to other travelers. For all that she'd never been outside the bounds of her own village, she knew what she needed out of a town. Nolton was the nearest city with enough musicians to give her a choice in teachers—dozens of inns and taverns, she'd been told, with all manner of entertainers.

Musicians could make a good living in Nolton. The rich had their own, family musicians as retainers—there were several Guild Halls which often hired singers and players, even whole ensembles. There were even instrument-makers in Nolton, enough of them that they had their own section in the weekly market. It was *not* in the direction of the Midsummer Faire, but she wouldn't be ready for the trials for at least a year, maybe two. So direction didn't much matter at the moment. What did matter was finding a good teacher, quickly.

She hadn't once considered how big a city would have to be in order to provide work for that many musicians. The number of ordinary folk that meant simply hadn't entered her mind; she'd simply pictured, in a vague sort of way, a place like her own village, multiplied a few times over.

Now she found herself standing on the edge of the road, looking down on a place that contained more people than she had ever imagined lived in the whole world, and suddenly found herself reluctant to enter it.

With all those people—the abundance of musicians abruptly became more than just a wide choice of teachers. It had just occurred to her that all those teachers were also *competition*. Suddenly her plan of augmenting her savings with her fiddling seemed a lot riskier. What if she wasn't good enough?

But the Ghost thought I was. The weight of the coins she'd sewn into the linen belt she wore under her shirt served as a reminder of that.

Still—she was good in a little village, she was passable in the country inns; but here she was likely to be just one more backwater fiddler. The tunes she knew could be hopelessly outdated, or too countrified to suit townsfolk. And she'd heard that everything was more expensive in cities; her hoard of coins might not be enough to keep her for any length of time. Apprehension dried her mouth as she stared at the faraway roofs. Maybe she just ought to forget the whole idea; turn back, and keep on as she had been, fiddling for food and a place to sleep in little wayside inns, traveling about, picking up a few coppers at weddings and Faires.

Tempting; it was the easy way out. It was the way her mother would have counseled. *Stick with the sure thing.*

But the thought of Stara's counsel made her stiffen her back. Maybe she should—but no. That wasn't what she *wanted* to do. It wasn't enough. And look where Stara's counsel had gotten *her*.

She gave herself a mental shake, and squared her shoulders under her pack. It wasn't enough—and besides, practically speaking, this fiddling about was a fine life in the middle of summer, but when winter came, she'd be leading a pretty miserable existence. Many inns closed entirely in the winter, and it would be much harder to travel then. Her pace would be cut to half, or a third, of what it was now. She'd be spending a lot of time begging shelter from farmers along the road. Some of them were friendly; some weren't. Then there were robbers, highwaymen, bandits—she hadn't run afoul of any of them yet, but that had been because she was lucky and didn't look worth robbing. In winter, anything was worth robbing.

No, there was no hope for it. The original plan was the best.

She took a deep breath, remembered the Ghost—with a bit of a chuckle to think that she was finding comfort in the memory of *that* creature—and joined the stream of humanity heading into the city.

She kept her eyes on the road and the back of the cart in front of her, watching to make sure she didn't step in anything. The pace slowed as people crowded closer and closer together, finally dropping to a crawl as the road reached the outskirts of the city. There was no wall, but there *was* a guard of some kind on the roadway, and everyone had to stop and talk to him for a moment. Rune was behind a man with an ox cart full of sacks of new potatoes, so she didn't hear what the guard asked before she reached him herself.

A wooden barrier dropped down in front of her, startling her into jumping back. The guard, a middle-aged, paunchy fellow, yawned and examined her with a bored squint, picking his teeth with his fingernail. She waited, stifling a cough, as he picked up a piece of board with paper fastened to it; a list of some kind. He studied it, then her, then it again.

"Name?" he said, finally.

"Rune," she replied, wishing her nose didn't itch. She was afraid to scratch it, lest he decide she meant something rude by the gesture. He scribbled a few things on the list in his hand.

"Free, indentured or Guild?" came the next question. She wrinkled her forehead for a moment, puzzled by that middle term. He looked at her impatiently, and swatted at a horsefly that was buzzing around his ears.

"What's matter, boy?" he barked. "Deaf? Or dumb?"

For a moment she was confused, until she remembered that she had decided to wear her loose shirt, vest, and breeches rather than attract unwelcome attention. "Boy," was her. But what on Earth was he asking her? Well, she wasn't Guild, and if she didn't know what "indentured" was, she probably wasn't that, either. "No, sir," she said, hesitantly. "I—uh—"

"Then answer the question! Free, indentured or Guild?" He swatted at the fly again.

"Free, sir." She was relieved to see him make another note. He didn't seem angry with *her,* just tired and impatient. Well, she was pretty hot and tired herself; she felt a trickle of sweat running down the back of her neck, and her feet hurt.

"From Westhaven, sir," she added. "My mother is Stara at the Hungry Bear."

He noted that, too.

"Profession?" That at least she could answer. She touched the strap of Lady Rose and replied with more confidence.

"Fiddler, sir. Musician, sir, but not Guild."

He gave her another one of those sharp glances. "Passing through, planning to stay a while?"

She shook her head. "Going to stay, sir. Through winter, anyway."

He snorted. "Right. They all are. All right, boy. You bein' not Guild, you can busk in the street, 'or you can take up with a common inn or a pleasure-house, but you *can't* take no gentry inns an' no gentry jobs 'less you get Guild permission, an' you stay outa the parks—an' you got a three-day to get a permit. After that, if you be caught street-buskin', you get fined, maybe thrown in gaol. Here." He shoved a chip of colored wood at her with a string around it. She took it, bewildered. "That shows what day ye come in. Show it when yer buskin' or when innkeeper asks fer it, till ye get yer permit. Mind what I said. Get that permit." He raised the barrier, and she stepped gingerly past him and into the town.

"An' don't think t' come back through an' get another chit!" he shouted after her. "Yer down on the list! Constables will know!"

Constables? What on Earth is a constable? She nodded as if she understood, and got out of the way of a man leading a donkey who showed the guard a piece of paper and was waved through. The fellow with the ox cart had disappeared into the warren of streets that led from the guard-post, and she moved off to the side of the road and the shade of some kind of storage building to study the situation.

She stood at the edge of a semicircular area paved with flat stones, similar to streets she had seen in some of the larger villages and in the courtyards of the Church hostels. That only made sense; with all these people, a dirt street would be mud at the first bit of rain, and dust the rest of the time. Storage buildings, padlocked and closed up, made a kind of barricade between the open fields and the edge of town. The streets led between more of these buildings, with no sign of houses or those inns the guard spoke of.

She watched the steady stream of travelers carefully as she rubbed her nose, looking for a system in the way people who seemed to know what they were doing selected one of the streets leading from this crossing.

She took off her hat and fanned herself with it, the sweat she had worked up cooling in the shade of the building. No one seemed inclined to make her move on, which was a relief. Finally she thought she had a pattern worked out. There weren't so many streets as she had thought; just a half dozen or so. The people with the bits of paper, the ones with beasts laden with foodstuffs, were taking the street farthest left.

That probably leads to a market. There won't be any inns there; too noisy and too smelly.

The three streets on the right were being followed by folks who were plainly Church, Guild or noble; mounted and well-dressed. The street directly before her was taken only by commoner folk, or by guards, they were all people who'd been waved through without being stopped, so it probably led to homes. A wide assortment of folks, the kind questioned by the guard before he let them in, were taking the market-street or the one next to it. After a moment, she decided to take the latter.

She made her way across the fan-shaped crossing-area, darting under the noses of placid oxen, following in the wake of a peddler leading a donkey loaded with what looked like rolls of cloth. As she had hoped, he took that second street, and she continued to follow him, being jostled at every turn before she got the knack of avoiding people. It was a little like a dance; you had to watch what they were going to do, but there was a kind of rhythm to it, although she lost her guide before she figured it all out. After a few moments, she settled into the pace, a kind of bobbing walk in which she took steps far shorter than she was used to, and began looking around her with interest.

All the buildings here were of wood with slate roofs, two or three stories tall; the upper stories overhung the street, and some were near enough to each other that folk sat in their open windows and gossiped above the heads of the crowd like neighbors over a fence. For the most part there was scarcely enough room for a dog to squeeze between the buildings, and the street itself was several degrees darker for being over-shadowed. A gutter ran down the center of the street, and she assumed at first that it was for the dung of the beasts—but a moment later, she saw a little old man with a barrow and a shovel, adroitly skipping about his side of the street and scooping up every fragrant horse-apple in sight, often before anyone had a chance to tread on it.

He acted as if he was collecting something valuable; he certainly didn't miss much. And what he didn't get, the sparrows lining the rooftops swooped down on, scattered it, and picked it over, looking for undigested grain.

Behind the fellow with the barrow came another, with a dog cart drawn by a huge mongrel, holding a barrel with boards bulging and sprung so that it leaked water in every direction. Rune stared at it, aghast at what she thought was his loss through foolishness or senility—and then realized it was on purpose. The water washed whatever the dung-collector had missed into the gutter, where it ran away, somewhere.

It wasn't the arrangement itself that caught her by surprise, it was what it implied. Here were people who spent all day, every day, presumably making a living—*keeping the streets clean*. The very idea would have made someone from her own village stare and question the sanity of anyone who proposed such an outlandish notion. This was not just a new world she'd jumped into, it was one that entertained things she'd never even dreamed of as commonplaces.

She felt dizzy, rootless—and terribly alone. How could she have enough in common with these townsfolk to even begin to entertain them?

But the next moment she heard the familiar sounds of a jig she knew well—"Half a Penny"—played on some kind of fife or pipe. She craned her neck to try and spot the player, waiting impatiently for the flow of the traffic to take her close enough to see him. Finally she spotted him, wedged in a little nook under the overhanging second story of one of the houses, with his hat on the stones in front of him, and a bit of paper pinned to his hat. He was surrounded by a mix of people, none very well-born, but of all ages and trades, clapping in time to his piping.

She focused on that brightly colored bit of paper. *That must be the permit the guard told me I had to get—*

She tried to get over to him, to ask him where he'd gotten it, but the crowd carried her past and she wasn't sure enough of her way to try and fight her way back. Still, his hat had held a fair amount of coin—which meant that *someone* thought country jigs were good enough entertainment. . . .

The houses began to hold shops on the lower level, with young 'prentices outside, crying the contents. The street widened a bit as well, and she began to spot roving peddlers of the sort that walked the Faires, trays of goods carried about their necks. The peddlers seemed mostly to be crying foodstuffs: meat pies, roast turnips, nuts; bread-and-cheese, muffins, and sweets. One of them passed near enough to her that she got a good whiff of his meat-pies, and the aroma made her stomach growl and her mouth water. It had been a long time since noon and her hoarded turnip.

But it wasn't only caution that kept her from reaching for her purse of coppers; it was common sense. No use in letting any thief know where her money was; she'd felt ghostly fingers plucking at her outer sash-belt a number of times, and at her pack, but the clever knots she'd tied the pack with foiled them, and the pouch, lean as it was, she had tucked inside her belt. If she let pickpockets see where that pouch was, she had a shrewd idea it wouldn't stay there long. She mentally blessed Raven for warning her to make a cloth belt to wear inside her clothes for most of any money she had, once she was on the road.

"It won't keep you safe from true robbers," he'd said. *"Not the kind that hit you over the head and strip you—but it'll save you from cut-purses."*

There was more advice he'd given her, and now that she was a little more used to the city, some of it was coming back, though she hadn't paid a lot of attention to it originally. The lessons in music had seemed a lot more important.

"Never ask for directions except from somebody wearing a uniform or from an innkeeper. If you find yourself on a street that's growing deserted, turn around and retrace your steps quickly, especially if the street seems very dirty and dark, with the buildings closed up or in bad repair. If a friendly passerby comes up out of nowhere and offers to help you, ignore him; walk away from him or get by him before he can touch you. Never do anything that marks you as a stranger, especially as a stranger from the country. That'll show you as an easy mark for robbers or worse."

All right then, exactly how was she going to find an inn, and a place where she might be able to set herself up as the resident musician?

This was a street of shops—but sooner or later there had to be an inn, didn't there?

Maybe. Then again, maybe not. There were other streets branching off this one; maybe the inns were on these side streets. She'd never know—

She spotted a dusty hat just ahead of her; a hat that had once been bright red, but had faded to a soft rose under sun and rain. Something about the set of the rooster feathers in it seemed familiar; when the crowd parted a little, she realized that it belonged to one of the journeymen who had been in the same inn she'd played at last night, and had tossed her a copper when she played the tune he'd requested.

She'd overheard him talking quite a bit to a fellow in the Apothecary's Guild. She remembered now that he had said he wasn't from Nolton himself, but he was familiar with the city, and had recommended a number of inns and had given directions to the other man. She hadn't paid attention then—the more fool her—she'd thought she would have no trouble, as an inn-brat herself, in finding plenty of places.

But he bobbed along in the crowd with a purposeful stride; he obviously knew exactly where he was going. An inn? It was very likely, given the time of day. And any inn he frequented would likely be the sort where her playing would be welcome.

She darted between two goodwives with shopping baskets over their arms, and scraped along a shop front past a clutch of slower-paced old men who frowned at her as she scooted by. The feathers bounced in the breeze just ahead of her, tantalizingly near, yet far enough away that she could all too easily lose their owner in the press. She found herself stuck behind a brown-clad, overweight nursemaid with a gaggle of chattering children on their way home from the Church school. The two eldest, both girls, one in scarlet and one in blue, and both wearing clothing that cost more than every item she'd ever owned in her life bundled together, looked down their noses at her in a vaguely threatening fashion when she made as if to get past them. She decided not to try to push her way by. They might think she was a thief, and get a guard or something. In fact, they might do it just to be spiteful; the pinched look about their eyes put her in mind of some of the more disagreeable village girls. She loitered behind them, and fumed.

But they were moving awfully slow, as the nursemaid called back the littler ones from darting explorations of store fronts, time and time again. The rooster feathers were bobbing away, getting ahead of her, their owner making a faster pace than she dared.

Then, suddenly, as she strained her neck and her eyes, trying to keep them in sight, Red-Hat turned into a side street, the rooster feathers swishing jauntily as he ducked his head to cut across the flow of traffic. Then hat and feathers and all disappeared behind a building.

Oh, no— Heedless now of what the unfriendly girls might say or do, Rune dashed between them at the first break, ignoring their gasps of outrage as she wormed her way through the crowd to the place where Red-Hat had vanished. She used her elbows and thin body to advantage, ignoring the protests of those whose feet she stepped on or who got an elbow in the ribs, taking care only to protect Lady Rose and her pack.

She broke out of the crowd directly under the nose of a coach horse.

It snorted in surprise, and came to a hoof-clattering halt. She flung herself against the wall, plastering herself against the brick to let the coach pass. The driver cursed her and the other foot-travelers roundly, but the well-trained, placid horse simply snorted again at her, as if to register his surprise when she had appeared under his nose, and ignored her once she was out of his way. The wheels of the coach rumbled by her feet, missing them by scant inches, the driver now too busy cursing at the other folk in his way to pay any more attention to her.

She sighed, and wiped her sweating brow when he had passed. That was a lot closer than she cared to come to getting run over, and if the horse hadn't been a particularly stolid beast, she could have gotten trampled or started a runaway. But now that the coach was gone, she saw that this street carried a lot less traffic than the main street; it should be easy to find Red-Hat.

She peered down the cobblestone street, but the conspicuous hat was nowhere to be seen. For a moment her heart sank, but then she raised her eyes a little, and couldn't help but grin. There, not twenty feet from her, swung a big, hand-painted sign proclaiming the "Crowned Corn Public House, Drink & Vittles," superimposed over a garish yellow painting of a barley-sheaf with a crown holding the straws in place. Beside it swung a huge wooden mug with carved and white-painted foam spilling over the sides, for the benefit of the illiterate. Whether or not Red Hat was in there, the presence of the beer mug meant that it was a "common" place, and its clientele shouldn't be too different from the travelers she'd been entertaining. If she couldn't strike up a bargain here, she could probably get directions to a place that could use a musician. If the owner proved unfriendly, at least now she knew that the inns *were* on the side streets.

I can retrace my steps if I have to, and find another. She trotted the remaining few steps to the door, and pushed it open.

She blinked, trying to get her eyes to adjust quickly to the dark, smoky interior. The aroma that hit her, of smoke, baking bread and bacon, of stew and beer, was so like the way the Hungry Bear smelled that she could have been there instead of here. But the crowds! This place was packed full, with more people than the Bear ever saw except at the height of Harvest Faire. There were five or six girls in bright, cheap skirts and tight-laced bodices, and young men in leather aprons, breeches, and no-color shirts scurrying about the room, tending to the customers. She despaired of being able to catch anyone's eye to ask directions to the owner, but one of the girls must have caught the flicker of movement at the door, for she bustled over as soon as she'd finished gathering the last of the mugs from an empty table.

She appraised Rune with a knowing eye, a little disappointed that it wasn't a paying customer, but willing to see what Rune wanted. "Ye be a musicker, boy?" she asked, and Rune nodded. "Come wi' me, then," she said, and turned on her heel to lead the way through the crowd, her striped skirts swishing jauntily with every step. There evidently wasn't any prohibition *here* about fondling the help, and the many pats and pinches the girl got made Rune very glad for her boy's garb.

She pushed past two swinging half-doors into what could only be the kitchen; it was hot as the inside of a bake-oven and overcrowded with people. On the wall nearest the door stood a pair of dish-tubs on a tall bench or narrow table, with a draggle-haired girl standing beside it and working her way through a mountain of mugs and bowls. Rune's guide heaved her own double-handful of wooden mugs up onto the table with a clatter, then turned to the rest of the room. It was dominated by the bake-ovens at the far end, all of them going full blast; three huge windows and the door open to the yard did little to ease the burden of heat the roaring fires beneath the ovens emitted. There was a big table in front of the ovens, with a man and a woman rolling out crust for a series of pies at one end, and cooling loaves stacked at the other. Another table, next to that, held a man cutting up raw chickens; beside him was another woman slicing some kind of large joint of cooked meat. A third table held six small children cleaning and chopping vegetables. There were other folks darting in and out with food or the dirty dishes, and a knot of people at the oven end.

"Mathe!" the serving girl shouted over the din. "Mathe! Sommut t' see ye!"

A short, round, red-faced man in a flour-covered apron detached himself from the clump of workers beside the ovens, and peered across the expanse of the kitchen toward them. His bald head, shiny with sweat, looked like a ripening tomato.

"What is it?" he yelled back, wiping his brow with a towel he tucked back into his waistband.

"Musicker!" the girl called, a bit impatiently. "Wants a job!"

Mathe edged around the end of the table by the oven, then squeezed in between the wall with the windows and the children cleaning vegetables to make his way towards them. Rune waited for him, trying not to show any anxiety. The serving girl watched them both with avid curiosity as Mathe stopped a few feet away.

The owner planted both fists on his hips and stood slightly straddle-legged, looking her up and down with bright black eyes. As keen as his eyes seemed to be, however, she got the feeling he didn't realize she wasn't a boy. Plenty of young men wore their hair longer than hers, and her thin face and stick-straight body wasn't going to set any hearts aflame even when she was in skirts. Certainly the serving girl had made the same mistake that the gate-guard had made, and she wasn't going to correct any of them.

"Musicker, eh?" Mathe said at last. "Guild?"

She shook her head, wondering if she had doomed herself from the start. What had the gate-guard said about jobs she could take? There had been something about inns—

"Good," Mathe said in satisfaction. "We can't afford Guild fees. From country, are ye? Singer or player?"

"From down near Beeford. I'm a player, sir," she replied. "Fiddle, sir."

"Got permit? When ye come in?" he asked. "Where's yer chit?" These city-folk spoke so fast she had to listen carefully to make out what they were saying.

Wordlessly she showed him her scrap of wood. He took a quick glance at it.

"Today, hmm?" He examined her a moment more. "You know 'Heart to the Ladies'?" he asked, and at her nod, said, "Unlimber that bit'a wood and play it."

She dropped her pack on the flagstone floor and took Lady Rose out of her traveling bag, tuning her hastily, with a wince for her in this overheated room. She set the bow to the strings, and played—not her best, but not her worst—though it was hard to make the music heard in the noisy kitchen. Still, the serving girl's foot was tapping when Mathe stopped her at the second chorus.

"Ye'll do," he said. "If we c'n agree, ye got a one-day job. Here's how it is. We got a reg'lar musicker, but he took a job at a weddin'. We was gonna do wi'out t'night, but music makes the beer flow better, an since here ye be, I don't go lookin' a gift musicker i' the mouth."

He chuckled, and so did Rune, though she didn't get the joke, whatever it was.

"Now, here's the bargain," Mathe continued, wiping the back of his neck with his towel. It was a good thing he was mostly bald, or his hair would have been in the same greasy tangles as the dishwasher girl's. "I feeds ye now; ye plays till closin'. Ye gets a place by th' fire t' sleep— this ain't no inn, an' I'm not s'pposed t' be puttin' people up, but you bein' on yer three-day chit th' law'll look 'tother way. Ye put out yer hat, I get two coins outa every three.''

That wasn't as good a bargain as she'd been getting on the road, but it sounded like he was waiting for her to make a counteroffer. She shook her head. ''Half, and I get bread and stew in the morning.''

''Half, an' ye get bread'n dripping,'' he countered. ''Take it or leave it, it's m'last offer.''

Bread and butter, or bread and honey, would have been better—but butter and honey could be a lot more expensive in the city, where there were neither cows nor bees. ''Done,'' she said, putting out her hand. They shook on it, solemnly.

''All right, then,'' he said, rubbing his hands together in satisfaction. ''Beth there'll show ye where t'set up, and gi' ye the lay'a the land, an' she'll see to yer feedin'. Don' touch th' girls 'less they invite it, or m'barkeep'll have yer hand broke. Oh, one other thing. I don' let me musickers get dry, but I don' let 'em get drunk, neither. Small beer or cider?''

''Cider,'' Rune said quickly. The last thing she needed was to get muddle-headed in a strange eating-house in a strange city, and although small beer didn't have a lot of punch to it, drinking too much could still put you under the table, and if it was this hot all night, she'd be resorting to her mug fairly often.

Mathe had given her an interesting piece of information. So inns didn't necessarily take sleepers here? That was worth noting. She reckoned that would suit Stara just fine—it would mean less than half the work . . . but this place wasn't called an ''inn,'' it was something called a ''public house.'' They must be two different things—

''Good lad,'' Mathe replied with satisfaction. ''Don't talk much, sensible, and ye drive a good bargain. Ye'll do. Now get 'long wi' ye, I got my work t' tend.''

Beth laughed and wrinkled her nose at him, and Rune picked up her pack and followed the serving girl out. Her hips waggled saucily, and Rune wondered just what constituted an ''invitation.'' Certainly the girl was trying to see if this new musician could be tempted.

Too bad for her I'm not a boy. I'm afraid I'm going to disappoint her if she wants a sweaty-palm reaction.

There was just enough of a clear path behind the benches and tables to walk without bumping into the customers. They edged around the wall until they came to a corner with a stool and a shelf very near the bar, and the massive bartender presiding over the barrels of beer and ale; his expression impassive, statue-like.

"Here," Beth said, gesturing at the stool, flipping her dark hair over her shoulder. If she was disappointed that Rune hadn't answered her flirtations, she didn't show it. Maybe she was completely unaware she'd been flirtatious. Manners could be a lot different here than what Rune was used to. "This be where ye set up an' play. We likes country-tunes here, an' keep it lively. If they gets t' clappin', they gets t' drinkin'."

Rune nodded, and tucked her pack behind the stool. Lady Rose was still in her hand, and she set the fiddle down on top of the pack gently, so that the instrument was cradled by the worn fabric of the pack and the clothing it contained.

"Look sharp here, boy," Beth said, and Rune looked up. "Ye see how close ye are t' the bar?" She pointed with her chin at the massive barrier of wood that stood between the customers and the barrels of beer and wine.

Rune nodded again, and Beth grinned. "There's a reason why we put th' musicker here. Most of ye ain't big 'nuff t' take care'a yerselves if it comes t' fightin'. Now, mostly things is quiet, but sometimes a ruckus comes up. If there's a ruckus, ye get yer tail down behin' that bar, hear? Ain't yer job t' stop a ruckus. Tha's Boony's job, an' he be right good at it."

Beth tossed her curly tangle of hair over her shoulder again, and pointed at a shadowy figure across the room, in a little alcove near the door. She hadn't noticed it when she first came in, because her back had been to it, and the occupant hadn't moved to attract her attention. Rune squinted, then started. Surely she hadn't seen what she thought she'd seen—

Beth laughed, showing that she still had most of her teeth, and that they were in good shape. "Ain't never seen no Mintak, eh, fiddler? Well, Boony's a Mintak, an' right good at keepin' the peace. So mind what I said an' let him do what he's good at, 'f it come to it."

Rune blinked, and nodded. She wanted to stare at the creature across the room, but she had the vague feeling that too many people already stared at Boony, openly or covertly, and she wasn't going to add to their rudeness.

A Mintak . . . she'd heard about the isolated pockets of strange creatures that were scattered across the face of Alanda, but no one in her village had ever seen so much as an elven forester, much less a Mintak. They were supposed to have bodies like huge humans, but the heads of horses. The brief glimpse she'd gotten didn't make her think of a horse so much as a dog, except that the teeth hadn't been the sharp, pointed rending teeth of a canine, but the flat teeth of an herbivore. And the eyes had been set on the front of the head, not the sides. But the Mintak loomed a good head-and-a-half above the bartender, and that worthy was one of the tallest men Rune had ever seen.

Beth came bustling back with a bowl of stew, a mug, and a thick slice of bread covered in bacon drippings in one hand, and a pitcher with water beading the sides in the other. "Take this, there's a good lad." She'd evidently decided that Rune was terribly young, too young and girl-shy to be attracted, and had taken a big-sisterly approach to dealing with her. "You get dry an' look to run short, you nod at me or one'a th' other girls. Ol' Mathe, he don't like his musickers goin' dry; you heard him sayin' that, an' he meant it."

She put the pitcher on the floor beside the stool, shoved the rest into Rune's hands, and scampered off, with a squeal as one of the customers' pinches got a little closer to certain portions of her anatomy than she liked. She slapped the hand back and huffed away; the customer started to rise to follow—

And Boony stepped forward into the light. Now Rune saw him clearly; he wore a pair of breeches and a vest, and nothing else. He carried a cudgel, and he was a uniform dark brown all over, like a horse, and he had the shaggy hair of a horse on his face and what could be seen of his body. His eyes seemed small for his head; he had pointed ears on the top of his head, peeking up through longer, darker hair than was on his face, and that hair continued down the back of his neck like a mane. He looked straight at the offending customer, who immediately sat down again.

So Boony kept the peace. *It looks like he does a good job,* Rune mused.

But there was dinner waiting, and beyond that, a room full of people to entertain. She wolfed down her food, taking care not to get any grease on her fingers that might cause problems with the strings of her fiddle. The sooner she started, the sooner she could collect a few coins.

And hopefully, tonight Boony's services wouldn't be needed. Nothing cooled a crowd like a fight, and nothing dried up money faster.

She put out her hat, wedging it between her feet with one foot on the brim to keep it from being "accidentally" kicked out into the room, and re-tuned Lady Rose.

Cider or no, with all these people and only herself to entertain them, it was going to be a long night.

"Seventeen, eighteen, nineteen," Rune counted out the coins on the table under Mathe's careful eye. "That's the whole of it, sir. Nineteen coppers.'' The candle between them shone softly on the worn copper coins, and Mathe took a sip of his beer before replying.

"Not bad," Mathe said, taking nine and leaving her ten, scooping his coins off the table and into a little leather pouch. "In case ye were wonderin' lad. That's not at all bad for a night that ain't a feast nor Faire-day. Harse don' do much better nor that.''

He set a bowl down in front of her, and a plate and filled mug. "Ye did well 'nough for another meal, boy. So, eat whiles I have my beer, an' we'll talk.''

This time the stew had meat in it, and the bread had a thin slice of cheese on top. Getting an extra meal like that meant that she'd done more than "all right." She could use it, too; she was starving.

The public house was very quiet; Beth and the other girls had gone off somewhere. Whether they had lodgings upstairs or elsewhere, Rune had no idea, for they'd left while Rune was packing up, going out the back way through the kitchen. Presumably, they'd gotten their meals from the leftovers on their way through. Boony slept upstairs; she knew that for certain. So did Mathe and one of the cooks and all of the children, who turned out to be his wife and offspring.

Right now, she was thinking about how this would have meant a month's take in Faire-season at home. She shook her head. "It seems like a lot—" she said, tentatively, "—but people keep telling me how much more expensive it is to live in the city.''

Mathe sipped his own beer. "It is, and this'd keep ye for 'bout a day; but it's 'cause'a the rules, the taxes, an' the Priests," he said. "Ye gotta tithe, ye gotta pay yer tax, an' ye gotta live where they say. Here— lemme show ye—''

He stretched out his finger and extracted two coppers, and moving them to the side. "That's yer tithe—ye gotta pay tithe an' tax on what ye made, *b'fore* I took my share." He moved two more. "That's yer tax. Now, ye got six pence left. Rules say ye gotta live in res'dential distrik, 'less yer a relative or a special kinda hireling, like the cooks an' the kids and Boony is. Musickers don' count. So—there's fourpence a day fer a place w' decent folks in it, where ye c'n leave things an' know they ain't gonna make legs an' walk while ye're gone. That leaves ye tuppence fer food.''

Rune blinked, caught off guard by the way four pennies evaporated— close to half her income for the day. "Tax?" she said stupidly. "Tithe?'' Fourpence, gone—and for what?

Mathe shook his head. "Church *is* the law round 'bout towns," he told her, a hint of scolding in his voice. "Ye *tithe*, lad, an' ye base it

on what ye took in. Same fer taxes. If ye don' pay, sooner 'r later they
cotch up wi' ye, or sommut turns ye in, an' then they fine ye. They fine
ye *ten times* what they figger ye owe.''

''But how would they know what I owe them?'' she asked, still confused. '' 'Specially if I work the street—''

''They know 'bout what a musicker like you should make in a night,
barrin' windfalls,'' he replied. ''Twenny pence. That's two fer Church
an' two fer tax. An' if ye get them windfalls, the lad as drops bit'a gold
in yer hat an' the like, ye best r'port 'em too. Could be sommut saw it
go in yer hat, an's gone t' snitch on ye. Could be 'tis a Priest in disguise,
belike, testin' ye.''

This all seemed terribly sinister. ''But what happens if I couldn't pay?''
she asked. ''I mean, what if I'd been holding back for a year—'' *Ten times*
tuppence times—how many days in a year? The figures made her head
swim. It was more than she'd ever seen in her life, except for the
windfall of the silver. And she panicked over that for a moment, until
she realized that no one knew about it but her—nor ever would, if she
kept her mouth shut.

''Happened to a girl'a mine,'' Mathe said warningly. ''She owed 'em
fer 'bout three year back; spent it all, a' course, stupid cow. Couldn't
pay. She got indentured t' pay the bill.''

Indentured? There was that word again. ''What's 'indentured,'
Mathe?'' she asked.

''Worse than slavery,'' boomed a voice over her head, so that she
jumped. ''Worse than being chattel.''

''Ol' Boony, he's got hard feelin's 'bout bein' indentured,'' Mathe
offered, as Boony moved around to the other side of the table and sat
down on the bench, making it creak under his weight.

''There are laws to keep a slave from being beaten,'' Boony rumbled.
''There are laws saying he must be fed so much a day, he must have
decent clothing and shelter. The Church sees to these laws, and fines the
men who break them. There are no such laws for the indentured.''

The Mintak nodded his massive head with each word. Now that he
was so close, he looked less animal-like and more—well, human wasn't
the word, but there was ready intelligence in his face; he had expressions
Rune was able to read. His face was flatter than a horse's, and his mouth
and lips were mobile enough to form human speech without difficulty.
His hands only had three broad fingers, though, and the fingers had one
less joint than a human's, though the joints seemed much more flexible.

''Boony didn' know 'bout tithin' an taxes when he come here,'' Mathe
said, as Boony took a turnip from the bowl at the end of the table and

began stolidly chewing it. "He got indentured t' pay 'em. An' he's right, the way indenturin' works is that ye work fer yer wage. But yer wage goes first t' yer master, t' pay off yer debt, an' there ain't no law saying how much he c'n take, so long as he leaves ye a penny a day."

And a penny, as she had just learned, wouldn't go far in this city.

"I was bought by a greedy man who used my strength in his warehouse, took all, and left me with nothing," Boony said. "He thought I was stupid." A dark light in his eyes told her he'd somehow managed to turn the tables on his greedy owner, and was waiting for her to ask how he'd done it.

"What did you do?" she asked, obediently.

Boony chewed up the last of the turnip, top and all, confirming her notion that he was herbivorous. He laughed, a slow, deep laugh that sounded like stones rolling down a hill. "I was so *very* stupid that I did not know my own strength," the Mintak said, smiling. "I began to break things. And when he ordered me beaten, I would catch the hand of the overseer, and ask him, ever so mildly, why he did this to me. Soon I was costing the scum much, and there was no one in his employ willing to face me, much less beat me."

"That's when I bought 'im out," Mathe said. "I've had a Mintak cust'mer or twain here, an' I knew th' breed, d'ye see. He earned back 'is fine a long time agone, but he reckoned on stayin' wi' me, so we've got 'im listed as adopted so's he c'n live here." He and the Mintak exchanged backslaps, the Mintak delivering one that looked like a fly-swat and staggered his employer. "He'll run th' place fer the wife when I'm gone, won't you, old horse?"

"May God grant that never come to be," the Mintak said piously. "But admit it—you are the exception with indentures."

Mathe shrugged. "Sad, but Boony's got the right 'f it. And 'member, boy—if ye get indentured, the law says ye work at whatever yer bond-holder says ye do. That means 'f he runs a boy-brothel. . . ."

"Which is where a-many young men and women go," Boony rumbled. "Into shame. The law says nothing about that. Nor the Church."

Mathe made a shushing motion. "Best not t' get inta *that*. Best t' jest finish warnin' the young'un here." He took another pull on his beer, and Boony chomped up a couple of carrots and a head of lettuce, jaws moving stolidly. She took the opportunity to finish her food.

"All right," Mathe said after a moment of silence. "Tonight, ye sleep on that straw mat by th' fire—which's what payin' customers'd get if I took any—an' in the mornin' I feeds ye, an' yer on yer way. Now, ye know where ye go first?"

"To get a permit?" she ventured. He shook his head.

"Not 'less ye got a silver penny on ye; that's th' cost 'f a street-buskin' permit. No, ye go straight t' Church-box on t'end 'a this street, an ye pay yer tithe an' tax from today. Church clerk'll put down yer name, an' that goes in at end 'f day t' Church Priest-house w' th' rest on the records. *Then* ye busk on street, outside Church-box. By end'a day, ye'll have th' silver penny, ye' get the permit. Go get *that* fr'm same place; Church-box. Then ye busk where the pleasure-houses be, thas on Flower Street, 'till ye can't stay awake no more. That'd be dawn, an' ye'll have 'nough for tithe an' tax from t'day."

"This is the one time you may safely skim a little, to pay for the permit, in all the time you may be here," the Mintak rumbled. "They will not expect you to play enough to earn double wages."

She nodded. "But—" she began, then hesitated.

"So?" Mathe said, as his wife shooed her children up the stairs behind them to their living quarters.

"Don' be t' long, eh sweeting?" she called. "Boy's a good'un, but ye both needs sleep."

Mathe waved at her, his eyes fixed on Rune. She dropped her eyes to her hands. "What I—really came here for, to Nolton, I mean, was lessons. I—want to join the Guild."

"I told you," Boony said, booming with satisfaction. "Did I not tell you he knew more than to be simple busker?"

"Ye did, ye did, I heerd ye," Mathe replied. "Ye won yer bet, old horse. Now, boy, lemmee think." He rubbed his bare chin and pursed his lips. "There's places t' get secondhand instruments, an' places t' get lessons. Sometimes, they be th' same place. Tell ye what, I gi' ye a map i' th' mornin'. Tell ye what else, sommut 'em gonna know where there's places lookin' fer musickers. If ye got a place, ye don' need no permit—or ye c'an git one, an' play double, by day fer pennies i' th' street, an' by night fer yer keep."

Rune could hardly restrain herself. This was far more than she'd expected in the way of help. "I don't know how to thank you, sir," she said, awkwardly. "I mean—"

"Hush," Mathe said. "Thank yon Beth an' Boony. 'Twas she brought ye back; 'twas he tol' me I'd best sit ye down an' 'splain how things is 'round here, afore ye got yersel' in a mess."

"I've already thanked Beth, sir," she said, truthfully, for she'd asked the girl what her favorite tunes were, and had played them all. "It was kindness to take me back to you and not show me the street."

"Well, she said ye had th' look'a sommut that knew his way about an inn," Mathe replied, blushing a little. "I figgered if ye did, ye knew what t' play t' please m' custom. An' ye did; sold a good bit'a beer t'night. Ye done good by me."

"I'm glad," she replied sincerely. "And thank *you*, sir," she said, turning to Boony. "Although I'm sure I know your reasons—that you didn't want to see a weaker creature put in the same position you'd been in. I've heard many good things about the Mintak; I will be glad to say in the future that they are all true."

Boony laughed out loud. "And I will say that it is true that Bards have silver tongues and the gift of making magic with word and song," he replied. "For I am sure you will be a Bard one day. It pleases me to have saved a future Bard from an unpleasant fate. And now—" he looked significantly at Mathe.

The man laughed. "All right, old horse. It's off t' bed for all of us, or m'wife 'll have Boony carry me up. G'night, young Rune."

He and Boony clumped up the stairs, taking the candle, but leaving the fire lit so she could see to spread her blankets out on the sack of clean straw they'd given her to sleep on.

She had thought that she'd be too excited to sleep, but she was wrong. She was asleep as soon as she'd found a comfortable position on the straw sack, and she slept deeply and dreamlessly.

CHAPTER SIX

Breakfast, dished up by Mathe's wife after the morning cleaning crew rousted her out of her bed, was not bread and drippings nor leftover stew; it was oat-porridge with honey and a big mug of fresh milk. When Rune looked at her with a lifted eyebrow, she shrugged, and cast a half-scornful look at Mathe's back.

" 'Tis what my younglings get," she said. "Ye need a healthy morning meal, ye do. And I told Mathe, I did, that you're not much bigger nor they. Bread and drippings, indeed, for a growing boy! Ye'd think the man had no childer of his own!" And she sniffed with disdain.

Rune knew when to leave well enough alone, and she finished the porridge with appreciation. She gathered up her things, slung her pack and Lady Rose over her back, and headed for the outer door. She found the owner there, as if he was waiting for her, and somehow she wasn't surprised when Mathe slipped a packet into her hand as she bade him farewell. The cooks from last night were already hard at work in the kitchen; the serving-boys were scrubbing down tables, benches and floor, while the girls swept the fireplaces and cleaned beer mugs. Mathe took her outside, and stood on the door-sill, closing the door behind them.

The street before them had a few carts on it, but not many. By the angle of the sunlight it was about an hour past dawn. In the country, folks would already be out in their fields, working; here in the city, it seemed that most people weren't even awake yet. Since Rune had always preferred lying late abed, she had the feeling she was going to like being a city person.

"Ye go straight down this street, east," Mathe said, waving his hand down the quiet, sunlit lane. Dust-motes danced in the shaft of light that ran between the overhanging buildings. "At second crossing, there be a little black stall. That be Church-box; there be priest inside, ye gi' him yer tithe an' tax, an make sure ye gi' him separate. Elsewise, he'll write all fourpence down as tithe, an' leave ye owin' fourpence tax."

And I wonder how many people that's happened to? I bet the Church

wouldn't give it back, either, even if you could get them to admit that
a mistake was made.

She nodded, slipping the packet into the pocket in her vest. It felt like
bread; maybe even bread and cheese. That would be welcome, in a few
hours. It meant something more she wouldn't have to buy.

And courtesy of Mathe's wife, too, she had no doubt. That was a
good woman, and very like Rose.

Mathe continued with his directions and instructions. "Now, then ye
go 'cross street; there be couple stalls sells vittles. Play there. There's
always a crowd there—ye got the people as come t' pay tax an' tithe,
ye got people as wants a bit t'eat. It's a bit too noisy fer a singer, but
ye'll do fine. Nobody got that as set yet, that I heerd of. Here's bit'a
map." He handed her a folded paper, and watched as she unfolded it;
the maze of lines was incomprehensible at first, until she resolved it into
streets, and even found the one the public house stood on, the gate she'd
come in by, and the street she had followed. "See, this here, this's
where we be. These little red dots, thas some'a them teachers an' in-
str'ment makers. See if any on 'em'll do ye." He nodded as she folded
it up and stowed it in her belt-pouch, where the ten pennies from her
evening's labor chinked. "Now, if I was in yer shoes, I'd play till after
nuncheon, thas midmeal, when people stop buyin' things at stall, an then
I'd go look up some'a them teachers and the like. But thas me. Think
ye'll do?"

"You've done more for me than I ever hoped, sir," she replied honestly. "I can't begin to thank you."

And I don't know why you've done it, either. I'm glad you did, but I
wish I knew why. . . .

He flushed a little with embarrassment. "Ah, musickers done me a
good turn or twain, figger this helps pay back. When I was jest startin'
this place, musickers came round t' play jest fer the set-out, 'till I could
afford t' feed 'em. Then I got my reg'lar man, an' he bain't failed me.
So—I gi' ye a hand, ye gi' sommut else one 'f it's needed—"

Someone inside called him, urgently, and he turned. "Can't be away
a breath an' they need me. God be wi' ye, youngling. Watch yerself."

And he dashed back inside, shouting, "All right! All right! I'm gettin'
there fast as I can!"

Rune headed up the street, in the same direction Mathe had pointed.
It was considerably quieter in the early hours of the morning. Shops
were just opening, merchants taking down massive wooden shutters, and
laying displays in the windows behind thinner wooden grates to foil
theft.

The shops here seemed to tend to clothing; materials, or clothing ready-made. She passed a shop full of stockings, hats and gloves, a shoemaker, and several shops that appeared to be dressmakers and tailors. The Crowned Corn seemed to be the only inn or public house on this street, although there were vendors of foodstuffs already out with their trays about their necks. They weren't crying their wares, though; the streets weren't so full that customers couldn't see them. They ignored Rune for the most part, as being unlikely to have enough spare coin to buy their goods.

A cart passed, and Rune noticed another odd contrivance, just under the horse's clubbed tail. This was a kind of scoop rigged to the cart that caught any droppings. A good notion, given the number of animals here. That would mean only those carts without the scoop and horses being ridden would be leaving refuse. The city, while not exactly sweet-smelling, would be a lot worse without the care taken to keep it clean.

The merchants were doing their part, too; there were folks out scrubbing their doorsteps, and the street immediately in front of the shop, right up to the gutter-line. How the folk back in the village would stare!

Not even the late Rose was that fanatical about cleanliness.

On the other hand, there weren't that many people in the village. With all these people, all these animals, there would have to be extra precautions against the illnesses that came from dirt and contaminated water.

The little black stall that Mathe had called the "Church-box" was plainly visible as soon as she crossed the first street. It had an awning above it, supported by carved wooden angels instead of simple props. And without a doubt, the awning was decorated with painted saints distributing alms, to remind the pious and impious alike where their tithes were going.

In all probability, the stall was the last business to close at night, and the first to open in the morning. The Church never lost an opportunity to take gifts from her children.

There was a grill-covered window in the front of the stall, and beneath it, a slot. Behind the window sat a bored young novice-Priest in his plain, black robes, yawning and making no attempt to cover his indifference to his surroundings. He blinked at her without interest, and reached for a pen when he saw she was going to stop and give him something to do. Or rather, force him to do something.

"Name?" he mumbled. She gave it; likewise her occupation, and that she was beginning her second day in Nolton. He noted all of it down, and warned her, in a perfunctory manner, that she would have to purchase her permit to busk before the fourth day. From him, of course. And that it would be a silver penny. He did *not* issue any of the warnings Mathe had, about what it would mean if she neglected to do so.

"Here's my two-pence tithe for yesterday, sir," she said, pushing the pennies across the counter to him, through the slit. He took it, with a slightly wrinkled nose, as if in disdain for the tiny amount, but he took it, nevertheless. She noted that he seemed well-fed; very well-fed in fact, round-cheeked and healthier than most. His hands were soft, and white where the ink of his occupation hadn't stained them. He dropped the two coins into something beneath the counter, just out of sight, and made a notation after her name. "And here's my two-pence tax," she said, shoving those coins across when she knew he'd made his first notation and couldn't change it.

He frowned at her as he took the two coins. "You could have given it to me all at once," he grumbled, making a second notation. She blinked, and contrived to look stupid, and he muttered something under his breath, about fools and music, and waved her off.

She turned away from the window. Well, that was that; fourpence lighter, and nothing to show for it. Could have been worse, she supposed. If she hadn't been warned, sooner or later the Church would have caught up with her. . . . Boony's description of his treatment as a bondservant hadn't been inviting.

Although the idea of seeing a bondholder's face when he realized that the boy he'd thought he'd bought off was a girl was amusing, she didn't care to think about what would have followed that discovery. Probably something very unpleasant.

Across the street were the two food-stalls Mathe had described for her, with a bit of space in between for a tall counter where folk could eat standing up; one was red-painted, and one was blue. She crossed the street under the disdainful gaze of the novice-Priest and approached the first stall-holder.

"Would you mind if I put out my hat here, sir?" she asked politely of the thin fellow frying sausage rolls in deep skillets of lard. He glanced up at her, and shook his head.

"So long as ye don' drive th' custom away, 'tis nobbut t' me," he replied absently. Encouraged, she repeated her question at the second stall, which sold drink, and got the same answer.

So she found a place where she wasn't going to be in the way of people buying or eating, and set her hat at her feet, with her pack to hold it down. She took the fiddle from her carrying bag, gave Lady Rose a quick tuning, and began playing, choosing a simple jig, bright and lively.

Although she quickly attracted a small crowd, they were mostly children and people who didn't look to have much more money than she. Still, they enjoyed her music, and one or two even bought something at the stalls on either side of her, so she was accomplishing that much. And as long as her listeners bought something, she wasn't likely to be chased away.

By noon bell, she'd acquired a grand total of three pennies, a marble dropped in by a solemn-faced child, a little bag of barley-sugar candy added by a young girl, a bit of yellow ribbon, and at least a dozen pins. She'd never collected pins before, but any contribution was better than nothing. Once she'd straightened and cleaned them, pins were worth a penny the dozen, so that wasn't so bad, really.

The bad part was that she'd fiddled most of the morning and not even gained half what she'd gotten in the public house last night. She was a long way from the silver penny that permit would cost her. She took a moment for a breather, to look over the traffic on the street.

Early days yet, she told herself, as the crowds thickened, the street filling with folk looking for a bit to eat. The first noon bell seemed to signal a common hour for nuncheon, which the people back home called midmeal. She took her eyes off her hat and fixed them on the faces about her, smiling as if she hadn't a care in the world. *When you're fiddling, think about music,* Raven had admonished her. *Don't think about your dinner, or where you're going to sleep tonight. Tell yourself you're happy, and put that happiness into the way you're playing. Make people feel that happiness. . . .*

The faces of those about her changed as they got within earshot of the fiddle. They generally looked surprised first, then intrigued. Their eyes searched the edge of the crowd for the source of the music, then, when they found it, a smile would creep onto their lips. And, most times, they'd stop for a moment to listen. She found herself looking for those smiles, trying to coax them onto otherwise sour faces; playing light, cheerful tunes, tunes meant to set feet tapping.

Her efforts began to pay off, now that she was looking to those smiles for her reward and not the money in the hat. A couple of children broke into an impromptu jig at her feet once; and a young couple with the look of the infatuated did an entire dance-set beside her until the glare and a word from a passing Priest sent them laughing away.

She played a mocking run on her fiddle to follow the fat, bitter man, and thought then how odd it was that the Church seemed to frown upon everything that was less than serious—

But frivolity puts no coins in their coffers, she reminded herself—and realized that the crowds had thinned again; the second noon-bell had rung, and the stall-keepers on either side of her were cleaning their counters instead of cooking or serving customers. She finished the piece, then looked down at her hat, and saw that the three pennies had multiplied to nine, there was a second bag of sweets beside the first, and a veritable rain of pins covered the bottom of the hat.

"Eh, lad," said the second stall-keeper, leaning out to examine the contents of her hat with interest. " 'F ye got no plans fer them pins, I trade 'em fer ye. Fifteen pins fer a mug'a cider, an' don' matter what shape they be in, I'll swap. Wife c'n allus use pins."

"Same here," said the sausage-roll vendor. "Fifteen pins fer a roll."

Well, that would take care of her nuncheon with nothing out of her pocket, and she'd be saved the trouble of straightening the pins herself. And dealing with them; she hadn't a paper to stick them in, and she didn't relish the idea of lining them up in rows on her hat. She'd probably forget they were there and put her hand on them. "Done, to both of you," she replied, "and grateful, too."

"Good enough," said the sausage vendor. And when a count proved her to have forty-three, offered her two rolls for what was left when she got her cider. She stowed the rest of her take in her pouch and pack, put away Lady Rose, drank her cider, and considered what to do with the rest of her day, devouring her rolls while she thought.

It really wasn't worth playing her fingers off for only three pennies, not when she needed to find a place to live, a teacher, and a second instrument, in that order. So, with a wave of farewell to the two vendors, she packed herself up, and took out her map.

After a few times of getting turned around, she learned the trick of following it. It was too bad that none of the places Mathe had marked were terribly nearby, but there were three that were kind of in a row, and she headed in their direction.

The first shop was in the middle of a neighborhood where her shabby clothing drew dubious looks; nearly everyone she saw on the street wore clothing like the wealthier farmers' sons and daughters wore to Church services back home. One look in the shop window convinced her that this was no place for her. The instruments hung on the wall were polished and ornamented with carving and inlay work; they might well be second-hand, but they were still beyond her reach, and so, likely, was the teaching to be had.

The second place was much like the first, and she caught sight of some of the students waiting their turns. They were very well dressed, hardly a patch or a darn or let-down hem to be seen, and most of them were much younger than she. From the bored expressions they wore, she had the notion that the only reason they were taking music lessons at all was because it was genteel to do so.

She left the brightly painted shops behind, passed through a street of nothing but wrought-iron gates set into brick walls a story tall, gates giving onto small, luxurious gardens. The gardens were beautiful, but she didn't linger to admire them. Some of those gates had men in livery behind them, and those men wore weapons, openly. No point in giving them a reason to think she was here by anything other than accident.

That street became a street of shops; food shops this time, vegetables, fruit, wooden replicas of meat and fish and poultry, all displayed enticingly inside open windows, with the real meat and dairy products lying on counters inside, or hanging from the rafters and hooks on the walls. Here, the clothing of the folk in the street had a kind of uniform feel to it; all sober colors, with white aprons and caps or dark hats. *Servants,* she decided. Sent from those houses behind her to buy the goods for dinner. How strange to have a servant to send out—what a thought! To wait, doing whatever it was that rich folk did, until dinner appeared like magic, without ever having to raise a finger to make it all happen! And then to go up to a room, and find a bath hot and waiting, and a bed warmed and ready—a book, perhaps, beside it. And in the morning, to find clean clothing set out, breakfast prepared. . . .

She daydreamed about this as she wormed her way down street after street, each one getting progressively narrower, and gradually shabbier. Finally she found herself on a street much too narrow for a cart, unless it was one of the dog carts; a street that even a ridden horse would probably find uncomfortably confining.

There was only one shop in the street that had three instruments hanging in the window, although it had other things there as well; cheap copper jewelry, religious statues, cards of lace and tarnished trim that showed bits of thread on the edge where it had been picked off a garment, knives and a sword, a tarnished silver christening-goblet. . . .

A small sign in the window said "We Buy and Sell" and "Loans Made." Another sign beneath it showed two pairs of hands; one offering a knife, the other a silver coin. A third, smaller sign said "Music Lessons."

She looked back up at the instruments, a lute, a harp, and a guitar; they were old, plain, but well-cared-for. There wasn't a speck of dust on them anywhere. The strings looked a little loose, which meant they weren't kept tuned—something that would warp an instrument's neck if it wasn't taken down and played often. Whoever had hung them there knew what he was doing.

The street itself was quiet; one of those "residential" areas Mathe had spoken of. There was another food-shop on the corner, but otherwise, this seemed to be the only store in this block of buildings. The rest were all wooden, two-storied, with slate roofs; they had single doors and a window on either side of the door, with more windows in the overhanging second story. A rat might have been able to scurry in the spaces between them, but nothing larger.

The buildings themselves were old, in need of a new coat of paint, and leaned a little. They reminded Rune of a group of old granddams and grandsires, shabby, worn, but always thinking of the days when they had been young.

Instruments and lessons—and a place where she might find somewhere to live. This was the most promising area, at least insofar as her purse was concerned, that she had encountered yet. She opened the door and went inside.

The interior of the shop was darker than the public house had been, and smelled of mildew and dust. When she closed the door behind her, a bell jangled over it, and a voice from the back of the store said, "Be patient a moment, please! I'm up on a ladder!" The voice matched the store; a little tired, old, but with a hint that it had been richer long ago.

Rune waited, letting her eyes adjust to the darkness of the shop. The place was crowded with all sorts of oddments, even more so than the tiny window. Behind and in front of her were floor-to-ceiling shelves; on them were books, stuffed animals, neatly folded clothing, statues of all sorts, not just religious, one or two of which made her avert her eyes in flushed embarrassment. There were dusty crystals, strange implements of glass and metal, lanterns, and cutlery. All of it was used, much of it was old, and some of it looked as if it had sat there for centuries. Every object had a little paper tag on it; she couldn't imagine why.

Suspended from the rafters were cloaks and coats, each with moth-bane festooning the hems. The shop itself was barely large enough for Rune, the shelves, and the tiny counter at the rear of the shop.

After a moment, an old man dressed in a dust-colored shirt and breeches pushed aside the curtain behind the counter and peered at her, then shook his gray, shaggy head.

"I'm sorry, lad," he said regretfully. "I'm not buying today—"

"And I'm not selling, sir," she interrupted, approaching the counter so he could get a better look at her.

He blinked, looked again, and chuckled; a rich, humor-filled sound that made her want to like him. He reminded her of Raven, a little. And a little of that Guild Minstrel. "And you're no lad, either. Forgive me, lass. What can I do for you?"

A little surprised, since no one else had seen her true sex through her purposefully sexless clothing, she took another step forward. "My name is Rune. I'm a player, sir," she said, hesitantly. "I was told that I could find an instrument and lessons here."

"That's true," the old man said, his sharp black eyes watching her so closely she felt as if her skin were off. "You can, as you know if you saw the signs in the windows. But there's more to it than that—the things that brought you to this shop in this city. Now, I like a good tale as well as any man, and it's late and near time to close up. If you'd care to share a cup of tea with me—and tell me your tale?"

Part of her said not to trust this man—here he was a stranger, and offering to share his hospitality with another stranger—

But the rest of her thought—what could he possibly *do* to her? He was old, he moved slowly; he couldn't possibly out-wrestle her in a bad situation. Where was the harm in indulging him?

And there was more of Raven's advice. *If you find yourself with someone who cares for his instruments, no matter how old, or how plain—or even how cheap—you can trust him. He's a man who knows that all value isn't on the surface. And he may have some of that hidden value himself.*

"I'd like that, sir," she said, finally. But he had already raised his tiny counter on the hinges at one side, and was motioning her through as if he had never expected she would do anything other than accept. She pushed the curtains aside, hesitantly, and found herself in another narrow room, with a staircase at the farther end leading up to a loft. This room was just as crowded as the shop. There was a stove with a tiny fire in it, with a kettle atop; a broken-down bed that seemed to be in use as seating, since it was covered with worn-out cushions in a rainbow of faded materials. There seemed to be more furniture up in the loft, but the shadows up there were so thick that it was hard to see.

Besides the bed, there was a basin and ewer on a stand, a couple of tables piled with books, two chairs, and a kitchen-cupboard next to the stove. Everything stood within inches of the furniture beside it. There wasn't any possible way one more piece of furniture could have been crammed in here.

Rune took a seat on one of the chairs, placing her pack and Lady Rose at her feet. The only light came from a window at the rear of the room, below the loft, covered in oiled paper; and from a lantern on the table beside her.

There was a *thump,* as of heavy shutters closing, the door-bell jangled, and then a scraping sound of wood on wood came to her ears as the old man pushed the bar into place across his shutters. A moment later, he pushed aside the curtains and limped into the room.

Instead of speaking, he went straight to the stove at the rear and took a kettle off the top, pouring hot water into a cracked teapot that was missing its lid and stood on the shelf of the kitchen-cupboard beside him. He brought the pot and a pair of mugs with him, on a tarnished tray, which he sat down on the table beside her, next to the lamp, pushing the books onto the floor to make room for the tray.

"Now," he said, taking the other chair, "My name's Tonno. Yours, you said, is Rune, as I believe. While we wait for the herbs to steep, why don't you tell me about yourself? You're obviously not from Nolton, and your accent sounds as if you're from—hmm—Beeford, or thereabouts?"

She nodded, startled.

He chuckled and smiled, a smile that turned his face into a spiderweb of tiny lines, yet made him look immensely cheerful. "So, how is it that a young lady like you finds herself so far from home, and alone?"

She found herself telling him everything, for somehow his questions coaxed it all out of her; from the bare facts, to how she had managed to come here, to her desire for a place in the Guild. As the light beyond the oiled paper dimmed, and her confidence in him grew, she even told him about the Ghost, and her secret hoard of coins. Somehow she felt she could trust him even with that, and he wouldn't betray her trust.

He pursed his lips over that. "Have you told anyone else about this?" he asked sternly. She shook her head. "Good. Don't. The Church would either take a lion's share, or confiscate it all as coming from demons. I'll give you a choice; either you can keep them hidden and safe, or you can give them to me, and I'll provide you with that instrument you want and a year's worth of lessons—and give you whatever's left over, but I'll have it all changed into smaller coins. Smaller coins won't call attention to you the way silver would. I can probably manage that just on what I've saved."

She thought about that; thought about how easy it would be for the money to just trickle away, without her ever getting the lessons or the instrument. If she paid him now—

"This won't be just lessons in learning tunes, mind," Tonno said abruptly. "I'll teach you reading music, and writing it—you'll have the freedom to read any book in this shop, and I'll expect you to read one a week. I'm a hard teacher, but a fair one.''

She nodded; this was more than she had expected.

''Can you play me a tune on that little fiddle of yours?'' he asked— and once again, Rune took her lady from her case, and tuned her. This time, with care—for Tonno was a fellow musician, and she wanted to give him her very best.

She played him three pieces; a love song, a jig, and one of the strange Gypsy tunes that Nightingale had taught her. The last seemed to fill the shadows of the room with life, and turn them into things not properly of the waking world. It wasn't frightening, but it was certainly uncanny. She finished it with gooseflesh crawling up her arms, despite the fact that she had played the tune herself.

When she'd finished, Tonno sighed, and his eyes were a little melancholy. ''I'll tell you something else,'' the old man said, slowly, ''and I'm not ashamed to admit it, not after listening to you. I'm no better than a talented amateur. I knew better than to try and make a living at music, but I promise you that I know how to play every instrument in this shop, and I'm quite good enough to give you basic lessons. And believe me, child, if you've learned this much on your own, basic lessons in a new instrument, the ways of reading and writing the tunes you surely have in your head, and all the education you'll get from reading whatever you can get your hands on for the next year will be all that you need.'' He shook his head again. ''After that you'll need more expert help than that, and I can probably find someone to give it to you. But I don't think that you'll need it for at least a year, and tell the truth, I wonder if some people who heard you now might not hold you back out of jealousy to keep you from outstripping them. When you get beyond me, I can send you out to others for special lessons, but until then—''

She let out the breath she'd been holding in a sigh.

''Can we chose an instrument now, sir?'' she asked. ''I'd like to make this a firm bargain.''

They picked out a delicate little lute for her; she fell in love with its tone, and decided against the harp that Tonno thought might suit her voice better. Besides, the lute only had four strings; it would be easier to tune and keep tuned in the uncertain climes a traveling musician was likely to encounter. They agreed on a price for it and the year of lessons, and Rune retired behind a screen to take off her belt of silver coins. She knew she had spent a lot getting to Nolton; even augmenting her cash with playing on the road, the coins had been spent a lot faster than she'd liked. There was some left when they got through reckoning up how much three hours of lessons every day for a year would cost. Not much, but some. She could go ahead and buy her permit; and she would have a hedge against a lean spell.

When the commercial exchange had been accomplished, an awkward silence sprang up between them. She coughed a little, and bit her lip, wondering what to say next.

"I probably should go," she said, finally. "It's getting darker, and I've taken up too much of your time as it is. I'll come about the same time tomorrow for my first lesson—"

"Now what are your plans?" he asked, interrupting her. "Never mind what you're going to do tomorrow, what are you planning on doing tonight? You don't know the city—you could get yourself in a bad area, wandering about."

"I need a place to live," she said, now uncertain. Daylight was long spent, and she wasn't certain if those who took in lodgers would open their doors to a stranger after dark.

"What about a place to earn your keep?" he asked. "Or part of it, anyway—I—know someone looking for a musician. She could offer you a good room in exchange for playing part of the night. Possibly even a meal as well."

There was something about his manner that made her think there was a great deal more about the place than he was telling her, and she said as much.

He nodded, reluctantly. "It's a public house—a real one, but a small one. In part. And—well, the rest I'd rather Amber told you herself. If you want to go talk to her."

Tonno's diffident manner convinced her that there was something odd going on, but she couldn't put her finger on what it was. She frowned a little.

He shrugged, helplessly. "It's only a few blocks away," he said. "And it's in the area where there are a lot of—places of entertainment. If you don't like Amber, or she doesn't like you, you can try somewhere else. *That* area is safe enough you could even busk on the street-corner and *buy* yourself a room when you have the two pence." He smiled apologetically. "I often go there for my dinner. I would be happy to walk you there, and introduce you to Amber."

She thought about it; thought about it a long time. In the end, what decided her was Tonno's expression. It wasn't that of a man who was planning anything, or even that of a man who was trying to keep his plans hidden. It was the anxious look of someone who has a friend of dubious character that he likes very much—and wants his new friend to like as well.

Rune was well enough acquainted with the way the world wagged to guess what Tonno's friend Amber was. A public house—"of sorts," hmm? A small one? That might be what it was below-stairs, but above . . .

Amber probably has pretty girls who serve more than just beer and wine, I'd reckon.

On the other hand, it couldn't hurt to go look. People who came to a whorehouse had money, and were ready to spend it. They might be willing to toss a little of it in the direction of a player. As long as Amber knew she was paying for the music, and not the musician.

Besides, if there was one thing the Church Priests preached against, it was the sins of the flesh. It would ease the burden of having to pay the Priests their damned tithe knowing that the money came from something they so violently disapproved of.

"All right," she said, standing up and catching Tonno by surprise. "I'll see this friend of yours. Let's go."

And I can always say no, once I've met her.

CHAPTER SEVEN

In the streets of Nolton darkness was total, and at first the only light they had to show them their footing were the torches at the crossroads, and the occasional candle or rushlight in a window at street level. Tonno kept a brisk pace for such an old man; Rune had to admire him. It helped that he knew the way, of course, and she didn't. He kept pointing out landmarks as they passed—a building that dated back several hundred years, a place where some significant event in the history of the city had occurred, or the site of someone's birth or death. She would strain her eyes, and still see only one more shapeless bulk of a building, with a furtive light or two in the windows. Finally she gave up trying to see anything; she just nodded (foolish, since he wouldn't be able to see the nod), and made an appreciative grunt or a brief comment.

The street Tonno led her to was not one she would have found on her own; it was reached only by passing through several other side streets, and the street itself was about a dozen houses long, and came to a dead end, culminating in a little circle with an ornamental fountain in the center of it. It was, however, very well lit, surprisingly so after the darkness of the streets around it; torches outside every door, and lanterns hanging in the windows of the first and second stories saw to that. There was an entire group of musicians and a dancer busking beside the fountain, and from the look of the money they'd collected on the little carpet in front of the drummer, the pickings were pretty good here. The fountain wasn't one of the noisy variety; it would be easy enough even for a single singer to be heard over it. A good place to put out a hat, it would seem.

The musicians looked familiar, in the generic sense; finally she realized that they were dressed in the same gaudy fashion as the Gypsies the harpist Nightingale traveled with. If this "Amber" didn't prove out, perhaps she'd see if they'd let her join them. They didn't have a fiddler, and they might recognize Nightingale's name or description, and be willing to let her join them on the basis of a shared acquaintance.

Most of the places on the circle itself were large, with three stories and lights in every window, sometimes strings of lanterns festooning the balconies on the second and third stories, as if it were a festival. There were people coming and going from them in a steady stream; men, mostly. And, mostly well-dressed. Whenever a door opened, Rune heard laughter and music for a moment, mingling with the music of the quartet by the fountain. There were women leaning over the balconies and out of the windows; most disheveled, most wearing only the briefest of clothing, tight-laced bodices and sleeveless under-shifts that fluttered like the drapes of the Ghost—

She shivered for a moment with a chill, then resolutely put the memory out of her mind. There was no Ghost here—and anyway, he'd favored her, he hadn't harmed her.

Sheer luck, whispered the voice of caution. She turned her attention stubbornly to her surroundings. Here was warmth and light and laughter, however artificial. There were no ghosts here.

All of the women, she had to admit, were very attractive—at least from this distance. They flirted with fans, combed their hair with languid fingers, or sometimes called out to the men below with ribald jokes.

She'd have to be a simpleton not to recognize what kind of a district this was. It might even be the same street Mathe had mentioned as a good place to busk at night. Her guise of a boy would probably keep her safely unmolested here—she'd seen no signs that these brothels catered to those whose tastes ran to anything other than women.

But Tonno took her to a tiny place, just two stories tall, tucked in beneath the wings of the biggest building on the circle. There were lights in the windows, but no women hanging out of them, and no balcony at all, much less one festooned with willing ladies. The sign above the door said only, "Amber's." And when Tonno opened the door, there was no rush of light and sound. He invited Rune in with a wave of his hand, and she preceded him inside while he shut the door behind them.

The very first thing she noticed were the lanterns; there was one on every table—and every table seemed to have at least one customer. So whatever this place was or did, it wasn't suffering from lack of business. The common room was half the size of the Bear's, but the difference was in more than size. Here, there were no backless benches, no trestle tables. Each square table was made of some kind of dark wood, and surrounding it were padded chairs, and there were padded booths with tables in them along the walls. The customers were eating real meals from real plates, with pewter mugs and forks to match. And the whiff Rune got of beef-gravy and savory was enough to make her stomach growl. She told it sternly to be quiet, promising it the bread and cheese still tucked into her pack. No matter what came of this meeting, she had a meal and the price of a room on her—and tomorrow would be another day to try her luck.

She'd certainly been lucky today, so far. It was enough to make her believe in guardian spirits.

Across the room, a woman presiding over a small desk beside a staircase saw them, smiled, and rose to greet them. She was middle-aged; probably a little older than Stara, and Rune couldn't help thinking that *this* was what Stara was trying to achieve with her paints and her low-cut bodices, and failing. Her tumbling russet curls were bound back in a style that looked careless, and probably took half an hour to achieve. Her heart-shaped face, with a wide, generous mouth, and huge eyes, seemed utterly ageless—but content with whatever age it happened to be, rather than being the face of a woman trying to hold off the years at any cost. The coloring of her complexion was so carelessly perfect that if Rune hadn't been looking for the signs, and seen the artfully painted shadows on lids and the perfect rose of the cheeks, she'd never have guessed the woman used cosmetics. Her dress, of a warm, rich brown, was of modest cut—but clung to her figure as if it had been molded to it, before falling in graceful folds to the floor.

Any woman, presented with Stara and this woman Amber, when asked to pick out the trollop, would point without hesitation to Stara, ignoring the other entirely. And Rune sensed instinctively that any man, when asked which was the youngest, most nubile, attractive, would select Amber every time. The first impression of Amber was of generosity and happiness; the first impression of Stara was of discontent, petulance, and bitterness.

She found herself smiling in spite of herself, and in spite of her determination not to let herself be charmed into something she would regret later.

"Tonno!" Amber said, holding out both hands to him, as if he was the most important person in the world. He clasped them both, with a pleased smile on his lips, and she held them tightly. "I had given up on seeing you tonight! I am *so* pleased you decided to come after all! And who is this young lad?"

She turned an inquiring smile on Rune that would likely have dazzled any real "lad," and yet was entirely free of artifice. It didn't seem designed to dazzle; rather, that the ability to dazzle was simply a part of Amber's personality.

"Amber, this *lass* is my new pupil, Rune. And, I hope, is the musician you've been asking me to find." Tonno beamed at both of them, but the smile that he turned to Rune held a hint of desperation in it, as if he was begging Rune to like this woman.

We'll see how she reacts to being told I'm a girl, first—if all she's interested in is what she can get out of someone, and she knows that as a woman I'm not as likely to be manipulated—

"A lass!" Amber's smile didn't lose a bit of its brightness. In fact, if anything, it warmed a trifle. "Forgive me, Rune—I hope you'll take my mistake as a compliment to your disguise. It really is very effective! Was this a way to avoid trouble in public? If it is, I think you chose very well."

Rune found herself blushing. "It seemed the safest way to travel," she temporized. "I never wore skirts except when I planned to stay at a hostel."

"Clever," Amber replied with approval. "Very clever. Now what was this about your being a musician? I take it you have no place yet? Tonno, I thought you said she was your student—" She interrupted herself with a shake of her head. "Never mind. Let's discuss all this over food and drink, shall we?"

Rune glanced sideways at the customer nearest her. She knew what *she* could afford—and she didn't think that this place served meals for a penny.

She thought she'd been fairly unobtrusive, but Amber obviously caught that quick sideways glance. And had guessed what it meant—though that could have been intuited from the threadbare state of Rune's wardrobe. "Business before pleasure, might be better, perhaps. If you'd feel more comfortable about it, we can discuss this now, in my office, and Tonno can take his usual table. Would that be more to your liking?"

Rune nodded, and Amber left her for a moment, escorting Tonno to a small table near the door, then returning with a faint swish of skirts. Rune sighed a little with envy; the woman moved so gracefully she turned the mere act of walking into a dance.

"Come into my office will you?" she said, and signaled to one of the serving girls to take care of Tonno's table. Obediently, Rune followed her, feeling like an awkward little donkey loaded down with packs, carrying as she was her worldly goods and the fiddle and lute cases.

The office was just inside the door to the staircase, and held only a desk and two chairs. Amber took the first, and Rune the other, for the second time that day dropping her packs down beside her. Amber studied her for a moment, but there was lively interest in the woman's eyes, as if she found Rune quite intriguing.

"Tonno is a very good friend, and has advised me on any number of things to my profit," she said at last. "He's very seldom wrong about anything, and about music, never. So perhaps you can explain how you can be both his student and the musician I've needed here?"

"I'm self-taught, milady," Rune replied with care. "Last night, my first in the city, the owner of the Crowned Corn said I was good enough to expect the same profit as anyone else who isn't a Guild musician. But that's on the fiddle—and I can't read nor write music, can't read much better than to puzzle out a few things in the Holy Book. So that's how I'm Tonno's student, you see—on the lute, and with things that'll make me ready for the Guild trials."

Amber nodded, her lips pursed. "So you've ambitions, then. I can't blame you; the life of a common minstrel is not an easy one, and the life of a Guild musician is comfortable and assured."

Rune shrugged; there was more to it than that, much more, but perhaps Amber wouldn't understand the other desires that fired her—the need to find the company of others like herself, the thirst to learn more, much more, about the power she sensed in music—and most especially, the drive to leave something of herself in the world, if only one song. As she knew the names of the Bards who had composed nearly every song in her repertory except the Gypsy ballads, so she wanted to know that in some far-off day some other young musician would learn a piece of hers, and find it worth repeating. Perhaps even—find it beautiful.

No, she'd never understand that.

"I will be willing to take Tonno's assessment of your ability as a given. This is what I can offer: a room and one meal a day of your choice. This is what your duty would be: to play here in the common room from sundown until midnight bell. I should warn you that you can expect little in the way of tips here; as you have probably guessed already, this is not an inn as such."

"It's a—pleasure-house, isn't it?" She had to think for a moment before she could come up with a phrase that wouldn't offend.

Amber nodded. "Yes, it is—and although many clients come here only for the food, the food is not where the profit is; it is merely a sideline. It serves to attract customers, to give them something to do while they wait their turn. Your capacity would be exactly the same. You would *not* be expected to serve above-stairs, is that clear?"

The relief must have been so obvious in spite of Rune's effort not to show it that Amber laughed. "My dear Rune—you are a very pleasant girl, but a *girl* is all you are, no matter how talented you might be in other areas. This house serves a very specific set of clients, by appointment only. And let me tell you that the four young ladies entertaining above are quite a peg beyond being either girls or merely pleasant. Beside them, I am a withered old hag indeed, and their talents and skills far outstrip mine!''

Irrationally, Rune felt a little put out at being called a ''pleasant young girl''—but good sense got the better of her, and she contemplated the offer seriously for the first time since Tonno had brought the possibility up.

This meant one sure meal a day, a particularly good meal at that, and a room. She need only play until midnight bell; she would have the morning and noon and part of the afternoon to busk before her lessons with Tonno. Not a bad arrangement, really. It would let her save a few pennies, and in the winter when it was too cold to busk, she could stay inside, in a building that would, by necessity, be warmly heated. Still, this was a whorehouse . . . there were certain assumptions that would be made by the clients, no matter what Amber claimed. If Amber wanted her to dress as a female, there could be trouble.

''No one will bother you,'' Amber said firmly, answering the unspoken question. ''If you like, you can keep to that boy's garb you've taken, although I would prefer it if you could obtain something a little less— worn.''

Rune looked down reflexively at her no-color shirt, gray-brown vest and much-patched breeches, all of which had been slept in for the past three days, and flushed.

''Tonno can help you find something appropriate, I'm sure,'' Amber continued, with a dimpling smile. ''I swear, I think the man knows where every second-hand vendor in the city is! As for the clients and your own safety—I have two serving girls and two serving boys below-stairs; you may ask them if they have ever been troubled by the clients. The ladies do not serve meals; the below-stairs folk do not serve the clients. Everyone who comes here knows that.''

Rune licked her dry lips, took a deep breath, and nodded. ''I'd like to try it then, Lady Amber.''

''Good.'' Amber nodded. ''Then let's make your meal for the day a bit of dinner with Tonno, and we can call tonight's effort your tryout. If you suit us, then you have a place; if not—I'll let you have the room for the rest of the night, and then we'll see you on your way in the morning.''

A short trial-period, as these things went, and on generous terms. But she had nothing to lose, and if nothing else, she'd gain a dinner and a place to sleep for the night. She followed Amber back out into the common room, where she sat at Tonno's table, ate one of the best beef dinners she had ever had in her life, and listened while Amber and Tonno talked of books. The only time she'd ever eaten better was when the Sire had sent a bullock to the village to supply a feast in celebration of his own wedding, and Rune had, quite by accident she was sure, been given a slice of the tenderloin. The beef she'd normally eaten was generally old, tough, and stewed or in soup.

During that time, she saw several men leave by the stairs, and several more ascend when summoned by a little old man, so bent and wizened he seemed to be a thousand years old. They were all dressed well, if quietly, but for the rest, they seemed to fit to no particular mold.

As soon as she'd finished, she excused herself, and returned to Amber's office for Lady Rose, figuring that the office was the safest place to leave her gear for the moment. Fiddle in hand, she came back to the table, and waited for a break in the conversation.

"Lady Amber, if you please, where would you like me to sit, and what would you prefer I played?" she asked, when Amber made a point that caused Tonno to turn up his hands and acknowledge defeat in whatever they were discussing. They both turned to her as if they had forgotten she was there. Tonno smiled to see her ready to play, and Amber nodded a little in approval.

Amber's brows creased for a moment. "I think—over there by the fireplace, if you would, Rune," she said, after a moment of glancing around the room for the best place. "And I would prefer no dance tunes, and no heart-rending laments. Anything else would be perfectly suitable. Try to be unobtrusive—" She smiled, mischievously. "Seduce them with your music, instead of seizing them, if you will. I would like the clients relaxed, and in a good mood; sometimes they get impatient when they are waiting, and if you can make the wait enjoyable instead of tedious, that would be perfect."

Rune made her way around the edge of the room, avoiding the occupied tables, a little conscious of Amber's assessing eyes and Tonno's anxious ones. That was an interesting choice of music, for normally innkeepers wanted something lively, to heat the blood and make people drink faster. Evidently the "inn" was not in the business of selling liquor, either. It must be as Amber had said, that their primary income came from the rooms above. Rune would have thought, though, that an intoxicated client would be easier to handle.

On the other hand, maybe you wouldn't want the clients drunk; they might be belligerent; might cause trouble or start fights if they thought they'd waited longer than they should. So—must be that I'm supposed to keep 'em soothed. Soothing it is.

She found a comfortable place to sit in the chimney-corner, on a little padded bench beside the dark fireplace. She set her bow to her strings, and began to play an old, old love song.

This was a very different sort of playing from everything she'd done in inns up to this moment. There she had been striving to be the center of attention; here she was supposed to be invisible. After a moment, she began to enjoy it; it was a nice change.

She played things she hadn't had a chance to play in a while; all the romantic pieces that she normally saved for the odd wedding or two she'd performed at. Keeping the volume low, just loud enough to be heard without calling attention to the fact that there was a musician present, she watched her audience for a while until she became more interested in what she was playing than the silent faces at the tables. The serving-girls and men gave her an appreciative smile as they passed, but that was all the reward she got for her efforts. It was as if the men out there actually took her playing for granted.

Then it dawned on her that this was exactly the case; these were all men of some means, and no doubt many of them had household musicians from the Bardic Guild whose only duty was to entertain and fill the long hours of the evening with melody. That was why Amber had warned her she should expect little in the way of remuneration. Men like these didn't toss coins into a minstrel's hat—they fed him, clothed him, housed him, saw to his every need. And on occasion, when he had performed beyond expectation or when they were feeling generous, they rewarded him. But that only happened on great occasions, and in front of others, so that their generosity would be noted by others. They never rewarded someone for doing what she was doing now; providing a relaxing background.

Ah well. If I become a Guild musician, this may well be my lot. No harm in getting used to it.

After a while, she lost herself in the music—in the music itself, and not the memories it recalled for her. She began to play variations on some of the pieces, doing some improvisational work and getting caught up in the intricacies of the melody she was creating. She closed her eyes without realizing she'd done so, and played until her arm began to ache—

She opened her eyes, then, finished off the tune she'd been working on, and realized that she must have been playing for at least an hour by the way her arms and shoulders felt. The customers had changed completely; Tonno was gone, and Amber was nowhere to be seen. One of the serving-girls glided over with a mug of hot spiced cider; Rune took it gratefully. They exchanged smiles; Rune found herself hoping she'd be able to stay. Everything so far indicated that all Amber had claimed was true. She hadn't seen the serving-girls so much as touched. And both the girls, pretty in their brown skirts and bodices, one dark-haired and one light, had been friendly to her. They acted as if they were glad to have her there, in fact. Perhaps the clients were making fewer demands on them with Rune's playing to occupy their thoughts.

When she had shaken the cramps out, and had massaged her fingers a bit, she felt ready to play again. This time she didn't lose herself in the spell of the music; she watched the customers to see what their reaction was to her playing.

A head or two nodded in time to the music. There were two tables where there were pairs of men involved in some kind of game; it wasn't the draughts she was used to, for the pieces were much more elaborate. Those four ignored her entirely. There were another three involved in some kind of intense conversation who didn't seem to be paying any attention either. Then she noticed one richly dressed, very young man— hardly more than a boy—in the company of two older men. The boy looked nervous; as an experiment, she set out deliberately to soothe *him*. She played, not love songs, but old lullabies; then, as he began to relax, she switched back to love songs, but this time instead of ballads, she chose songs of seduction, the kind a young man would use to lure a girl into the night and (hopefully, at least from his point of view) into his bed.

The young man relaxed still further, and began to smile, as if he envisioned himself as that successful lover. He sat up straighter; he began to sip at his drink instead of clutch it, and even to nibble at some of the little snacks his companions had ordered for their table. By the time the wizened man summoned them, he was showing a new self-assurance, and swaggered a bit as he followed the old man up the stairs. His two companions chuckled, and sat back to enjoy their drink and food; one summoned one of the serving-boys, and a moment later, they, too, were embroiled in one of those games.

At first Rune was amused. But then, as she started another languid ballad, she felt a twinge of conscience. If the boy had actually responded to what she'd been doing, rather than simply calming normally, then she had manipulated him. She'd had her own belly full of manipulation; was it fair to do that to someone else, even with the best of intentions?

Did I do that, or was it just the liquor? And if it was me, what gave me the right?

She wondered even more now about these invisible "women" Amber employed. Did they enjoy what they were doing? Were they doing it by choice, or because of some kind of constraint Amber had on them? Were they pampered and protected, or prisoners? Just what kind of place was this, exactly?

She had finished her second mug of cider and was well into her third set, when the midnight bell rang, signaling the end of her stint. There was no sign that the custom had abated any, though; the tables were just as full as before. While she wondered exactly what she should do, Amber herself glided down the stairs and into the room, and nodded to her. She finished the song, slid Lady Rose into her carrying bag, and stood up, a little surprised at how stiff she felt. She edged past the fireplace to Amber's side, without disturbing anyone that she could tell. Amber drew her into the hall of the staircase, and motioned that she should go up.

"At this point, the gentlemen waiting are in no hurry," she said. "At this late hour, the gentlemen have usually exhausted their high spirits and are prepared to relax; past midnight I probably won't ever need your services to keep them occupied."

They got to the top of the stairs, where there was a hall carpeted in something thick and plushly scarlet, paneled in rich wood, and illuminated by scented candles in sconces set into the walls. She started to turn automatically down the candlelit hallway, but Amber stopped her before she'd gone a single pace. "Watch this carefully," the woman said, ignoring the muffled little sounds of pleasure that penetrated into the hall and made Rune blush to the hair. "You'll have to know how to do this for yourself from now on."

She tried to ignore the sounds herself, and watched as Amber turned to the shelves that stood where another hall might have been. She reached into the second set of shelves, grasped a brass dog that looked like a simple ornament, and turned it. There was a *click,* and a door, upon which the set of shelves had been mounted, swung open, revealing another hall. Amber waved Rune through and shut the door behind them.

This was a much plainer hallway; lit by two lanterns, and with an ordinary wooden floor and white-painted walls. "This subterfuge is so that the customers don't 'lose their way,' and blunder into our private quarters," Amber said, in a conversational voice. "I never could imagine why, but some people seem to think that anything ordinary in a pleasure-house must conceal something extraordinary. The serving-girls got very tired of having clients pester them, so I had the shelves built to hide the other hall. I took the liberty of having old Parro bring your things up to your new room so you wouldn't have to; I imagine that you're quite fatigued with all your walking about the streets today."

Rune tried to imagine that poor, wizened little man hauling her pack about, and failed. "He really didn't have to," she protested. "He—he doesn't—"

"Oh, don't make the mistake of thinking that because he's small and a bit crippled that he's weak," Amber said. "He wouldn't thank you for that. He's quite fiercely proud of his strength, and I have him as my summoner for a good reason. He can—and has—brought strong guardsmen to their knees, and men constantly underestimate him because of the way he looks."

"Oh," Rune said weakly.

"You'll meet everyone tomorrow; I thought you'd rather get to sleep early tonight," Amber continued, holding open a door for her. "This is your room, by the way. You did very well, just as well as Tonno said you would. I'm happy to welcome you to my little family, Rune."

Rune stepped into the room before the last remark penetrated her fatigue. "You are?" she said, a little stupidly.

Amber nodded, and lit a candle at the lantern outside the door, placing it in a holder on a little table just inside. "The bathroom is at the end of the hall, and there should be hot water in the copper if you want to wash before you go to bed. In the morning, simply come downstairs when you're ready, and either Parro or I will introduce you. Goodnight, Rune."

She had closed the door before Rune had a chance to say anything. But what could she say, really? "Wait, I'm not sure I should be doing this?" That wasn't terribly bright. "Just what is going on around here?" She *knew* what was going on. This was a whorehouse. She was going to entertain here. The madam was a gracious lady, of impeccable manners and taste, but it was still a house of pleasure—

But this was certainly the oddest bawdy-house she'd ever heard of.

She looked around at her room—*her* room, and what an odd sound that had! There wasn't much: a tiny table, a chair, a chest for clothing, and the bed. But it was a real bed, not a pallet on the floor like she'd had all her life. And it was much too narrow for two, which in a way, was reassuring.

There's no way anyone would pay to share that with Amber, much less with me.

The frame was the same plain wood as the rest of the furniture; the mattress seemed to be stuffed with something other than straw. Not feathers, but certainly something softer than she was used to; she bounced on it, experimentally, and found herself grinning from ear to ear.

There were clean, fresh sheets on the bed, and blankets hung over the footboard, with clean towels atop them. The plain wooden floor was scrubbed spotless, as were the white-painted walls. There was one window with the curtains already shut; she went to it and peeked out. Less than an arm's length away loomed the wooden side of the house next door; there were windows in it, but they were set so that they didn't look into any windows in this building, thus ensuring a bit of privacy. Not much of a view, but the window would probably let in some air in the summer, as soon as the warmer weather really arrived. It was better than being in the attic, where the sun beating down on the roof would make an oven of the place in summer, and the wind whistling under the eaves would turn it into the opposite in winter.

Her room. *Her* room, with a latch on the inside of the door, so she could lock it if she chose. Her room, where no one could bother her, a room she didn't have to share with anyone. Maybe it was the size of a rich man's closet, but it was all hers, and the thrill of privacy was heady indeed.

She looked longingly at the bed—but she knew she was filthy; she hadn't had a bath in several days, and to lie down in the clean sheets unwashed seemed like a desecration. It also wouldn't give Amber a very good impression of her cleanliness; after all, the woman had gone out of her way to mention that there was water ready for washing even at this late hour. That could have been a hint—in fact, it probably was.

She took the towels and went to the end of the hall to find the promised bathroom. And indeed, it was there, and included the indoor privies she had seen in the Church hostels, which could be flushed clean by pulling a chain that sluiced down a measured amount of water from a reservoir on the roof. There were two privies in stalls, and two bath-basins behind tall screens. One was big enough to soak in, but the other wouldn't take as long to fill, and she was awfully tired. Both the baths were fixed to the floor, with permanent drains in their bottoms.

She filled the shallow bath with equal measures of hot and cold water, dipped from the copper and a jar, both of which were also fed by the roof-reservoir. As she dipped the steaming water out of the top of the cauldron, she longed more than ever to be able to take a good long soak—

But that could wait until she had a half-penny to spare for the public baths and steam-house. Then she could soak in the hot pools, swim in the cold, and go back to soak in the hot pools until every pore was cleansed. She could take an afternoon from busking, perhaps the Seventh-Day, when people would be going to Church in the morning and spending the afternoon at home. That would mean there'd be fewer of them in the streets, and her take wouldn't be that much anyway; it wouldn't hurt her income as much to spend the afternoon in the bath-house.

But for now, at least, she could go to bed clean.

She scrubbed herself hastily, rinsed with a little more cold water, and toweled herself down, feeling as if she were a paying patron. And if *this* was the treatment that the help got, how *were* the patrons treated?

With that thought in mind, she returned to her room, locked herself in for the night, and dug out her poor, maltreated bread and cheese. It was squashed, but still edible, and she found herself hungry enough to devour the last crumb.

And with the last of her needs satisfied, she blew out the candle and felt her way to her bed, to dream of dancing lutes dressed in Gypsy ribbons, and fiddles that ran fiddle-brothels where richly dressed men came to caress their strings and play children's lullabies, and strange, wizened old men who lifted houses off their foundations and placed them back down, wrong-way about.

She woke much later than she had intended, much to her chagrin. She hurried into the only clean set of clothing she had—a shirt and breeches that had seen much better days—and resolved to find herself more cloth-ing before Amber had a chance to comment on the state of her dress.

When she found her way down to the common room, she discovered the exterior doors locked tight, and a half-dozen people eating what looked like breakfast porridge, and talking.

One of those was the most stunning young woman Rune had ever seen. Even in a simple shift with her hair combed back from her face, she looked like—

An angel, Rune thought wonderingly. She was inhumanly lovely. No one should look that lovely. No one *could*, outside of a ballad.

The girl was so beautiful it was impossible to feel jealousy; Rune could only admire her, the way she would admire a rainbow, a butterfly, or a flower.

Her hair was a straight fall of gold, and dropped down past her waist to an inch or two above the floor; her eyes were the perfect blue of a summer sky after a rain. Her complexion was roses and cream, her teeth perfect and even, her face round as a child's and with a child's inno-cence. Her figure, slight and lissome, was as delicate as a porcelain figure of an idealized shepherdess.

Her perfect rosebud mouth made a little "o" as she saw Rune, and the person sitting with her, who Rune hadn't even noticed at that mo-ment, turned. It was Amber.

"Ah, Rune," she said, smiling. "Come here, child. I'd like you to meet Sapphire. She is one of the ladies I told you about last night."

Rune blinked, and made her way carefully to the table. *Anyone with that much beauty can't be human. She probably has the brains of a pea—*

"Hello, Rune," Sapphire said, with a smile that eclipsed Amber's. "That isn't my real name, of course—Amber insisted we all take the names of jewels so when I leave here and retire, I can leave 'Sapphire' behind and just be myself."

Amber nodded. "It will happen, of course. This is not a profession one can remain in for long."

"Oh," Rune said, awkwardly. "Then—"

"Amber is not my real name, either—at least, it isn't the one I was born with," Amber said easily.

"I'll probably become 'Amber' when I take over as Madam," Sapphire continued. "Since there's always been an 'Amber' in charge here. This Amber decided to take me as her 'prentice, so to speak. I already help with the bookkeeping, but I'm going to need a lot more schooling in handling people, that much I know."

Rune nearly swallowed her tongue; *this* delicate, brainless-looking creature was doing—bookkeeping?

Sapphire laughed at the look on her face; Rune felt like a fool. "You're not the first person who's been surprised by Sapphire," Amber said indulgently. "I told you the ladies were all something very special."

"So are you, love," Sapphire replied warmly. "Without you, we'd all be—"

"Elsewhere," Amber interrupted. "And probably just as successful. All four of you have brains and ambition; you'd probably be very influential courtesans and mistresses."

"But not wives," Sapphire replied, and her tone was so bitter that Rune started.

"No," Amber said softly. "Never wives. That's the fate of a lovely woman with no lineage and no money. The prince doesn't fall in love with you, woo you gently, carry you away on his white horse and marry you over his father's objections."

"No, the prince seduces you—if you're lucky. More often than not he carries you off, all right, screaming for your father who doesn't dare interfere. Then he rapes you—and abandons you once he knows you're with child," Sapphire said grimly, her mouth set in a thin, hard line.

"And that is the prerogative of princes," Amber concluded with equal bitterness. "Merchant princes, princes of the trades, or princes by birth."

They both seemed to have forgotten she was there; she felt very uncomfortable. This was not the sort of thing one heard in ballads. . . .

Well, yes and no. There were plenty of ballads where beautiful women *were* seduced, or taken against their will. But in those ballads, they died tragically, often murdered, and their spirits pursued their ravagers and brought them to otherworldly justice. Or else they retired to a life in a convent, and only saw their erstwhile despoilers when the villains were at death's door, brought there by some other rash action.

Apparently, it wasn't considered to be in good taste to survive one's despoiling as anything other than a nun.

"Well, I'm not going to let one damn fool turn me into a bitter old hag," Sapphire said with a sigh, and stretched, turning from bitter to sunny in a single instant. "That's over and done with. In a way, he did me a favor," she said, half to Rune, half to Amber. "If he hadn't carried me off and abandoned me here, I probably would have married Bert, raised pigs, and died in childbed three years ago."

Amber nodded, thoughtfully. "And I would have pined myself over Tham wedding Jakie until I talked myself into the convent."

Sapphire laughed, and raised a glass of apple juice. A shaft of sunlight lancing through the cracks in the shutters pierced it, turning it into liquid gold.

"Then here's to feckless young men, spoiled and ruthless!" she said gaily. "And to women who refuse to be ruined by them!"

Amber solemnly clinked glasses with her, poured a third glass for Rune without waiting for her to ask, and they drank the toast together.

"So, Rune, how is it that you come here," Sapphire asked, "with your accent from my own hills, and your gift of soothing the fears out of frightened young men?"

Rune's jaw dropped, and Amber and Sapphire both laughed. "You thought I hadn't noticed?" Amber said. "That was the moment when I knew you were for us. If you can soothe the fears out of a young man, you may well soothe the violence out of an older one. That is a hazard of our profession. Oh, our old and steady clients know that to come here means that one of the ladies will be kind and flattering, will listen without censure, and will make him feel like the most virile and clever man on Earth—but there are always new clients, and many of them come to a whore only because they hate women so much they cannot bear any other relationship."

"Then—I did right?" Rune asked, wondering a little that she brought a question of morality to a whore—but unable to believe that these two women were anything but moral. "I thought—it seemed so calculating, to try and calm him down—"

"The men who come here, come to feel better," Amber said firmly. "That is why I told you we serve a very special need. We hear secrets they won't even tell their Priests, and fears they wouldn't tell their wives or best friends. If all they wanted was lovemaking, they could go to any of the houses on the street—"

"Unskilled sex, perhaps," Sapphire commented acidly, with a candor that held Rune speechless. "Not lovemaking. That takes ability and practice."

"Point taken," Amber replied. "Well enough. Our clients come to us for more than that. Sapphire, Topaz, Ruby, and Pearl are more than whores, Rune."

"I'm—" she said, and coughed to clear her throat. "I'm, uh—beginning to see that."

"So how *did* you come here, Rune?" Sapphire persisted. "When I heard you speak, I swear, you carried me right back to my village!"

Once again, Rune gave a carefully edited version of her travels and travails—though she made light of the latter, sensing from Sapphire's earlier comments that *her* experiences had been a great deal more harrowing than Rune's. She also left out the Skull Hill Ghost; time enough to talk about him when she'd made a song out of him and there'd be no reason to suspect that the adventure was anything more than a song.

Sapphire sat entranced through all of it, though Rune suspected that half of her "entrancement" was another skill she had acquired; the ability to listen and appear fascinated by practically anything.

When Rune finished, Sapphire raised her glass again. "And here's to a young lady who refused to keep to her place as decreed by men and God," she said. "And had the gumption to pack up and set out on her own."

"Thank you," Rune said, flattered. "But I've a long way to go before I'm a Guild apprentice. Right now I intend to concentrate on keeping myself fed and out of trouble until I master my second instrument."

"Good." Amber turned a critical eye on her clothing, and Rune flushed again. "Please talk to Tonno about finding you some costumes, would you?"

That was a clear dismissal if ever Rune had heard one. And since she had decided to take advantage of her promised meal by making it supper—especially if she was going to dine like she had last night—she took her leave.

But she took to the streets in search of a busking-corner with her head spinning. Nothing around here was the way she had thought it would be. The folk who should have been honest and helpful—the Church—were taking in money and attempting to cheat over it at every turn. And the folk who should have been the ones to avoid—Amber and her "ladies"—had gone out of their way to give her a place. Of course, she was going to have to work for that place, but still, that didn't make things any less than remarkable. Amber was about as different from the fellow who set up at the Faires as could be imagined—and the ladies, at least Sapphire, as different from his hard-eyed dancers. They seemed to think of themselves as providing a service, even if it was one that was frowned upon by the Church.

Then again, it was the Church who frowned upon anything that didn't bring money to its coffers and servants to its hands. Doubtless the Church had found no way for the congress between men and women to bring profit to them—so they chose instead to make it, if not forbidden, then certainly not encouraged.

Rune shook her head and stepped out into the sunlight surrounding the fountain. It was all too much for her. Those were the worries of the high and mighty. *She* had other things to attend to—to find breakfast, pay her tax and tithe, buy her permit, and set up for busking until it was time for her lessons.

And that was enough for any girl to worry about on a bright early summer morning.

CHAPTER EIGHT

Midmorning found her back on the corner between the drink-stall and the sausage-stall, and both owners were happy to see her; happier still to see the badge of her permit pinned to the front of her vest. She set herself up with a peculiar feeling of permanence, and the sausage roll vendor confirmed that when he asked her if she planned to make this her regular station. She didn't have a chance to answer him then, but once the nuncheon rush was over and he had time again to talk, he brought it up again.

She considered that idea for a moment, nibbling at her lip. This wasn't a bad place; not terribly profitable, but not bad. There was a good deal of traffic here, although the only folks that passed by that appeared to have any money at all were the Church functionaries. Still, better spots probably already had "residents." This one might even have a regular player later in the day, when folk were off work and more inclined to stop and listen.

"I don't know," she said truthfully. "Why?"

"Because if ye do, me'n Jak there'll save it for ye," the sausage-man told her, as she exchanged part of her collection of pins for her lunch. "There's a juggler what has it at night, but we c'n save it fer ye by day. Th' wife knows a seamstress; th' seamstress allus needs pins." He leaned forward a bit, earnestly, his thin face alive with the effort of convincing her. "Barter's no bad way t'go, fer a meal or twain. An 'f ye get known fer bein' here, could be ye'll get people comin' here t' hear ye a-purpose."

"An we'll get th' custom," the cider-vendor said with a grin, leaning over his own counter to join the conversation. "Ain't bad fer ev'body."

Now that was certainly true; she nodded in half-agreement.

"Ye get good 'nough, so ye bring more custom, tell ye what we'll do," the cider-vendor Jak said, leaning forward even farther, and half-whispering confidentially. "We'll feed ye fer free. Nuncheon, anyway. But ye'll have t' bring us more custom nor we'd had already."

After a moment of thought, the sausage-vendor nodded. "Aye, we c'n do that, if ye bring us more custom. 'Nough t' pay th' penny fer yer share, anyway,'' he said. "That'll do, I reckon.''

His caution amused her, even while she felt a shade of annoyance at their penny-pinching. Surely one sausage roll and a mug of cider wasn't going to ruin their profits in a day! "How would I know?" Rune asked with a touch of irony. "I mean, I'd only have your word that I hadn't already done that.''

"Well now, ye'd just haveta trust us, eh?" Jak said with a grin, and she found herself wondering what the juggler thought of these two rogues. "What can ye lose? Good corners are hard t' find. A' when ye find one, mebbe sommut's already there. An' ye *know* ye can trade off yer pins here, even if we says ye hain't brought in 'nough new business t' feed ye free. Not ev'body takes pins. Ask that blamed Church vulture t'take pins, he'll laugh in yer face.''

That was true enough. She looked the corner over with a critical eye. It seemed to be adequately sheltered from everything but rain. The wind wouldn't whip through here the way it might a more open venue. Sure, it was summer now, but there could be cold storms even in summer, and winter was coming; she was going to have to think ahead to the next season. She still had to eat, pay her tax and tithe on the trade-value of what she was getting from Amber, and enlarge her wardrobe. Right now she had no winter clothes, and none suitable for the truly hot days of summer. She'd have to take care of that, as well.

" 'F it rains, ye come in here," Jak said, suddenly. "I reckon Lars'd offer, but he's got that hot fat back there, an' I dunno how good that'd be fer th' fiddle there. Come winter, Lars peddles same, I peddle hot cider wi' spices. Ye can come in here t'get yer fingers an' toes warm whene'er ye get chilled.''

That settled it. "Done," Rune replied instantly. It wasn't often a street-busker got an offer of shelter from a storm. That could make the difference between a good day's take and a poor one—shelter meant she could play until the last moment before a storm broke, then duck inside and be right back out when the weather cleared. And a place out of the cold meant extra hours she could be busking. That alone was worth staying for. These men might be miserly about their stock, but they were ready enough to offer her what someone else might not.

She left the corner for the day feeling quite lighthearted. On the whole, her day so far had been pretty pleasant, including the otherwise unpleasant duty of paying the Church. She'd been able to annoy the priest at the Church-box quite successfully; playing dunce and passing over first her tithe, counted out in half-penny and quarter-pennies, then her tax, counted out likewise, and then, after he'd closed the ledger, assuming she was going to move on, her permit-fee, ten copper pennies which were the equivalent of one silver. She'd done so slowly, passing them in to him one at a time, much to the amusement of a couple of other buskers waiting to pay their own tithes and taxes. *They* knew she was playing the fool, but he didn't. It almost made it worth the loss of the money. He had cursed her under his breath for being such a witling, and she'd asked humbly when she finished for his blessing—he'd had to give it to her—and he'd been so annoyed his face had been poppy-red. The other buskers had to go around the corner to stifle their giggles.

Now it was time to go find Tonno's shop—she needed at least one "new" outfit to satisfy Amber's requirements, and Tonno knew where she was going to be able to find the cheapest clothes. That expenditure wasn't something she was looking forward to, for the money for new clothing would come out of her slender reserve, but she had no choice in the matter. Amber's request had the force of a command, if she wanted to keep her new place, and even when she'd gotten her old clothing clean, it hadn't weathered the journey well enough to be present-able "downstairs." It would do for busking in the street, where a little poverty often invited another coin or two, but not for Amber's establishment.

On the other hand, the money for her lodging was *not* coming out of her reserves, and that was a plus in her favor. And she did need new clothes, no matter what.

When she pushed open the door, she saw that Tonno had a customer. He was going over a tall stack of books with a man in the long robes of a University Scholar, probably one of the teachers there. She hung back near the door of the shop until she caught his eye, then waited patiently until the Scholar was engrossed in a book and raised her eyebrows in entreaty. He excused himself for a moment; once she whispered what she needed, he took Lady Rose and her lute from her to stow safely behind the counter until lesson time, then gave her directions to Patch Street, where many of the old clothes sellers either had shops or barrows. She excused herself quickly and quietly—a little disappointed that he wouldn't be able to come with her. She had the feeling that he'd be able to get her bargains she hadn't a chance for, alone.

It was a good thing that she'd started out with a couple of hours to spend before her first lesson. Patch Street was not that far away, but the number of vendors squeezed into a two-block area was nothing less than astonishing. The street itself was thick with buyers and sellers, all shouting their wares or arguing price at the tops of their lungs. The cacophony deafened her, and she began to feel a little short of breath from the press of people the moment she entered the affray. The sun beat down between the buildings on all of them impartially, and she was soon limp with heat as well as pummeled by noise and prodded by elbows.

She now was grateful she had left Lady Rose with Tonno; there was scarcely room on this street to squeeze by. She tried to keep her mind on what she needed—good, servicable clothing, not too worn—but there were thousands of distractions. The woman in her yearned for some of the bright silks and velvets, worn and obviously second-hand as most of them were, and the showman for some of the gaudier costumes, like the ones the Gypsies had worn—huge multicolored skirts, bright scarlet sashes, embroidered vests and bodices—

She disciplined herself firmly. *Under-things first. One pair of breeches; something strong and soft. Two new shirts, as lightweight as I can get them. One vest. Nothing bright, nothing to cry out for attention. I'm supposed to be inconspicuous. And nothing too feminine.*

The under-things she found in a barrow tended by a little old woman who might have been Parro's wizened twin. She suspected that the garments came from some of the houses of pleasure, too; although the lace had been removed from them, they were under-things meant to be seen—or rather, they had been, before they'd been torn. Aside from the tears, they looked hardly used at all.

She picked up a pair of underdrawers; they were very lightweight, but they were also soft—not silk, but something comfortable and easy on the skin. Quite a change from the harsh linen and wool things she was used to wearing. The tears would be simple enough to mend, though they would be very obvious. . . .

Then again, Rune wasn't likely to be in a position where anyone was going to notice her mended underwear. The original owners though—it probably wasn't good for business for a whore to be seen in under-things with mends and patches.

It was odd, though; the tears were all in places like shoulder-seams, or along the sides—where the seams themselves had held but the fabric hadn't. As if the garments had been torn from their wearers.

Maybe they had been. Either a-purpose or by chance.

Perhaps the life of a whore wasn't all that easy. . . .

Her next acquisition must be a pair of shirts, and it was a little hard to find what she was looking for here. Most shirts in these stalls and barrows were either ready to be turned into rags, or had plainly been divested of expensive embroidery. The places where bands of ornamentation had been picked off on the sleeves and collars were distressingly obvious, especially for someone whose hands and arms were going to be the most visible parts of her. Although Rune wasn't the most expert seamstress in the world, it looked to her as if the fine weave of the fabrics would never close up around the seam-line. It would always be very clear that the shirt was second-hand, and that wouldn't do for Amber's. As she turned over garment after garment, she wondered if she was going to be able to find *anything* worth buying. Or if she was going to have to dig even deeper into her resources and buy new shirts. She bit her lip anxiously, and went back to the first barrow, hoping against hope to find *something* that might do—

" 'Scuse me, dearie." A hand on her arm and a rich, alto voice interrupted her fruitless search. Rune looked up into the eyes of a middle-aged, red-haired woman; a lady with a busking-permit pinned to the front of *her* bodice, and a look of understanding in her warm green-brown eyes. "I think mebbe I c'n help ye."

She licked her lips, and nodded.

"Lissen, boy," the woman continued, when she saw she'd gotten Rune's attention, leaning towards Rune's ear to shout at her. "Can ye sew at all? A straight seam, like? An' patch?"

What an odd question. "Uh—yes," Rune answered, before she had time to consider her words. "Yes, I can. But I can't do any more than that—"

"Good," the woman said in satisfaction. "Look, here—" She held up two of the shirts Rune had rejected, a faded blue, and a stained white, both of lovely light material, and both useless because the places where bands of ornament had been picked off or cut away were all too obvious. "Buy these."

Rune shook her head; the woman persisted, "Nay, hear me out. Ye go over t' *that* lass, th' one w' th' ribbons." She pointed over the heads of the crowd at a girl with a shoulder-tray full of ribbons of various bright colors. "Ye buy 'nough plain ribbon t' cover th' places where the 'broidery was picked out, an' wider than' the 'broidery was. Look, see, like I done wi' mine."

She held up her own arm and indicated the sleeve. Where a band of embroidery would have been at the cuff, there was a wide ribbon; where a bit of lace would have been at the top of the sleeve, she'd put a knot of multicolored ribbons. The effect was quite striking, and Rune had to admit that the shirt did not look as if it had come from the rag-bin like these.

The woman held up the white one. "This 'un's only stained at back an' near th' waist, ye see?" she said, pointing out the location of the light-brown stains. "Sleeves 'r still good. So's top. Get a good vest, sew bit'a ribbon on, an nobbut'll know 'tis stained."

Rune blinked, and looked at the shirts in the woman's hands in the light of her suggestions. It would work; it would certainly work. The stained shirt could even be made ready by the time Rune needed to take up her station at Amber's tonight.

"Thank you!" she shouted back, taking the shirts from the woman's hands, and turning to pay the vendor for them. "Thank you very much!"

"Think nowt on't," the woman shouted back, with a grin. " 'Tis one musicker to 'nother. Ye do sommut else the turn one day. 'Sides, me niece's th' one w' the ribbon!"

She bought the shirts—dearer than she'd hoped, but not as bad as she'd feared—and wormed her way to the ribbon vendor's side. A length of dark blue quite transformed the faded blue shirt into something with dignity, and a length of faded rose—obviously also picked off something else—worked nicely on the stained white. And who knew? Maybe someone at Amber's would know how to take the stains out; they looked like spilled wine, and there was undoubtably a lot of spilled wine around a brothel.

Now for the rest; she had better luck there, thankful for her slight frame. She was thin for a boy, though tall—her normal height being similar to the point where a lad really started shooting up and outgrowing clothing at a dreadful rate. Soon she had a pair of fawn-colored corduroy breeches, with the inside rubbed bare, probably from riding, but that wouldn't show where she was sitting—and a slightly darker vest of lined leather that laced tight and could pass for a bodice when she wore her skirts. The seams on the vest had popped and had not been mended; it would be simplicity to sew them up again. With the light-colored shirt, the breeches, and the new vest, she'd be fit for duty this evening, and meanwhile she could wash and dry her blue breeches and skirt, and her other three shirts. Once they were clean, she could see how salvageable they were for night-duty. If they were of no use, she could come back here, and get a bit more clothing. And they'd be good enough for street-busking; it didn't pay to look too prosperous on the street. People felt sorry for you if you looked a bit tattered, and she didn't want that nosy Church-clerk to think she was doing too well.

She wormed her way out of the crowd to find that two hours had gone by—as well as five pennies—and it was time to return to Tonno.

Rune's head pounded, and her hands hurt worse than they had in years.

Blessed God. She squinted and tried to ignore the pain between her eyebrows, without success. Her fingers and her head both hurt; she was more than happy to take a break from the lesson when Tonno ran his hand through his thick shock of gray hair and suggested that she had quite enough to think about for the moment. She had always known that the lute was a very different instrument from the fiddle, but she hadn't realized just how different it was. She shook her left hand hard to try and free it from the cramps, and licked and blew on the fingertips of her right to cool them. There wouldn't be any blisters, but that was only because Tonno was merciful to his newest pupil.

Playing the lute was like playing something as wildly different from the fiddle as—a shepherd's pipe. The grip, and the action, for instance; it was noticably harder to hold down the lute's strings than the fiddle's. And now she was required to *do* something with her right hand—bowing required control of course, but all of her fingers worked together. Now she was having to pick in patterns as complicated as fingering . . . more so, even. She was sweating by the time Tonno called the break and offered tea, and quite convinced that Tonno was earning his lesson money.

It didn't much help that she was also learning to read music—the notes on a page—at the same time she was learning to play her second instrument. It was hard enough to keep notes and fingerings matched now, with simple melodies—but she'd seen some music sheets that featured multiple notes meant to be played simultaneously, and she wasn't sure she'd *ever* be ready for those.

"So, child, am I earning my fee?" Tonno asked genially.

She nodded, and shook her hair to cool her head. She was sweating like a horse with her effort; at this rate, she'd have to wash really well before she went on duty tonight. "You're earning it, sir, but I'm not sure I'm ever going to master this stuff."

"You're learning a new pair of languages, dear," he cautioned, understanding in his eyes. "Don't be discouraged. It will come, and much more quickly than you think. Trust me."

"If you say so." She put the lute back in its carrying case, and looked about at the shop. There were at least a dozen different types of instruments hanging on the wall, not counting drums. There were a couple of fiddles, another lute, a guitar, a shepherd's pipe and a flute, a mandolin, a hurdy-gurdy, a trumpet and a horn, three harps of various sizes, plus several things she couldn't identify. "I can't imagine how you ever learned to play all these things. It seems impossible."

"Partially out of curiosity, partially out of necessity," Tonno told her, following her gaze, and smiling reminiscently. "I inherited this shop from my father; and it helps a great deal to have a way to bring in extra money. But when he still owned it and I was a child, he had no way of telling if the instruments he acquired were any good, so when I showed some aptitude for music, he had me learn everything so that I could tell him when something wasn't worth buying.''

"But why didn't you—" Rune stopped herself from asking why he hadn't become a Guild musician. Tonno smiled at her tolerantly and answered the question anyway.

"I didn't even try to enter the Guild, because I have no real talent for music," he said. "I have a knack for picking up the basics, but there my abilities end. I'm very good at *teaching* the basics, but other than that, I am simply a gifted amateur. Oh—and I can tell when a musician has potential. I am good enough to know that I am not good enough, you see."

Rune felt inexplicably saddened by his words. She couldn't imagine not pursuing music, at least, not now. Yet to offer sympathy seemed rude at the least. She kept her own counsel and held her tongue, unsure of what she could say safely.

"So," Tonno said, breaking the awkward silence. "It's time for your other lessons. What do you think you'd like to read? Histories? Collected poems and ballads? Old tales?"

Reading! She'd forgotten that was to be part of her lessoning. Her head swam at the idea of something more to learn.

"Is there anything easy?" she asked desperately. "I can't read very well, just enough to spell things out in the Holy Book."

Tonno got up, and walked over to the laden shelves without answering, scrutinizing some of the books stacked there for a moment.

"Easy, hmm?" he said, after a moment or two. "Yes, I think we can manage that. Here—"

He pulled a book out from between two more, and blew the dust from its well-worn cover. "This should suit you," he told her, bringing the book back to where she sat with her lute case in her lap. "It's a book of songs and ballads, and I'm sure you'll recognize at least half of them. That should give you familiar ground to steady you as you plunge into the new material. Here—" He thrust it at her, so that she was forced to take it before he dropped it on her lute. "Bring it back when you've finished, and I'll give you something new to read. Once you're reading easily, I'll start picking other books for you. It isn't possible for a minstrel to be too widely read."

"Yes, sir," she said hastily. "I mean, no, sir."

"Now, run along back to Amber's," he said, making a shooing motion with his hands. "I'm sure you'll have to do something with those new clothes of yours to make them fit to wear. I'll see you tomorrow."

How he had known that, she had no idea, but she was grateful to be let off. Right now her fingers stung, and she wanted a chance to rest them before the evening—and she did, indeed, have quite a bit of mending and trimming to do before her garments were fit for Amber's common room.

The first evening-bell rang, marking the time when most shops shut their doors and the farmer's market was officially closed. She hurried back through the quiet streets, empty of most traffic in this quarter, reaching Amber's and Flower Street in good time.

None of the houses on the court were open except Amber's, and Rune had the feeling that it was only the "downstairs" portion that was truly ready for business. There were a handful of men, and even one woman sitting in the common room, enjoying a meal. As Rune entered the common room, her stomach reminded her sharply that it would be no bad thing to perform with a good meal inside her. As she hesitated in the stairway, one of the serving-girls, the cheerful one who had smiled at her last night, stopped on her way to a table.

"If you'd like your meal in your room," she said, quietly, "go to the end of the corridor, just beyond the bathroom. There's a little staircase in a closet there that leads straight down into the kitchen. You can get a tray there and take it up, or you can eat in the kitchen—but Lana is usually awfully busy, so it's hard to find a quiet corner to eat in. This time of night, she's got every flat space filled up with things she's cooking."

"Thanks," Rune whispered back; the girl grinned in a conspiratorial manner, and hurried on to her table.

Rune followed her instructions and shortly was ensconced in her own room with a steaming plate of chicken and noodles, a basket of bread and sliced cheese, and a winter apple still sound, though wrinkled from storage. Although she was no seamstress, she made a fairly quick job of mending the vest and trimming the light shirt, taking a stitch between each couple of bites of her supper. The food was gone long before the mending was done, of course; she was working by the light of her candle when a tap at her door made her jump with startlement.

"Y-yes?" she stuttered, trying to get her heart down out of her throat.

"It's Maddie," said a muffled voice. "Lana sent me after your dishes."

"Oh—come in," she said, standing up in confusion, as the door opened, revealing the serving-girl who'd told her the way to the kitchen. With her neat brown skirt and bodice and apron over all, she looked as tidy as Rune felt untidy. Rune flushed. "I'm sorry, I meant to take them down—I didn't mean to be any trouble—"

The girl laughed, and shook her head until her light brown hair started to come loose from the knot at the back of her neck. "It's no bother," she replied. "Really. There's hardly anyone downstairs yet, and I wanted a chance to give you a proper hello. You're Rune, right? The new musician? Carly thought you were a boy—she is going to be so mad!"

Rune nodded apprehensively. The girl seemed friendly enough—she had a wonderful smile and a host of freckles sprinkled across her nose that made her look like a freckled kitten. She looked as if she could have been one of the village girls from home.

Which was the root of Rune's apprehension. Those girls from home hadn't ever been exactly friendly. And now this girl had been put out of her way to come get the dishes, and had informed her that the other serving-girl was going to be annoyed when she discovered the musician wasn't the male she had thought.

"Well, I'm Maddie," the girl said comfortably, picking up the tray, but seeming in no great hurry to leave with it. "I expect we'll probably be pretty good friends—and I expect that Carly will probably hate you. She's the other server, the blond, the one as has the sharp eyes and nose. She hates everyone—every girl, anyway. But she's Parro's daughter, so Lady Amber puts up with her."

"What's Carly's problem?" Rune asked, putting her sewing down.

"She wants to work upstairs," Maddie said with a twist of her mouth. "And there's no way. She's not nowhere good enough. Or nice enough." Maddie shrugged, at least as much as the tray in her arms permitted. "She'll probably either marry some fool and nag him to death, or end up down the street at the Stallion or the Velvet Rope. There's men enough around that'll pay to be punished that she'd be right at home."

Rune found her mouth sagging open at Maddie's matter-of-fact assessment of the situation. And at what she'd hinted. Back at home—

Well, she wasn't back at home.

She found herself blushing, and Maddie giggled. "Best learn the truth, Rune, and learn to live with it. We're on Flower Street, and that's the whore's district. There's men that'll pay for whores to do weirder things than just nag or beat 'em, but that doesn't happen here. But this's a whorehouse, whatever else them 'nice' people call it; the ladies upstairs belong to the Whore's Guild, and they got the right to make a living like any other Guild. Got Crown protection and all."

Rune's mouth sagged open further. "They—do?" she managed.

"Surely," Maddie said, with a firm nod. "I know, 'tis a bit much at first. Me, my momma was a laundry-woman down at Knife's Edge, so I seen plenty growing up. . . . and let me tell you, I was right glad to get a job *here* instead of there! But young Shawm, he's straight from the country like you, and Carly made his life a pure misery until me and Arden and Lana took him in hand and got him used to the way things is. Like we're gonna do with you."

Rune managed a smile. "Thanks, Maddie," she said weakly, still a little in shock at the girl's frankness. "I probably seem like a real country-cousin to you—"

Maddie shook her head cheerfully. "Nay. Most of the people here in town think just like you—fact is, Amber's had a bit of a problem getting a good musicker because of that. Whoring is a job, lass, like any other. Whore sells something she can *do,* just like a cook or a musicker. Try thinking on it that way, and things'll come easier." She tilted her head to one side, as Rune tried not to feel too much a fool. At the moment, she felt as naive as a tiny child, and Maddie, though she probably wasn't more than a year older, seemed worlds more experienced.

"I got to go," the other girl said, hefting the tray a little higher. "Tell you what, though, if you got clothes what need washing, you can give 'em to me and I'll take 'em to Momma with Lana and Shawm's and mine tonight. 'Twon't cost you nothing; Momma does it 'cause Lana gives her what's left over. Lady Amber don't allow no leftovers being given to our custom."

"Oh—thank you!" Rune said, taken quite aback. "But are you sure?"

Maddie nodded. "Sure as sure—and sure I won't *never* do the same for Carly!" She winked, and Rune stifled a giggle, feeling a sudden kinship with the girl. "I'll come by in the morning and you can help me carry it all down to Momma, eh?"

Rune laughed. "Oh, I see! This way you get somebody to help you carry things!"

Maddie grinned. "Sure thing, and I don't want to ask Shawm. I got other things I'd druther ask him to do."

Rune grinned a little wider—and dared to tease her a little. "Maddie, are you sweet on Shawm?"

To her surprise, the girl blushed a brilliant scarlet, and mumbled something that sounded like an affirmative.

Rune could hardly believe Maddie's sudden shyness—this from the girl who had just spoke about being brought up in a whorehouse with the same matter-of-factness that Rune would have used in talking about her childhood at the Hungry Bear. "Well, don't worry," she said impulsively, "I won't tell him *or* Carly. If that's what you want."

Maddie grinned gratefully, still scarlet. "Thanks. I knew you were a good'un," she said. "Now I really *do* have to go. The custom's gonna start coming in right soon, and Shawm's down there by himself."

"I'll see you down there in a little bit," Rune replied. "And if you can think of anything you'd like to hear, let me know. If I don't know it, I bet Tonno does, and I can learn it from him."

"Thanks!" Maddie said with obvious surprise. "Hey—you know, 'Ratcatcher'? I really like that song, and I don't get to hear it very often."

"I sure do!" Rune replied, happy to be able to do something for Maddie right away in return for the girl's kindness. "I'll play it a couple times tonight, and if you think of anything else, tell me."

"Right-oh!" Maddie said, and turned to go. Rune held the door open for her, then trotted down to the end of the hall to hold open the door to the stairway as well.

She returned to put the last touches on her costume for tonight and get Lady Rose in tune, feeling more than a little happy about the outcome of the day so far. She'd gotten her first lesson, a permanent busking site with some extra benefits, acquired the first "new" clothing she'd had in a while, been warned about an enemy—

And found a friend. That was the most surprising, and perhaps the best part of the day. She'd been half expecting animosity from the other girls—but she was used to that. She'd never expected to find one of them an ally.

She slipped into her new garb and laced the vest tight, flattening her chest—what there was of it—and looking down at herself critically. Neat, well-dressed—and not even remotely feminine looking. That would do.

Time to go earn her keep. She grinned at the thought. *Time to go earn my keep. At a house of pleasure. With my fiddle. And my teacher thinks I'm going to be good. Go stick that in your cup and drink it, Westhaven.*

And she descended the front stairs with a heady feeling of accomplishment.

CHAPTER NINE

"I can't imagine what Lady Amber thinks she's doing, hiring that scruffy little catgut-scraper," Carly said irritably—and very audibly—to one of the customers, just as Rune finished a song. "I should think she'd drive people away. She gives *me* a headache."

Rune bit her tongue and held her peace, and simply smiled at Carly as if she hadn't been meant to overhear that last, then flexed her fingers to loosen them.

Bitch. She'd fit right in at Westhaven. Right alongside those other sanctimonious idiots.

"I think it's very pleasant," the young man said in mild surprise. He looked over to Rune's corner and lifted a finger. "Lass, you wouldn't know 'Song of the Swan,' would you?"

"I surely would, my lord," she said quickly, and began the piece before Carly could react, keeping her own expression absolutely neutral. No point in giving the scold any more ammunition than she already had. Rune got along fine with everyone else in the house; it was only Carly who was intent on plaguing her life. Why, she didn't know, but it was no use taking tales to Lady Amber; Amber would simply fix her with a chiding look, and ask her if it was *really* so difficult to get along with one girl.

The young man looked gratified at being called "my lord"; Amber had told her to always call men "my lord" and the few women who frequented the place "my lady." "It does no harm," Amber had said with a lifted eyebrow, "and if it makes someone feel better to be taken for noble, then it does some good."

That seemed to be the theme of a great many things that Amber said. She even attempted to make the sour-tempered Carly feel more contented. Of course, the girl *did* do her work, quickly, efficiently, and expertly—she could serve more tables than Shawm, Maddie, or Arden. That was probably one of the things that saved her from getting the sack, Rune reflected. If she'd shirked her work, there would be no way that even Amber would put up with her temper.

Now that summer was gone, and autumn nearly over as well, Rune was a standard fixture at Amber's and felt secure enough there that she had dropped the boy disguise, even when she wore her breeches instead of skirts. The customers never even hinted at services other than music, for she, along with the rest of the downstairs help, did *not* sport the badge of the Whore's Guild. And that made her absolutely off-limits, at least in Amber's. In one of the other houses on the street, that might not be true, but here she was safe.

She knew most of the regular customers by sight now, and some by name as well. Tonno's friends she all knew well enough even to tease them a bit between sets—and they frequently bought her a bit of drink a little stronger than the cider she was allowed as part of her keep. A nice glass of brandy-wine did go down very well, making her tired fingers a little less tired, and putting a bit more life in her hands at the end of a long night. That was the good part; the bad part was that her income had fallen off. There were fewer people on the street seeking nuncheon during the day, the days themselves were shorter, and winter was coming on very early this year. Jak and his fellow vendor had been looking askance at the weather, and Jak had confessed that he thought they might have to close down during the bitterest months this year, shutting up the stalls and instead taking their goods to those public houses that didn't serve much in the way of food.

If that happened, Rune would still have her corner, but no shelter. Already she had lost several days to rotten weather; rains that went on all day, soaking everything in sight, and so cold and miserable that even Amber's had been shy of custom come the evening hours.

The winter did not look to be a good one, so far as keeping ahead of expenses went. The best thing she could say for it was that at least she had a warm place to live, and one good, solid meal every day—she still had her teacher, and a small store of coin laid up that might carry her through until spring. If only she didn't have the damned tax and tithe to pay. . . .

No one made any further suggestions, so Rune let her wandering mind and fingers pick their own tunes. Today had been another of those miserable days; gray and overcast, and threatening rain though it never materialized. The result was that her take was half her norm: five pennies in half and quarter pence and pins, and out of that was taken three pence for tithes and taxes. The only saving grace was that since her corner was right across from the Church-box, the Priest could see for himself how ill she was doing and didn't contest her now that she was paying less. Nor, thank God, had he contested her appraisal of her food and lodging as five pennies. She hadn't told him where it was, or she suspected he'd have levied it higher. She'd seen the clients paying over their bills, and the meal alone was generally five copper pennies.

It's a good thing I've already got my winter clothes. I'd never be able to afford them now. The local musicians had a kind of unofficial uniform, an echo of what the Guild musicians wore. Where Guildsmen always wore billowy-sleeved shirts with knots of purple and gold or silver ribbons on the shoulders of the sleeves, the non-Guild Minstrels wore knots of multicolored ribbons instead. Rune had modified all her shirts to match; and since no one but a musician ever sported that particular ornament, she was known for what she was wherever she went. During the summer she'd even picked up an odd coin now and again because of that, being stopped on the street by someone who wanted music at his party, or by an impromptu gathering on a warm summer night that wanted to dance.

But that had been this summer—

A blast of cold wind hit the shutters, shaking them, and making the flames on all the lanterns waver. Rune was very glad of her proximity to the fireplace; it was relatively cozy over here. Maddie and Carly wore shawls while they worked, tucking them into their skirt bands to keep their hands free. She couldn't wear a shawl; she had to keep hands and arms completely free. If she hadn't been in this corner, she'd be freezing by now, even though fiddling was a good way to keep warm.

The winter's going to be a bad one. All the signs pointed in that direction. For that matter, all the signs pointed to tomorrow being pretty miserable. *Maybe I ought to just stay here tomorrow. . . .*

Carly passed by, scowling. Just to tweak the girl's temper, Rune modulated into "I've A Wife." Since it was quite unlikely that Carly would ever attain the married state, it was an unmistakable taunt in her direction. Assuming the girl was bright enough to recognize it as such.

On the other hand, staying here tomorrow means I'd have to put up with her during the day. I can't stay in bed all day reading, and it's too cold to stay up there the whole day. It's not worth it.

Maybe Tonno could use some help in his shop. . . .

She changed the tune again, to "Winter Winds," as another blast hit the shutters and rattled them. She told herself again that it could be worse. She could be on the road right now. She could be back in Westhaven. There were a hundred places she *could* be; instead she was here, with a certain amount of her keep assured.

Sapphire drifted down the stairs, dressed in a lovely, soft kirtle of her signature blue. That was a rarity, the ladies didn't usually come down-

stairs after dark. Rune was a little surprised; but then she saw why
Sapphire had come down. While luxurious, the lady's rooms were meant
for one thing only—besides sleep. And then, it got very crowded with
more than two. If clients wanted simple company, and in a group rather
than alone, well, the common room was the best place for that. There
were four older gentlemen waiting eagerly for Sapphire at their table, a
pentangle board set up and ready for play.

If all they wanted was to play pentangle with a beautiful woman who
would tease and flatter all of them until they went home—or one or more
of them mustered the juice to take advantage of the other services here—
then Amber's would gladly provide that service. And now Rune knew
why Carly was especially sour tonight. Bad enough that *she* wasn't good
enough to take her place upstairs. Worse that one of the ladies came
down here, into her sphere, to attract all eyes and remind her of the fact.
For truly, there wasn't an eye in the place that wasn't fastened on Sapphire, and well she knew it. Though Carly was out-of-bounds, she liked
having the men look at her; now no one would give her any more
attention than the lantern on the table.

Sapphire winked broadly at Rune, who raised her eyebrows and played
her a special little flourish as she sat down. Rune knew all the ladies
now, and to her immense surprise, she found that she liked all of them.
And never mind that one of them wasn't human. . . .

That was Topaz; a lady she had met only after Maddie had taken her
aside and warned her not to show surprise if she could help it. What
Topaz was, Rune had never had the temerity to ask. Another one of
those creatures who, like Boony, came from—elsewhere. Only Topaz
was nothing like Boony; she was thin and and wiry and completely
hairless, from her toe and finger-claws to the top of her head. Her golden
eyes were set slantwise in her flat face, which could have been catlike;
but she gave an impression less like a cat and far more like a lizard with
her sinuosity and her curious stillness. Her skin was as gold as her eyes,
a curious, metallic gold, and Rune often had the feeling that if she looked
closely enough, she'd find that in place of skin Topaz really had a hide
covered in tiny scales, the size of grains of dust. . . .

But whatever else she looked like, Topaz was close enough to human
to be very popular at Amber's. Or else—

But Rune didn't want to speculate on that. She was still capable of
being flustered by some of the things that went on here.

Her fingers wandered into "That Wild Ocean"—which made her think
of Pearl, not because Pearl was wild, but because she reminded Rune of
the way the melody twisted and twined in complicated figures, for all

that it was a slow piece. Pearl was human, altogether human, though of a different race than anyone Rune had ever seen. She was tiny and very pale, with skin as colorless as white quartz, long black hair that fell unfettered right down to the floor, and black, obliquely slanted eyes. She and Topaz spent a great deal of their free time together; Rune suspected that there were more of Topaz's kind where Pearl came from, although neither of them had ever said anything to prove or disprove that. Occasionally Rune would catch them whispering together in what sounded like a language composed entirely of sibilants, but when Rune had asked Pearl if that was her native tongue, the tiny woman had shaken her head and responded with a string of liquid syllables utterly unlike the hissing she had shared with Topaz.

But for all their strangeness, Pearl and Topaz were very friendly, both to her and to Maddie, Shawm, and Arden. Maddie frankly adored Pearl, and would gladly run any errand the woman asked of her. Shawm, white-blond and bashful, with too-large hands and feet, was totally in awe of all the ladies, and couldn't even get a word out straight when they were around. Arden, tall and dark, like Rune, teased them all like a younger brother, and took great pleasure in being teased back. He was never at a loss for words with any of them—

Except for one; the fourth lady, Ruby, who was the perfect compliment to Sapphire. Her eyes were a bright, challenging green, in contrast to Sapphire's dreamy blue. Her hair was a brilliant red, cut shorter than Rune's. Her figure was athletic and muscular, and she kept it that way by running every morning when she rose, and following that by two hours of gymnastic exercises. Where Sapphire was soft and lush, she was muscle and whipcord. Where Sapphire was gentle, she was wild. Where Sapphire was languid, she was quicksilver; Sapphire's even temper was matched by her fiery changeability.

Predictably enough, *they* were best friends.

And where Arden could tease Sapphire until she collapsed in a fit of giggles, he became tongue-tied and silent in the presence of Ruby.

And Carly *hated* that.

Well, fortunately Ruby was fully occupied at the moment—so Arden could tease Sapphire as she teased the old gentlemen at her table, and Carly only glowered, she didn't fume.

All four of them, plus Maddie, were the first female friends Rune had ever had. She found herself smiling a little at that, and smiled a bit more when she realized that her fingers had started "Home, Home, Home." Well, this *was* the closest thing she'd ever had to a home. . . .

One by one, the four ladies had introduced themselves over the course

of her first few weeks at Amber's, and gradually Rune had pieced together their stories. Topaz's history was the most straightforward. Topaz,
like Boony, had been a bondling, and had been taken up for the same
reason; failure to pay tax and tithe. She had been a small merchant-
trader until that moment. Amber had bought her contract from one of
the other houses at Pearl's hysterical insistence when the tiny creature
learned that Topaz was in thrall there.

"And just as well," Topaz had said, once. "One more night there,
and . . . something would have been dead. It might have been a client.
It might have been me. I cannot say."

Looking at her strange, golden eyes, and the wildness lurking in them,
Rune could believe it. It was not that Topaz had objected to performing
what she called "concubine duties." Evidently that was a trade with no
stigma attached in her (and Pearl's) country. It was some of the other
things the house had demanded she perform. . . .

Her eyes had darkened and the pupils had widened until they were all
that was to be seen when she'd said that. Rune had not asked any further
questions.

Pearl had come as a concubine in the train of a foreign trader; when
he had died, she had been left with nowhere to go. By the laws of her
land, she was property—and should have been sent back with the rest
of his belongings. But by the laws of Nolton, even a bondling was freed
by the death of his bondholder, and no one was willing to part with the
expense of transporting her home again.

But she had learned of Flower Street and of Amber's from her now-
dead master, and had come looking for a place. Originally she had
intended to stay only long enough to earn the money to return home,
but she found that she liked it here, and so stayed on, amassing savings
enough to one day retire to a place of her own, and devote herself to
her other avocation, the painting of tiny pictures on eggshells. As curiosities, her work fetched good prices, and would be enough to supplement
her savings.

Sapphire's story was the one she had obliquely referred to that first
morning when Rune had met her; carried off and despoiled by a rich
young merchant's son, she had been abandoned when her pregnancy first
became apparent. She had been befriended by Tonno, who had found
her fainting on his doorstep, and taken to Amber. What became of the
child, Rune did not know, though she suspected that Amber had either
rid the girl of it or she had miscarried naturally. Amber had seen the
haggard remains of Sapphire's great beauty, and had set herself to bringing it back to full bloom again. And had succeeded. . . .

Then there was Ruby, who had been a wild child, willful, and determined to be everything her parents hated and feared. Possibly because they had been *so* determined that she become a good little daughter of the Church—perhaps even a cleric-Priest or a nun. She had run away from the convent, got herself deflowered by the first man she ran across (a minstrel, she had confided to Rune, "And I don't know who was the more amazed, him or me") and discovered that she not only had a talent for the games of man and maid, she *craved* the contact. So she had come to Nolton ("Working my way"), examined each of the brothels on Flower Street, then came straight to Amber, demanding a place upstairs.

Amber, much amused by her audacity and impressed by her looks, had agreed to a compromise—a week of trial, under the name "Garnet," promising her a promotion to "Ruby" and full house status if she did well.

She was "Ruby" within two days.

Ruby was the latest of the ladies, a fact that galled Carly no end. Carly had petitioned Amber for a trial so many times that the lady had forbidden her to speak of it ever again. She could not understand *why* Ruby had succeeded where she had failed.

Sapphire left the gentlemen for a moment and drifted over to Rune's corner. Seeing where she was headed, Rune brought her current song to an end, finishing it just as Sapphire reached the fireplace. The young gentleman who had earlier requested a song hardly breathed as he watched her move, his eyes wide, his face a little flushed.

"Rune, dear, each of the gentleman has a song he'd like you to play, and I have a request too, if you don't mind," Sapphire said softly, with an angelic smile. "I know you must be ready for a break, but with five more songs, I think dear Lerra might be ready to—you know."

Rune smiled back. "Anything for you ladies, Sapphire, and you know it. I didn't get to play much out on the street today; my fingers aren't the least tired."

That was a little lie, but five more songs weren't going to hurt them any.

"Thank you, dear," Sapphire breathed, her face aglow with gratitude. That was one of the remarkable things about Sapphire; whatever she felt, she felt *completely,* and never bothered to hide it. "All right, this is what we'd like. 'Fair Maid of The Valley,' 'Four Sisters,' 'Silver Sandals,' 'The Green Stone,' and 'The Dream of the Heart.' Can you do all those?"

"In my sleep," Rune told her, with a grin. Sapphire rewarded her with another of her brilliant smiles, and started to turn to go—

But then she turned back a moment. "You know, I must have thought this a thousand times, and I never told you. I am terribly envious of your talent, Rune. You were good when you first arrived—you're quite good now—and some day, people are going to praise your name from one end of this land to the other. I wish I had your gift.''

"Well—" Rune said cautiously, "I don't know about that. I've a long way to go before I'm that good, and a hundred things could happen to prevent it. Besides—" she grinned. "It's one Guild Bard in a thousand that ever gets *that* much renown, and I doubt I'm going to be that one.''

But Sapphire shook her head. "I tell you true, Rune. And I'll tell you something else; for all the money and the soft living and the rest of it, if I had a fraction of your talent, I'd never set foot upstairs. I'd stay in the common room and be an entertainer for the rest of my life. All four of us know how very hard you work, we admire you tremendously, and I want you to know that.''

Then she turned and went back to her little gathering, leaving Rune flattered, and no little dumbfounded. *They* admired *her*? Beautiful, graceful, with everything they could ever want or need, and they admired *her*?

This was the first time she had ever been admired by anyone, and as she started the first of the songs Sapphire had requested, she felt a little warm current of real happiness rising from inside her and giving her fingers a new liveliness.

Even Jib thought I was a little bit daft for spending all my time with music, she thought, giving the tune a little extra flourish that made Sapphire half turn and wink at her from across the room. *Tonno keeps thinking about what I should be learning, Maddie doesn't understand how I feel about music, and even to Lady Amber I'm just another part of the common room. That's the very first time anyone has ever just thought that what I did was worth it, in and of itself.*

The warm feeling stayed with her, right till the end of the fifth song, when Sapphire laughingly drew one of the gentlemen to his feet and up the stairs after her.

She played one more song—and then she began to feel the twinges in her fingers that heralded trouble if she wasn't careful. Time for a break.

She threw the young gentleman a good-natured wink, which he returned, and set off to the kitchen for a bit of warm cider, since it was useless to ask Carly for anything.

They admire me. Who'd have thought it. . . .

Rune let her fingers prance their way across her lute-strings, forgetting that she was chilled in the spell of the music she was creating. Tonno listened to her play the piece she had first seen back in the summer, and thought impossible, with all its runs and triple-pickings, with his eyes closed and his finger marking steady time.

She played it gracefully, with relish for the complexities, with all the repeats and embellishments. She couldn't believe how easy it seemed—and how second-nature it was to read and play these little black notes on the page. She couldn't have conceived of this back in the summer, but one day everything had fallen into place, and she hadn't once faltered since. She came to the end, and waited, quietly, for her teacher to say something. When he didn't, when he didn't even open his eyes, she obeyed an impish impulse and put down the lute, picking up Lady Rose instead.

Then she started in on the piece again—this time playing it on the fiddle. Of course, it was a little different on the fiddle; she stumbled and faltered on a couple of passages where the fingering that was natural for the lute was anything but on the fiddle, but she got through it intact. Tonno's eyes had flown open in surprise at the first few bars; he stared at her all through the piece, clearly dumbfounded, right up until the moment that she ended with a flourish.

She put the fiddle and bow down, and waited for him to say something.

He took a deep breath. "Well," he said. "You've just made up my mind for me, dear. If ever I was desirous of a sign from God, that was it."

She wrinkled her brow, puzzled. "What's that supposed to mean?" she asked. "It was just that lute-piece, that's all."

"Just the lute-piece—which you proceeded to play through on an instrument it wasn't intended for." Tonno shook his head. "Rune, I've been debating this for the past two weeks, but I can't be selfish anymore. You're beyond me, on both your instruments. I can't teach you any more."

It was her turn to stare, licking suddenly dry lips, not sure of what to say. "But—but I—"

This was too sudden, too abrupt, she thought, her heart catching with something like fear. She wasn't ready for it all to end; at least, not yet. *I'm not ready to leave. There's still the whole winter yet, the Faire isn't until Midsummer—what am I supposed to do between now and then?*

"Don't look at me like that, girl," Tonno said, a little gruffly, rubbing his eyebrow with a hand encased in fingerless gloves. "Just because you're beyond my teaching, that doesn't mean you're ready for what you want to do."

"I'm—not?" she said dazedly, not certain whether to be relieved or disappointed.

"No," Tonno replied firmly. "You're beyond my ability to contribute to your teaching—*in music*—but you're not good enough to win one of the Bard apprenticeships. And I've heard some of your tunes, dear; you shouldn't settle for less than a Bardic position. Of all the positions offered at the Faire, only a handful are for Bardic teaching, and you are just not good enough to beat the ninety-nine other contenders for those positions."

Good news *and* bad, all in the same bite. "Will I ever be?" she asked doubtfully.

"Of course you will!" he snapped, as if he was annoyed at her doubt. "I have a damned good ear, and I can tell you when you will be ready. What we'll have to do is find some of my truly complicated music, the things I put away because they were beyond my meager capabilities to play. You'll practice them until your fingers are blue, and then you'll learn to transpose music from other instruments to yours and play *that* until your fingers are blue. Practice is what you need now, and practice, by all that's holy, is what you're going to get."

I guess it's not over yet. Not even close. She sighed, but he wasn't finished with his plans for her immediate future.

"Then there's the matter of your other lessons," he continued inexorably. "I've taught you how to read music; now I'll teach you how to write it as well—by ear, without playing it first on your instruments. I'll see that you learn as much as I know of other styles, and of the work of the Great Bards. And *then*, my dear, I'm going to drill you in reading, history in particular, until you think you've turned Scholar!"

"Oh, no—" she said involuntarily. While she was reading with more competence, it still wasn't something that came easily. Unlike music, she still had to work at understanding. History, in particular, was a great deal of hard work.

"Oh, yes," he told her, with a smile. "If you're going to become a Guild Bard, you're going to have to compete with boys who've been learning from Scholars all their lives. You're going to have to know plenty about the past—who's who, and more importantly, *why*, because if you inadvertently offend the wrong person—"

He sliced his finger dramatically across his neck.

She shuddered, reflexively, as a breath of cold that came out of nowhere touched the back of her neck.

"Now," he said, clearing the music away from the stand in front of her, and stacking it neatly in the drawer of the cabinet beside him. "Put your instruments back in their cases and come join me by the stove. I want you to know some hard truths, and what you're getting yourself into.''

She cased the lute and Lady Rose obediently, and pulled her short cloak a little tighter around her shoulders. Tonno's stove didn't give off a lot of heat, partially because fuel was so expensive that he didn't stoke it as often as Amber fueled her fireplaces. Rune would have worried more about him in this cold, except that he obviously had a lot of ploys to keep himself warm, He spent a lot of time at Amber's in the winter, Maddie said; nursing a few drinks and keeping some of the waiting clients company with a game of pentangle or cards, and Amber smiled indulgently and let him stay.

I wonder what it is that he did for her, that they're such good friends?

Rune followed him to the back of the living-quarters, bringing her chair with her, and settled herself beside him as he huddled up to the metal stove.

He wrapped an old comforter around himself, and raised his bushy gray eyebrows at her. ''Now, first of all, as far as I know, there are no girls in the Guild,'' he stated flatly. ''So right from the beginning, you're going to have a problem.''

She nodded; she'd begun to suspect something of the sort. She'd noticed that no one wearing the purple ribbon-knots was female—

And she'd discovered her first weeks out busking that every time she wore anything even vaguely feminine out on the street, she got propositions. Eventually, she figured out why.

There were plenty of free-lance whores out on the street, pretending to busk, with their permits stuck on their hats like anyone else. She found out why, when she'd asked the dancers that performed by the fountain every night. The permit for busking was cheaper by far than the fees to the Whore's Guild, so many whores, afraid of being caught and thrown into the workhouse for soliciting without a permit or Guild badge, bought busking permits. The Church, which didn't approve of either whores *or* musicians, ignored the deception; the city frowned, but looked the other way, so long as those on the street bought *some* sort of permit. Real musicians wore the ribbon knots on their sleeves, and whores didn't, but most folk hadn't caught on to that distinction. So, the result was undoubtedly that female musicians had a reputation in the Guild for being something else entirely.

But still—the auditions should weed out those with other professions. Shouldn't they? And why on Earth would a whore even *come* to the trials?

"The reason there aren't any females in the Guild," he continued, "is because they aren't allowed to audition at the Faire. Ever."

She stared at him, anger warming her cheek at the realization that he hadn't bothered to say anything to her about this little problem with her plans before this.

"I imagine you're wondering why I didn't tell you that in the first place." He raised an eyebrow, and she blushed that he could read her so easily. "It's simple enough. I didn't think it would be a problem as long as you were prepared for it. You've carried off the boy-disguise perfectly well; I've seen you do it, and fool anyone who just looks at the surface of things. I don't see any reason why you can't get your audition as a boy, and tell them the truth after you've won your place."

She flushed again, this time at her own stupidity. She should have figured that out for herself. "But won't they be angry?" she asked, a little doubtfully.

Tonno shrugged. "That, I can't tell you. I don't know. I do know that if you've been so outstanding that you've surprised each and every one of them, if they are any kind of musician at all, they'll overlook your sex. They might make you keep up the disguise while you're an apprentice, but once you're a master, you can do what you want and they can be hanged."

That seemed logical, and she could see the value of the notion. So long as she went along with their ideas of what was proper, they'd give her what she wanted—but once she had it, she would be free of any restraints. They weren't likely to take her title away; once you were a Master Bard, you were always a Master, no matter what you did. They hadn't even taken away the title from Master Marley, who had lulled his patron, Sire Jacoby, to sleep, and let in his enemies by the postern gate to kill him and all his family. They'd turned him over to the Church and the High King for justice, but they'd left him his title. Not that it had done much good in a dungeon.

"I intend you to leave here with enough knowledge crammed into that thick head of yours—and enough skill in those fingers—to give every boy at the trials a run for his money," Tonno said firmly. "I trust you don't plan to settle for less than an apprenticeship to a Guild Bard?" He raised one eyebrow.

She shook her head, stubbornly. Guild Minstrels only played music; Guild Bards created it. There were songs in her head dying to get out—

"Good." Tonno nodded with satisfaction. "That's what I hoped you'd say. You're too good a musician to be wasted busking out in the street. You should have noble patrons, and the only way you're going to get that is through the Guild. That's the only way to rise in any profession; through the Guilds. Guildsmen keep standards high and craftsmanship important. And that's not all. If you're good enough, the Guild will make certain that you're rewarded, by backing you.''

"Like what?" she asked, curiously, and tucked her hands under her knees to warm them.

"Oh, like Master Bard Gwydain," Tonno replied, his eyes focused somewhere past her head, as if he was remembering something. "I heard him play, once, you know. Amazing. He couldn't have been more than twenty, but he played like no one I've ever heard—and that was twenty years ago, before he was at the height of his powers. Ten years ago, the High King himself rewarded Master Gwydain—made him Laurel Sire Gwydain, and gave him lands and a royal pension. A great many of the songs I've been teaching you are his—'Spellbound Captive,' 'Dream of the Heart,' 'That Wild Ocean,' 'Black Rose,' oh, he must have written hundreds before he was through. Amazing.''

He fell silent, as the light in the shop began to dim with the coming of evening. Soon Rune would have to leave, to return to Amber's, but curiosity got the better of her; after all, if Gwydain had been twenty or so, twenty years ago, he couldn't be more than forty now. Yet she had never heard anyone mention his name.

"What happened to him?" she asked, breaking into Tonno's reverie. He started a little, and wrinkled his brow. "You know, that's the odd part," he said slowly. "It's a mystery. No one I've talked to knows what happened to him; he seems to have dropped out of sight about five or ten years ago, and no one has seen nor heard of him since. There've been rumors, but that's all.''

"What kind of rumors?" she persisted, feeling an urgent need to know, though she couldn't have told why.

"Right after he vanished, there was a rumor he'd died tragically, but no one knew how—right after that there was another that he'd taken vows, renounced the world, and gone into Holy Orders.'' Tonno shook his head. "I don't believe either one, if you want to know the truth. It seems to me that if he'd really died, there'd have been a fancy funeral and word of it all over the countryside. And if he'd taken Holy Orders, he'd be composing Church music. There's never been so much as a hint of scandal about him, so that can't be it. I just don't know.''

Rune had the feeling that Tonno was very troubled by this disappearance—well, so was she. It left an untidy hole, a mystery that cried to be cleared up. "What if he gave up music for some reason?" she asked. "Then if he'd gone into the Church, he'd have just vanished.''

"Give up music? Not likely," Tonno snorted. "You can't keep a Bard from making music. It's something they're born to do. No," he shook his head vehemently. "Something odd happened to him, and that's for sure—and the Guild is keeping it quiet. Maybe he had a brainstorm, and he can't play, or even speak clearly. Maybe he took wasting fever and he's too weak to do anything. Maybe he ran off to the end of the world, looking for new things. But something out of the ordinary happened to him, I would bet my last copper on it. It's a mystery."

He changed the subject then, back to quizzing Rune on the history she'd been reading, and they did not again return to the subject of Master Bard Gwydain. Eventually darkness fell, and it was time for her to leave.

She bundled herself up in her cloak, slung her instruments across her back underneath it to keep them from the cold, and let herself out of the shop, wanting to spare Tonno the trip up through the cold, darkened store. As she hurried along the street towards Amber's, the wind whipping around her ankles and crawling under her hood until she shivered with cold, she found herself thinking about the mystery.

She agreed with Tonno; unless *she* were at death's door, or otherwise crippled, she would not be able to stop making music. If Gwydain still lived, he must be plying his birthright, somewhere.

And if he was dead, someone should know about it. If he was dead, and the Guild was keeping it quiet, there must be a reason.

And I'll find it out, she decided, suddenly. *When I get into the Guild, I'll find it out. No matter what. They can't keep it a secret forever. . . .*

CHAPTER TEN

Rune fitted the key Tonno had given her into the old lock on the front door of the shop, and tried to turn it. Nothing happened.

Frozen again, she thought, and swore under her breath at the key, the ancient lock, and the damned weather. She pulled the key out and tucked it under her armpit to warm it, wincing as the cold metal chilled her through her heavy sweater, and flinching again as a gust of wind blew a swirl of snow down her neck. She glanced up and down the silent street; the only traffic was a pair of tradesmen muffled in cloaks much heavier than hers, probably hurrying to open their own shops, and a couple of apprentice-boys out on errands. Other than that, there was no one. The slate-colored sky overhead spilled thin skeins of flurries, and the wind sent them skating along the street like ghost-snakes.

Whatever could have been in God's mind when He invented winter? Thrice-forsaken season. . . .

It didn't *look* like a good day for trade—but Scholars made up half of Tonno's business, and days like today, she had learned, meant business from Scholars. They'd be inside all day, fussing over their libraries or collections of curiosities, and discover they had somehow neglected to buy that book or bone or odd bit of carving they'd looked at back in the summer. And now, of course, they simply *must* have it. So they'd wait until one of their students arrived for a special lesson, and the hapless youth would be sent out On Quest with a purchase-order and a purse, will-he, nill-he. Those sales made a big difference to Tonno, especially in winter, and made it worth keeping the shop open.

She pulled out the key and stuck it back into the lock quickly, before it had a chance to chill down again. This time, when she put pressure on it, the lock moved. Stiffly, but the door did unlock, and she hurriedly pushed it open and shoved it closed against another snow-bearing gust of wind.

"Tonno?" she called out. "I'm here!"

She flipped the little sign in the window from "Closed" to "Open," and made her way back to the counter, where she raised the hinged part and flipped it over. "Tonno?" she called again.

"I'm awake, Rune," he replied, his voice distant and a little weak. "I'm just not—out of bed yet."

She frowned; he didn't sound well. She'd better get back to him before he decided to be stubborn and open the shop himself. In weather like this, or so Amber told her, Tonno did better to stay in bed.

She pushed the curtain in the doorway aside and hurried over to his bedside. Before he had a chance to struggle out of the motley selection of comforters, quilts, and old blankets he had piled, one atop the other so that the holes and worn spots in each of them were compensated for by the sound spots in the others, she reached him and had taken his hand in both of hers, examining the joints with a critical eye. As she had expected, they were swollen, red, and painful to look at.

"You aren't going anywhere," she said firmly. "There's a storm out there, and it's mucking up your hands and every other bone you've got, I'd wager."

He frowned, but it was easy to see his heart wasn't in the protest. "But I didn't get up yesterday except—"

"So you don't get up today. What's the difference?" she asked, reasonably. "I can mind the shop. We'll probably get a customer or two, but not more. That's hardly work at all. And I'm *not* busking today; it's too damned cold and I'll not risk Lady Rose to weather like this. I might just as well mind the shop and give your lessons to—who is it today— Anny and Ket? I thought so. They're bare beginners. Easy. I could teach them half asleep. And their parents don't care if it's me or you who teaches them, so long as they get the lessons they've paid for."

"But you aren't benefiting by this—" Tonno said fretfully. "You should be out earning a few coppers—"

She shrugged. "There's no one out there to earn coppers from. I picked up a little in my hat at Amber's last night, enough for the tax and tithe. And I am benefiting—" She gave him a wide grin. "If I'm here, I'm not there, and I don't have to listen to Carly's bullying and whining."

"You haven't been tormenting her, have you?" Tonno asked sharply, with more force than she expected. She gave him a quizzical look, wondering what notion he'd gotten into his head. Surely Carly didn't deserve any sympathy from Tonno!

"Not unless you consider ignoring her to be tormenting her," she replied, straightening his bedcovers, then putting a kettle on the stove and a brick to heat beneath it. "I try not to let her bother me, but she does bully me every chance she gets, and she says nasty things about my playing to the customers. She'd probably say worse than that about me, but the only thing she can think of is that since I dress like a boy sometimes, I might be a poppet or an androgyn. That's hardly going to be an insult in a place like Amber's! It's just too bad for her that the clients all have ears of their own, and they don't agree with her. Maddie is the one who teases her.''

Tonno relaxed. "Good. But be careful, Rune. I've been thinking about her, and wondering why Amber keeps her on, and I think now I know the reason. I think she's a spy for the Church.''

"A *what*?" Rune turned from her work to gape at him. "Carly? Whatever for? What reason would the Church have to spy on a brothel?''

"I can think of several reasons," he said, his face and voice troubled. "The most obvious is to report on how many clients come and go, and how much money they tip in the common room, to make certain that all taxes and tithes have been paid for. That's fairly innocuous as things go, since we both know perfectly well that all the fees are paid at Amber's and on time, too. There's another reason, too, though; and it's one that would just suit the girl's sour spirit right down to the core.''

"Oh?" she asked, a cold lump of worry starting in the pit of her stomach. "What's that?''

She couldn't imagine what interest the Church would find in a brothel—and if she couldn't imagine it, it must be something darkly sinister. She began wondering about all those rumors she'd heard of Church Priests being versed in dark magics, when his next words cleared her mind entirely. "Fornication," he said. "Fornication is a sin, Rune. Although the laws of the city say nothing about it, the only lawful congress by the Church's rule, is between man and woman who are wedded by Church ceremony. And, by Church rule, sins must be confessed and paid for, either by penance or donation.''

Her first impulse had been to laugh, but second thought proved that Tonno's concern was real, though less sinister than *her* fears. She nodded, thoughtfully. "So if Carly keeps a list of who comes and goes, and gives it to the Church, the next time Guildsman Weaver shows up to confess and do penance, if he *doesn't* list his visit to Amber's—he's in trouble.''

Tonno sighed, and reached eagerly for the mug of hot tea she handed to him. "And for the men of means who visit Amber's, the trouble will mean that the Priest will confront them with their omission, impress them with his 'supernatural' understanding, and assign additional penance—''

"Additional guilt-money, you mean," she finished cynically. "And meanwhile, no doubt, Carly's record-keeping is paying off *her* sins for working in a brothel in the first place." She sniffed, angrily. "Oh, that makes excellent sense, Tonno. And it explains a lot. Since Carly can't have a place at Amber's, she'll do her best to foul the bedding for everyone else. And *she'll* come out sanctimoniously lily-white."

She picked up the hot brick and tucked it into the foot of the bed, replacing it under the stove with another. The heat did a great deal of good for Tonno; already there was a bit more color in his face, and some of the lines of pain around his eyes and mouth were easing.

He took another sip of tea, and nodded. "Do you see what I mean by suiting the girl's nature? Likely she's even convinced herself that this was why she came to work there in the first place, to keep an eye on the welfare of others' souls."

"No doubt," Rune said dryly. She stirred oatmeal into a pot of water, and set it on top of the stove beside the kettle to cook. "She'll always want the extreme of anything; if she can't be a highly paid whore, she'll be a saint. What I can't understand is why Amber lets her stay on—you pretty much implied that she knows what Carly's up to."

Tonno laughed, though the worry lines about his mouth had not eased any. "That's the cleverness of our Lady Amber, dear. As long as Carly is in place, she *knows* who the spy is. If there is truly someone whose reputation with the Church is so delicate that he *must not* be seen at Amber's, then all the lady needs to do is make certain Carly doesn't see him. And I suspect Lady Amber has whatever official Carly reports to quite completely bribed."

Wiser in the ways of bribery than she had been a scant six months ago, Rune nodded. "If she got rid of Carly, someone else might get *his* agent in, and she'd have to find out what *his* price was."

"But if she stopped bribing the old official, he'd report on what Carly had given him already." Tonno shrugged. "Amber knows what's going on, what's being reported, and saves money this way as well. And what does Carly cost her, really? Nothing she wouldn't be paying anyway. She'd have to bribe someone in the Church to be easy with the clients, no matter what."

Rune shook her head. "I guess I'll have to put up with it, and be grateful that I personally don't care that much about the state of my soul to worry about what working in a whorehouse is going to do to it. I'm probably damned anyway, for having the poor taste to be born on the wrong side of the blankets."

"That's the spirit!" Tonno laughed a little, and she cheered up herself, seeing that he was able to laugh without hurting himself. She gave the room a sketchy cleaning, and washed last night's supper dishes. By then the oatmeal was ready and she spooned out enough for both of them, sweetening it with honey. She ate a lot faster than he did; he wasn't even half finished with his portion when she'd cleaned her bowl of the last spoonful. She put the dish into the pan of soapsuds just as the bell to the front door tinkled.

He started to get up from sheer habit, but she glared at him until he sank back into the pillows, and hurried to the front of the shop.

As she'd anticipated, since it was too early for either of the children having music lessons to arrive, the person peering into the shop with a worried look on his face was one of the University Students. The red stripe on the shoulders of his cloak told her he was a Student of Philosophy. Good. They had money—and by extension, so did their teachers. Only a rich man could afford to let his son idle away his time on something like Philosophy. And rich men paid well for their sons' lessons.

"Can I help you, my lord?" she said into the silence of the shop, startling him. He jumped, then peered short-sightedly at her as she approached.

"Is this the shop of—" he consulted a strip of paper in his hand "—Tonno Alendor?"

"Yes it is, my lord," she said, and waited. He looked at her doubtfully.

"I was told to seek out this Tonno himself," he said. The set of his chin told her that he was of the kind of nature to be stubborn, but the faint quiver of doubt in his voice also told her he could be bullied. Another of Tonno's lessons: how to read people, and know how to deal with them.

"Master Tonno is ill. I am his niece," she lied smoothly. "He entrusts everything to me."

The soft, round chin firmed as the spoiled young man who was not used to being denied what he wanted emerged; in response to that warning, so did her voice. "If you *truly* wish to disturb him, if you feel you *must* pester a poor, sick old man, I can take you to his bedside"—*and I'll make you pay dearly for it in embarrassment,* her voice promised— "but he'll only tell you the same thing, young man."

Her tone, and the scolding "young man," she appended to her little speech, gave him the impression she was much older than he had thought. Nearsighted as he was, and in the darkness of the shop, he would probably believe it. And, as she had hoped, he must have a female relative somewhere that was accustomed to browbeating him into obedience; his resistance collapsed immediately.

"Scholar Mardake needs a book," he said meekly. "He looked at it last summer, and he was certain he had purchased it, but now he finds he hadn't, and he *has* to have it for his monograph, and—"

She let him rattle on for far too long about the monograph, the importance of it, and how it would enhance Scholar Mardake's already illustrious reputation. And, by extension, the reputations and status of all of Mardake's Students.

What a fool.

She tried not to yawn in his face, but it was difficult. Jib had more sense in his big toe than this puffed-up popinjay had in his entire body. And of all the things to be over-proud of—this endless debate over frothy nothings, like the question of what a "soul" truly consisted of, made her weary to the bone. If they would spend half the time on questions of a practical nature instead of this chop-logic drivel, the world would be better run. Finally he came to the point: the name of the book.

"By whom?" she asked, finally getting a word in. Of all of the Scholars, the Philosophers were by far and away the windiest.

"Athold Derelas," he replied, loftily, as if he expected that she had never heard of the great man.

"Ah, you're in luck," she replied immediately. "We have *two* copies. Does your master prefer the annotated version by Wasserman, or the simple translation by Bartol?"

He gaped at her. She stifled a giggle. In truth, she wouldn't have known the books were there if she hadn't replaced a volume of history by Lyam Derfan to its place beside them the day before. It was bad enough that she'd known of the book; but she'd offered two choices, and he didn't know how to react. He'd loftily assumed, no doubt, that she was the next thing to illiterate, and she'd just confounded him.

He'd have been less startled to hear a pig sing, or an ape recite poetry.

She decided to rub the humiliation in. "If your master is doing a monograph covering Derelas' work as a whole, he would probably want the annotated version," she continued blithely, "but if all he wants is Derelas' comments on specific subjects, he'd be better off with the Bartol translation."

Now the young man had to refer to the slip of paper in his hand. He looked from it, to her, and back again, and couldn't seem to come to a decision. His face took on a pinched look of miserable confusion.

"Perhaps he'd better have both," she suggested. "No knowledge is ever wasted, after all. The Wasserman is rare; he may find enough of interest in it for an entirely new monograph."

The Student brightened up considerably. "Yes, of course," he said happily, and Rune had no doubt that he would parrot her words back to his Scholar as if they were his own, and suggesting that the shop-girl hadn't known what a rarity the Wasserman was, so that he'd gotten the book at a bargain price.

Before he could change his mind—it was his master's money he was spending, after all, and not his own—she rolled the floor-to-ceiling ladder over to the "D" section, and scampered up it. The Student virtuously averted his eyes, blushing, lest he have an inadvertent glimpse of feminine flesh. As if there was anything to be seen under her double skirts, double leggings, and boots.

Besides being the most long-winded, Philosophers were also the most prudish of the Scholars—at least the ones that Rune had met. She much preferred the company of the Natural Scientists and the Mathematicians. The former were full of the wonders of the world, and eager to share the strange stories of birds and beasts; the latter tended to make up for the times when they lost themselves in the dry world of numbers with a vengeance. And both welcomed women into their ranks far oftener than the Philosophers.

Doubtless because women are too sensible to be distracted for long by maunderings about airy nothings.

She came down with both books clutched in her hand, eluding his grasp for them so easily he might not even have been standing there, and took them behind the counter. There she consulted the book where Tonno noted the prices of everything in the shop, by category. It was a little tedious, for things were listed in the order he had acquired them, and not in the alphabetical order in which they were ranked on the shelves. But finally she had the prices of both of them, and looked up, reaching beneath the counter for a piece of rough paper to wrap them in.

"The Wasserman, as I said, is rare," she said, deftly making a package and tying it with a bit of string. "Master Tonno has it listed at forty silver pieces."

His mouth gaped, and he was about to utter a gasp of outrage. She continued before he had a chance. "The other is more common as I said; it is only twenty. Now, as it is Master Tonno's policy to offer a discount to steady clients like your Scholar, I believe I can let you have both for fifty." She batted her eyelashes ingenuously at him. "After all,

Master Tonno does trust me in all things, and it isn't often we have a fine young man like you in the shop.''

The appeal to his vanity killed whatever protest he had been about to make. His mouth snapped shut, and he counted out the silver quickly, before she could change her mind. He knew very well—although he did not know that *she* knew—his Scholar was anything but a steady customer; he bought perhaps a book or two in a year. What he did not know—and since he was not a regular customer, neither would his Scholar—was that she had inflated the listed prices of both books by ten silver pieces each. She had heard other Scholars speaking when she had tended the shop before, chuckling over Tonno's prices. She heard a lot of things Tonno didn't. The Scholars tended to ignore her as insignificant.

So whenever she had sold a book lately, she had inflated the price. Scholars would never argue with her, assuming no woman would be so audacious as to cheat a Scholar; their Students never argued with her because she bullied and flattered them the same way she had treated this boy, and with the same effect. And when she added the nonsense about a ''discount,'' they generally kept their mouths shut.

She handed him the parcel, and he hurried out into the cold. She dropped the taxes and tithes into the appropriate boxes, and pocketed the rest to take back to Tonno. Merchants with shops never went to a Church stall the way buskers and peddlers did; they kept separate tax and tithe boxes which were locked with keys only the Church Collectors had. The Collectors would come around once a week with a city constable to take what had accumulated in the boxes, noting the amounts in their books. Rune actually liked the Collector who serviced Tonno's shop; she hadn't expected to, but the first day he had appeared when she was on duty he had charmed her completely. Brother Bryan was a thin, energetic man with a marvelously dry sense of humor, and was, so far as she could tell, absolutely honest. Tonno seemed convinced of his honesty as well, and greeted him as a friend. And whenever she was here and Tonno was ill, he would make a point of coming to the back of the shop to see how the old man was faring, pass the time of day with him, and see if he could find some way to entertain Tonno a little before he continued on his rounds of the other shops.

She dipped a quill in a bit of ink and ran a delicate line through the titles of the two books to indicate they had been sold, and returned to Tonno.

He sat up with interest, and demanded to know what had happened. He shook his head over her duplicity with the spurious ''discount,'' but she noted that he did not demand that she refund the extra ten silvers.

"You should update your prices," she said, scolding a little. "You haven't changed some of them from the time when your father ran this shop. I know you haven't, because I've seen the prices still in his handwriting."

He sighed. "But people come here for bargains, Rune," he replied plaintively. "Even when father had the shop, this district was changing over from shops to residences. Now—it's so out of the way that no one would ever come here at all if they didn't know they'd get a bargain."

"You can make them think you've given them a bargain and still not cheat yourself," she said, taking the empty bowl from the floor beside his bed and swishing it in the painfully cold wash-water until it was clean.

"I hope you put what was due in the tax box, and not what was in the book," he said suddenly.

She grimaced, but nodded. "Of course I did. Although I can't for the life of me see *why*. That Scholar isn't likely to tell anyone how much he paid, and you need every silver you can get. We may not have another sale for a week or more!" She put the bowl back on the shelf with a thud.

"Because it's our responsibility, Rune," he replied, patiently, as if she was a child. He said that every time she brought up the subject of taxes, and she was tired to death of hearing it. He never once explained what he meant, and she just couldn't see it. There were too many rich ones she suspected of diddling the tax rolls to get by with paying less than they should.

"*Why* is it our responsibility?" she asked fiercely. "And why *ours*? I don't see anyone else leaping forward to throw money in the tax and tithe boxes! You and Amber keep saying that, and I don't see any reason for it!"

He just looked at her, somberly, until she flushed. He made her feel as if she had said something incredibly irresponsible, and that made no sense. She didn't know why she should feel embarrassed by her outburst, but she did, and that made her angry as well.

"Rune," he said slowly, as if he had just figured out that she was serious. "There truly is a reason for it. Now do you really want to hear the reason, or do you want to be like all those empty-headed fools out there who grumbled about taxes and cheat when they can, and never once think about who or what they're cheating?"

"Well, if there's a reason, I'd certainly like to hear it," she muttered, skeptically, and sat down in the chair beside his bed. "Nothing I've seen yet has given me a reason to think differently, and *you're* the one who taught me to trust my eyes and not just parrot what I've been told!"

"You've lived here for almost half a year," Tonno replied. "I know that there's a world of difference between Nolton and your little village; there are things we do here that no one would ever think of doing back in Westhaven." She made a face, but he continued. "I know I'm saying something obvious, but because it's obvious, you might not have thought about it. There are things that people take for granted after they've been here as long as you have; things that are invisible, but that we couldn't do without. Dung-sweepers, for instance. Who cleans up the droppings in Westhaven?"

"Well, no one," she admitted. "It gets kicked to one side or trodden into the mud, that's about it."

"But if we did that here, we'd be knee-deep in manure in a week," Tonno pointed out, and she nodded agreement. "Who do you think *pays* the dung-sweepers?"

"I never wondered about it," she admitted with surprise. "I thought the dung must be valuable to someone—for composting, or some-thing—"

"It is, and they sell it to farmers, but that's not enough to compensate a man for going about with a barrow all day collecting it," Tonno pointed out. "The city pays them—right out of that tax box." She rubbed her hands together to warm them, about to say something, but he continued. "Who guards the streets of Westhaven by day or night from robbers, drunks, troublemakers and thieves?"

She laughed, because it was something else that would never have occurred to her old village to worry about. "No one. Nobody's abroad very late, and if they are, there's no one to trouble them. If a drunk falls on his face in the street, he can lie there until morning."

But she couldn't keep the laughter from turning uneasy. It might not have occurred to them, but it would have been a good thing if it had. A single constable could have prevented a lot of trouble in the past. If there'd been someone like the city guard or constables around, would those bullies have tried to molest her that day? Even one adult witness would likely have prevented the entire incident. How many times had something like that happened to someone who couldn't defend herself?

Was that how Stara had gotten into trouble in the first place, as a child too young to know better? Was that why she had gone on to trade her favors so cheaply?

If that incident with Jon and his friends hadn't occurred, would Rune have been quite so willing to seek a life out in the wider world?

"That will do for a little village, but what would we do here?" Tonno asked gently. "There are thousands of people living here; most are honest, but some are not. What's a shopkeeper to do, spend his nights waiting with a dagger in hand?"

"Couldn't people—well—band together, and just have one of them watch for all?" she asked, self-consciously, flushing; knowing it wasn't any kind of a real answer. "I suppose they could pay him for his troubles—" Then she shook her head. "That's basically what the constables are, aren't they? That's what you're trying to tell me. And they're paid from taxes too."

"Constables, dung-sweepers, the folk who repair and maintain the wells and the aqueducts, and a hundred more jobs you'd never think of and likely wouldn't see. Rat-catchers and street-tenders, gate-keepers and judges, gaolers and the men who make certain food sold in the marketplace is what it's said to be." Tonno leaned forward, earnestly, and she saw that the light was fading.

"I suppose you're right." She lit a candle at the stove, but he wasn't going to be distracted from his point.

"That's what a government is all about, Rune," he said, more as if he was pleading with her than as if he was trying to win an argument. "Taking care of all the things that come up when a great many people live together. And yes, most of those things each of us could do for himself, taking care of his own protection, and his family's, and minding the immediate area around his home and shop—but that would take a great deal of time, and while the expenses would be less, they would come in lumps, and in the way of things, at the worst possible time." He laughed ruefully, and so did she. It hadn't been that long ago they'd had one of those lump expenses, when the roof sprang a leak and they'd had it patched.

She could see his point—but not his passion. And for something as cold and abstract as a government. "But you don't like paying taxes either," she said in protest, and he nodded.

"No, I don't. That's quite true. There are some specific taxes that I think are quite unfair. I pay a year-tax leavened against the shop simply because I own it, rather than renting, and when my father died, I paid a death-tax in order to inherit. I don't think those taxes are particularly fair. But"—he held up his hand to forestall her comments—"those are only two taxes, with a government that could leaven far more taxes than it does. I've heard of cities where they tax money earned, then tax the goods sold, then tax every stage a product goes through as it changes hands—"

She shook her head, baffled. "I don't understand—" she said. "How can they do that?"

He explained further. "Take a cow; it is taxed when it is sold as a weanling, taxed again when it is brought to market, the rawhide is taxed when it comes into the hands of the tanners, taxed again when it goes to the leather-broker, taxed when it is sold to the shoemaker, then taxed a final time when the shoes are sold."

Her head swam at the thought of all those taxes.

"That kind of taxation is abusive; when the time comes that the price of an object is doubled to pay the taxes on it, that is abusive. And governments of that nature are generally abusive of the people that live under them as well." Tonno leaned back into his pillows, and he looked like a man who was explaining something he cared about, deeply.

As deeply as I care about music, she thought in surprise. She had found his secret passion. And it was nothing like what she would have expected.

"Before you ask," he told her, carefully, as if he was weighing each word for its true value, "I can tell you that you'll get a different definition of an abusive government from nearly everyone who cares to think about such things. In general, though, I would say that when a government is more concerned with keeping itself in power, and keeping its officials in luxury, whether they were elected to the posts, appointed, or inherited the position, then that government is abusive as well. Government is what takes care of things beyond you. Good government cares for the well-being of the people it serves. Abusive government cares only for its own well-being. The fewer the people, the less government you need. Does that seem clear to you?"

She thought about it for a moment. She'd begun listening to this mostly because she respected Tonno, and this seemed to mean a great deal to him. But the more he'd said, the more she began to get a glimmering of a wider sphere than the one she was used to dealing with—and it intrigued her in the way the things the Mathematicians said intrigued her. And now she realized that Amber had said basically the same things, in cryptic little bits, over the past several months. Reluctantly, she had to agree that they were right.

Still—this was the real world she was living in, and not some Philosopher's book, where everyone did as he should, and everything was perfect. "But what about the stories I keep hearing?" she protested, taking one last shot at disproving his theories. "The things about the inspectors who take bribes, and the gaolers who turn people loose no matter what they've done, so long as they've got money enough? What about the clerics at the Church stalls, who'll take all your money as tax or tithe, then insist you owe as much over again for the one you didn't pay? I bet *they* pocket the difference!''

Tonno shrugged, then chuckled a little, though sadly. "You're dealing with people, Rune, and the real world, not a Philosopher's ideal sphere,'' he said, echoing her very thoughts. "People are corruptible, and any time you have money changing hands, someone is likely to give in to temptation. So I'll give you another definition: since there's always going to be corruption, a good government is one where you have a manageable level of corruption!''

He laughed at that one. She made a face, but laughed with him. "Right, I'll grant your stand on taxes, but what about tithes? What's the Church doing to earn all that money? They take in as much as the city, and *they* aren't hiring the rat-catchers!''

"What's the Church doing—or what is it *supposed* to be doing, rather?'' he asked, his expression hardening. "What it's supposed to be doing is to care for those who can't care for themselves—to feed and clothe the impoverished, to heal the sick, to bring peace where there is war, to be family to the orphaned, find justice for those who have been denied it. The Priests are bound to make certain every child can read and write and cipher, so that it can grow up to find a place or earn a living without being cheated. That's what it's *supposed* to be doing. That, and give the time to God that few of us have the leisure for, so that, hopefully, God will know when we have need of His powers, having run out of solutions for ourselves.''

She nodded. That was, indeed, what the village Priest was supposed to deal with—when he wasn't too busy with being holy, that is. He seemed to spend a great deal of time convincing the villagers that he was much more important than they were. . . .

Tonno took note of her abstracted nod. "And we all pay tithes to see that it gets done—because one day I may be too ill to care for myself, you may find yourself in a town on the brink of war, your friend's child may lose its parents, you might find yourself in the right—but up against the Sire himself, with no hope from his courts. And some of that is done.''

"But?'' she asked, a little more harshly than she intended. Nobody had seen that justice was done for her—or Jib. Had she been raped, would the Priest have lifted a finger to see that the bullies paid? Not a chance. More likely he'd have condemned her for leading them on.

"But not enough to account for the enormous amount of money the Church takes in,'' Tonno replied, his mouth a tight, grim line. "And I could be in very deep trouble if you were ever to repeat my words to a Church official other than, say, Brother Bryan. The Church is an example of an abusive government; it punishes according to whim, or according to who can afford to buy it off. Within Church ranks, dissenters must walk softly, and reform by infinitesimal degrees if at all. The Church is a dangerous enemy to have—and there's only one reason why it isn't more dangerous than it is. It is so involved in its own internal politics that it rarely moves to look outside its walls. And for that, I am profoundly grateful."

This last colloquy aroused intense feelings of disquiet in Rune's heart; she was glad when he fell silent. She'd never thought much about the Church—but the few glimpses she'd had from inside, in the hostels, only confirmed what Tonno had just told her. If the Church as a whole ever decided to move against something—

—say, for instance, the Church were to declare non-humans as unholy, anathema, as they had come very close to doing, several times, according to the history books she'd read—

She shivered, and not from the cold. Boony, Topaz—they were as "human" as she was. There was nothing demonic about them. And when would the Church end, once it had begun? Would exotics, like Pearl, also fall under the ban?

What if they decided to ban—certain professions? Whores, or even musicians, dancers, anyone who gave pleasure that was not tangible? That sort of pleasure *could* be construed as heretical, since it took attention away from God.

And what about all those rumors of dark sorceries that some priests practiced, using the mantle of the Church to give them protection?

She was glad to hear the shop bell, signaling the arrival of one of the two youngsters due for lessons today. Ket was due first; he was late, but that was all right. Her thoughts were all tangled up, and too troubled right now. It would be a relief to think about simpler things, like basic lute lessons.

She forgot about her uneasiness as she gave Ket his teaching, then drilled Anny in her scales. The children were easier to deal with than they normally were; this kind of weather didn't tempt anyone to want to play outside, not even a child. And Anny was home alone with her governess, a sour old dame who sucked all the joy out of learning and left only the withered husks; she was glad for a chance to get away and do something entirely different. The lute lessons and the sessions she had with her dancing teacher were her only respites from the heavy hand of the old governess.

So it wasn't until after they'd left that Tonno's words came back to trouble her—and by then she had convinced herself that she had fallen victim to the miserable weather. She made a determined effort to shake off her mood, and by the time she left Tonno curled up in his blankets with bread and toasted cheese beside him and a couple of favorite books to read, she was in as cheerful a mood as possible, given her long walk back to Amber's through the dark and blowing snow.

And by midnight, she'd forgotten it all entirely.

But her dreams were haunted by things she could not recall clearly in the morning. Only—the lingering odor of incense.

CHAPTER ELEVEN

Rune sailed in the door of Tonno's shop singing at the top of her lungs, with a smile as wide and sunny as the day outside, and a bulging belt-pouch.

"Well!" Tonno greeted her, answering her smile with one of his own. "What's all this?"

She leaned over the counter and kissed him soundly on the cheek. He actually blushed, but could only repeat, "Well! Welladay!"

She laughed, pulled her pouch off her belt, and spread her day's takings out on the countertop for him to see. "Look at that! Just *look* at it! Why, that's almost ten whole silver pennies, and a handful of copper! Can you believe it?"

"What did you do, rob someone?" Tonno asked, teasingly.

"No indeed," she said happily. "Do you remember that city ordinance that was passed at Spring Equinox session? The one that was basically about female buskers?"

He sobered, quickly. "I do, indeed," he replied. The ordinance had troubled him a great deal; he had fretted about it incessantly until it was passed, and he had warned Rune not to go out on the streets as a musician in female garb once it was passed. Not that she *ever* did, at least, not to busk. The ordinance had been aimed squarely at those females who were using busking to cover their other business; it licensed inspectors who were to watch street and tavern musicians to be certain that their income was derived entirely from music. A similar ordinance, aimed at dancers, had also passed. Rune, of course, had either not come under scrutiny—at least that she was aware of—because of her habit of taking on boy-disguise, or she had passed the scrutiny easily. For some reason it never occurred to the inspectors or to those who had passed the ordinance that males might be operating the same deceptions. But the ordinance had pretty much cleared the streets of those women who had bought cheaper busking licenses and were using them to cover their other activities. The ordinance directed that any such woman be made to tender up not one, but *two* years' dues in the Whore's Guild, and buy a free-lancer's license as well. The Whore's Guild and the Bardic Guild had backed it; the Whore's Guild since it obviously cut down on women who were practicing outside the rules and restrictions of the Guild, which set prices and ensured the health of its members. Amber hadn't said much, but Rune suspected that she both approved and worried.

She partially approved of it, obviously, because she felt the same way about those women who were abusing the busker's licenses as Rune felt about amateur musicians who thought they could set up with an instrument they hardly knew how to play and a repertoire of half a dozen songs and call themselves professionals. But Rune knew that Amber and Tonno both worried about this law because the Church had also been behind it—and they feared it might be the opening move in a campaign to end the Whore's Guild altogether, and make the Houses themselves illegal.

It had been hard for Rune to feel much concern about that, when the immediate result had been to free up half the corners in Nolton to *honest* musicians and dancers, and to send even more clients to Amber's than there had been before. Amber had been forced to add a fifth and sixth lady; both of whom had passed their trial periods with highest marks— which had made Carly even more sour than before. Carly now stalked the hall of the private wing with a copy of the Holy Book poking ostentatiously out of her pocket. And she spent most of her time off at the Church, at interminable "Women's Prayer Meetings." She had even tried to drag the boys off to a "Group Prayer Meeting," but both of them had told her to her face that they'd rather scrub chamber pots.

The two new ladies, Amethyst and Diamond, got along perfectly well with the other four; Rune liked them both very much, especially Diamond, who had the most abrasive and caustic sense of humor she'd ever encountered. It was Diamond who had suggested her current project.

Diamond was an incredibly slender woman with pure white hair— naturally white, claimed Maddie, who often helped Diamond with the elaborate, though revealing, costumes she favored. Diamond had been in the common room one night (dressed—so to speak—mostly in strings of tiny glass beads made into a semblance of a dress) when Rune had played a common song called "Two Fair Maids" at a client's request. Diamond had politely waited until that client had gone upstairs before she said anything, but *then* she had them all in stitches.

"Just once—" she'd said vehemently, "just *once* I'd like to hear a song about that situation that makes some sense!"

One of the gentlemen with her, who Rune had suspected for some time really *was* nobly born, had said, ingenuously, "What situation?"

That had pretty much confirmed Rune's suspicions, since it would have been hard to be a commoner and not have heard "Two Fair Maids" often enough to know every word of every variant.

Diamond, however, had simply explained it to him without betraying that. "It's about two sisters in love with the same man," she told him. "He's been sleeping with the older one, who thinks he's going to have to marry her—but he proposes to the younger one, who accepts. When the older one finds out, she shoves the younger one in the river." She turned to Rune, then, and included her in the conversation. "Rune, what *are* all the various versions of it after that?"

"Well," Rune had answered, thinking, "There's three variations on how she dies. One, the older girl holds her under; two, she gets carried off by the current and pulled under the millrace; three, that the miller sees her, wants her gold ring, and drowns her. But in all of the versions, a wandering harpist-Bard finds her—or rather, what's *left* of her after the fish get done—and makes a harp of her bones and strings it with her long, gold hair."

"Dear God!" the gentleman exclaimed. "That's certainly gruesome!"

"And pretty stupid," Rune added, to Diamond's great delight. "I can't imagine why *any* musician would go making an instrument out of human bone when there are perfectly good pieces of wood around that are much better suited to the purpose! And I can't imagine why anyone would want to *play* such a thing!" She shivered. "I should think you'd drive customers into the next kingdom the first time they caught sight of it! But anyway, that's what this fool does, and he takes it to court and plays it for the Sire. And, *of course,* the moment the older sister shows up, the harp begins to play by itself, and sing about how the little idiot got herself drowned. And *of course,* the sister is burned, and the miller is hung, and the bastard that started it in the first place by seducing the first sister gets off free." She curled her lip a little. "In fact, in one of the versions he gets all kinds of sympathy from other stupid women because his syrupy little true love drowned."

"And that's what I mean by I wish that someone would write a sensible version," Diamond said, taking up where Rune left off. "I mean, if I was the wronged sister, I wouldn't blame my brainless sib, I'd go after the motherless wretch that betrayed me! And if I was the younger sister, if I found out about it, I'd *help* her!" She turned to Rune, then, with a mischievous look on her face that made her pale blue eyes sparkle like the stone she was named for. "You're a musician," she said, gleefully. "Why don't you do it?"

At first Rune could only think of all the reasons why it wouldn't work—that people were used to the old song and would hate the new version, that the Bardic Guild would hate it because their members had written a great many of the variants, and that it wasn't properly romantic.

But then she thought of all the reasons why, if she chose her audience properly, picking mostly young people who were in a mood to laugh, it *would* work. There were not a great many comic songs out in the world, and she could, if she managed this successfully, get quite a following for herself based on the fact that she had written one. In fact, there were a great many really stupid, sentimental ballads like "Two Fair Maids" in existence; if she wrote parodies of them, she could have an entire repertory of comic songs.

And songs like that were much more suited to the casual atmosphere of street-busking than the maudlin ones were.

She'd started on the project in late spring; she already had four. She'd moved to a new corner, vacated by one of the buskers-that-weren't, on a very busy crossroads. It wasn't a venue usually suited to busking, but she'd made a bargain with one of the Gypsy-dancers who had reappeared at the fountain in Flower Street with the spring birds. Rune would play the fiddle for her to dance from exactly midday until second bell and split the take, if the Gypsies would hold the corner for her to play from two hours before midday till the dancer showed up. No one wanted to argue with the Gypsies, who were known to have tempers and be very quick with their knives, so the corner was Rune's without dispute.

Now what she had planned to do, was to alternate lively fiddling with comic songs, to see how well they did, and if she could hold a rowdy crowd with them.

She had discovered this afternoon that not only could she hold the crowd, she now had a reputation for knowing the funny songs, and there were people coming to her corner at lunch just to hear them.

And furthermore, they were willing to *pay* to hear them. Every time she'd tried to go back to the fiddle today, someone had called out for one of her songs. And when she'd demurred, protesting that she'd already done it, or that people must be getting tired of it, at least three coins were tossed into her hat as an incentive. In the end, she had made as much during her stint alone as she and the dancer had together.

She explained all that to Tonno, who looked pleased at first, then troubled. "You didn't write anything—satiric, did you?" he asked, worriedly. "These were just silly parodies of common songs, am I understanding you correctly?"

She sighed, exasperated. He was beating around the bush again, rather than asking her directly what he wanted to know, and she was tired of it. "Tonno, just what, exactly, are you asking me? Get to the point, will you? I'm not one of your Scholar customers, that you have to build a tower of logic for before you get a straight answer."

He blinked in surprise. "I suppose—did you make fun of anyone high-ranking enough to cause you trouble? Or did you sing *anything* satirical about the Church?"

"If anybody in one of those songs resembles someone in Nolton, *I* don't know about it," she told him in complete honesty. "And I must admit that I had considered doing something about a corrupt Priest, but I decided against it, after seeing Carly leaving my room. It would be just like her to take a copy to the Church with her, when she goes to one of her stupid Prayer Meetings, and find a way to get me in trouble."

Tonno let out a deep sigh of relief. "I'd advise you to keep to that decision," he said, passing his hand over his hair. "At least for now, when you have no one to protect you. Later, perhaps, when you have Guild status and protection, you can write whatever you choose." He smiled, weakly. "Who knows; with the force of a Guild Bard behind a satiric song, you might become an influence for good within the Church."

"What are you so worried about, really?" she asked, putting her instruments down on the counter. "Did Brother Bryan tell you something? Is the Church planning on backing more of those ordinances you don't like?"

He shook his head. "No—no, it's that I've been debating doing something for a while, and I've been putting it off because I didn't have the connections. Remember when I started sending you to other people for lessons this spring?"

She nodded. "Mandar Cray for lute, and Geor Baker for voice. You told me you weren't going to be useful for anything with me except for reading and writing." Mandar and Geor were two of the people she had considered as teachers when she first came to Nolton, as it turned out. Both of them were Guild musicians; both had very wealthy students. Had she approached them on her own, she probably would have gotten brushed off.

But both were clients and friends of both Tonno and Amber, and both had heard her sing and play. They were two very different men; Mandar tall and ascetic, Geor short and muscular; Mandar hardly ever ate, at least at Amber's, and Geor ate everything in sight. Mandar fainted at the thought of bloodshed, let alone the sight of blood, and Geor was a champion swordsman. But they had one other thing in common besides being clients and friends of Amber and Tonno—they both adored music.

For the opportunity to teach someone who loved it as much as they did, and had talent, as opposed to the rich, bored children who were enduring their lessons, both of them cut their lesson-rates to next-to-nothing.

They wouldn't teach her for free—for one thing, that could get them in trouble with the Guild—for another, they felt, like Tonno, that *paying* for something tended to make one pay attention to it. But they weren't charging her any more than Tonno had, and she was learning a great deal he simply could not show her.

"I've been wanting to find someone who could teach you composition," Tonno said, his expression still worried, "But the only Bards I knew of in the city were either in a Great Household, or—in the Church."

Rune's mouth formed a silent "O" of understanding. Now all of Tonno's fussing made some sense. If he'd wanted to find her a teacher and she'd gotten herself in trouble with the Church—

But he wasn't finished. "I didn't have the contacts to get you lessons with any of the Church Bards," he continued. "But last week Brother Bryan mentioned that he'd listened to you playing out on the street and that he thought you were amazing. He still thinks you're a boy, you understand—"

Rune nodded. Brother Bryan had never seen her in female garb; she and Tonno had judged that the best idea. Many Church *men* felt very uneasy around females for one thing—and it seemed no bad idea to have her female persona unknown to the Church, after all the ordinances and the snooping Carly was doing. They might not connect the "Rune" that busked with the "Rune" that played at Amber's. And even if they did, they might not know that Rune was really a girl, if Carly hadn't gone out of her way to tell them. Rune didn't think she had; she just reported the activities going on, but because *she* knew Rune's sex, she would probably assume the Church did, too.

"Well, Brother Bryan was very impressed by what he'd heard. He asked if you composed, then before I could say anything, he offered to see if he couldn't get Brother Pell to take you in his class." Tonno was clearly torn between being proud and being concerned at a Church Collector's interest in his pupil. "That's why I wanted to know what your comic songs were about; if you'd done anything to annoy the Church officials, going to that class could be walking you into a trap. The Church has no power outside the cloister, but once they had you inside, they could hold you for as long as they cared to, and the city couldn't send anyone to get you out. Assuming they'd even bother to try, which I doubt. The only people the constables and guards are likely to exert themselves for have more money than you and I put together.''

Rune's mouth went dry at the bare thought of being held by the Church for questioning. She recalled the high walls around the cloister all too well—walls that shut out the world. And held in secrets? "They wouldn't—''

He saw her terrified expression, and laughed, easing her fear. "Oh, all they'd do, most likely, is try to frighten you; to bully you and make you promise never to write something like that again.'' He cocked his head sideways, for a moment, and his expression sobered. "But if they connected you with the musician at Amber's, they could threaten other punishments, and make you promise to spy at Amber's in return for being set free. I doubt Carly is terribly effective.''

"I wouldn't do that!'' she exclaimed, hotly.

"You might, if you were frightened enough,'' he admonished her. "I'm not saying you also wouldn't go straight to Amber afterwards and tell her what they'd gotten from you, but don't ever underestimate the power of a skilled Church interrogator. They could make you promise to do almost anything for them, and you'd weep with gratitude because they had forgiven you for what you'd done to them. They are very skilled with words—with innuendo—with making threats they have no intention of carrying out. And they are a force unto themselves on their own ground.''

"And maybe they're as skilled with magic as they are with words?'' Rune frowned; those were some of the whispered rumors she'd heard. That the Church harbored Priests and Brothers who were powerful magicians, who could make people do what they wanted them to with a few chosen words and a spell to take over their will.

"Possibly,'' Tonno conceded wearily. "Possibly; I don't know. I've never seen a Church mage, and I don't know of anyone who has, but that doesn't mean anything, does it? Since you haven't angered them, and don't *intend* to, you're unlikely to see one either. Let's face it, Rune, you and I are just too small for them to take much notice of. It's not worth the time they'd spend.''

"Something to be said for being insignificant,'' she commented sardonically.

He nodded. "At any rate, I'm quite confident that you'll be in no danger whatsoever, if you want to take these lessons. Brother Bryan told me that Brother Pell is—well, 'rather difficult to get along with,' is the way he put it. I pressed him for details, but he couldn't tell me much; I gather he has a bad temper and a sour disposition. He doesn't like much of anybody, and even someone as even-tempered as Bryan has a hard time finding good things to say about him.''

"Sounds like taking lessons from Carly," she said, with a wry twist to her mouth.

"Perhaps," Tonno replied thoughtfully. "But there is this; Bryan said that by all reports, even of those who don't like him at all, Pell is the best composition teacher in all of Nolton."

"Huh," Rune said thoughtfully. "I'd be willing to take lessons even from Carly if she was that good. Am I supposed to be a boy or a girl?"

"Boy," Tonno told her firmly. "Women have very little power in the Church, at least here in Nolton, and I gather that Pell in particular despises the sex. Go as a girl, and he'll probably refuse to teach you on the grounds that you'll just go off and get married and waste his teaching." He gave her a long, level look, as he realized exactly what she'd said. "I take it that you want the lessons, then?"

"I said I'd even take lessons from Carly if she had anything worth learning," Rune replied firmly. "When can I start?"

She didn't feel quite so bold a few days later, as she meekly showed her pass to the Brother on watch at the cloister gate. In the year she'd been here, she'd never once been inside the huge cathedral in the center of Nolton, big enough to hold several thousand worshipers at once. In fact, she avoided it as much as possible. That wasn't too difficult, since there was no use in busking anywhere near it; the Priests and Brothers made a busker feel so uncomfortable by simply standing and staring with disapproval that it was easier to find somewhere else to play.

It was an imposing, forbidding edifice, carved of dark stone, with thousands of sculptures all over its surface; there wasn't a single square inch that didn't hold a carving of something. Down near the base, it was ordinary people doing Good Works, and the temptations of the Evil One trying to waylay them. Farther up, there were carvings of the lives of the saints and all the temptations that they had overcome. The next level held the bliss of Paradise. The uppermost level was carved with all the varied kinds of angels, from the finger-length Etherials, to the Archangels that were three times the height of a man.

There was a sky-piercing tower in the middle of it, carved with abstract water and cloud shapes, that held the bells that signaled the changes of the hours for everyone in the city. Inside, she had been told, it was different; not dark and foreboding at all, full of light and space—those carved walls held hundreds of tiny windows filled with glass, and most of the ones near the ground were of precious colored glass. Every saint's shrine, every statue inside had been gilded or silvered; places where the light couldn't reach were covered with banks of prayer candles. When the sun shone, or so Tonno claimed, the eye was dazzled. Even when it didn't, there were lights and reflective surfaces enough to make the interior bright as day in an open meadow.

She hadn't cared enough to want to see it, although it was quite an attraction for visitors just to come and gawk at. Behind the cathedral was the cloister; a complex of buildings including convents for men and for women, a school, and the Church administrative offices. All that was held behind a high wall pierced with tiny gates, each guarded day and night by a Brother. Rune had never been inside those walls, and didn't know anyone who had.

Plenty of people had been inside the cathedral though. The High Priest of Nolton was said to be a marvelous speaker, although, again, Rune couldn't have said one way or another. She hadn't cared to see *him*, either, though Carly went to the service he preached at as faithfully as the bells rang.

From the little she saw outside the walls, the cloister was twice as forbidding as the cathedral, because it had none of the cathedral's ornamentation. Now that she was *inside* the walls, it was worse, much worse. The place looked like a prison. The buildings were carved of the same dark stone, with tiny slits for windows. It looked as if it was a place designed to keep people from escaping; Rune hoped she'd never have occasion to discover that her impression was true.

The Brother at the gate, anonymous in his dark gray robe, directed her to go past the building immediately in front of her and take the first door she saw after that. She walked slowly across the silent, paved courtyard; nothing behind her but the wall with its small postern gate, nothing on either side of her or before her but tall, oblong buildings with tiny passages between them. Nothing green or growing anywhere, not even a weed springing up between the cobblestones. It seemed unnatural. A few robed figures crossed the courtyard ahead of her; none looked at her, no one spoke. In their dark, androgynous robes, she couldn't even tell if they were men or women.

Once past the first building, she felt even more hemmed in and confined. *How can anyone bear to live like this?* she wondered. No need to look for a reason why Brother Pell was so sour; if she had to live here, she'd be just as bitter as he was.

There was another Brother at the door of the building, sitting behind a tiny desk; once again, she showed her pass, and was directed to a second-floor room. She looked back over her shoulder for a moment as she climbed the stair; the Brother was watching her—to be certain she went where she was told? Possibly. That might be simple courtesy on the part of the Brothers. It might be something else. There was no point in speculating; she was just here for composition lessons, not anything sinister. She didn't want to stay here a moment longer than she had to. Let the Brother watch; he'd see only a young boy obeying, doing exactly what he was told.

She opened the designated doorway and went inside. There was no one there, and nothing but one large desk and six smaller ones. She discovered that she was the first to arrive of a class of six, including her. The classroom was a tiny cubicle, narrow, with enough space for their six desks arranged two by two, with Brother Pell's large desk facing them, and behind that, a wall covered in slate.

Brother Pell appeared last, a perfectly average man, balding slightly, with his hands tucked into the sleeves of his gray robe and a frown so firmly a part of his face that Rune could not imagine what he would look like if he ever smiled. If he had been anything other than a Brother, she would have guessed at Scholar or clerk; he had that kind of tight-lipped look.

There was a nagging sense of familiarity about him; after a moment, she knew what it was. She had seen this man often, out on the street, ever since the ordinance against pseudo-buskers had been passed. Presumably he was one of the inspectors. And now that she thought about it, she realized that there were a great many more Brothers and Sisters out on the street since the ordinance had been passed. Interesting; she had never thought of *them* as being inspectors, but it made sense. The inspectors were being paid very little, about the same as a lamp-lighter or a dung-sweeper. Unless you had no other job, it wasn't one you'd think of taking. A few of the real buskers had become inspectors by day, and did their busking at night. But Church clerics—well, it wouldn't matter to them how small the fee was. It was very probable that, since everyone in the Church took a vow to own nothing, their fees as inspectors went to the Church itself.

Very interesting, and not very comforting, that the Church who had backed the law should send its people out into the streets as an army of enforcers of that law. She'd have to tell Tonno about her suspicion and see what he said.

Brother Pell did not seem to recognize her, however, although she recognized him; his eyes flitted over her as they did the other five boys in the class without a flicker of recognition. He consulted a list in his hand.

"Terr Capston of Nolton," he said, and looked up. His voice, at least, was pleasant, although cold. A good, strong trained tenor.

"Here, sir," said a sturdy brown-haired boy, who looked back at the Brother quite fearlessly. Of all of them, he seemed the most used to being in the tutelage of Brothers.

"And why are you here, Terr Capston?" Brother Pell asked, without any expression at all.

Terr seemed to have been ready for this question. "Brother Rylan wants me to find out if I have Bardic material in me," the boy said. "I'm for the Church either way, but Brother wants to know if it will be as just a player or—"

"Stop right there, boy," Brother Pell said fiercely, and his cold face wore a forbidding frown. "There is no such thing as 'just' a player, and Brother Rylan is sadly to blame if that's the way he's taught you. Or is that *your* notion?"

The boy hung his head, and Brother Pell grimaced. "I thought so. I *should* send you back to him until you learn humility. Consider yourself on probation. Lenerd Cattlan of Nolton."

"Here—sir." The timid dark-haired boy right in front of Rune raised his hand.

"And why are you here?" the Brother asked, glaring at him with hawk-fierce eyes. The boy shrank into his seat and shook his head.

"You don't know?" Pell said, biting off each word. He cast his eyes upward. "Lord, give me patience. Rune of Westhaven."

"Sir," she said, nodding, and matching his stare with a stare of her own. *You don't frighten me one bit. And I'm not going to back down to you, either.*

She had expected the same question, but he surprised her. "No last name? Why not?"

That was rude at the very least—but she had a notion that Brother Pell was never terribly polite. She decided to see if she could startle or discomfort him with the truth. "I don't know who my father is," she replied levelly. "And I judged it better than to claim something I have no right to."

One of the other boys snickered, and Pell turned a look on him that left Rune wondering if she scented scorched flesh in its wake. The boy shrank in his seat, and gulped. "You're an honest boy," he barked, turning back to Rune, "and there's no shame in being born a bastard. The shame is on your mother who had no moral sense, not on you. *You* did not ask to be born; that was God's will. You are doing well to repudiate your mother's weak morals with strong ones of your own. God favors the honest. Perhaps your mother will see your success one day, and repent of her ways.''

If Rune hadn't agreed with him totally about her mother's lack of sense, moral or otherwise, she might have resented that remark. As it was, she nodded, cautiously.

"Why are you here, Rune?" *Now* came the question she expected.

"Because there is music in my head, and I don't know how to write it down the way I hear it," she replied promptly. "I can find harmonies and counter-melodies when I sing, but I don't know how to get *them* down, either, and sometimes I lose things before I even manage to work them out properly." He looked a little interested, so she continued. "Brother Bryan heard me on the street and told my first teacher that he'd get me a recommendation into this class if I wanted it. I wanted it. I want to be more than a street busker, if it's in me. And if it's God's will," she added, circumspectly.

Pell barked a laugh. "Good answer. Axen Troud of Nolton."

Brother Pell continued the litany until he had covered all six of them, and Rune realized after she watched him listening to their answers that he had formed a fairly quick impression of each of them from both their words, and the way they answered. And as he began the first session and she bent all of her attention to his words and the things he was writing down on the slate behind him, she also realized that unlike Tonno, Brother Pell was not going to *help* anyone. He would never explain things twice. If you fell behind, that was too bad. You would keep up with *him* in this class, or you would not stay in it.

She had a fairly good idea that the timid boy would not be able to keep up. Nor would one of the boys who had answered after her; a stolid, unimaginative sort who was more interested in the mathematics of music than the music itself. And they might lose the first boy, who was plainly used to being cosseted by his teacher.

At the end of that first lesson, she felt as drained and exhausted as she had been at the end of her first lute lesson. If this had been the first time she'd ever felt that way, she likely would have given up right there—which was what the first boy looked ready to do.

But as she gathered up her notes under Pell's indifferent eye and filed out with the rest, she knew that if nothing else, she was going to get her money's worth out of this class. Pell *was* a good teacher.

And I've been hungry, cold, nearly penniless. I fiddled for the Skull Hill Ghost and won. If the Ghost didn't stop me, neither will Brother Pell.

No one will. Not ever.

CHAPTER TWELVE

Rune rang the bell outside the Church postern gate again, though she had no expectation of being answered this time, either. When after several minutes there was no sound of feet on stone, she beat her benumbed, mittened hands together and continued pacing up and down the little stretch of pavement outside the Gate. Her heart pounded in her chest at the audacity of what she was about to do, but she wasn't going to let fear stop her. Not now. Not when the stakes were this high.

She told her heart to be still, and the lump in her throat to go away. Neither obeyed her.

Tonno had taken a chill when he'd been caught between the market and his shop three weeks ago, on the day of the great blizzard, and it had taken him hours to stumble back home. The blizzard had piled some of the city streets so deeply with snow that people were coming and going from the second-floor windows of some places, although that was not the case with Amber's or with Tonno's shop. Rune had been busy with helping to shovel once the storm was over, and it had taken her two days to get to him. By then, the damage was done. He was sick, and getting sicker.

She had gone out every day to the Church since then, to the Priests who sent out Doctors to those who had none of their own. Each day she had been turned away by the Priest in charge, who had consulted a list, told her brusquely that there were those with more need than Tonno, and then ignored her further protests. Finally, today, one of the other women in line had explained this cryptic statement to her.

"Your master's old, boy," the woman had whispered. "He's old, he's never been one for making more than the tithe to the Church, no doubt, and he's got no kin to inherit. And likely, he's not rich enough to be worth much of a thanks-gift if a Doctor came out and made him well. They figure, if he dies, the Church gets at least half his goods, if not all—and if he lives, it's God's will."

That had infuriated and frightened her; it was obvious that she was never going to get any help for Tonno—and when she'd arrived today, he'd been half delirious with a fever. She'd sent a boy to get Maddie to come watch him while she went after a Doctor—again. And this time, by all that was holy, she was not going to return without one.

She had been in and out of the cloister enough to know who came and went by all the little gates; one lesson the Brothers had never expected her to learn, doubtless. She knew where the Doctors' Gate was, and she was going to wait by it until she spotted one of the physician-Brothers. They were easy enough to pick out, by the black robe they wore instead of gray, and by the box of medicines they always carried. When she saw a Doctor, or could get one to answer the bell, she was going to take him to Tonno—by force, if need be.

Her throat constricted again, and she fought a stinging in her eyes. Crying was not going to help him. Only a Doctor could do that, and a Doctor was what she was waiting for. She tried not to think about what he'd looked like when she left him; transparent, thin, and old—so frail, as if a thought would blow him away.

She stopped her pacing long enough to cough; like everyone else, it seemed, she'd picked up a cold in the past two weeks. She hadn't paid it much attention. Beside Tonno's illness, it was hardly more serious than a splinter. As she straightened up, she heard the sound of feet approaching; hard soles slapping wearily on the stonework. The *Church* certainly didn't lack hands to see that the streets about the cathedral and the cloisters were shoveled clean. . . .

She turned; approaching from a side street to her left was a man in the black robe of a Church Doctor, laden with one of those black-leather-covered boxes. He walked with his head down so that she couldn't see his face, watching his step on the icy cobbles.

She hurried to intercept him, her heart right up in her throat and pounding so loudly she could hardly hear herself speak.

"Excuse me, sir," she said, trotting along beside him, then putting herself squarely in his path when he wouldn't stop. She held out her empty, mittened hands to him, and tried to put all the terror and pleading she felt into her face and voice. "Excuse me—my master's sick, he's got a fever, a dry fever and a dry cough that won't stop, he's been sick ever since the blizzard and I've been here every day but the Priest won't send anybody, he says there's people with greater need, but my master's an old man and he's having hallucinations—" She was gabbling it all out as fast as she could, hoping to get him to listen to her before he brushed her aside. He frowned at her when she made him stop, and frowned even harder when she began to talk—he put out a hand to move her away from his path—

But then he blinked, as if what she had said had finally penetrated his preoccupation, and stayed his hand. "A fever? With visions, you say?" She nodded. "And a dry, racking cough that won't stop?" She nodded again, harder. If he recognized the symptoms, sure, surely he knew the cure!

He swore—and for the first time in months of living at Amber's, she was shocked. Not at the oath; she'd heard enough like it from the carters and other rough laborers who visited some of the other Houses on the street. That a Brother should utter a hair-scorching oath like that—*that* was what shocked her. But it seemed that this was no ordinary Brother.

His face hardened with anger, and his eyes grew black. "An old man with pneumonia, lying untreated for two weeks—and instead of taking care of him, they send me out to tend a brat with a bellyache from too many sweets—" He swore again, an oath stronger than the first. "Show me your master, lad, and be hanged to Father Genner. Bellyache my ass!"

Rune hurried down the street towards Tonno's with the Brother keeping pace beside her, despite the hindering skirts of his robe. "I'm Brother Anders," he said, trotting next to her and not even breathing hard. "Tell me more about your master's illness."

She did, everything she could recall, casting sideways glances at the Brother as she did so. He was a large man, black-bearded and black-haired; he made her think of a bear. But his eyes, now that he wasn't frowning, were kind. He listened carefully to everything she said, but his expression grew graver and graver with each symptom. And her heart sank every time his expression changed.

"He's not in good shape, lad," the Brother said at last. "I won't lie to you. If I'd seen him a week ago—or better, when he first fell ill—"

"I came then," she protested angrily, forcing away tears with the heat of her outrage. "I came every day! The Priest kept telling me that there were others with more need, and turning me away!" She wanted to tell him the rest, what the old woman had told her—but something stopped her. This was a Brother, after all, tied to the Church. If she maligned the Church, he might not help her.

"And I simply go where the Priests tell me," Brother Anders replied, as angry as she was. "Father Genner didn't see fit to mention *this* case to any of us! Well, there's going to be *someone* answering for this! I took my vows to tend to *all* the sick, not just fat merchants with deep pockets, and their spoiled children who have nothing wrong that a little less coddling and cosseting wouldn't cure!"

There didn't seem to be anything more to add to that, so Rune saved her breath for running, speeding up the pace, and hoping that, despite Brother Anders' words, things were not as grave as they seemed. But she was fighting back tears with every step. And the old woman's words kept echoing in her head. If the Church wanted Tonno to die, what hope did she have of saving him?

But this Brother seemed capable, and caring. He was angry that the Priests hadn't sent him to Tonno before this. He would do everything in his power to help, just for that reason alone, she was certain.

After all, many Doctors probably exaggerated the state of an illness, to seem more skilled when the patient recovered—didn't they?

She had left the door unlocked when she went out; it was still unlocked. She pushed it open and motioned to the Brother to follow her through the dark, cold, narrow shop.

Maddie looked up when Rune came through the curtain. "Rune, he's getting worse," she said worriedly. "He doesn't know who I am, he thinks it's summer and he keeps pushing off the blankets as fast as I put them back—" Then she saw the Brother, as he looked up, for his black robe had hidden him in the shadows. "Oh!" she exclaimed with relief. "You got a Doctor to come!"

"Aye, he did," the Brother rumbled, squinting through the darkness to the little island of light where Tonno lay. "And not a moment too soon, from the sound of it. You go on home, lass; this lad and I will tend to things now."

Maddie didn't wait for a second invitation; she snatched up her cloak and hurried out, pushing past them with a brief curtsy for the Doctor. Brother Anders hardly noticed her; all his attention was for the patient. Rune heard the door slam shut behind Maddie, then she ignored everything except Tonno and the Doctor.

"Get some heat in this place, lad," the Brother ordered gruffly, shoving his way past the crowded furnishings to Tonno's bedside. Rune didn't hesitate; she opened the stove door and piled on expensive wood and even more expensive coal. After all, what did it matter? Tonno's life was at stake here. She would buy him more when he was well.

And if he dies, the Church gets it all anyway, she thought bitterly, rubbing her sleeve across her eyes as they stung damply. *Why should I save it for them?*

Then she pushed the thought away. Tonno would *not* die, she told herself fiercely, around the lump of pain and fear that filled her. He would get better. This was a conscientious Doctor, and she sensed he'd fight as hard for Tonno as he would for his own kin. Tonno would get well—and she would use some of the money saved from last summer to buy him more wood and coal—yes, and chicken to make soup to make him strong, and medicine, and anything else he needed.

"Boil me some water, will you, lad?" the Doctor said as the temperature in the room rose. Tonno mumbled something and tried to push Brother Anders' hands away; the Doctor ignored him, peering into Tonno's eyes and opening his mouth to look at his throat, then leaning down to listen to his chest.

"There's some already, sir," she replied. He turned in surprise, to see her holding out the kettle. "I always had a fresh kettle going. I kept giving him willow-bark tea, sir. At first it helped with the fever, and even when it didn't, it let him sleep some—"

"Well done, lad." Brother Anders nodded with approval. "But he's going to need something stronger than that if he's to have any chance of pulling through. And do you think you can get me some steam in here? It'll make his breathing easier, and I have some herbs for his lungs that need steam."

She put the kettle back on the top of the stove, as he rummaged in his kit for herbs and a mortar and pestle to grind them. *Steam. How can I get steam over to the bed—* If she put a pan of water on the stove, the steam would never reach as far as the bed; if she brought a pan to boil and took it over beside the bed, it would stop steaming quickly, wasting the precious herbs.

Then she thought of the little nomads' brazier out in the shop; one of the curiosities that Tonno had accumulated over the years that had never sold. If she were to put a pan of water on that, and put the whole lot beside the bed—

Yes, that would work. She ran out into the shop to get it; it was up on one of the shelves, one near the floor since it was ceramic and very heavy. It was meant, Tonno had said, to use animal-droppings for fuel. If she took one of the burning lumps of coal out of the stove and dropped it into the combustion chamber, that should do. As an afterthought, she picked up the wooden stool she used to get things just out of her reach, and took that with her as well. There was a slab of marble in the living area that Tonno used to roll out dough on; if she put that on the stool, and the brazier on that, it would be just tall enough that she could fan steam directly onto Tonno's face. And the marble would keep the wooden stool from catching fire.

She set up the stool with the marble and brazier atop it, then carefully caught up a lump of bright red coal in the tongs and carried it over, dropping it into the bottom on the brazier to land on the little iron grate there. Then she got an ornamental copper bowl, put it atop the brazier, and filled it with water. She didn't look at Tonno; she couldn't. She couldn't bear to see him that way. When the water began to steam, and she started fanning it towards Tonno's face, the Doctor looked up in surprise and approval.

"Keep that up, lad," he said, and dropped a handful of crushed herbs into the water. The steam took on an astringent quality; refreshing and clean-smelling. It even seemed to make her breathing easier.

She tried not to listen to Tonno's. His breath rasped in his throat, and wheezed in his chest, and there was a gurgling sound at the end of each breath that sounded horrible. The Doctor didn't like it either; she could tell by the way his face looked. But he kept mixing medicines, steeping each new dose with a little hot water, and spooning them into Tonno's slack mouth between rattling breaths.

She lost track of time; when the water in the bowl got low, she renewed it. At the Doctor's direction, she heated bricks at the stove and kept them packed around Tonno's thin body. When she wasn't doing either of those things, she was fanning the aromatic steam over Tonno's face.

And despite all of it, each breath came harder; each breath was more of a struggle. Tonno showed no signs of waking—and the hectic fever-spots in his cheeks grew brighter as his face grew paler.

Finally, just before dawn, he took one shallow breath—the last.

Rune huddled in the chair beside the bed, silent tears coursing down her cheeks and freezing as they struck the blanket she'd wrapped herself in. The Doctor had gently given Tonno Final Rites, as he was authorized to do, then covered him, face and all, so that Rune didn't have to look at the body. He'd told her to go home, that there was nothing more to do, that the Priests would come and take care of everything—then he'd left.

But she couldn't leave. She couldn't bear the idea of Tonno being left alone here, with no one to watch to see that he wasn't disturbed.

She let the fire go out, though, after piling on the last of the wood and coal. There was no point in saving it for the damned Priests—

Let them buy their own, or work in the cold, she thought savagely. *I hope their fingers and toes fall off!*

But she just couldn't see the point of buying any more, either. After all, Tonno didn't need the warmth any more. . . .

It's all my fault, she told herself, as the tears continued to fall, *I should have gone after a Doctor before. I should never have gone to the Priests. I should have found Brother Bryan and had him help me. I should have seen if Brother Pell was any use. I should have told Amber that Tonno was sicker than I thought—*

But what could Amber have done? Oh, there were Herb-women attached to the Whore's Guild that kept the members of the Guild healthy and free of unwanted pregnancies, but did they know anything about pneumonia?

Probably not—but I should have tried! I should have gone to everyone I knew—

If she'd done that, Tonno would probably be alive now.

She'd spent hours talking to the empty air, begging Tonno's forgiveness, and promising him what she was going to do with the rest of her life because of what he'd taught her, and trying to say good-bye. She'd cursed the Priests with every curse she knew, three times over, but the essential blame lay with her. There was no getting around it. So she stayed, as the shop grew colder, the water in the pan beside the bed froze over, and the square of sun cast through the back window crept across the floor and up the wall. It wasn't much of a penance, but it was something.

She'd long ago talked herself hoarse. Now she could only address him in thought. Even if her voice hadn't been a mere croak, she couldn't have said anything aloud around the lump of grief that choked her.

I'm sorry, Tonno, she said silently to the still, sheet-shrouded form on the bed. *I'm sorry—I did everything I could think of. I just didn't think of things soon enough. I really tried, honestly I did. . . .*

And the tears kept falling, trickling down her cheeks, though they could not wash away the guilt, the pain, or the loss.

The Priests finally arrived near sunset, as another snowstorm was blowing up, when she was numb within and without, from cold and grieving both. A trio of hard-faced, vulturine men, they seemed both surprised and suspicious when they saw her beside Tonno's bed.

When they asked her what she was doing there, she stammered something hoarsely about Tonno being her master, but that wasn't enough for them. While two of them bundled the body in a shroud, the third questioned her closely as to whether she was bonded or free, and what her exact relationship to Tonno had been.

She answered his questions between fits of coughing. He was not pleased to discover that she was free—and less pleased to discover that Tonno was nothing more than her teacher. She had the feeling that this one had been counting on her to have been a bonded servant, and thus part of the legacy.

I'd rather die than work for you bastards, she thought angrily, though she held her tongue. *I can just imagine what the lives of your bonded servants are like!*

"I see no reason why you should have been here," the Priest finally said, acidly. "You did your duty long ago; you should have been gone when we arrived." He stared at her as if he expected that she had been up to something that would somehow threaten a single pin that the Church could expect out of Tonno's holdings. That was when she lost her temper entirely.

"I was his *friend*," she snapped, croaking out her words like an asthmatic frog. "That's reason enough, sir—or have you forgotten the words of your own Holy Book? 'You stayed beside me when I was sick, you fed me when I was hungry, you guided me when I was troubled, and you asked no more than my love—blessed are they who love without reward, for they shall have love in abundance'? I was following the words of the Book, whether or not it was *prudent* to do so!"

The Priest started, taken aback by having the Holy Words flung in his face. It didn't look to her like he was at all familiar with that particular passage, either in abstract or in application.

She dashed angry tears away. "He gave me something more precious than everything in this shop—he gave me *learning*. I could never repay that! Why shouldn't I watch by him—" She would have said more, but a coughing fit overcame her; she bent over double, and by the time she had gotten control of herself again, the Priest who was questioning her had gone out into the shop itself. She looked outside at the snowstorm, dubiously, wondering if she should just try to stay the night here. It wouldn't have been the first time—in fact, she'd been sleeping on the couch, just to keep an eye on him these past two weeks. Then one of the other two Priests came back into the room and cleared his throat so that she'd look at him.

"You'll have to leave, boy," the Priest said coldly. "You can't stay here. There'll be someone to come collect the body in a moment, but you'll have to leave now."

"In this snow?" she replied, without thinking. "Why? And what about thieves—"

"We'll be staying," the Priest said, his voice and eyes hard and unfriendly. "We'll be staying and making certain the contents of this place match the inventory. There might be a will, but there probably isn't, and if there isn't, everything goes to the Church anyway. That's the law."

What would I do if I didn't have anyplace else to go? she wondered—

but it didn't look as though the Priest cared. He'd have turned anyone out in the snow, like as not—old woman or young child. Unless, of course, they were bonded. Then, no doubt, he'd have been gracious enough to let them sleep on the floor.

He stared at her, and she had the feeling that he expected her to have a fortune in goods hiding under her cloak. She took it off and shook it, slowly and with dignity, trying not to shiver, just to show them that there wasn't anything under it but one skinny "boy." Then she put it back on, stepped right up to him as if she was about to say something, and deliberately sneezed on him. He started back, with the most dumb-founded and offended look on his face she'd ever seen. If she hadn't been so near to tears, and so angry, she'd have laughed at him.

"Excuse me," she said, still wrapped in dignity. "I've been tending him for two weeks now. Out of charity. I must have caught a chill myself."

Then she pushed rudely past him, and past the other two, who were already out in the shop with Tonno's books, candles, and pens. She managed to cough on them, too, on her way out, and took grim pleasure in the fact that there wasn't a stick of fuel in the place. And at this time of night, there'd be no one to sell them any. Unless they sent one of their number back to the cloister to fetch some, which meant going out into the storm, they'd be spending a long, cold night. There wasn't any food left, either; she'd been buying soup for him from one of his neighbors.

I hope they freeze and starve.

She wrapped her cloak tighter around herself before stepping out of the door—which she left open behind her. One of the Priests shouted at her, but she ignored him. *Let him shut his own damn door,* she thought viciously. Then the wind whipped into her, driving snow into her face, and she didn't have a breath or a thought to spare for anything else but getting back to Amber's.

This wasn't as bad a storm as the one that had killed Tonno, but it was pure frozen hell to stagger through. She lost track of her feet first, then her hands, and finally, her face. She was too cold to shiver, but under the cloak she was sweating like a lathered horse. It seemed to take forever to beat her way against the wind down the streets she usually traveled in a half hour or less. The wind cut into her lungs like knives; every breath hurt her chest horribly, and her throat was so raw she wept for the pain of it and tried not to swallow. She was horribly thirsty, but icicles and snow did nothing but increase the thirst. She wondered if she'd been the one that had died, and this was her punishment in the afterlife. If so, she couldn't imagine what it had been that she'd done that warranted anything *this* bad.

When she got to Flower Street, she couldn't bear to go around the back; she staggered to the front door instead. Amber would forgive her this once. She could clean up the snow later, or something, to make up for it. All she wanted was her bed, and something hot to drink . . . her head hurt, her body hurt, everything hurt.

She shoved open the front door, too frozen to think, and managed to get it slammed shut behind her.

She turned in the sudden silence and shelter from the wind to find herself the center of attention—and there wasn't a client in the place. All of the ladies were downstairs, gathered in the common room, around the fire, wearing casual lounging robes in their signature colors. And all seven sets of eyes—Amber's included—were riveted to her, in shocked surprise.

That was when the heat hit her, and she fainted dead away.

She came to immediately, but by then she was shivering despite the heat; her teeth chattering so hard she couldn't speak. She was flat on her back, in a kind of crumpled, twisted pile of melting snow and heavy cloak. Sapphire and Amber leaned over her, trying to get her cloak off, trying to pry her hands open so they could get her unwrapped from the half-frozen mass of snow-caked wool. Amber's hand brushed against her forehead, as Rune tried to get enough breath to say something—and the woman exclaimed in surprise.

"I-I-I'm s-s-s-sorry," Rune babbled, around her chattering teeth. "I-I-I'm j-j-just c-c-c-cold, that's all." She tried to sit up, but the room began to spin.

"Cold!" Amber said in surprise. "Cold? Child, you're burning up! You must have a fever—" She gestured at someone just out of sight, and Topaz slid into view. "Topaz, you're stronger than any of the boys, can you lift her and get her into bed?"

The strange, slit-pupiled eyes did not even blink. "Of course," Topaz replied gravely. "I should be glad to. Just get her out of the cloak, please? I cannot bear the touch of the snow."

"I'm all r-r-r-right, really," she protested. "Th-th-this is s-s-silly—"

Rune had forgotten the cloak; she let go of the edges and slid her arms out of it. Sapphire pulled it away, and before Rune could try again to get to a sitting position, Topaz had scooped her up as easily as if she weighed no more than a pillow, and was carrying her towards the stairs.

I didn't know she was so strong, Rune thought dazedly. *She must be stronger than most men. Or—maybe I've just gotten really light—* She felt that way, as if she would flutter off like a leaf on the slightest wind.

"No—" Amber forestalled her, as Topaz started for the staircase. "No, I don't think her room is going to be warm enough, and besides, I don't want her alone. We'll put her on the couch in my rooms."

"Ah," was all that Topaz said; Amber led the way into her office, then did—something—with the wall, or an ornament on the wall. Whatever, a panel in the wall opened, and Topaz carried her into a small parlor, like Rose had in the private quarters back at the Hungry Bear. But this was nothing like Rose's parlor—it was lit with many lanterns, the air was sweet with the smell of dried herbs, the honey-scent of beeswax, and a faint hint of incense.

But that was when things stopped making sense, for Topaz turned into Boony, and the couch she was put on was on the top of Skull Hill, and she was going to have to play for the Ghost, only Tonno was in the Ghost's robes—she tried to explain that she'd done her best to help him, but he only glared at her and motioned for her to play. She picked up her fiddle and tried to play for him, but her fingers wouldn't work, and she started to cry; the wind blew leaves into her face so she couldn't see, and she couldn't hear, either—

And she was so very, very cold.

She began to cry, and couldn't stop.

Someone was singing, very near at hand. She opened gritty, sore eyes in an aching head to see who it was, for the song was so strange, less like a song than a chant, and yet it held elements of both. It was nothing she recognized, and yet she thought she heard something familiar in the wailing cadences.

There was a tall, strong-looking old woman sitting beside her, a woman wearing what could only be a Gypsy costume, but far more elaborate than anything Rune had ever seen the Gypsies wear. Besides her voluminous, multicolored skirts and bright blouse, the woman had a shawl embroidered with figures that seemed to move and dance every time she breathed, and a vast set of necklaces loaded with charms carved of every conceivable substance. They all seemed to represent animals and birds; Rune saw mother-of-pearl sparrows, obsidian bears, carnelian fish, turquoise foxes, all strung on row after row of tiny shell beads. The woman looked down at her and nodded, but did not stop her chanting for a moment.

Everything hurt; head, joints, throat—she was alternately freezing and burning. She closed her eyes to rest them, and opened them again when she felt a cold hand on her forehead. Amber was looking down at her with an expression of deep concern on her face. She tried to say something, but she couldn't get her mouth to work, and the mere effort was exhausting. She closed her eyes again.

She felt herself floating, away from the pain, and she let it happen. When her aching body was just a distant memory, she opened her eyes, to find that she was somewhere up above her body, looking down at it.

Amber was gone, but the strange Gypsy woman was back again, sitting in the corner, chanting quietly. Rune realized then that she *felt* the chanting; the song wove a kind of net about her that kept her from floating off somewhere. As she watched, with an oddly dispassionate detachment, Pearl and Diamond entered the room; Pearl carrying a large bowl of something that steamed which she set down on the hearth, Diamond with a tray of food she set down beside the Gypsy.

Diamond kept glancing at the Gypsy out of the corner of her eye. "That's not one of the Guild Herb-women," she said finally to Pearl, as she moved a little away.

"No," Pearl confirmed. "No, this is someone Amber knows. How?" Pearl shrugged expressively. "Amber has many friends. Often strange. Look at us!"

Diamond didn't echo Pearl's little chuckle. "Ruby says she's elf-touched," the young woman said with a shiver. "Ruby says she's a witch, and elf-touched."

Pearl shook her head. "She may be, for all I know. The Gypsies, the musicians, they know many strange creatures."

"Not like this," Diamond objected. "Not elf-touched! That's perilous close to heresy where I come from." She shuddered. "Have you ever seen what the Church does to heretics, and those who shelter them? I have. And I don't ever want to see it again."

Pearl cocked her head to one side, as if amused by Diamond's fear. "We—my people—we have old women and old men like her; they serve the villages in many ways, as healers of the sick, as speakers-to-the-Others, and as magicians to keep away the dark things that swim to the surface of the sea at the full moon. She deserves respect, I would say, but not fear."

"If you say so," Diamond said dubiously. "Is she—I mean, is Rune—" She cast a glance at the couch where Rune lay wrapped in a cocoon of blankets, her face as pale as the snow outside, with the same fever-spots of bright red that Tonno had on his cheeks.

"Yes," Pearl replied with absolute certainty. "She has told Amber that the girl will live, and if she makes such a pledge, she will keep it. Such as she is cannot lie—"

Rune would have liked to listen to more—in fact, she would have liked to see if she couldn't float off into another room and see what was going on there—but at that moment the old woman seemed to notice that she was up there. The tone of her chant took on a new sharpness, and the words changed, and Rune found herself being pulled back down into the body on the couch. She tried resisting, but it was no use.

Once back in her body, all she could think of was Tonno, and once again she began crying, feebly, for all the things she had not done.

Her head hurt, horribly, and her joints still ached, but she wasn't so awfully cold, and she didn't feel as if she was floating around anymore. She felt very solidly anchored inside her body, actually. She opened her eyes experimentally.

Maddie was sitting in the chair where the old woman had been sitting, working on her mending. Rune coughed; Maddie looked up, and grinned when she saw that Rune was awake.

"Well! Are you back with us again?" the girl said cheerfully.

Rune tested her throat, found it still sore, and just nodded.

"Hang on a moment," Maddie told her, and put her mending away. She went over to the hearth, where there was a kettle on the hob beside the steaming bowl of herbs—herbs that smelled very like the ones Brother Anders had used for Tonno. That—it seemed as if it had happened years ago—

Something had happened to her grief while she slept. It was still with her, but no longer so sharp.

Maddie picked up the kettle and poured a mug of something, bringing it over to the couch. Rune managed to free an arm from her wrappings to take it. Her hand shook, and the mug felt as if it weighed a thousand pounds, but she managed to drink the contents without spilling much.

It was some kind of herb tea, heavily dosed with honey, and it eased the soreness in her throat wonderfully.

"What happened?" she said, grateful beyond words to hear her voice come out as a whispered version of her own, and not a fever-scorched croak.

"Well," Maddie said, sitting herself down in the chair again. "You made a very dramatic entrance, that's for certain. Nighthawk said that she thinks you got pneumonia—Nighthawk's the Gypsy-witch Amber knows that treats us all for things the Guild Herb-women can't. Anyway, Nighthawk says you got pneumonia, but that your voice is going to be all right, so don't worry. It's just that you're going to be all winter recovering, so don't think you can go jumping out of bed to sing.''

"Oh," Rune said vaguely. "What—what am I doing here?" She gestured at Amber's neat little parlor, in which she was the only discordant note.

"Amber says you're staying here where we can all keep an eye on you until you stop having fevers," Maddie said fiercely—and something in her voice told Rune that her recovery hadn't been nearly as matter-of-fact as Maddie made it out to be. "Then you can go back to your room, but you're going to stay in bed most of the time until spring. That's orders from Amber.''

"But—" Rune began.

"That's orders from *Amber*," Maddie repeated. And the tone of her voice said that it was no use protesting or arguing. "And she says you're not to worry about what all this is costing. Or about the fact that you're not playing in the common room for your keep. You've been part of Amber's for more than a year, and Amber takes care of her people.''

Rune nodded, meekly, but when Maddie finally left, she lay back among her pillows and tried to figure out exactly *why* Amber was doing all this for her. It wasn't as if this was the same set of circumstances as when she'd nursed Tonno—

—or was it?

She fell asleep trying to puzzle it all out, without much success.

She dreamed of Jib; dreamed of the Hungry Bear. Like her, he was two years older—but unlike her, he was still doing exactly the same things as he'd been two years ago. Still playing stable-hand and general dogsbody. His life hadn't altered in the slightest from when she'd left, and she was struck with the gloomy certainty that it never would, unless fate took an unexpected hand.

She woke again to near-darkness; the only light was from the banked fire. There was another full mug on a little table beside her, this time with doctored apple cider in it. She sipped it and stared into the coals for a long time, wondering how much of her dream was reality and how much was her fever-dreams.

What was going to happen to Jib? He'd been her friend, her only friend, and she'd run off without even a good-bye. She hadn't ever worried about what was going to happen to him with her gone. Was he all right? Had the bullies found something better to do, or were they still making his life a torment?

Was he satisfied? How *could* he be? How could anyone be satisfied in the position he held? It was all right for a boy, but no job for a man.

But unless something changed for him, that was what he'd be all his life. Someone's flunky.

Now she remembered what he'd wanted to do, back in the long-ago days when they'd traded dreams. He'd wanted to be a horse-trader; a modest enough ambition, and one he could probably do well at if he stuck to the kind of horses he had experience with. Farm-stock, donkeys, rough cobs—sturdy beasts, not highly bred, but what farmers and simple traders needed. Jib knew beasts like that; could tell a good one from a bad one, a bargain from a doctored beast that was about to break down.

She tried to tell herself that what happened to him wasn't her responsibility, but if that was true, then it was also true that what happened to *her* was not Amber's responsibility. Yet Amber was caring for her.

Jib was old enough to take care of himself.

Well, that was true—but Jib had no way to get himself out of the rut he was in. He had no talent at all, except that of working well with animals. If he went somewhere else, he'd only be doing the same work in a different place. Would that be better or not? And would he even think of doing so? She knew from her own experience how hard it was to break ties and go, when things where you were at the moment were only uncomfortable, not unbearable. It was easy to tell yourself that they'd get better, eventually.

She fell asleep again, feeling vaguely bothered by yet more guilt. If only there was something she could have done to help him. . . .

Weak, early-spring sunshine reflected off the wall of the House across from her window, and she had the window open a crack just for the sake of the fresh air. She'd been allowed out of bed, finally, two weeks ago; she still spent a lot of time in her room, reading. Even a simple trip down to the common room tended to make her legs wobbly. But she persisted; whether she was ready or not, she would have to make Midsummer Faire this year, and the trials. For her own sake, and for the sake of Tonno's memory.

If only she didn't owe Amber so much. . . . Her indebtedness troubled her, as it did not seem to trouble Amber. But at the least, before she left, Rune had determined to walk the length and breadth of Nolton, listening to buskers and talking to them, to find Amber a replacement musician for the common room. That wouldn't cancel the debt, but it would ease it, a little.

"Rune?" Maddie tapped on the half-open door to her room; Rune looked up from the book she was reading. It was one of Tonno's, but she'd never seen fit to inform the Church that she had it, and no one had ever come asking after it. She had a number of books here that had been Tonno's, and she wasn't going to give them back until someone came for them. She reasoned that she could always use her illness as an excuse to cover why she had never done so.

She smiled at Maddie, who returned it a little nervously. "There's a visitor below," she said, and the tone of her voice made Rune sit up a little straighter. "It's a Priest. He wants to see you. He was with Amber for a while and she said it was all right for him to talk to you—but if you don't want to, Rune—"

She sighed, exasperated. "Oh, it's probably just about the books I have from the shop. The greedy pigs probably want them back." She tugged at her hair and brushed down her shabby breeches and shirt. "Do I look like a boy, or a girl?"

Maddie put her head to one side and considered. "More like a girl, actually."

"Damn. Oh well, it can't be helped. You might as well bring him up." She gritted her teeth together. He *would* show up now, when she was just getting strong enough to enjoy reading.

Maddie vanished, and a few moments later, heavy footsteps following her light ones up the kitchen stairs heralded the arrival of her visitor.

Rune came very near to chuckling at the disgruntled look on the Priest's face. Bad enough to have to come to a brothel to collect part of an estate—*worse* that he was taken up the back stairs to do so, like a servant.

That's one for you, Tonno, she thought, keeping the smile off her lips somehow. *A small one, but there it is.*

"Are you Rune of Westhaven?" the balding, thin Priest asked crossly. He was another sort like Brother Pell, but *he* didn't even have the Brother's love of music to leaven his bitterness. Rune nodded. She waited for him to demand the books; she was going to make him find them all, pick them up, and carry them out himself. Hopefully, down the back stairs again.

But his next words were a complete shock.

"Tonno Alendor left a will, filed as was proper, with the Church, and appointing Brother Bryan as executor of the estate," the Priest continued, as if every word hurt him. "In it, everything except the tithe of death-duties and death-taxes was left to you. The shop, the contents, everything."

He glared at her, as if he wanted badly to know what she had done to "make" the old man name her as his heir. For her part, she just stared at him, gaping in surprise, unable to speak. Finally the Priest continued in an aggrieved tone.

"Brother Bryan has found a buyer for the shop and contents, with the sole exception being a few books that Tonno mentions specifically that he wanted you to keep. Here's the list—"

He handed it to her with the tips of his fingers, as if touching her or it might somehow contaminate him. She took it, hands shaking as she opened it. As she had expected, they were all the books Tonno had insisted she keep here, at her room.

"If you have no objections," the Priest finished, his teeth gritted, "Brother Bryan will complete the purchase. The Church will receive ten percent as death-tithe. He, as executor, will receive another ten percent. City death-taxes are a remaining ten percent. You will receive the bulk of the moneys from the sale. It won't be much," he finished, taking an acid delight in imparting *that* bad news. "The shop is in a bad location, and the contents are a jumble of used merchandise, mostly curiosities, and hard to dispose of. But Brother Bryan will have your moneys delivered here at the conclusion of the sale, and take care of the death-duties himself. Unless you have something else from the shop you would like to keep as a memorial-piece." Again he pursed his lips sourly. "The value of that piece, will, of course, be pro-rated against your share."

She thought quickly, then shook her head. There was nothing *there* that she wanted. Everything in the shop would be forever tainted with the horrid memories of Tonno's sickness and unnecessary death. Let someone else take it, someone for whom the place would have no such memories. Not even the instruments would be of any use; she could only play fiddle and lute, and Tonno had sold the last of those months ago, during the height of summer.

The Priest took himself out, leaving her still dazed.

She didn't know what to think. How much money *was* "not very much"? Assuming that Brother Bryan only got a fraction of what the contents of the shop were worth—and she did not doubt that he would drive a very hard bargain indeed, both for her sake, and the Church's— that was still more money than she had ever had in her life. What was she to do with it? It beggared the pouch full of silver she'd gotten from the Ghost. . . .

She fell asleep, still trying to comprehend it.

This time, her dreams about Jib were troubled. He was plainly un-happy; scorned by the villagers, abused by Stara, ordered about by every-one. And yet, he had nowhere to go. He had no money saved, no prospects—

The village toughs still bullied him, and without Rune to protect him, he often sported bruises or a black eye. They laughed at him for being a coward, but what was he to do? If he fought them, they'd only hurt him further or complain that he had picked the fight, not they. They never came at him by ones or twos, only in a gang.

He'd had an offer from a horse-trader a month ago, an honest man who had been stopping at the Bear for as long as Jib could recall—if he had some money, the man would let him buy into the string and learn the business, eventually to take it over when the trader settled down to breeding. *That* was the answer to his prayers—but he had no money. The trader would keep the offer open as long as he could, but how long would he wait? A year? More? No matter how long he waited, Jib would still never have it. He got no pay; he'd *get* no pay for as long as Stara was holding the purse-strings. If he went elsewhere, he might earn pay in addition to his keep, but only if he could produce a good reference, and Stara would never let Jeoff give him one if he left.

He worked his endless round of chores with despair his constant companion. . . .

Rune woke with a start. And she knew at that moment exactly what she was going to do.

The days were warm now, and so were the nights—warm enough to sleep out, at any rate. Now was the time to leave; she'd be at the Faire when it opened if she left now.

But leaving meant good-byes. . . .

She hugged everyone, from Ruby to the new little kitchen-boy, with a lump in her throat. She'd been happier here than anyplace else in her life. If Tonno were still alive, she might have put this off another year.

Not now. It was go now, or give up the dream. Tonno's memory wouldn't let her do that.

"We're sorry to see you leave, Rune," Amber said with real regret, when Rune hugged her good-bye, her balance a little off from the unaccustomed weight of her packs. "But Tonno and I always knew this place wouldn't hold you longer than a year or two. We're glad you stayed this long."

Rune sighed. "I'm sorry too," she confessed. "But—I can't help it, Amber. This is something I *have* to do. At least I found you a replacement for me."

"And a good one," Diamond said, with a wink. "She'll do just fine. She's already giving Carly hives."

"*She* doesn't want to do anything else but work as a street-busker, so you'll have her for as long as you want her," Rune continued. "I was very careful about that."

"I know you were, dear," Amber said, and looked at the pouch of coin in her hand. "I wish you'd take this back. . . ."

Rune shook her head stubbornly. "Save it, if you won't use it. Save it for an emergency, or use it for bribes; it's not a lot, but it ought to keep the lower-level Church clerks happy. I know that's what Tonno would like, and it'd be a good way to honor his memory."

Half of the money she'd gotten from the sale of the shop she'd given to Amber, to repay her for all the expense she'd gone to in nursing Rune back to health. A quarter of it had been sent to Jib, via the Gypsies, with a verbal message—"Follow *your* dream." There were things the Gypsies were impeccably honest about, and one of them was in keeping pledges. They'd vowed on their mysterious gods to take the money to Jib without touching a penny. Once it had gone, she'd ceased to have nightmares about him.

The remaining quarter, minus the Gypsies' delivery-fee, and the things she'd needed for the trip, ought to be just enough to get her to the Midsummer Faire and the trials for the Bardic Guild. She had a new set of faded finery, a new pack full of books, and the strength that had taken so long to regain was finally back. She was ready.

Amber kissed her; the way a fond mother would. "You'd better go now, before I disgrace myself and cry," the Madam ordered sternly. "Imagine! Amber, in tears, on the steps of her own brothel—and over a silly little fiddler-girl!" She smiled brightly, but Rune saw the teardrops trembling at the corners of her eyes and threatening to spill over.

To prevent that, she started another round of hugs and kisses that included all of them. Except Carly, who was nowhere to be seen.

Probably telling the Church that I'm running away with my ill-gotten gains.

"Well, that's it," she said at last, as nonchalantly as if she was about to cross the town, not the country. "I'm off. Wish me luck!"

She turned and headed off down the street for the east gate, turning again to walk backwards and wave good-bye.

She thought she saw Amber surreptitiously wipe her eyes on the corner of her sleeve, before returning the wave brightly. Her own throat knotted up, and to cover it, she waved harder, until she was forced to round a corner that put them all out of sight.

Then she squared her shoulders beneath her pack, and started on her journey; destination, the Midsummer Faire.

And Tonno, she thought, as she passed below the gates and took to the road. *This one's for you, too. Always for you.*

CHAPTER THIRTEEN

All the world comes to the Midsummer Faire at Kingsford.

That's what they said, anyway—and it certainly seemed that way to Rune, as she traveled the final leg down from Nolton, the Trade Road that ran from the Holiforth Pass to Traen, and from there to Kingsford and the Faire Field across the Kanar River from the town. She wasn't walking on the dusty, hard-packed road itself; she'd likely have been trampled by the press of beasts, then run over by the carts into the bargain. Instead, she walked with the rest of the foot-travelers on the road's verge. It was no less dusty, what grass there had been had long since been trampled into powder by all the feet of the fairgoers, but at least a traveler was able to move along without risk of acquiring hoof-prints on his anatomy.

Rune was close enough now to see the gates of the Faire set into the wooden palisade that surrounded it, and the guard beside them. This seemed like a good moment to separate herself from the rest of the throng, rest her tired feet, and plan her next moves before entering the grounds of the Faire.

She elbowed her way out of the line of people, some of whom complained and elbowed back, and moved away from the road to a little hillock under a forlorn sapling, where she had a good view of the Faire, a scrap of shade, and a rock to sit on. The sun beat down with enough heat to warm the top of her head through her soft leather hat. She plopped herself down on the rock and began massaging her tired feet while she looked the Faire over.

It was a bit overwhelming. Certainly it was much bigger than she'd imagined it would be. Nolton had been a shock; this was a bigger one. It was equally certain that there would be nothing dispensed for free behind those log palings, and the few coppers Rune had left would have to serve to feed her through the three days of trials for admission to the Bardic Guild. After that—

Well, after that, she should be an apprentice, and food and shelter would be for the Guild and her master to worry about. Or else, if she somehow failed—

She refused to admit the possibility of failing the trials. She couldn't— not after getting this far.

Tonno would never forgive me.

But for now, she needed somewhere to get herself cleaned of the road-dust, and a place to sleep, both with no price tags attached. Right now, she was the same gray-brown as the road from head to toe, the darker brown of her hair completely camouflaged by the dust, or at least it felt that way. Even her eyes felt dusty.

She strolled down to the river, her lute thumping her hip softly on one side, her pack doing the same on the other. There were docks on both sides of the river; on this side, for the Faire, on the other, for Kingsford. Close to the docks the water was muddy and roiled; there was too much traffic on the river to make an undisturbed bath a viable possibility, and too many wharf-rats about to make leaving one's belongings unattended a wise move. She backtracked upstream a bit, while the noise of the Faire faded behind her. She crossed over a small stream that fed into the river, and penetrated into land that seemed unclaimed. It was probably Church land, since the Faire was held on Church property; she'd often seen Church land left to go back to wilderness if it was hard to farm. Since the Church owned the docks, and probably owned all fishing rights to this section of river, they weren't likely to permit any competition.

The bank of the river was wilder here, and overgrown, not like the carefully tended area by the Faire docks. Well, that would discourage fairegoers from augmenting their supplies with a little fishing from the bank, especially if they were townsfolk, afraid of bears and snakes under every bush. She pushed her way into the tangle and found a game-trail that ran along the riverbank, looking for a likely spot. Finally she found a place where the river had cut a tiny cove into the bank. It was secluded; trees overhung the water, their branches making a good thick screen that touched the water, the ground beneath them bare of growth, and hollows between some of the roots were just big enough to cradle her sleeping roll. Camp, bath, and clear water, all together, and within climbing distance on one of the trees she discovered a hollow big enough to hide her bedroll and those belongings she didn't want to carry into the Faire.

She waited until dusk fell before venturing into the river, and kept her eyes and ears open while she scrubbed herself down. She probably wasn't the only country-bred person to think of this ploy, and ruffians preferred places where they could hide. Once clean, she debated whether or not to change into the special clothing she'd brought tonight; it might be better to save it—then the thought of donning the sweat-soaked, dusty traveling gear became too distasteful, and she rejected it out of hand.

I've got shirts and under-things for three days. That'll do.

She felt strange, and altogether different once she'd put the new costume on. Part of that was due to the materials—except for when she'd tried the clothing on for fit, this was the first time in her life she'd ever worn silk and velvet. Granted, the materials were all old; bought from a second-hand vendor back in Nolton and cut down from much larger men's garments by Maddie. She'd had plenty of time on the road to sew them up. The velvet of the breeches wasn't *too* rubbed; the ribbons on the sleeves of the shirt and the embroidered trim she'd made when she was sick should cover the faded and frayed places, and the vest should cover the stains on the back panels of each shirt completely. That had been clever of Maddie; to reverse the shirts so that the wine-stained fronts became the backs. Her hat, once the dust was beaten out of it and the plumes she'd snatched from the tails of several disgruntled roosters along the way were tucked into the band, looked both brave and professional enough. Her boots, at least, were new, and when the dust was brushed from them, looked quite respectable. She tucked her remaining changes of clothing and her bedroll into her pack, hid the lot in the tree-hollow, and felt ready to face the Faire.

The guard at the gate, a Church cleric, of course, eyed her carefully. "Minstrel?" he asked suspiciously, looking at the lute and fiddle she carried in their cases, slung from her shoulders. "You'll need a permit to busk, if you plan to stay more than three days."

She shook her head. "Here for the trials, m'lord. Not planning on busking."

Which was the truth. She wasn't *planning* on busking. If something came up, or she was practicing and people chose to pay her—well, that wasn't planned, was it?

"Ah." He appeared satisfied. "You come in good time, boy. The trials begin tomorrow. The Guild has its tent pitched hard by the main gate of the Cathedral; you should have no trouble finding it."

She thanked him, but he had already turned his attention to the next in line. She passed inside the log walls and entered the Faire itself.

The first impressions she had were of noise and light; torches burned all along the aisle she traversed; the booths to either side were lit by lanterns, candles, or other, more expensive methods, like perfumed oil-lamps. The crowd was noisy; so were the merchants. Even by torchlight it was plain that these were the booths featuring shoddier goods; second-hand finery, brass jewelry, flash and tinsel. The entertainers here were—surprising. She averted her eyes from a set of dancers. It wasn't so much that they wore little but imagination, but the *way* they were dancing embarrassed even her; Amber had never permitted anything like *this* in her House. And the fellow with the dancers back at the Westhaven Faire hadn't had his girls doing anything like this, either.

Truth to tell, they tended to move as little as possible.

She kept a tight grip on her pouch and instruments, tried to ignore the crush, and let the flow of fairgoers carry her along.

Eventually the crowd thinned out a bit (though not before she'd felt a ghostly hand or two try for her pouch and give it up as a bad cause). She followed her nose then, looking for the row that held the cook-shop tents and the ale-sellers. She hadn't eaten since this morning, and her stomach was lying in umcomfortably close proximity to her spine.

She learned that the merchants of tavern-row were shrewd judges of clothing; hers wasn't fine enough to be offered a free taste, but she wasn't wearing garments poor enough that they felt she needed to be shooed away. Sternly admonishing her stomach to be less impatient, she strolled the length of the row twice, carefully comparing prices and quantities, before settling on a humble tent that offered meat pasties (best not ask what beast the meat came from, not at these prices) and fruit juice or milk as well as ale and wine. Best of all, it offered seating at rough trestle-tables as well. Her feet were complaining as much as her stomach.

Rune took her flaky pastry and her mug of juice and found a spot at any empty table where she could eat and watch the crowds passing by. No wine or ale for her; not even had she the coppers to spare for it. She dared not be the least muddle-headed, not with a secret to keep and the first round of competition in the morning. The pie was more crust than meat, but it was filling and well-made and fresh; that counted for a great deal.

She watched the other customers, and noted with amusement that there were two sorts of the clumsy, crude clay mugs. One sort, the kind they served the milk and juice in, was ugly and shapeless, too ugly to be worth stealing but was just as capacious as the exterior promised. No doubt, that was because children were often more observant than adults gave them credit for—and very much inclined to set up a howl if something didn't meet implied expectations. The other sort of mug, for wine and ale, was just the same ugly shape and size on the *outside*, though a different shade of toad-back green, but had a far thicker bottom, effectively reducing the interior capacity by at least a third. Which a thirsty adult probably wouldn't notice.

"Come for the trials, lad?" asked a quiet voice in her ear.

Rune jumped, nearly knocking her mug over, and snatching at it just in time to save the contents from drenching her shopworn finery. And however would she have gotten it clean again in time for tomorrow's competition? There hadn't been a sound or a hint of movement, or even the shifting of the bench to warn her, but now there was a man sitting beside her.

He was of middle years, red hair just going to gray a little at the temples, smile-wrinkles around his mouth and gray-green eyes, with a candid, triangular face. Well, that said nothing; Rune had known highwaymen with equally friendly and open faces. His costume was similar to her own, though; leather breeches instead of velvet, good linen instead of worn silk, a vest and a leather hat that could have been twin to hers. But the telling marks were the knots of ribbon on the sleeves of his shirt—and the neck of a lute peeking over his shoulder. A minstrel!

Of the Guild? Could it be possible that here at the Faire there'd be Guild musicians working the "streets"? Rune rechecked the ribbons on his sleeves, and was disappointed. Blue and scarlet and green, not the purple and silver of a Guild Minstrel, nor the purple and gold of a Guild Bard. This was only a common busker, a mere street-player. Still, he'd bespoken her kindly enough, and God knew not everyone with the music-passion had the skill or the talent to pass the trials—

Look at Tonno. He'd never even gotten as far as busking.

"Aye, sir," she replied politely. "I've hopes to pass; I think I've the talent, and others have said as much."

Including the sour Brother Pell. When she'd told him good-bye and the reason for leaving, he'd not only wished her well, he'd actually cracked a smile, and said that of all his pupils, *she* was the one he'd have chosen to send to the trials.

The stranger's eyes measured her keenly, and she had the disquieting feeling that her boy-ruse was fooling *him* not at all. "Ah well," he replied, "There's a-many before you have thought the same, and failed."

"That may be—" She answered the challenge in his eyes, stung into revealing what she'd kept quiet until now. "But I'd bet a copper penny that none of *them* fiddled for a murdering ghost, and not only came out by the grace of their skill but were rewarded by that same spirit for amusing him!"

"Oh, so?" A lifted eyebrow was all the indication he gave of being impressed, but somehow that lifted brow conveyed volumes. And he believed her; she read that, too. "You've made a song of it, surely?"

Should I sing it now? Well, why not? After the next couple of days, it wouldn't be a secret anymore. "Have I not! It's to be my entry for the third day of testing."

"Well, then . . ." he said no more than that, but his wordless attitude of waiting compelled Rune to unsling her fiddle case, extract her instrument, and tune it without further prompting.

"It's the fiddle that's my first instrument," she said, feeling as if she must apologize for singing with a fiddle rather than her lute, since the lute was clearly his instrument. "And since 'twas the fiddle that made the tale—"

"Never apologize for a song, child," he admonished, interrupting her. "Let it speak out for itself. Now let's hear this ghost tale."

It wasn't easy to sing while fiddling, but Rune had managed the trick of it some time ago. She closed her eyes a half-moment, fixing in her mind the necessary changes she'd made to the lyrics—for unchanged, the song would have given her sex away—and began.

"I sit here on a rock, and curse my stupid, bragging tongue,
And curse the pride that would not let me back down from a boast
And wonder where my wits went, when I took that challenge up
And swore that I would go and fiddle for the Skull Hill Ghost!"

Oh, that was a damn fool move, Rune. And you knew it when you did it. But if you hadn't taken their bet, you wouldn't be here now.

"It's midnight, and there's not a sound up here upon Skull Hill
Then comes a wind that chills my blood and makes the leaves blow wild—"

Not a good word choice, but a change that had to be made—that was one of the giveaway verses.

"And rising up in front of me, a thing like shrouded Death.
A voice says, 'Give me reason why I shouldn't kill you, child.' "

The next verse described Rune's answer to the spirit, and the fiddle wailed of fear and determination and things that didn't rightly belong on Earth. Then came the description of that night-long, lightless ordeal she'd passed through, and the fiddle shook with the weariness she'd felt, playing the whole night long.

Then the tune rose with dawning triumph when the thing not only didn't kill her outright, but began to warm to the music she'd made. Now she had an audience of more than one, though she was only half aware of the fact.

"At last the dawnlight strikes my eyes; I stop, and see the sun
The light begins to chase away the dark and midnight cold—
And then the light strikes something more—I stare in dumb surprise—
For where the ghost had stood there is a heap of shining gold!"

The fiddle laughed at Death cheated, thumbed its nose at spirits, and chortled over the revelation that even the angry dead could be impressed and forced to reward courage and talent.

Rune stopped, and shook back brown locks dark with sweat, and looked about her in astonishment at the applauding patrons of the cook-tent. She was even more astonished when they began to toss coppers in her open fiddle case, and the cook-tent's owner brought her over a full pitcher of juice and a second pie.

"I'd'a brought ye wine, laddie, but Master Talaysen there says ye go to trials and mustna be a-muddled," she whispered as she hurried back to her counter.

But this hadn't been a performance—at least, not for more than one! "I hadn't meant—"

"Surely this isn't the first time you've played for your supper, child?" The minstrel's eyes were full of amused irony.

She flushed. "Well, no, but—"

"So take your well-earned reward and don't go arguing with folk who have a bit of copper to fling at you, and who recognize the Gift when they hear it. No mistake, youngling, you *have* the Gift. And sit and eat; you've more bones than flesh. A good tale, that."

She peeked at the contents of the case before she answered him. *Not a single pin in the lot. Folks certainly do fling money about at this Faire.*

"Well," Rune said, and blushed, "I did exaggerate a bit at the end. 'Twasn't gold, it was silver, but silver won't rhyme. And it was that silver that got me here—bought me my second instrument, paid for lessoning, kept me fed while I was learning. I'd be just another tavern-musician, otherwise—" She broke off, realizing who and what she was talking to.

"Like me, you are too polite to say?" The minstrel smiled, then the smile faded. "There are worse things, child, than to be a free musician.

I don't think there's much doubt your Gift will get you past the trials—but you might not find the Guild to be all you think it to be.''

Rune shook her head stubbornly, taking a moment to wonder why she'd told this stranger so much, and why she so badly wanted his good opinion. Maybe it was just that he reminded her of a much younger Tonno. Maybe it was simply needing the admiration of a fellow musician. ''Only a Guild Minstrel would be able to earn a place in a noble's train. Only a Guild Bard would have the chance to sing for royalty. I'm sorry to contradict you, sir, but I've had my taste of wandering, singing my songs out only to know they'll be forgotten in the next drink, wondering where my next meal is coming from. I'll never get a secure life except through the Guild, and I'll never see my songs live beyond me without their patronage.''

He sighed. ''I hope you never regret your decision, child. But if you should—or if you need help, ever, here at the Faire or elsewhere—well, just ask around the Gypsies or the musicians for Talaysen. Or for Master Wren; some call me that as well. I'll stand your friend.''

With those surprising words, he rose soundlessly, as gracefully as a bird in flight, and slipped out of the tent. Just before he passed out of sight among the press of people, he pulled his lute around to the front, and struck a chord. She managed to hear the first few notes of a love song, the words rising golden and glorious from his throat, before the crowd hid him from view and the babble of voices obscured the music.

She strolled the Faire a bit more; bought herself a sweet-cake, and watched the teaser-shows outside some of the show-tents. She wished she wasn't in boy-guise; there were many good-looking young men here, and not all of them were going about with young women. Having learned more than a bit about preventing pregnancy at Amber's, she'd spent a little of her convalescence in losing her virginity with young Shawm. The defloration was mutual, as it turned out; she'd reflected after she left that it might have been better with a more experienced lover, but at least they'd been equals in ignorance. Towards the end they'd gotten better at it; she had at least as much pleasure out of love-play as he did. They'd parted as they'd begun—friends. And she had the feeling that Maddie was going to be his next and more serious target.

Well, at least I got him broken in for her!

But it was too bad that she was in disguise. Even downright plain girls seemed to be having no trouble finding company, and if after a day or two it turned into more than company—

Never mind. If they work me as hard as I think they will in the Guild,

*I won't have any time for dalliance. So I might as well get used to
celibacy again.*

But as the tent-lined streets of the Faire seemed to hold more and
more couples, she decided it was time to leave. She needed the sleep,
anyway.

Everything was still where she'd left it. Praying for a dry night, she
lined her chosen root-hollow with bracken, and settled in for the night.

Rune was waiting impatiently outside the Guild tent the next morning,
long before there was anyone there to take her name for the trials. The
tent itself was, as the Faire guard had said, hard to miss; purple in the
main, with pennons and edgings of silver and gilt. Almost—*too* much;
it bordered on the gaudy. She was joined shortly by three more striplings,
one well-dressed and confident, two sweating and nervous. More trickled
in as the sun rose higher, until there was a line of twenty or thirty
waiting when the Guild Registrar, an old and sour-looking Church cleric,
raised the tent-flap to let them file inside. He wasn't wearing Guild
colors, but rather a robe of dusty gray linen; she was a little taken aback
since she hadn't been aware of a connection between the Guild and the
Church before, other than the fact that there were many Guild musicians
and Bards who had taken vows.

Would they have ways to check back to Nolton, and to Amber's?
Could they find out she was a girl before the trials were over?

Then she laughed at her own fears. Even if they had some magic that
could cross leagues of country in a single day and bring that knowledge
back, *why would they bother*? There was nothing important about her.
She was just another boy at the trials. And even if she passed, she'd
only be another apprentice.

The clerk took his time, sharpening his quill until Rune was ready to
scream with impatience, before looking her up and down and asking her
name.

"Rune of Westhaven, and lately of Nolton." She held to her vow of
not claiming a sire-name. "Mother is Stara of Westhaven."

He noted it, without a comment. "Primary instrument?"

"Fiddle."

Scratch, scratch, of quill on parchment. "Secondary?"

"Lute."

He raised an eyebrow; the usual order was lute, primary; fiddle, secondary. For that matter, fiddle wasn't all that common even as a secondary instrument.

"And you will perform—?"

"First day, primary, 'Lament Of The Maiden Esme.' Second day, secondary, 'The Unkind Lover.' Third day, original, 'The Skull Hill Ghost.' " An awful title, but she could hardly use the *real* name of "Fiddler Girl." "Accompanied on primary, fiddle."

He was no longer even marginally interested in her. "Take your place."

She sat on the backless wooden bench, trying to keep herself calm. Before her was the raised wooden platform on which they would all perform; to either side of it were the backless benches like the one she warmed, for the aspirants to the Guild. The back of the tent made the third side of the platform, and the fourth faced the row of well-padded chairs for the Guild judges. Although she was first here, it was inevitable that they would let others have the preferred first few slots; there would be those with fathers already in the Guild, or those who had coins for bribes who would play first, so that *they* were free to enjoy the Faire for the rest of the day, without having to wait long enough for their nerves to get the better of them. Still, she shouldn't have to wait too long—rising with the dawn would give her that much of an edge, at least.

She got to play by midmorning. The "Lament" was perfect for fiddle, the words were simple and few, and the wailing melody gave her lots of scope for improvisation. The style the judges had chosen, "florid style," encouraged such improvisation. The row of Guild judges, solemn in their tunics or robes of purple, white silk shirts trimmed with gold or silver ribbon depending on whether they were Minstrels or Bards, were a formidable audience. Their faces were much alike; well-fed and very conscious of their own importance; you could see it in their eyes. As they sat below the platform and took unobtrusive notes, they seemed at least mildly impressed with her performance. Even more heartening, several of the boys yet to perform looked satisfyingly worried when she'd finished.

She packed up her fiddle and betook herself briskly out—to find herself a corner of the cathedral wall to lean against as her knees sagged when the excitement that had sustained her wore off.

I never used to react that badly to an audience.

Maybe she hadn't recovered from her sickness as completely as she'd thought. Or maybe it was just that she'd never had an audience this important before. It was several long moments before she could get her legs to bear her weight and her hands to stop shaking. It was then that she realized that she hadn't eaten since the night before—and that she was suddenly ravenous. Before she'd played, the very thought of food had been revolting.

The same cook-shop tent as before seemed like a reasonable proposition. She paid for her breakfast with some of the windfall-coppers of the night before; this morning the tent was crowded and she was lucky to get a scant corner of a bench to herself. She ate hurriedly and joined the strollers through the Faire.

Once or twice she thought she glimpsed the red hair of Talaysen, but if it really was the minstrel, he was gone by the time she reached the spot where she had thought he'd been. There were plenty of other street-buskers, though. She thought wistfully of the harvest of coin she'd reaped the night before as she noted that none of them seemed to be lacking for patronage. And no one was tossing pins into the hat, either. It was all copper coins—and occasionally, even a silver one. But now that she was a duly registered entrant in the trials, it would be going against custom, if not the rules, to set herself up among them. That much she'd picked up, waiting for her turn. An odd sort of custom, but there it was; better that she didn't stand out as the only one defying it.

So instead she strolled, and listened, and made mental notes for further songs. There were plenty of things she saw or overheard that brought snatches of rhyme to mind. By early evening her head was crammed full—and it was time to see how the Guild had ranked the aspirants of the morning.

The list was posted outside the closed tent-flaps, and Rune wasn't the only one interested in the outcome of the first day's trials. It took a bit of time to work her way in to look, but when she did—

By God's saints! There she was, "Rune of Westhaven," listed *third.* She all but floated back to her riverside tree-roost.

The second day of the trials was worse than the first; the aspirants performed in order, lowest ranking to highest. That meant that Rune had to spend most of the day sitting on the hard wooden bench, clutching the neck of her lute in nervous fingers, listening to contestant after contestant and sure that each one was *much* better on his secondary instrument than she was. She'd only had a year of training on it, after all. Still, the song she'd chosen was picked deliberately to play up her voice and de-emphasize her lute-strumming. It was going to be pretty difficult for any of these others to match her high contralto (a truly cunning imitation of a boy's soprano), since most of them had passed puberty.

At long last her turn came. She swallowed her nervousness as best she could, took the platform, and began.

Privately she thought it was a pretty ridiculous song. Why on Earth any man would put up with the things that lady did to him, and all for the sake of a "kiss on her cold, quiet hand," was beyond her. She'd parodied the song, and nothing she wrote matched the intrinsic silliness of the original. Still, she put all the acting ability she had into it, and was rewarded by a murmur of approval when she'd finished.

"That voice—I've seldom heard one so pure at that late an age!" she overheard as she packed up her instrument. "If he passes the third day— you don't suppose he'd agree to being gelded, do you? I can think of half a dozen courts that would pay red gold to have a voice like his in service."

She smothered a smile—imagine their surprise to discover that it would *not* be necessary to eunuch her to preserve her voice!

She played drum for the next, then lingered to hear the last of the entrants. And unable to resist, she waited outside for the posting of the results.

She nearly fainted to discover that she'd moved up to second place.

"I told you," said a familiar voice behind her. "But are you still sure you want to go through with this?"

She whirled, to find the minstrel Talaysen standing in her shadow, the sunset brightening his hair and the warm light on his face making him appear scarcely older than she.

"I'm sure," she replied firmly. "One of the judges said today that he could think of half a dozen courts that would pay red gold to have my voice."

He raised an eyebrow. "Bought and sold like so much mutton? Where's the living in that? Caged behind high stone walls and never let out of the sight of m'lord's guards, lest you take a notion to sell your services elsewhere? Is *that* the life you want to lead?"

"Trudging down roads in the pouring cold rain, frightened half to death that you'll take sickness and ruin your voice—maybe for good? Singing with your stomach growling so loud it drowns out the song? Watching some idiot with half your talent being clad in silk and velvet and eating at the high table, while you try and please some brutes of guardsmen in the kitchen in hopes of a few scraps and a corner by the fire?" she countered. "No, thank you. I'll take my chances with the Guild. Besides, where else would I be able to *learn*? I've got no more silver to spend on instruments or teaching."

Tonno, you did your best, but I've seen the Guild musicians. I heard Guild musicians in the Church, at practice, back in Nolton. I have to become that good. I have to, if I'm to honor your memory.

"There are those who would teach you for the love of it—" he said, and her face hardened as she thought of Tonno, how he had taught her to the best of his ability. She was trying to keep from showing her grief. He must have misinterpreted her expression, for he sighed. "Welladay, you've made up your mind. As you will, child," he replied, but his eyes were sad as he turned away and vanished into the crowd again.

Once again she sat the hard bench for most of the day, while those of lesser ranking performed. This time it was a little easier to bear; it was obvious from a great many of these performances that few, if any, of the boys had the Gift to create. By the time it was Rune's turn to perform, she judged that, counting herself and the first-place holder, there could only be five real contestants for the three open Bardic apprentice slots. The rest would be suitable only as Minstrels; singing someone else's songs, unable to compose their own.

She took her place before the critical eyes of the judges, and began.

She realized with a surge of panic as she finished the first verse that they did *not* approve. While she improvised some fiddle bridges, she mentally reviewed the verse, trying to determine what it was that had set those slight frowns on the judicial faces.

Then she realized; she had said she had been *boasting*. Guild Bards simply did not admit to being boastful. Nor did they demean themselves by reacting to the taunts of lesser beings. Oh, God in heaven—

Quickly she improvised a verse on the folly of youth; of how, had she been older and wiser, she'd never have gotten herself into such a predicament. She heaved an invisible sigh of relief as the frowns disappeared.

By the last chorus, they were actually nodding and smiling, and one of them was tapping a finger in time to the tune. She finished with a flourish worthy of a Master, and waited, breathlessly.

And they *applauded*. Dropped their dignity and *applauded*.

The performance of the final contestant was an anticlimax.

None of them had left the tent since this last trial began. Instead of a list, the final results would be announced, and they waited in breathless anticipation to hear what they would be. Several of the boys had already approached Rune, offering smiling congratulations on her presumed first-place slot. A hush fell over them all as the chief of the judges took the platform, a list in his hand.

"First place, and first apprenticeship as Bard—Rune, son of Stara of Westhaven—"

"Pardon, my lord—" Rune called out clearly, bubbling over with happiness and unable to hold back the secret any longer. "But it's not son—it's *daughter.*"

She had only a split second to take in the rage on their faces before the first staff descended on her head.

They flung her into the dust outside the tent, half-senseless, and her smashed instruments beside her. The passersby avoided even looking at her as she tried to get to her feet and fell three times. Her right arm dangled uselessly; it hurt so badly that she was certain that it must be broken, but it hadn't hurt half as badly when they'd cracked it as it had when they'd smashed her fiddle; that had broken her heart. All she wanted to do now was to get to the river and throw herself in. With any luck at all, she'd drown.

But she couldn't even manage to stand.

"Gently, lass," someone said, touching her good arm. She looked around, but her vision was full of stars and graying out on the edges. Strong hands reached under her shoulders and supported her on both sides. The voice sounded familiar, but she was too dazed to think who it was. "God be my witness, if ever I thought they'd have gone this far, I'd never have let you go through with this farce."

She turned her head as they got her standing, trying to see through tears of pain, both of heart and body, with eyes that had sparks dancing before them. The man supporting her on her left she didn't recognize, but the one on the right—

"T-Talaysen?" she faltered.

"I told you I'd help if you needed it, did I not?" He smiled, but there was no humor in it. "I think you have more than a little need at the moment—"

She couldn't help herself; she wept, like a little child, hopelessly. The fiddle, the gift of Rose—and the lute, picked out by Tonno—both gone forever. "Th-they broke my fiddle, Talaysen. And my lute. They broke them, then they beat me, and they broke my arm—"

"Oh, Rune, lass—" There were tears in *his* eyes, and yet he almost seemed to be laughing as well. "If *ever* I doubted you'd the makings of a Bard, you just dispelled those doubts. *First* the fiddle, *then* the lute— and only *then* do you think of your own hurts. Ah, come away lass, come where people can care for such a treasure as you—"

Stumbling through darkness, wracked with pain, carefully supported and guided on either side, Rune was in no position to judge where or how far they went. After some unknown interval however, she found herself in a many-colored tent, lit with dozens of lanterns, partitioned off with curtains hung on wires that criss-crossed the entire dwelling. Just now most of these were pushed back, and a mixed crowd of men and women greeted their entrance with cries of welcome that turned to dismay at the sight of her condition.

She was pushed down into an improvised bed of soft wool blankets and huge, fat pillows. A thin, dark girl dressed like a Gypsy bathed her cuts and bruises with something that stung, then numbed them, and a gray-bearded man tsk'd over her arm, prodded it once or twice, then, without warning, pulled it into alignment. When he did that, the pain was so incredible that Rune nearly fainted.

By the time the multicolored fire-flashing cleared from her eyes, he was binding her arm up tightly with bandages and thin strips of wood, while the girl was urging her to drink something that smelled of herbs and wine.

Where am I? Who are these people? What do they want?

Before she had a chance to panic, Talaysen reappeared as if conjured at her side.

"Where—"

He understood immediately what she was asking. "You're with the Free Bards—the *real* Bards, not those pompous puff-toads of the Guild," he said. "Dear child, I thought that all that would happen to you was that those inflated bladders of self-importance would give you a tongue-lashing and throw you out on your backside. If I'd had the slightest notion that they'd do *this* to you, I'd have kidnapped you away and had you drunk insensible 'till the trials were over. I may never forgive myself. Now, drink your medicine."

"But how—why—who *are* you?" Rune managed between gulps.

" 'What are you?' I think might be the better place to start. Tell her, will you, Erdric?"

"We're the Free Bards," said the gray-bearded man, "as Master Talaysen told you. He's the one who banded us together, when he found that there were those who, like himself, had the Gift and the Talent but were disinclined to put up with the self-aggrandizement and politics and foolish slavishness to form that the Guild requires. We go where we wish and serve—or not serve—who we will, and sing as we damn well please and no foolishness about who'll be offended. We also keep a sharp eye out for youngsters like you, with the Gift, and with the spirit to fight the Guild. We've had our eye on you these—oh, it must be near a half-dozen years, now."

Six years? All this time, and I never knew? "You—but how? Who was watching me?"

"Myself, for one," said a new voice, and a bony fellow with hair that kept falling into his eyes joined the group around her. "You likely don't remember me, but I remember you—I heard you fiddle in your tavern when I was passing through Westhaven, and I passed the word."

"And I'm another." This one, standing near the back of the group, Rune recognized; she was the harpist with the Gypsies, the one called Nightingale. "Another of my people, the man you knew as Raven, was sent to be your main teacher until you were ready for another. We knew you'd find another good teacher for yourself, then, if you were a true musician."

"You see, we keep an eye out for all the likely lads and lasses we've marked, knowing that soon or late, they'd come to the trials. Usually, though, they're not so stubborn as you," Talaysen said, and smiled.

"I should hope to live!" the lanky fellow agreed. "They made the same remark my first day about wanting to have me stay a liltin' soprano the rest of me days. That was enough for me!"

"And they wouldn't even give *me* the same notice they'd have given a flea," the dark girl laughed. "Though I hadn't the wit to think of passing myself off as a boy for the trials."

"That was my teacher's idea," Rune admitted.

"It might even have worked," Talaysen told her, "if they weren't so fanatic about women. It's part of Guild teachings that women are lower than men, and can *never* have the true Gift of the Bards. You not only passed, you beat every other boy there. They couldn't have that. It went counter to all they stand for. If they admitted you could win, they'd have to admit that many other things they teach are untrue." He grinned. "Which they are, of course. That's why *we're* here."

"But—why are you—together?" Rune asked, bewildered. She was used to competition among musicians, not cooperation.

"For the same reason as the Guilds were formed in the first place. We band together to give each other help; a spot of silver to tide you over an empty month, a place to go when you're hurt or ill, someone to care for you when you're not as young as you used to be," the gray-haired man called Erdric said.

Nightingale spoke up from the rear. "To teach, and to learn as well. And we have more and better patronage than you, or even the Guild, suspects."

A big bear of a man laughed. "Not everyone finds the precious style of the Guild songsters to their taste, especially the farther you get from the large cities. Out in the countryside, away from the decadence of courts, they like their songs to be like their food. Substantial and heartening.''

"But why does the Guild let you get away with this, if you're taking patronage from them?'' Rune couldn't help feeling apprehensive, despite all their easy assurance.

"Bless you, child, they couldn't do without us!'' Talaysen laughed. "No matter what you think, there isn't a single creative Master among 'em! Gwyna, my heart, sing her 'The Unkind Lover'—your version, I mean, the real and original.''

Gwyna, the dark girl who had tended Rune's bruises, flashed dazzling white teeth in a vulpine grin, plucked a guitar from somewhere behind her, and began.

Well, it was the same melody that Rune had sung, and some of the words—the best phrases—were the same as well. But this was no ice-cold princess taunting her poor chivalrous admirer with what he'd never touch; no, this was a teasing shepherdess seeing how far she could harass her cowherd lover, and the teasing was kindly meant. And what the cowherd claimed at the end was a good deal more than a ''kiss on her cold, quiet hand.'' In fact, you might say with justice that the proceedings got downright heated!

It reminded her a bit of her private ''good-bye'' with Shawm, in fact. . . .

"That 'Lament' you did the first day's trial is another song they've twisted and tormented; most of the popular ballads the Guild touts as their own are ours,'' Talaysen told her with a grin.

"As you should know, seeing as you've written at least half of them!'' Gwyna snorted.

"But what would you have done if they had accepted me anyway?'' Rune wanted to know.

"Oh, you wouldn't have lasted long; can a caged lark sing? Soon or late, you'd have done what I did—'' Talaysen told her. "You'd have escaped your gilded cage, and we'd have been waiting.''

"Then, *you* were a Guild Bard?'' Somehow she felt she'd known that all along. "But I never hear of one called Talaysen, and if the 'Lament' is yours—''

Talaysen coughed, and blushed. "Well, I changed my name when I took my freedom. Likely though, you wouldn't recognize it—''

"Oh, she wouldn't, you think? Or are you playing mock-modest with us again?'' Gwyna shook back her abundant black hair. "I'll make it known to you that you're having your bruises tended by Master Bard Gwydain, himself.''

"Gwydain?" Rune's eyes went wide as she stared at the man, who coughed, deprecatingly. "But—but—I thought Master Gwydain was supposed to have gone into seclusion—or died—or took vows!"

"The Guild would hardly want it known that their pride had rejected 'em for a pack of Gypsy jonguelers, now would they?" the lanky fellow pointed out.

"So, can I tempt you to join with us, Rune, lass?" the man she'd known as Talaysen asked gently.

"I'd like—but I can't," she replied despairingly. "How could I keep myself? It'll take weeks for my arm to heal. And—my instruments are splinters, anyway." She shook her head, tears in her eyes. "They weren't much, but they were all I had. They were—from friends."

Tonno, Rose, will you ever forgive me? I've not only failed, but I've managed to lose your legacy to me. . . .

"I don't have a choice; I'll have to go back to Nolton—or maybe they'll take me in a tavern in Kingsford. I can still turn a spit and fill a glass one-handed." Tears spilled down her cheeks as she thought of going back to the life she'd thought she'd left behind her.

"Ah lass, didn't you *hear* Erdric?" the old man asked. "There's nothing for you to worry about! You're one of us; you won't need to go running off to find a way to keep food in your mouth! We take care of each other—we'll care for you till you're whole again—"

She stared at them all, and every one of them nodded. The old man patted her shoulder, then hastily found her a rag when scanning their faces brought her belief—and more tears.

"As for the instruments—" Talaysen vanished and returned again as her sobs quieted. "I can't bring back your departed friends. 'They're splinters, and I loved them' can't be mended, nor can I give you back the memories of those who gave them to you. But if I can offer a poor substitute, what think you of these twain?"

The fiddle and lute he laid in her lap weren't new, nor were they the kind of gilded, carved and ornamented dainties Guild musicians boasted, but they held their own kind of quiet beauty, a beauty of mellow wood and clean lines. Rune plucked a string on each, experimentally, and burst into tears again. The tone was lovely, smooth and golden, and these were the kind of instruments she'd never dreamed of touching, much less owning.

When the tears had been soothed away, the various medicines been applied both internally and externally, and introductions made all around,

Rune found herself once again alone with Talaysen—or Gwydain, though on reflection, she liked the name she'd first known him by better. The rest had drawn curtains on their wires close in about her little corner, making an alcove of privacy.

"If you're going to let me join you—" she said, shyly.

"Let!" He laughed, interrupting her. "Haven't we made it plain enough we've been trying to lure you like cony-catchers? Oh, you're one of us, Rune, lass. You've just been waiting to find us. You'll not escape us now!"

"Then—what am I supposed to do?"

"You heal," he said firmly. "That's the first thing. The second, well, we don't have formal apprenticeships amongst us. By the Lady, there's no few things you could serve as Master in, and no question about it! You could teach most of us a bit about fiddling, for one—"

"But—" She felt a surge of dismay. *Am I going to have to fumble along on my own now?* "One of the reasons I wanted to join the Guild was to *learn*! I can barely read or write music, not like a Master, anyway; there's so many instruments I can't play"—her voice rose to a soft wail—"how am I going to learn if a Master won't take me as an apprentice?"

"Enough! Enough! No more weeping and wailing, my heart's over-soft as it is!" he said hastily. "If you're going to insist on being an apprentice, I suppose there's nothing for it. Will I do as a Master to you?"

Rune was driven to speechlessness, and could only nod. *Me? Apprentice to Gwydain?* She felt dizzy; this was impossible, things like this only happened in songs—

—like winning prizes from a ghost.

"By the Lady, lass, you make a liar out of me, who swore never to take an apprentice! Wait a moment." He vanished around the curtain for a moment, then returned. "Here—"

He set down a tiny harp. "This can be played one-handed, and learning the ways of her will keep you too busy to bedew me with any more tears while your arm mends. Treat her gently—she's my own very first instrument, and she deserves respect."

Rune cradled the harp in her good arm, too awe-stricken to reply.

"We'll send someone in the morning for your things, wherever it is you've cached 'em. Lean back there—oh, it's a proper nursemaid I am—" He chattered, as if to cover discomfort, or to distract her, as he made her comfortable on her pillows, covering her with blankets and moving her two—no, three—new instruments to a place of safety, but still within sight. He seemed to understand how seeing them made her feel. "We'll find you clothing and the like as well. That sleepy-juice they gave you should have you nodding shortly. Just remember one thing before you doze off. I'm not going to be an easy Master to serve; you won't be spending your days lazing about, you know! Come morning, I'll set you your very first task. You'll teach *me*"—his eyes lighted with unfeigned eagerness—"that Ghost song!"

"Yes, Master Talaysen," she managed to say—and then she fell deeply and profoundly asleep.

CHAPTER FOURTEEN

The Faire ran for eight weeks; Rune had arrived the first day of the second week. Not everyone who was a participant arrived for the beginning of the Faire. There were major events occurring every week of the Faire, and minor ones every day. She had known, vaguely, that the trials and other Guild contests were the big event of the second week—the first week had been horse races, and next week would be livestock judging, a different breed of animal every day. None of this had made any difference to her at the time, but it might now. The final week of Faire was devoted to those seeking justice, and it was entirely possible that the Guild might decide to wreak further justice on her, in trials of another sort. She spent the night in pain-filled dreams of being brought up before the three Church Justices on charges of trying to defraud the Bardic Guild.

Each time she half-woke, someone would press a mug of medicinal tea into her hands, get her to drink it down, and take it away when she'd fallen asleep again. When she truly woke the next morning, the big tent was empty of everyone except Gwyna, the dark Gypsy girl, Erdric, and a young boy.

It was the boy's voice that woke her; singing in a breathy treble to a harp, a song in a language she didn't recognize. The harp-notes faltered a little, as he tried to play and sing at the same time.

She struggled to sit up, and in the process rattled the rings of the curtain next to her against the wire strung overhead. There was no sound of footsteps to warn her that anyone had heard her, but Gwyna peeked around the curtain and smiled when she saw that Rune was awake.

"Everybody's gone out busking," she said, "except us." She pulled back the curtain to show who "us" was. "It's our turn to mind the tent and make sure no one makes off with our belongings. What will you have for breakfast?"

"A new head," Rune moaned. Moving had made both head and arm ache horribly. Her head throbbed in both temples, and her arm echoed the throbbing a half heartbeat after her head. She also felt completely filthy, which didn't improve matters any.

"How about a bath, a visit to the privy, and a mug of something for the aches?" Gwyna asked. "Once you're up, it'll be easier to get around, but for the first couple of days Redbird has said you ought to stay pretty much in bed." Wondering who "Redbird" was, Rune nodded, wordlessly, and Gwyna helped her up. "I think you'll have to borrow some of my clothes until yours can be washed," the girl added, looking at Rune's stained, filthy clothing. "If you've no objection to wearing skirts."

"No—I mean, the whole purpose of looking like a boy was to get in the trials. . . ." Rune sighed. "I don't really care one way or another, and if you'd be willing to lend some clothing, I'd be grateful. I left some other stuff, my bedroll and all, up a tree, but most of the clothing in my pack was dirty too." She described where she'd left it, as the boy left his harp with the old man, and came close to listen.

"I'll go get it!" the child said eagerly, and was off before anyone could say a word, flying out the front of the tent, where the two flaps stood open to let in air. Erdric shrugged.

"Hard to keep them to lessons at that age," the old man said, not without sympathy. "I know how I was. He'll be all right, and he'll get your things without touching the pack, he's that honest. Though I should warn you, if you've got anything unusual, you'd better show it to him before he gets eaten up with curiosity, imagining all sorts of treasures. That's my grandson, Rune. His name's Alain, but we all call him Sparrow."

The name suited him. "Well, if he gets back before we're done, would you tell him I thank him most kindly?" Rune said with difficulty, through the pain in her skull. The ache made her squint against all the light, and it made her tense up her shoulder muscles as well, which didn't help any. "Right now, I can't think any too well."

"Not to worry," Gwyna chuckled. "We all know how you must be feeling; I think every one of us has fallen afoul of someone and has ended up with a cracked bone and an aching head. I mind me the time a bitch of a girl in Newcomb reckoned I was after her swain and took after me with a fry-pan. I swear, my head rang like a steeple full of bells on a Holy Day. Come on, Lady Lark. Let me get you to some warm water to soak the aches out, and we'll worry about the rest later."

Rune hadn't really hoped for *warm* water, and she wondered how tent-dwellers, who presumably hadn't brought anything more than what they could carry, were going to manage it. She soon found out.

The Free Bards were camped outside the Faire palings, alongside of another little stream that fed the great river, on much hillier, rockier ground than Rune had crossed in her explorations of the river. It was an ingenious campsite; the huge tent lay athwart the entrance to a little hollow beside the stream. That gave them their own little park, free from prying eyes, screened by thick underbrush and trees that grew right up to the very edge of the bank on the other side. This was a wilder watercourse than the one Rune had crossed, upstream. It had a little waterfall at the top of the hollow, and was full of flat sheets of rock and water-smoothed boulders below the falls.

A hollow log carried water from the falls to a place where someone had cemented river-stones on the sides of a natural depression in one of those huge sheets of rock. There was a little board set into the rocks at the lower end like a dam, to let the water out again, and a fire on the flat part of the rock beside the rough bath-tub. The rock-built tub was already full.

"We've been coming here for years, and since we're here before anyone but the merchants, we always get this spot," Gwyna explained, as she shoveled rocks out of the heart of the fire, and dropped them into the waiting water with a sizzle. "We keep the tent in storage over in Kingsford during the year, with a merchant who sometimes lets it to other groups for outdoor revels. We've put in a few things that the wind and weather won't ruin over the years; this was one of the first. Do you know, those scurvy merchants over in the Faire charge a whole silver penny for a *bath*?" She bristled, as if she was personally offended. Rune smiled wanly. "You can't win," she continued. "You can get a bath for a copper in the public baths across the river in Kingsford, but you'd either get soaked going over the ford or pay four coppers coming and going on the ferry."

"That's a merchant for you," Rune agreed. "I suppose the Church has rules about bathing in the river."

"No, but no one would want to; up near the docks, it's half mud." She shook her head. "Well, when you're better, you'll have to do this for yourself, and remember, on your honor, you always leave the bath set up for the next person. He may be as sore and tired as you were when you needed it."

While she was talking, she was helping Rune get out of her clothing. Rune winced at the sight of all the bruises marking her body; it would be a long time before they all faded, and until then, it would be hard to find a comfortable position to sit or sleep in. And she'd have to wear long sleeves and long skirts, to keep people from seeing what had been done to her.

"In you go—" Gwyna said gaily, as if Rune didn't look like a patchwork of blue and black. "You soak for a while; I'll be back with soap."

Rune was quite content to lean back against the smooth rock, close her eyes, and soak in the warm water. It wasn't hot; that was too bad, because really hot water would have felt awfully good right now. But it was warmer than her own skin temperature, so it felt very comforting. A gap in the trees let sun pour down on her, and that continued to warm both the water and the rocks she rested on.

She must have dozed off, because the next thing she knew, Gwyna was shaking her shoulder, there was a box of soft soap on the rocks beside her. "Here, drink this. I'll do your hair," Gwyna said, matter-of-factly, placing a mug of that doctored wine in her good hand. "It's not fit to be seen."

"I can believe it," Rune replied. She took the mug, then sniffed the wine, wrinkled her nose, and drank it down in one gulp. As she had expected, it tasted vile. Gwyna laughed at her grimace, took the mug, and used it to dip out water to wet down her hair.

"We Gypsies only use the worst wine we can find for potions," Gwyna said cheerfully. "They taste so awful there's no use in ruining a good drink—and I'm told you need the spirits in wine to get the most out of some of the herbs." She took the box of soap, then, and began massaging it carefully into Rune's hair. Rune was glad she was being careful; there was an amazing number of knots on her skull, and Gwyna was finding them all. She closed her eyes, and waited for the aching to subside; about the third time Gwyna rinsed her hair, her head finally stopped throbbing.

She opened her eyes without wincing at the light, took the soap herself and began getting herself as clean as she could without wetting her splinted arm.

Finally they were both finished, and Rune rinsed herself off. "Can you stand a cold drench?" Gwyna asked then. "It'll probably clear your head a bit."

She considered it for a moment, then nodded; Gwyna let the water out by sliding out the board. Then she maneuvered the log over to its stand and let fresh, cold water run in; it swung easily, and Rune noted that it was set to pour water over the head of someone sitting beneath it in the tub. Rune rinsed quickly, getting the last of the soap off, and stuck her head under the water for as long as she could bear. Then she scrambled out, gasping, and Gwyna handed her a rough towel that might once have been part of a grain sack, and swung the log away again.

While Gwyna took the rocks out of the bottom of the pool, put them back beside the fire, then refilled the tub and built the fire back up, Rune dried herself off, wrapping her hair in the towel. There was clothing ready on the rocks in the sun; a bright skirt and bodice, and a minstrel's shirt with ribbons on the full sleeves, and some of her own under-things waiting for her. She got into them, and felt much the better; the medicine, the bath, and the clean clothing worked together to make her feel more like herself, especially after the worst of the bruises were covered. Even the ache in her head and arm receded to something bearable.

"Now what?" she asked Gwyna. "Where would you like me to go? I don't want to be in the way, and if there's anything I can do, I'd like to. I don't want to be a burden either."

The girl nodded towards the tent again.

"Back to bed with you," Gwyna said. "There's plenty you can do for us without being in the way. Erdric wants to hear some of those comic-songs Thrush said you did back in Nolton."

"Who?" she asked, astonished that anyone here knew about those songs. "How did you hear about those?"

"Thrush, I told you," Gwyna replied, a trifle impatiently. "You played for her to dance when her brothers were out busking the taverns at midday. The Gypsy, remember?"

"Oh," Rune said faintly. That was all the way back in Nolton! How on Earth had word of those songs gotten all the way here? How many of these Free Bards were there? And was there anything that they didn't know? "I didn't know—you all knew each other—" Then she burst out, impatiently, "Does *every* busker in the world belong to the Free Bards? Was I the only one who never heard of you before this?"

"Oh no—" Gwyna took one look at her angry, exasperated face, and burst out laughing. For some reason she found Rune's reaction incredibly funny. Rune wasn't as amused; in fact, she was getting a bit angry, but she told herself that there was no point in taking out her anger on Gwyna—

—even if she was being incredibly annoying.

Rune reined in her temper, and finally admitted to herself that she wouldn't be as exasperated if she wasn't still in pain. After all, what was she thinking—that the Free Bards had the same kind of information network as the Church? Now there was an absurdity!

"No, no, no," Gwyna finally said, when she'd gotten her laughter under control. "It's just the Gypsies. We're used to passing messages all over the Kingdoms. Anything that interests the Free Bards involves us, sooner or later.''

"Why?" Rune asked, her brow furrowed. "You Gypsies are all related in one way or another, if I understand right, but what does *that* have to do with the Free Bards?"

"Quite a bit," Gwyna said, sobering. "You see, Master Wren came to *us* when he first ran away from the Guild, and it was being with us that gave him the idea for the Free Bards. He liked the kind of group we are. He says we're 'supportive without being restrictive,' whatever that means.''

"All right, I can see that," Rune replied. "But I still don't understand what the Gypsies have to do with the Free Bards."

"For a start, it's probably fair to say that every Gypsy that's any kind of a musician is a Free Bard now. The Gift runs strong in us, when it runs at all. When anything calls us, music or dance, trading-craft, horse-craft, metal-craft, or mag—'' She stopped herself, and Rune had the startling idea that she was about to say "magic." Magic? If it was not proscribed by the Church, it was at the least frowned upon. . . .

"Well, anything that calls us, calls us strongly, so when we do a thing, we do it well." Gwyna skipped lightly over the grass and held open the tent-flap for Rune. "So if we'd chosen the caged-life, every male of us could likely be in the Guild. That wasn't our way, though, and seeing that gave Master Wren the idea for the Free Bards. Of you *gejo,* I'd say maybe one of every ten musicians and street-buskers are Free Bards. No more. The rest simply aren't good enough. You were good enough, so we watched you. We—that's Free Bards and Gypsies both.''

Rune sighed. That, at least, made her feel a little less like a child that hasn't been let in on a secret. The Free Bards weren't everywhere; they didn't have a secret eye on everyone. Just the few who seemed to promise they'd fit in the Free Bard ranks.

"There weren't any Free Bards in Nolton. The Gypsies, though, we have eyes and ears everywhere because we go everywhere. And since we're always meeting each other, we're always passing news, so what one knows, within months all know. We're a good way for the Free Bards to keep track of each other and of those who will fit in when they're ready." Gwyna showed her back to her own corner of the tent, which now held her bedroll and the huge cushions, her pack, as well as the instruments Talaysen had given her.

"Food first?" the girl asked. Rune nodded; now that her head and arm didn't hurt quite so much, she was actually hungry. Not terribly, which was probably the result of the medicine, but she wasn't nauseated anymore.

Gwyna brought her bread and cheese, and more of the doctored wine, while Erdric's grandson came and flung himself down on the cushions with the bonelessness of the very young and watched her as if he expected she might break apart at any moment. And as if he thought it might be very entertaining when she did.

She finished half the food before she finally got tired of the big dark eyes on her and returned him stare for stare. "Yes?" she said finally. "Is there something you wanted to ask me?"

"Did it hurt?" he asked, bright-eyed, as innocent and callous as only a child could be.

"Yes, it did," she told him. "A lot. I was very stupid, though nobody knew how stupid I was being. Don't ever put yourself in the position where someone can beat you. Run away if you can, but don't ever be as stupid as I was."

"All right," he said brightly. "I won't."

"Thank you for getting my things," she said, when it occurred to her that she hadn't thanked him herself. "I really appreciate it. There isn't anything special in my pack, but it's all I've got."

"You're welcome," he told her, serious and proper. Then, as if her politeness opened up a floodgate, the questions came pouring out. "Are you staying with the Free Bards? Are you partnering with Master Wren? Are you going to be his lover? He needs a lover. Robin says so all the time. Do you want to be his lover? Lots of girls want to be his lover, and he won't be. Do you like him? He likes you, I can tell."

"Sparrow!" Gwyna said sharply. "That's private! Do we discuss private matters without permission?"

"If she's with us, it isn't private, is it?" he retorted. "If she's a Free Bard she's part of the *romgerry* and it isn't private matters to talk about—"

"Yes it *is,*" Gwyna replied firmly. "Yes, she's staying, and yes, she's a Free Bard now, but the rest is private matters until Master Wren tells you different. You won't ask any more questions like that. Is that understood?"

For some reason that Rune didn't understand, Gwyna was blushing a brilliant scarlet. The boy seemed to sense he had pushed her as far as he dared. He jumped to his feet and scampered off. Gwyna averted her face until her blushes faded.

"What was that all about?" Rune asked, too surprised to be offended or embarrassed. After all, the boy meant no harm. She'd spent the night an arm's length away from Talaysen; it was perfectly natural for the child to start thinking in terms of other than "master and apprentice."

"We all worry about Master Wren," Gwyna said. "Some of us maybe worry a bit too much. Some of us think he spends too much time by himself, and well, there's always talk about how he ought to find someone who'd be good for him."

"And who is this 'Robin'?" she asked curiously.

"Me," Gwyna said, flushing again. "Gypsies don't like strangers knowing their real names, so we take names that anyone can use, names that say something about what our Craft is. A horse-tamer might be Roan, Tamer, or Cob, for instance. All musicians take bird-names, and the Free Bards have started doing the same, because it makes it harder for the Church and cities to keep track of us for taxes and tithes and— other things."

Yes, and I can imagine what those other things are. Trouble like I got myself into.

She turned a face back to Rune that might never have been flushed, once again the cheerful, careless girl she'd been a moment earlier. "Talaysen is Wren, Erdric is Owl, I'm Robin, Daran—that's the tall fellow that knew you—is Heron, Alain is Sparrow, Aysah is Nightingale. My cousin, the one who's making up your medicines, is Redbird. Reshan is Raven, you know him, too, the fellow who looks like a bandit. He's not here yet; we expect him in about a week." She tilted her head to one side, and surveyed Rune thoughtfully. "We need a name for you, although I think Wren tagged you with the one that will stick. Lark. Lady Lark."

Rune rolled the flavor of it around on her tongue, and decided she liked it. Not that she was likely to have much choice in the matter. . . . These folk tended to hit you like a wild wind, and like the wind, they took you where they wanted, without warning.

There's a song in that—

But she was not allowed to catch it; not yet. Erdric advanced across the tent-floor towards her, guitar in hand, and a look of determination on his face. She was a bit surprised at that; she hadn't thought there was anything anyone could want from her as badly as all that.

"My voice isn't what it was," Erdric said, as he sat down beside her. "It's going on the top and the bottom, and frankly, the best way I can coax money from listeners is with comedy. Now, I understand you have about a dozen comic songs that *no one else knows*. That's nothing short of a miracle, especially for me. You've no idea how hard it is to find comic songs."

"So the time's come to earn my bread, hmm?" she asked. He nodded.

"If you can't go out, you should share your songs with those that need them," Erdric replied. "I do a love song well enough, but I've no gift for satire. Besides, can you see a dried-up old stick like *me* a-singing a love ballad?" He snorted. "I'll give the love songs to you youngsters. You teach me your comedy. I promise you, I'll do justice to it."

"All right, that's only fair," she acknowledged. "Let's start with 'Two Fair Maids.'"

The Free Bards all came trickling back by ones and twos as the sun set, but only to eat and drink and rest a bit, and then they were off again. Mostly they didn't even stop to talk, although some of them did change into slightly richer clothing, and the dancers changed into much gaudier gear.

Erdric, his grandson, and Gwyna did quite a bit more than merely "watch the tent," she noticed. There was plain food and drink waiting for anyone who hadn't eaten at the Faire—though those were few, since it seemed a musician could usually coax at least a free meal out of a cook-tent owner by playing at his site. Still, there was fresh bread, cheese, and fresh raw vegetables waiting for any who needed it, and plenty of cold, clean water. And when darkness fell, it was Gwyna and Erdric who saw to it that the lanterns were lit, that there was a fire burning outside the tent entrance, and that torches were placed up the path leading to the Free Bard enclave to guide the wanderers home no matter how weary they might be.

Talaysen had not returned with the rest; he came in well after dark, and threw himself down on the cushions next to Rune with a sigh. He looked very tired, and just a trifle angry, though she couldn't think why that would be. Erdric brought him wine without his asking for it, and another dose of medicine for Rune, which she drank without thinking about it.

"A long day, Master Wren?" Erdric asked, sympathetically. "Anything we can do?"

"Very long," Talaysen replied. "Long enough that I shall go and steal the use of the bath before anyone else returns. And then, apprentice—" he cocked an eyebrow at Rune "—you'll teach me in that Ghost song." He drained half the mug in a single gulp. "There's been a lot of rumor around the Faire about the boy—or girl, the rumors differ—who won the trials yesterday, and yet has vanished quite out of ken. No one is talking, and no one is telling the truth." His expression grew just a little angrier. "The Guild judges presented the winners today, and they had their exhibition—and they all looked so damned smug I wanted to break *their* instruments over their heads. I intend the Guild to know you're with us and if they touch you, there'll be equal retribution.''

"Equal retribution?" Rune asked, swallowing a lump that had appeared in her throat when he'd mentioned broken instruments.

"When Master Wren came to us, the Guild didn't like it," Gwyna said, bringing Talaysen a slice of bread and cheese. " 'Twas at this very Faire that he first began to play with us in public. He wasn't calling himself Gwydain, but the Guildsmen knew him anyway. They set on him—they didn't break his arm, but they almost broke his head. We Gypsies went after every Guild Bard we caught alone the next day.''

Talaysen shook his head. "It was all I could do to keep them from setting on the Guildsmen with knives instead of fists.''

Erdric laughed, but it wasn't a laugh of humor. "If they'd hurt you more than bruises, you wouldn't have. They didn't dare walk the Faire without a guard—even when they wandered about in twos and threes, they're so soft 'twas no great task to beat them all black and blue. When we reckoned they'd gotten the point and when they started hiring great guards to go about with 'em, we left them alone. They haven't touched one of us since, any place there're Gypsies about.''

"But elsewhere?" Rune winced as her head throbbed. "Gypsies and Free Bards can't be everywhere.''

"Quite true, but I doubt that's occurred to them," Talaysen said. "At any rate"—he flicked a drop of water at her from his mug—"there. You're Rune no more. Rune is gone; Lark stands—or rather, sits—in her place. The quarrel the Bardic Guild has is with Rune, and I don't know anyone by that name.''

"As you say, Master," she replied, mock-meekly.

He saw through the seeming, and grinned. "I'm for a bath. Then the song; I'll see it sung all over the Faire tomorrow, and they'll know you're ours. When you come out with the rest of us in a week or two, they'll know better than to touch you.''

"Come out? In two weeks?" she exclaimed. "But my arm—"

"Hasn't hurt your voice any," Talaysen replied. "You can come with me and sing the female parts; teach me the rest of your songs, and I'll play while you sing." He fixed her with a fierce glare. "You're a Free Bard, aren't you?''

She nodded, slowly.

"Then you stand up to the Guild, to the Faire, to everyone; you stand up to them, and you let them know that *nothing* keeps a Free Bard from her music!'' He looked around at the rest of the Free Bards gathered in the tent; so did Rune, and she saw every head nodding in agreement.

"Yes, sir!'' she replied, with more bravery than she felt. She *was* afraid of the Guild; of the bullies that the Guild could hire, of the connection the Guild seemed to have with the Church. And the Church was everywhere. If the Church took a mind to get involved, no silly renaming would make her safe.

She hadn't been so shaken since Westhaven, when those boys had tried to rape her.

Talaysen seemed to sense her fear. He reached forward and took her good hand in his. "Believe in us, Lady Lark,'' he said, his voice trembling with intensity. "Believe in us—and believe in yourself. Together we can do anything, so long as we believe it. I *know*. Trust me.''

She looked into his green eyes, deep as the sea, and as restless, hiding as many things beneath their surface, and revealing some of them to her. There was passion there, that he probably didn't display very often. She found herself smiling, tremulously.

And nodded, because she couldn't speak.

He took that at face value; released her hand, and pulled himself up to his feet. "I'll be back,'' he said gravely, but with a twinkle. "And the apprentice had better be ready to teach when I return.'' He left the tent with a remarkably light step, and her eyes followed him.

When she pulled her eyes back to the rest, Rune didn't miss the significant glance that Erdric and Gwyna exchanged, but somehow she didn't resent it. Talaysen, though, might. She remembered all the questions that Sparrow had asked, and the tone of them, and decided to keep her observations to herself. It was more than enough that the greatest living Bard had taken her as his apprentice. Anything else would either happen or not happen.

A week later, it was Talaysen's turn to mind the tent, that duty shared by Rune's old friend Raven.

Raven had appeared the previous evening, to be greeted by all of his kin with loud and enthusiastic cries, and then underwent a series of kisses and backslapping greetings with each of the Free Bards.

Then he was brought to Rune's corner of the tent; she hadn't seen who had come in and had been dying of curiosity to see who it was. Raven was loudly pleased to see her, dismayed to see the fading marks of her beating, and angered by what had happened. It was all Talaysen and the others could do to keep him from charging out then and there, and beating up a few of the Guild Bards in retaliation. The judges in particular; he had the same notion as Talaysen, to break their instruments over *their* heads.

They managed to calm him, but after due thought, he judged that it was best he *not* go playing in the "streets" for a while, so he took his tent-duty early. He played mock-court to Rune, who blushed to think that she'd ever thought he might want to be her lover.

I didn't know anything *then,* she realized, as he bowed over her hand, but kept a sharp watch for Nightingale. She knew that once Nightingale appeared, he'd leave her side in a moment. She was not his type; not even in the Gypsy-garb she'd taken to wearing, finding skirts and loose blouses much more suited to handling one-handed than breeches and vests. All of his gallantry was in fun, and designed to keep her distracted and in good humor.

Oddly enough, Talaysen seemed to take Raven's mock-courtship seriously. He watched them with a faint frown on his face most of the morning. After lunch, he took the younger man aside and had a long talk with him. What they said, Rune had no idea, until Raven returned with a face full of suppressed merriment and his hands full of her lunch and her medicines.

"I've never in all me life had quite such a not-lecture," he whispered to her, when Talaysen had gone to see about something. "He takes being your Master right seriously, young Rune. I've just been warned that if I intend to break your heart by flirting with you, your Master there will be most unamused. He seems to think a broken heart would interfere more with your learning than yon broken arm. In fact, he offered to trade me a broken head for a broken heart."

Rune didn't know whether to gape or giggle; she finally did both. Talaysen found them both laughing, as Rune poked fun at Raven's gallantry, and Raven pretended to be crushed. Talaysen immediately relaxed.

But then he shooed Raven off and sat down beside her himself.

"It's time we had a real lesson," he said. "If you're going to insist I act like a Master, I'll give you a Master's lessoning." He then began a ruthless interrogation, having Rune go over every song she'd ever written. First he had her sing them until he'd picked them up, then he'd critique them, with more skill—and (which surprised her) he criticized them much harder even than Brother Pell had.

Of her comic songs, he said, "It's all very well to have a set of those for busking during the day, either in cities or at Faires, but there's more to music than parody, and you very well know it. If you're going to be a Bard, you have to live up to the title. You can't confine yourself to something as limited as one style; you can't even be *known* for just one style. You have to know all of them, and people must be aware that you're versed in all of them.''

Of ''Fiddler Girl,'' he approved of the tune, except that—''It's too limited. You need to expand your bridges into a whole new set of tunes. Make the listener feel what it was like to fiddle all night long, with Death waiting if you slipped! In fact, don't ever play it twice the same. Improvise! Match your fiddle-music to the crowd, play scraps of what you played then, so that they recognize you're recreating the experience, you're not just telling someone else's story.''

And of the lyrics, he was a little kinder, but he felt that they were too difficult to sing for most people. ''You and I and most of the Free Bards can manage them—*if* we're sober, *if* we aren't having a tongue-tied day— but what about the poor busker in the street? They look as if you just wrote them down with no notion of how hard they'd be to sing.''

When she admitted that was exactly what she'd done, he shook his head at her. ''At least *recite* them first. Nothing's ever carved in stone, Rune. Be willing to change.''

The rest of her serious songs he dismissed as being ''good for filling in between difficult numbers. Easy songs with ordinary lyrics.'' Those were the ones she'd composed according to Brother Pell's rules for his class, and while it hurt a bit to have them dismissed as ''ordinary,'' it didn't hurt as much as it might have. She'd chafed more than a bit at those rules; to have the things she'd done right out of her head given *some* praise, and the ones she'd done according to the ''rules'' called ''common'' wasn't so bad. . . .

Or at least, it wasn't as bad as it could have been.

Then he set her a task: write him a song, something about elves. ''They're always popular,'' he said. ''Try something—where a ruler makes a bargain with an elf, then breaks it. Make the retribution something original. No thunder and lightning, being turned into a toad, or dragged off to hell. None of that nonsense; it's trite.''

She nodded, and set to it as soon as he left. But she could see that he had not lied to her. He was not going to be an easy Master.

Talaysen left his instruments in the tent, and walked off into the Faire with nothing about him to identify who or what he was. He preferred to leave it that way, given that he was going to visit the cathedral—and that the Bardic Guild tent was pitched right up against the cathedral walls. Of course, there was always the chance that one of his old colleagues would recognize him, but now, at night, that chance was vanishingly slim. *They* would all be entertaining the high and the wealthy—

either their own masters, or someone who had hired them for the night. The few that weren't would be huddled together in self-satisfied smugness—though perhaps that attitude might be marred a little, since he'd begun singing "Fiddler Girl" about the Faire. The real story of the contest was spreading, through the medium of the Free Bards and the gypsies. In another couple of weeks it should be safe enough for Rune to show her face at *this* Faire.

He was worried about his young charge, though, because *she* troubled him. So he was going to talk with an old friend, one who had known him for most of his life, to see if she could help him to sort his thoughts out.

He skirted the bounds of the Guild tent carefully, even though a confrontation was unlikely. His bones were much older than the last time he'd been beaten, and they didn't heal as quickly anymore. But the tent was dark; no one holding revels in there, not at the moment. Just as well, really.

He sought out a special gate in the cathedral wall, and opened it with a key he took from his belt-pouch, locking the gate behind him again once he'd entered. The well-oiled mechanism made hardly a sound, but something alerted the guardian of that gate, who came out of the building to see who had entered the little odd-shaped courtyard.

"I'd like to see Lady Ardis," Talaysen told the black-clad guard, who nodded soberly, but said nothing. "Could you see if she is available to a visitor?"

The guard turned and left, still without a word; Talaysen waited patiently in the tiny courtyard, thinking that a musician has many opportunities to learn patience in a lifetime. *It seems as if I am always waiting for something. . . .*

This was, at least, a pleasant place to wait. Unlike the courtyards of most Church buildings, this one, though paved, boasted greenery in the form of plants spilling from tiers of wooden boxes, and trees growing from huge ceramic pots. Lanterns hanging from the wall of the cloister provided soft yellow light. Against the wall of the courtyard, a tiny waterfall trickled down a set of stacked rocks, providing a breath of moisture and the restful sounds of falling water.

At least, it did when the Faire wasn't camped on the other side of the wall. Music, crowd-noise, and laughter spilled over the walls, ruffling the serenity of the place.

He caught movement out of the corner of his eye, and turned. A tall, scarlet-clad woman whose close-cropped blond hair held about the same amount of gray as his, held out her hands to him. "Gwydain!" she exclaimed. "I wondered when you'd get around to visiting me!"

He strode towards her, and clasped both her hands in his. "I was busy, and so were you, my dear cousin. I truly intended to pay my respects when the trials were over. Then my latest little songbird got herself into a brawl with the Guild, and I had to extract her from the mess my lack of foresight put her in."

"Her?" One winglike brow rose sharply, and Ardis showed her interest. "I heard something of that. Was she badly hurt?"

"Bruised all over, and a broken arm—" he began.

"Which is disaster for a musician," she completed. "Can you bring her here? I can certainly treat her. That *is* what you wanted, isn't it?"

"Well, yes," he admitted, with a smile. "If that won't bring you any problems."

She sniffed disdainfully. "The Church treats its Justiciars well. It treats its mages even better. Rank does bring privileges; if I wish to treat a ragtag street-singer's broken arm, no one will nay-say me. But there will be a price—" she continued, taking her hand away from his, and holding up a single finger in warning.

"Name it," Talaysen replied with relief. With the mage-healing Lady Ardis could work, Rune's arm would be healed in half the time it would normally take; well enough, certainly, to permit her to play by the end of the Faire. More importantly, well enough so that when he and she went on the road together, it wouldn't cause her problems.

"You shouldn't be so quick to answer my demands," the lady replied, but with a serious look instead of the smile Talaysen expected. "This could be dangerous."

"So?" He shrugged. "I won't belittle your perception of danger, and I won't pretend to be a hero, but if I'd been afraid of a little danger, I would still be with the Guild."

"So you would." She studied his face for a moment. "There's a dark-mage among the Brotherhood, and I don't know who it is. I only know it's a 'he,' since there are only two female mages, and I know it isn't a Justiciar."

Talaysen whistled between his teeth in surprise and consternation. "That's not welcome news. What is it you want me to do?"

She freed her other hand, and walked slowly over to one of the planters, rubbing her wrists as she walked. He followed, and she turned abruptly. "It isn't quite true that I don't know who it is. I have a guess. And if my guess is correct, he'll take advantage of the general licentiousness of the Faire to sate some of his desires. What I want is for *you* to watch and wait, and see if there are rumors of a Priest gone bad, one who uses methods outside the ordinary to enforce his will."

Talaysen nodded, slowly. "It's true that a Bard hears everything—"

She laughed, shortly. "And everyone tells a Bard everything they know. A Free Bard, anyway. If you hear anything, bring it to me. If you can somehow contrive to bring him *before* me in my official capacity, that would be even better. I can be certain that the other two Justiciars with me would be mages and uncorrupted."

"I'll try," he promised, and gestured for her to seat herself. She took the invitation, and perched on a bench between two pots of fragrant honeysuckle.

"So, what else do you need of me, cousin?" she asked, a look of shrewd speculation creeping over her even features. "It has to do with this little songster, doesn't it?"

"Not so little," he replied, with a bit of embarrassment. "She's quite old enough to be wedded with children, by country standards. She's very attractive, Ardis. And that's the problem. I promised to give her a Master's teaching to an apprentice, and I find her very attractive."

"So?" A lifted shoulder told him Ardis didn't think that was much of a problem.

"So that's not *ethical*, dammit!" he snapped. "This girl is my student; if I took advantage of that situation, I'd be—dishonorable. And besides, I'm twice her age, easily."

Ardis shook her head. "I can't advise you, Gwydain. I agree with you that pushing yourself on the girl would not be ethical, but what if she's attracted to you? If she's as old as you say, she's old enough to know her own mind."

"It's still not ethical," he replied stubbornly. "And I'm still twice her age."

"Very well," she sighed. "If it isn't ethical, then be the same noble sufferer you've always been and keep your attraction hidden behind a mask of fatherly regard. If you keep pushing her away, likely she'll grow tired of trying and take her affections elsewhere. The young are very short of patience for the most part." She stood, and smoothed down the skirt of her robes with her hand. "The fact that you're twice her age doesn't signify; you know very well I was betrothed to a man *three* times my age at twelve, and if my father hadn't found it more convenient to send me to the Church, I'd likely be married to him now."

He tightened his jaw; her light tone told him she was mocking him, and that wasn't the answer he'd wanted to hear, either. She wasn't providing him with an answer.

"I'm not going to give you an answer, Gwydain," she said, echoing his very thought, in that uncanny way she had. "I'm not going to give you an excuse to do something stupid again. How someone as clever as you are can be so dense when it comes to matters of the heart—''

She pursed her lips in exasperation. "Never mind. Bring your little bird here tomorrow afternoon; I'll heal up her arm for you. After that, what you do with each other is up to you."

He bowed over her hand, since the audience was obviously at an end, and took a polite leave of her—

He sensed that she was amused with him, and it rankled—but he also sensed that part of her tormenting him was on account of her little problem.

Little! he thought, locking the gate behind him and setting off back through the Faire. *A dark-mage in the Kingsford Brotherhood—that's not such a little thing. What is it about the Church that it spawns both the saint and the devil?*

Then he shrugged. It wasn't that the Church spawned either; it was that the Church held both, and permitted both to run free unless and until they were reined in by another hand. To his mind, the venial were the more numerous, but then, he had been a cynic for many years now.

One of his problems was solved, at least. Rune would be cared for. If one of the Gypsies like Nighthawk had been available, he'd have sent the girl to her rather than subject her to his cousin and her acidic wit, but none of those with the healing touch had put in an appearance yet, and he dared not wait much longer.

He had hoped that Ardis would confirm his own assertions; that the child was *much* too young, and that he had no business being attracted to her. Instead she'd implied that he was being over-sensitive.

Still one of the things she'd said had merit. If he continued acting in a fatherly manner, she would never guess how he felt, and in the way of the young, would turn to someone more suitable. Young Heron, for instance, or Swift.

He clamped a firm lid down on the uneasy feelings of—was it jealousy?—that thought caused. Better, much better, to suffer a little and save both of them no end of grief.

Yes, he told himself with determination, as he wound through the press of people around a dancers' tent. *Much, much better.*

Rune hardly knew what to say when Talaysen ordered her to her feet the next afternoon—she had been feeling rather sick, and had a pounding head, and she suspected it was from too much of the medicine she'd been taking. But if she *didn't* take it, she was still sick with pain, her head still ached, and so did her arm. She simply couldn't win.

"Master Wren," she pleaded, when he held out his hand to help her to her feet, "I really don't feel well—I—"

"That's precisely why I want you to come with me," he replied, with a brisk nod. "I want someone else to have a look at your arm and head. Come along now; it isn't far."

She gave in with a sigh; she was *not* up to the heat and the jostling crowds, even if most of the fairgoers would be at the trials-concert this afternoon. But Talaysen looked determined, and she had the sinking feeling that even if she protested that she couldn't walk, he'd conjure a dog cart or something to carry her.

She got clumsily to her feet and followed him out of the tent and down to the Faire. The sun beat down on her head like a hammer on an anvil, making her eyes water and her ears ring. She was paying so much attention to where she was putting her feet that she had no idea where he was leading her.

No idea until he stopped and she looked up, to find herself pinned between the Guild tent and the wall of the Kingsford Cathedral Cloister.

She froze in terror as he unlocked the door in the wall there; she would have bolted if he hadn't reached for her good hand and drawn her inside before she could do anything.

Her heart pounded with panic, and she looked around at the potted greenery, expecting it to sprout guards at any moment. This was it: the Church had found her out, and they were going—

"We're not going to do anything to you, child," said a scarlet-robed woman who stepped out from behind a trellis laden with rosevines. She had a cap of pale blond hair cut like any Priest's, candid gray eyes, and a pointed face that reminded her sharply of someone—

Then Talaysen turned around, and the familial resemblance was obvious. She relaxed a little. Not much, but a little.

"Rune, this is my cousin, Ardis. Ardis, this is the young lady who was too talented for her own good." Talaysen smiled, and Rune relaxed a little more.

Ardis tilted her head to one side, and her pale lips stretched in an amused smile. "So I see. Well, come here, Rune. I don't bite—or rather, I don't bite people who don't deserve to be bitten."

Rune ventured nearer, and Ardis waved at her to take a seat on a bench. The Priest—for so she must be, although Rune had never seen a scarlet-robed Priest before—seated herself on the same bench, as Talaysen stood beside them both. She glanced at him anxiously, and he gave her a wink of encouragement.

"I might as well be brief," Ardis said, after a moment of studying

Rune's face. "I suppose you've heard rumors of Priests who also practice magic on behalf of the Church?"

She nodded, reluctantly, unsure what this had to do with her.

"The rumors are true, child," Ardis said, watching her face closely. "I'm one of them."

Rune's initial reaction was alarm—but simple logic calmed her before she did anything stupid. She trusted Talaysen; *he* trusted his cousin. There must be a reason for this revelation.

She waited for Ardis to reveal it.

"I have healing-spells," the Priest continued calmly, "and my cousin asked me to exercise one of them on your behalf. I agreed. But I cannot place the spell upon you without your consent. It wouldn't be ethical."

She smiled at Talaysen as she said that, a smile with just a hint of a sting in it. He chuckled and shook his head, but said nothing.

"Will it hurt?" Rune asked, the only thing she could think of to ask.

"A little," Ardis admitted. "But after a moment or two you'll begin feeling much better."

"Fine—I mean, please, I'd like you to do it, then," Rune stammered, a little confused by the Priest's clear, direct gaze. She sensed it would be difficult, if not impossible, to hide anything from this woman. "It can't hurt much worse than my head does right now."

The Priest's eyes widened for a moment, and she glanced up at Talaysen. "Belladonna?" she asked sharply. He nodded. "Then it's just as well you brought her here today. It's not good to take that for more than three days running."

"I didn't take any today," Rune said, plaintively. "I woke up with a horrid headache and sick, and it felt as if the medicine had something to do with the way I felt."

The Priest nodded. "Wise child. Wiser than some who are your elders. Now, hold still for a moment, think of a cloudless sky, and try not to move."

Obediently, Rune did as she was told, closing her eyes to concentrate better.

She felt the Priest lay her hand gently on the broken arm. Then there was a sudden, sharp pain, exactly like the moment when Erdric straightened the break. She bit back a cry—then slumped with relief, for the pain in both her head and her arm were gone!

No—not gone after all, but dulled to distant ghosts of what they had been. And best of all, she was no longer nauseous. She sighed in gratitude and opened her eyes, smiling into Ardis' intent face.

"You fixed it!" she said. "It hardly hurts at all, it's wonderful! How can I ever thank you?"

Ardis smiled lazily, and flexed her fingers. "My cousin has thanked me adequately already, child. Think of it as the Church's way of repairing the damage the Bardic Guild did."

"But—" Rune protested. Ardis waved her to silence.

"It was no trouble, dear," the Priest said, rising. "The bone-healing spells are something I rarely get to use; I'm grateful for the practice. You can take the splint off in about four weeks; that should give things sufficient time to mend."

She gave Talaysen a significant look of some kind; one that Rune couldn't read. He flushed just a little, though, as she bade him a decorous enough farewell and he turned to lead Rune out the tiny gate.

He seemed a little ill-at-ease, though she couldn't imagine why. To fill the silence between them, she asked the first thing that came into her head.

"Do all Priest-mages wear red robes?" she said. "I'd never seen that color before on a Priest."

He turned to her gratefully, and smiled. "No, actually, there's no one color for the mages. You can find them among any of the Church Brotherhoods. Red is the Justiciar's color—there *do* seem to be more mages among the Justiciars than any other Brotherhood, but that is probably coincidence."

He continued on about the various Brotherhoods in the Church, but she wasn't really listening. She had just realized as she looked at him out of the corner of her eye, what an extraordinarily handsome man he was. She hadn't thought of that until she'd seen his cousin, and noticed how striking *she* was.

How odd that she hadn't noticed it before.

. . . possibly because he was acting as if he was my father. . . .

Well, never mind. There was time enough to sort out how things were going to be between them. Maybe he was just acting oddly because of all the people around him; as the founder of the Free Bards he must feel as if there were eyes on him all the time—and rightly, given Sparrow's chattering questions the other day.

But once the Faire was over and the Free Bards dispersed, there would be no one watching them to see what they did. Then, maybe, he would relax.

And once he did, well—

Her lips curved in a smile that was totally unconscious. And Talaysen chattered on, oblivious to her thoughts.

CHAPTER FIFTEEN

Rune caught a hint of movement in the crowd out of the corner of her eye. She kept singing, but she thought she recognized the bright red skirt and bodice, and the low-cut blouse the color of autumn leaves. . . .

A second glance told her she was right. It was Gwyna, all right, and dressed to be as troublesome as she could to male urges and Church sensibilities. Tiny as she was, she had to elbow her way to the front of the crowd so Rune could see her, and by the look in her eyes, she knew she was causing mischief.

Her abundant black hair was held out of her eyes by a scarf of scarlet tied as a head-band over her forehead; beneath it, huge brown eyes glinted with laughter. There was no law against showing—and none against looking—and she always dressed to catch the maximum number of masculine attentions. She garnered a goodly share of appreciative glances as she sauntered among the fairgoers, from men both high and lowly born. She preened beneath the admiration like the bright bird she so strongly resembled.

Rune and Talaysen were singing "Fiddler Girl," though without the fiddle; Rune's arm was only just out of its sling, and she wasn't doing anything terribly difficult with it yet. Instead, she was singing her own part, and Talaysen was singing the Ghost, and making it fair blood-chilling, too. Even Gwyna shivered visibly, listening to them, and she'd heard it so many times she probably could reproduce every note of it herself in *both* their styles.

They finished to a deafening round of applause, and copper and silver showered into the hat set in front of them. As Gwyna wormed her way to the center of the crowd, Rune caught sight of another of the brotherhood just coming along the street—Daran, called "Heron." Tall, gangling, and bony, he was easy to spot, as he towered a good head above the rest of the crowd. He looked nothing like a musician, but he was second only to Talaysen in the mastery of guitar, and that daft-looking, vacuous face with empty blue eyes hid one of the cleverest satiric minds in their company. His voice was a surprising tenor, silver to Talaysen's gold.

And no sooner had Rune spotted him than she recalled a bit of wickedness the four of them had devised when she had first joined them out on the streets of the Faire, and her broken arm had prevented her from playing.

She whistled a snatch of the song—"My Lover's Eyes" it was, and as sickening and sticky-sweet a piece of doggerel as ever a Guild Bard could produce. She saw Talaysen's head snap up at the notes, saw his green eyes sparkle with merriment. He nodded, a grin wrapping itself around his head, then nodded at Gwyna to come join them. Daran had caught the whistle, too—he craned his absurdly long neck all about, blond forelock flopping into his eyes as usual, then sighted her and whistled back. That was all it took; while the crowd was still making up its collective mind about moving on, Gwyna and Daran edged in to take their places beside Talaysen and Rune, and the song was begun.

They sang it acappella, but all four of them had voices more than strong enough to carry over the crowd noise, and the harmony they formed—though they hadn't sung it since the fourth week of the Faire—was sweet and pure, and recaptured the fickle crowd's attention. The first verse of the ditty extolled the virtues of the singer's beloved, and the faithfulness of the singer-lover—Gwyna held Daran's hands clasped chin-high, and stared passionately into his eyes, as Rune and Talaysen echoed their pose.

So far, a normal sort of presentation, if more than a bit melodramatic. Ah—but the second verse was coming; and after all those promises of eternal fidelity, the partners suddenly dropped the hands they held and caught those of a new partner, and without missing a beat, sang the second verse just as passionately to a *new* "beloved."

Chuckles threaded the crowd. The audience waited expectantly for the next verse to see what the Bards would do.

They lowered their clasped hands, turning their heads away from their partners, as if in an agony of moon-struck shyness. At the end of the third verse, they dropped hands again, rolled their eyes heavenward as each lifted right hand to brow and the left to bosom, changed pose again (still without looking) and groped once again for the hands of the "beloved"—

Except that this time Talaysen got Daran's hands, and Gwyna got Rune's.

The crowd's chuckles turned into an appreciative roar of laughter when they turned their heads back to discover just whose hands they were clutching, and jumped back, pulling away as if they'd been burned.

The laughter all but drowned out the last notes of the song, sung to the eyes of their original partners.

As more coinage showered into the hat, one among the crowd turned away with a smothered oath, and a look of hatred. He wore the purple and gold ribbons of a Guild Bard.

"Well, here, my children—" Talaysen bent to catch up the laden hat. "Share and share alike. Feed your bodies that your voices not suffer; buy fairings to call the eyes of an audience, or other things—"

He poured a generous measure of the coinage into each of their hands. "Now off with you! We'll meet as usual, just at sundown, at the tent for dinner."

Gwyna slipped the money into her belt-pouch, and dropped Talaysen a mock-curtsy. "As you say, Master mine. Elsewhere, Tree-man, Master Heron, I'm minded to sing solos for a bit." Daran grinned and took himself off as ordered.

Rune noticed that his eyes had been following Gwyna for some time, and she reflected that *he* would be no bad company for the cheerful Gypsy. Gwyna had confided a great deal to Rune over the past few weeks; they'd become very good friends. Gwyna had said that she tended to take up with either Bards or Gypsies, but that she hadn't had a lover from amongst the Free Bards in four years.

Maybe she was thinking about it now.

As Gwyna strolled away, it seemed her thoughts were tending in that direction, for she pulled her guitar around in front of her and began a love song. Rune exchanged a glance full of irony with Talaysen, and they began her elf-ballad.

Gwyna didn't mind too carefully where she was wandering, until she noted that her steps had taken her away from the well-traveled ways and into the rows reserved for the finer goods. Here she was distinctly out of place, and besides, there were fewer fairgoers, and less of a chance for an audience. She turned to retrace her steps, only to find her path blocked.

He who blocked it was a darkly handsome man, as looks are commonly judged—but his gray eyes had a cruel glint to them that Gwyna did not in the least like, the smile on his thin, hard lips was a prurient one, and he wore the robes of a Church Priest. But they were winedark, and she thought she could see odd symbols woven into the hem of the robe, symbols which she found even less to her liking than the glint in his eyes.

"Your pardon, m'lord—" She made as if to step around him, but he moved like quicksilver, getting in front of her again.

"Stay, bright songbird—" He spoke softly, his voice pitched soft and low so as to sound enticing. "A word in your ear, if I may."

"I cannot prevent you, m'lord," Gwyna replied, becoming more uneasy by the heartbeat.

"You have no patron, else you would not be singing to the crowd— and I think you have, at present, no—'friend'—either." His knowing look gave another meaning entirely to the word "friend"; a prurient, lascivious meaning. "I offer myself in both capacities. I think we understand each other."

Although Gwyna was long past innocence, the blood rose to her cheeks in response to his words, and the evil, lascivious leer that lay thinly veiled behind them. Just listening to him made her feel used; and that made her angry as well as a little frightened.

"That I think we do *not,* 'my lord,' " she retorted, putting a good sharp sting in her reply. "Firstly, you are a Priest of the Church, and sworn to celibacy. If *you* will take no care for your vows, then I will! Secondly, I am a Free Bard, and I earn my way by song—naught else. I go where I will, I earn my way by *music,* and I do not sell myself to such as *you* for your caging. So you may take your 'patronage' and offer it among the dealers in swine and sheep—for I'm sure that *there* you'll find bedmates to your liking in plenty!"

She pushed rudely past him, her flesh shrinking from the touch of his robes, and stalked off with her head held high and proud. She prayed that he could not tell by her carriage how much she longed to take to her heels and run.

She prayed that he wouldn't follow her; it seemed her prayers were answered, for she lost sight of him immediately. And as soon as he was out of sight, she forgot him.

The Priest clenched his jaw in rage, and his saturnine face contorted with anger for one brief instant before settling into a mask of indifference. It was only a moment, but it was long enough for one other to see.

A plump, balding man, oily with good living, and wearing the gold and purple ribbons of a Guild Bard, stepped out from the shelter of a nearby awning and approached the dark-robed cleric.

"If you will forgive my impertinence, my lord," he began, "I cannot help but think we have an interest in common. . . ."

". . . so I told him to look for bedmates among the flocks," Gwyna finished, while Daran and Rune chuckled appreciatively. She took a hearty bite of her bread and cheese—no one among the brotherhood had had extraordinary good luck, so the fare was plain tonight—and grinned back at them. Neither Erdric nor Talaysen looked at all amused, however—Erdric was as sober as a stone, and Talaysen's green eyes were darkened with worry.

"That may not have been wise, Gypsy Robin," he said, sipping his well-watered wine. "It isn't wise to anger a Priest, and I would guess from your description that he is not among the lesser of his brethren. Granted, if you called him up before the justices this week, and you had witnesses, you could prove he meant to violate his vows—but even so, he is still powerful, and that is the worst sort of enemy to have made."

"So long as I stay within the Faire precincts, what can he do?" Gwyna countered, nettled at Talaysen's implied criticism of her behavior. "I *do* have witnesses if I care to call them, and if he dares to lay a hand on me—"

Her feral grin and a hand to the knife concealed in her skirts told the fate he could expect. Gwyna needed no man to guard *her* "honor"— such as it was.

"All right, Robin, I am rebuked. No one puts a tie on you, least of all me. Where away tonight?"

"A party—a most decorous party. Virtue, I tell you, will be my watchword this eve. I am pledged to play and sing for the name-day feast of the daughter of the jewel-smith Marek, she being a ripe twelve on this night. I am to sing nothing but the most innocent of songs and tales, and the festivities will be over before midnight. I will be there and back again in my bed before the night is half spent."

She drooped her eyelids significantly at Daran, who looked first surprised, then pleased. Talaysen bit his lip to keep from chuckling; he knew that tacit invitation. Gwyna would not be spending the last nights of the Faire alone.

"Then may the Lady see to it that the jewel-smith Marek rewards you and your songs with their true value. As for the rest of us—the Faire awaits! And we grow no richer dallying here."

They finished the last bites of their dinners, and rose from their cushions nearly as one, each to seek an audience.

Gwyna's pouch was the heavier by three pieces of gold, and she was wearing it inside her skirts for safety, as she made her way down the aisle of closed and darkened stalls. One gold piece would go to Erdric, with instructions to purchase a roast pig and wine for the company, and keep the remainder for himself. The other two would go to Goldsmith Nosta in the morning, to be put with her other savings. Gwyna firmly believed in securing high ground against rainy days.

With her mind on these matters, she did not see the dark shadow that followed her, mingling with the other shadows cast by the moon. Her sharp ears might have warned her of danger, but there were no footfalls for her to hear. There was only a sudden wind of ice and fear that blew upon her from behind, and hard upon that, the darkness of oblivion.

She woke with an aching head, her vision blurred and oddly distorted, her sense of smell gone, to find herself looking out through the bars of a black iron cage. She scrambled to her feet with a frightened squawk, and a flurry of wings, shaking so hard with a sudden onset of terror that every feather trembled.

Feathers? *Wings?*

A dun-colored hanging in front of her moved; from behind it emerged the dark, bearded Priest she had so foolishly insulted. Beside him was a fat little man in Guild purple and gold. She had heard of Priests who practiced magic; now she knew the rumors to be true.

"And the foolish little bird takes the baited grain. Not so clever now, are we?" the Guild Bard chortled. "Marek's invitation was his own, but two of those gold pieces you so greedily bore away were mine, with m'lord Revaner's spell upon them."

"Is the vengeance sweet enough, Bestif?" The Priest's deep voice was full of amusement.

"It will be in a moment, m'lord." Bestif bent down so that his face filled Gwyna's field of vision. She shrunk back away from him, until the bars of the cage prevented her going farther. "You, my fine *feathered* friend, are now truly feathered indeed, and you will remain so. Look at yourself! Bird-brained you were, to make a mock of my masterpiece, and bird you have truly become, the property of m'lord, to sing at his will. You would not serve him freely, so now you shall find yourself serving from within one of those cages you have so despised, and whether you will or no."

"And do not think, little songbird, that you may ever fly away," the Priest continued, his eyes shining with cheerful sadism. "Magic must obey laws; you wear the semblance of a bird, but your weight is that of the woman you were, as is your approximate size. Your wings could never carry you to freedom, attractive though they may be."

Gwyna stretched out one arm—no, wing—involuntarily; her head swiveled on a long neck to regard it with mournful eyes. Indeed, it was quite brilliantly beautiful, and if the rest of her matched the graceful plumage, she must be the most striking and exotic "bird" ever seen. The colors of her garb, the golds and reds and warm oranges, were faithfully preserved in her feathers—transformed from clothing to plumes, she supposed despairingly. Circling one leg was a heavy gold ring—which could only be the gold pieces that had been the instrument of her downfall, cunningly transmuted.

Black, bleak despair filled her heart, for how ever would any of her friends guess what had become of her? Had she been woman still, she would have sunk to the floor of her cage and wept in hopelessness—

Here the most cruel jest of all was played on her. Her neck stretched out, her beak opened involuntarily, and glorious liquid song poured forth.

Her amazement broke the despair for a moment, and the music ceased to come from her. The Priest read her surprise correctly, and smiled a predatory smile.

"Did we not say you would serve me, whether you would or no? I was not minded to have a captive that drooped all day on her perch. No, the spell binding you is thus; the unhappier you are, the more you will sing. Well, Bard, are you satisfied?"

"Very, my lord. Very."

The Priest clapped his hands, summoning two hulking attendants in black uniform tunics. These hoisted her cage upon their shoulders, and carried her outside the tent, where the cage was fastened to a chain and hoisted to the top of a stout iron pole.

"Now all the Faire shall admire my treasure, and envy my possessing it," the Priest taunted her from below, "while you shall look upon the freedom of your former friends—and sing for my pleasure."

As dawn began to color the tips of the tents and roofs of the Faire, Gwyna beat with utter futility on the bars of her cage with her wings, while glorious music fell on the tents below her in the place of her tears.

By midmorning there was a crowd of curiosity-seekers below her cage, and Gwyna had ceased her useless attempts at escape. Now she simply sat, eyes half-closed in despair, and sang. She had learned that while she could not halt the flow of music from her beak, she could direct it; to the wonderment of the onlookers, she was singing every lament and dirge she could remember.

Once she saw Daran below her, and her voice shook with hopelessness. She was singing Talaysen's "Walls of Iron" at the time; it seemed appropriate. Daran stared at her intently as she sang it with the special interludes she had always played on her guitar. She longed to be able to speak, even to throw a fit of some kind to attract his attention, but the spell holding her would not allow that. She thought her heart would break into seven pieces when he walked away at the end of the song.

The Priest had her cage brought down at sunset and installed on a special stand in his tent. She was scrupulously fed the freshest of fruit, and the water in her little cup was renewed. Despite the warnings that she could not fly away, she watched avidly for an opportunity to escape, but the cage was cleaned and the provisioning made without the door ever being opened. Revaner evidently had planned a dinner party; he greeted visitors, placing them at a table well within clear sight of her cage. When all were assembled, he lit branching candles with a wave of his hand, the golden light falling clearly upon her. The guests sighed in wonder—her spirits sank to their lowest ebb—she opened her beak and sang and her music was at its most lovely. The celebrants congratulated the Priest on his latest acquisition. He preened visibly, casting a malicious glance from time to time back at the cage where Gwyna drooped on her perch. It was unbearable, yet she had no choice but to bear it. Torture of the body would have been far, far preferable to this utter misery of the spirit.

At last the long, bitter day was over. A cover was placed over her cage; in the darkness, bird-instincts took over entirely, and despite sorrow and despair, Gwyna slept.

Talaysen questioned everyone who knew the Free Bards, and especially those who knew Gwyna herself. Always the answer was "no." No one had seen her since the previous day; the last to see her was Marek, and she had left his tent well within the time she had promised to return.

It was bad enough that she had not appeared last night, but as the day wore on, it became more and more obvious that she wasn't just dallying with a new, chance-met lover. She was *missing*. And since it was Robin, who truly could defend herself, that could only mean foul play.

As Talaysen searched the Faire for some sign of her, he could only think about the incident she had reported the previous evening. The Priest who had approached her—he wasn't one that Talaysen knew, which meant he wasn't one of the Priests attached to Kingsford.

He ran a hand through his hair, distractedly, and another thought occurred to him—one which he did not in the least like. Ardis had asked him to be on the watch for a Priest who might violate his vows to please his own desires—a Priest who would use extraordinary means to get what he wanted.

Could this Priest and the one that threatened Gwyna be the same?

Given that she had quite vanished from the Faire, it was not only possible, it seemed likely. Ardis had said that she didn't know the exact identity of this Priest, which meant he wasn't one she ordinarily worked with as a mage. So he would be new to Kingsford, and probably camped in the Priests' tents with the other visiting clerics. If he had Gwyna, in any form of captivity, he would keep her there. He wouldn't dare bring her into the cloisters, not with Ardis on the watch for him.

Talaysen made up his mind, called his Free Bards together, and passed the word. *Look for anything that reminds you of Gwyna, anything at all. And look for it especially among the Priests' tents.*

The next day was like the first, save only that she was left outside the tent when the sun set. Evidently since he had no reason to display her, the Priest saw no reason to bring her inside. Or perhaps this was but another sadism on his part—for now she was witness to the Faire's night life, with its emphasis on entertainments. The cage was lowered, cleaned and stocked, then raised again. Gwyna watched the lights of the Faire appear, watched the strollers wander freely about, and sang until she was too weary to chirp another note.

She was far too worn to notice that someone had come to stand in the shadows below her, until the sound of a whisper carried up to her perch.

"Gwyna? Bird, are you Gwyna?"

She fluttered her wings in agitation, unable to answer, except for strangled squawks.

A second voice whispered to the first: "Daran, this seems very far-fetched to me—"

"Rune, I tell you it's Gwyna! *Nobody* performs 'Walls of Iron' the way she does—but this bird replicated every damn note! *Gwyna! Answer me!*"

As a cloud of helplessness descended on her and her beak began to open to pour forth melody, she suddenly shook as an idea occurred to her. No, she couldn't talk, but she could most assuredly *sing*!

She sang the chorus of "Elven Captive"—

A spell-bound captive here am I
Who will not live and cannot die.

A bitten-off exclamation greeted the song. Rune gasped. "Wait, that's—"

Daran interrupted her. " 'Elven Captive'! No bird would pick that chorus just at this moment! It *is* Gwyna! Gypsy Robin, who did this to you?"

For answer Gwyna sang the first notes of "My Lover's Eyes" and the chorus of "The Scurvy Priest," a little ditty that was rarely, if ever, heard in Faires, but often in taverns of a particular clientele.

"Bestif and a Priest, probably the one she told us about. Oh hellfire, this is too deep for us to handle," Daran mumbled in a discouraged voice.

"Don't *ever* underestimate Talaysen, cloud-scraper." Rune sounded a bit more hopeful. "He's got resources you wouldn't guess—Gwyna, don't give up! We're going to leave you, but only to let Talaysen know what's happened. We'll be back, and with help! We'll get you back to us somehow, I swear it!"

There was a brief pattering of footsteps, and the space below her was empty again.

But the hope in her heart was company enough that night.

When dawn came, she looked long and hopefully for a sight of her friends among the swirling crowds, but there was no sign of them. As the day wore on, she lost hope again, and her songs rang out to the satisfaction of the Priest. When no one had appeared by sunset, the last of her hopes died. Talaysen must have decided that the idea of her transformation was too preposterous to consider—or that they simply were powerless to help her. She was so sunk in sadness that she did not notice the troupe of acrobats slowly making their way towards the Priest's dun-colored tent, tumbling and performing tricks as they came.

She only heard their noise and outcries when they actually formed up in the cleared space just in front of the tent and beneath her cage. Much to the displeasure of the Priest's chief servant, they began their routine right there, with a series of tumbles that ended with the formation of a human pyramid.

"Ho there—be off with you—away—!"

The major-domo was one to their many, and they simply ignored him, continuing with their act, much to the delight of the children that had followed them here. The pyramid collapsed into half-a-dozen somersaulting bodies, and the air and ground seemed full lithe, laughing human balls. The major-domo flapped his hands at them ineffectually as Gwyna watched, her unhappiness momentarily forgotten in the pleasure of seeing one of her captors discomfited.

This continued for several moments, until at last the Priest himself emerged to demand why his rest was being disturbed.

"Now!" cried a cloaked nonentity at the edge of the crowd—and Gwyna recognized Talaysen's voice with a start.

Everything seemed to happen at once—two of the acrobats flung a blanket over the Priest's head, enveloping him in its folds and effectively smothering his outcries. The rest jumped upon each other's shoulders, forming a tower of three men and a boy; the boy produced a lock-pick, and swiftly popped open the lock on Gwyna's cage. The door swung wide—

"Jump, Gwyna!" Talaysen and Daran held a second blanket stretched taut between them. She didn't pause to think, but obeyed. The ground rushed at her as she instinctively spread her wings in a futile hope of slowing her fall somewhat—

She landed in the blanket with one of her legs half-bent beneath her— it was painful, but it didn't hurt badly enough to have been broken. Before she could draw breath, Daran had scooped her up from the pocket of the blanket and bundled her under one arm like an oversized chicken; likely he was the only one of them big enough to carry her so. With Talaysen leading and the acrobats confusing the pursuit behind them, he set off at as hard a run as he could manage with the burden of Gwyna to carry. Gwyna craned her neck around in time to see the Priest free himself from the confines of the blanket, his face black with rage—then they were out of sight around a corner of one of the stalls.

They were hidden in the warm, near-stifling darkness of the back of a weaver's tent, in among bales of her work. Gwyna could hear Daran panting beside her, and clamped her bill tight on the first notes of a song. Her heart, high during the rescue, had fallen again. She was free, yes, but no nearer to being herself again than she had been in the cage.

There was a swish of material; Rune flung herself down beside them, breathing so hard she could hardly speak.

"Tal—Talaysen's gone to the cathedral, to the courts and the Justiciars—"

"Looking to the Church for help?" Daran whispered incredulously. "I thought the Wren cleverer than that! Why, all that bastard has to do is get there before him, lay a charge, and flaunt his robes—"

"There are Priests and Priests, Heron," Rune replied, invisible in the stuffy darkness. "And let me tell you, the Master's no fool. I thought the same as you, but he says he knows someone among the Justiciars today, and I think I know who it is. *He* knows who we can trust. He says to make a break and run as soon as we think it safe—I'm to get someone with the Gypsies, you're for the cathedral and the Court of Justice. The tumblers will do their best to scramble things again."

"All right—" Daran said doubtfully. "The Wren's never been wrong before, but—Lady bless, I hope he isn't now!"

All of them burst from the tent into the blinding sunlight—and behind them rose a clamor and noise; Gwyna looked back to see the Priest (how had he contrived to be so close to their hiding place?) in hot pursuit, followed by all of his servants and two of his helmeted and armed guards. If those caught them before they reached the goal Talaysen had in mind for them—

They burst into the Justice court of the cathedral itself, Revaner and his contingent hard on their heels; Talaysen was there already, gesturing to a robed man and woman and a younger man clad in the red robes of Church Justiciars.

"My lords—my lady—" he cried, waving at Daran and Gwyna. "Here is the one of whom I told you—"

"Justice!" thundered Revaner at the same time. "These thieves have stolen my pet—wrecked my tent—"

One of the guards seized Daran's arms. He responded by dropping Gwyna. She squawked in surprise at being dropped, then fled to the dubious safety of the feet of the three strangers before Revaner could grab more than one of her tail-feathers.

The lady reached down and petted Gwyna; comfort and reassurance passed from Priest to bird with her caress. Gwyna suddenly had far more confidence in Talaysen's scheme—this Priest was no ordinary, gold-grasping charlatan, but one with real power and a generous spirit!

The other two waited patiently for the clamor to die down to silence, quite plainly ready to wait all day if that was what it took.

At length even the yipping servants of the Priest ceased their noise.

"You claim, Bard Talaysen, that this bird is in fact one of your company, ensorceled into this shape," said the gray-haired man in Priest robes. "Yet what proof have you that this is so?"

"Mind-touch her, Lady Ardis—or have Lord Arran do so." Talaysen replied steadily. "Trust your *own* senses."

The man in red approached slowly, his hand held out as if to a shy animal. Gwyna needed no such reassurance. She ran limpingly to the young man's feet, chirping and squawking. She strove with all her might to project her *human* thoughts into the hireling's mind, spreading out the whole story as best she could.

Arran patted her feathers into smoothness, and from his touch came reassurance and comfort. More, words formed in Gwyna's mind, words as clear as speech.

Fear not, little singer; there is no doubt in my heart that you are wholly human.

The young man rose gracefully to his feet and faced the two mages.

"This one is bespelled indeed; she *is* the Free Bard Gwyna—more than that, the evil being that has so enslaved her is *that* one"—he pointed an accusing finger at Revaner—"he who claims her as his property and pet. His accomplice in this evil was the Guild Bard Bestif."

At that, the Priest paled, and tried to flee, only to be held by the guards he had brought with him. At the same time, Gwyna felt the Lady-Priest's hand on her head, and some instinct told her to remain utterly still. She saw Talaysen take Rune's hand, his face harden with anxiety. Daran clutched his bony hands together, biting his lip.

"We shall need your help," the Lady-Priest said to Talaysen and Rune. "I think you have some small acquaintance with magic yourselves. And you know her."

She saw Rune start with surprise, saw Talaysen nod—

Then all was confusion. The courtyard spun around in front of Gwyna's eyes, moving faster and faster until it was nothing but a blur of light and shadow. The courtyard vanished altogether. Then light blazed up, nearly blinding her, and a dark *something* separated from her own substance, pulling away from her with a reluctant shudder. She could feel it wanting to stay, clinging with an avid hunger, but the light drove it forth despite its will. Suddenly she was overcome with an appalling pain, and crumbled beneath the onslaught of it. Her flesh felt as if it were melting, twisting, reshaping, and it hurt so much she cried out in sheer misery—

A cry that began as a bird's call, and ended as the anguished sob of a human in mortal agony.

The pain cut off abruptly; Gwyna blinked, finding herself slumped on the stone of the courtyard, her skirts in a puddle of red, gold, and scarlet about her, her dark hair falling into her eyes, and three gold coins on the stone before her.

She stared at one hand, then at the other—then at the faces of the three who stood above her; the Lady-Priest, Talaysen and Rune. Their brown, green, and hazel eyes mirrored her own relief and joy—

From the other side of the courtyard came an uncanny shriek—something like a raven's cry, something like the scream of a hawk. All four turned as one to see what had made the sound.

Crouching where the dark Priest had stood, was an ugly, evil-looking bird, like none Gwyna had ever seen before. Its plumage was a filthy black, its head and crooked neck naked red skin, like a vulture. It had a twisted yellow beak and small, black eyes. It stood nearly waist-high to the two guards beside it. As they watched, it made a swipe at one of them with that sharp beak, but the man was not nearly so ale-sotted as he seemed, and caught the thing by the neck just behind the head.

"Evil spells broken often return upon their caster," said young Arran, soberly. "As this one has. Balance is restored. Let him be exhibited at the gate as a warning to those who would pollute the Holy Church with unclean magic; but tend him carefully and gently. It may be that one day God will warm to forgiveness if he learns to repent. As for the Guild Bard Bestif, let him be fined twelve gold pieces and banned forever from the Faire. Let one half of that fine be given to the minstrels he wronged, and one half to those in need. That would be my judgment."

"So be it, so let it be done," said the older man, silent until now.

They made as if to leave; Gwyna scrambled to her feet, holding out one of the three gold coins. "My lords—lady—this for my thanks, an' you will?"

The older Priest took it gravely. "We are true Priests of the Church; we do not accept pay for the performance of our duty—but if you wish this to be given to the offerings for the poor?"

Gwyna nodded; he accepted the coin and the three vanished into the depths of the cathedral.

Gwyna took the others and tossed them to Talaysen, who caught them handily.

"For celebration?" he asked, holding it up. "Shall we feast tonight?"

"Have I not cause to celebrate? Only one thing—"

"Name it, Gypsy Robin."

"If you love me, Master Wren—buy nothing that once wore feathers!"

CHAPTER SIXTEEN

Rune shooed Talaysen away, so that she could apportion their belongings into packs. "This is apprentice-work," she told him sternly. "You go do what a Master does." Grinning, he left her to it.

She had acquired a bit more clothing here at the Faire, but her load was still much lighter than his, and she elected to take their common stores of food along with her own things. The tent was still full of people, or seemed to be, anyway. It was much smaller when all of them were packing up, with gear spread all over, and there was much complaining about how it had all magically multiplied during the sojourn at the Faire. Rune hadn't had that much to start with, and Talaysen did not carry one item more than he needed, but some of the others were not so wise.

When one stayed in one place for any length of time, Rune suspected, it was easy to forget how much one could carry. There had been this same moaning and groaning for the past two days, as the Free Bards departed in groups, by morning and afternoon.

The only folk not involved in the throes of packing were Erdric and his grandson. They lived here in Kingsford the year round; Erdric had a permanent place in the King's Blade tavern, and young Sparrow was learning the trade at the hands of his grandfather. They would see to it that the two men the Free Bards had hired to take down the great tent would do so without damaging it, and haul it off in their cart to the merchant it was kept with the rest of the year.

More than three-fourths of the Free Bards had already gone their way by this morning; Talaysen would be the last to depart, so that no one lacked for a personal good-bye from their leader.

That meant he and Rune wouldn't be able to cover a great deal of ground their first day, but Rune didn't much mind. She'd gotten a great deal to think about over the past several weeks, and most of it was unexpected.

The Free Bards, for instance—contrasted with the Guild Bards. Talaysen's group was a great deal more in the way of what she had *thought* the Guild Bards would be like. The Free Bards took care of each other; she had seen with her own eyes right here at the Faire how the Guild Bards squabbled and fought among themselves for the plum jobs. And if someone were unfortunate to lose one of those jobs due to accident, illness or the like, well, his fellow Guild members would commiserate in public but rejoice in private, and all scramble for the choice tidbit like so many quarreling dogs under the table.

And the Church—there had been a set of shocks, though she'd been prepared for some of them from the rumors she'd heard. That though it officially frowned upon magic, it held a cadre of mages—well, she'd learned that was true enough, though Lady Ardis had warned her not to confirm the rumor to anyone. And though there were plenty of venial Priests, there were some like Lady Ardis, who would aid anyone who needed it, and valued honor and ethics above gold.

Then there was Talaysen—an enigma if ever she saw one. A Guild Bard once, he could still claim his place any time he wanted to—and he refused. Even though that refusal cost him in patronage and wealth.

She wasn't certain how he felt about her. He didn't treat her as a child, though she was his apprentice. He watched her constantly when he thought she wasn't looking, and the eyes he followed her with were the eyes of a starving man. But when he spoke with her or taught her, he had another look entirely; he teased her as if he was her elder brother, and he never once gave a hint that his feelings ran any deeper than that.

Yet whenever someone else seemed to be playing the gallant with her, he'd find himself watched so closely that he would invariably give up the game as not worth it. After all, no one wanted to invoke Talaysen's displeasure.

And no one wants to interfere with anyone that Master Wren is finally taking an interest in, she thought, with heavy irony. *The only problem is, the Master doesn't seem to know he's taken that interest.*

Gwyna had at least told her that Talaysen had remained virtually celibate for the last several years, though no one knew why. There didn't seem to be any great, lost loves in his life, although Lady Ardis had hinted that he might at least have had a dalliance that *could* have become a love, if he had pursued it. For some reason, he hadn't.

Well, if there's no lost loves, there's no ghosts for me to fight. I've got that much in my favor.

Rune had decided in the last week of the Faire how *she* felt about Master Wren. And there was nothing celibate about what she wanted. She had never in all her life met with a man who so exactly suited her in every way. Of course, she'd never seen him out of company—out on the road, he might turn surly, hard to get along with. But she didn't think so. He had a great deal to teach, and she to learn, but in performance, at least, they were absolute partners, each making up for the other's weaknesses. She had every reason to think that the partnership would continue when they were on their own.

Now if I can just warm it up to something more than "partnership."

She finished the packs; Talaysen was making farewells and giving some last-minute directions, so she had elected to pack up, and not because she was the apprentice and he expected it—which he didn't. It was because he was doing what his duties required, and she had free hands. The accord had been reached without either of them saying a word.

She set the packs aside and waited for him to return. Out beyond the Faire palings, the merchants were also breaking down and preparing to leave. The Midsummer Faire was over for another year.

She was surprised to feel an odd sense of loss, of uncertainty. For the past three weeks at least, ever since her splint had come off, she had known what every day would bring. Now it was completely new; she hadn't ever really traveled the roads for a living, and the idea was a little daunting.

Finally, as the sun crossed the zenith-line, he returned. "Well, are we ready?" he asked.

She nodded. "Packed and provisioned, Master Wren." She hefted her pack up and slung it over her back; her fiddle was safe inside, and her harp and lute were fastened securely on the outside. She wished briefly that Talaysen had a horse, or even a little donkey they could use to carry their supplies. With a beast their pace could be much faster, though it would be an added expense.

While you're wishing, Rune, why don't you wish for a pair of riding horses while you're at it?

Still, a donkey could eat almost anything; it wouldn't be that much of a burden unless they stayed in a town.

And a donkey makes you look more prosperous, and makes you a target for robbers.

Talaysen blinked in surprise, and hefted his own pack onto his back. "I hadn't expected you to be ready quite so soon," he said mildly. "I took you for town-bred, and not used to the road life."

She shrugged. "I walked from Westhaven to Nolton, from Nolton to here. I learned a bit."

"So I see." He shifted the pack into a comfortable position on his back. "Well, if you're ready, so am I."

So it was that simple, after all. They simply left the tent, with a farewell wave to Erdric as he gave the two hired men their instructions, and took their place in the steady stream of people leaving by the road to the north.

Talaysen seemed disinclined to talk, so she held her peace as they walked at a good pace along the verge. The press of people leaving was not as heavy as the one of those arriving had been, and most of them were driving heavily loaded wagons, not walking. *Their* pace was set by the pace of whoever was in the lead of this particular group of travelers. The other folk on foot, at least those that Rune saw, were limited to some small peddlers who had probably been vending impulse-goods from trays, and nondescript folk who could have been anything. The former toiled under packs that would have made a donkey blanch; the latter beneath burdens like their own. The pace that Talaysen set had them passing most other foot-travelers, and all the carts. The sun beat down on all of them, regardless of rank or station, and while there were frequent smiles and nods from those they passed, no one seemed inclined to talk. Halfway into the afternoon, though, they took the first turning to the right, a track so overgrown that she would never have picked it herself. It seemed no one else had chosen it either, at least not today. And no one followed them for as long as she could see the main road when she glanced behind them. She cast him a doubtful look that he never noticed, and followed along a step or two behind him, keeping a sharp watch for trouble.

Weeds grew ankle-high even in the ruts on the road itself, and were waist-high on the verge. Once under the shelter of overhanging trees, she was forced to revise her guess of how long it had been since the road had been used by other than foot traffic. From the look of the road— or rather, path—no one else had come this way since the beginning of the Faire at very best, unless they were foot-travelers like themselves. The weeds were not broken down the way they would be if cart wheels had rolled over them; she was, admittedly, no tracker, but it didn't seem to her that the weeds had been taken down by anything other than the passing of animals in days.

Trouble on a deserted way like this could come in several forms; least likely was in the form of humans, robbers who hunted up and down a seldom-traveled track precisely because they were unlikely to be caught on it and those they robbed were unlikely to be missed. Wild animals or farm animals run feral could give a traveler a bad time; particularly wild cattle and feral pigs. She didn't think that the larger predators would range this close to the Faire site and Kingsford, but that was a possibility that shouldn't be dismissed out of hand. There had once been a wild lion loose in the forest near Westhaven and there were always wolves about. But last of all, and most likely, was that it could be that the reason why this road was unused was the same reason the road through Skull Hill Pass was little used. Something really horrible could be on it. Something that had moved in recently, that Talaysen might not know about.

"Where are we going?" she asked Talaysen, not wanting to seem to question his judgment, but also not wanting to find herself facing something like the Ghost. The next uncanny creature might not be a music lover. And she was no hand at all with any kind of weapon.

"What's our next destination, do you mean?" he replied, "or where are we making for tonight?" He looked back over his shoulder at her to answer, and he didn't seem at all alarmed. Surely he knew about all the signs of danger on a road. . . . Surely he was better at it than her. . . .

"Both," she said shortly. The track widened a little, and she got up beside him so that he could talk to her without having to crane his neck around.

"Allendale Faire, ultimately," he told her. "That's about two weeks from now. The pickings there have been good for me in the past, and no one else wanted to take it this year, so I said we would. Tonight, there's a good camping spot I think we can make by moonrise; there's water, shelter, and high ground there. I've used it before. The track doesn't get any worse than this, so I don't see any problem with pressing on after sunset."

"After sunset?" she said doubtfully. "Master Wren, I don't think I'm up to struggling with tent poles in the dark."

"You won't have to," he said with a cheerful smile. "There won't be anyone there but us, and since the weather is fine, there's no need to worry about putting up a tent. With luck, the weather will hold until we reach Allendale in about two weeks."

Two weeks. That was a long time to walk through forest. She'd slept under the stars without a tent before, but never with company . . . still it wasn't that she was afraid something would happen, it was that she was afraid it *wouldn't*, without a little privacy to share. And she wasn't certain their provisions would hold out that long. "Is there anything on this road?" she asked.

"Quite a bit, after tonight. Small villages, a great deal like the one you came from, and about two days apart," he told her. "We ought to be able to pick up a few nights' worth of food and lodging for music on the way to Allendale Faire."

She frowned, not quite understanding why he was so certain of a welcome. "But they're so close to Kingsford—why would they bother to trade us for music so close to the city—and so close to Faire-time? In winter, now, I could see it—but now?"

He chuckled. "How often did the people in *your* village go even as far as the next one for anything? Maybe once or twice a year? The first village is close to a two-day walk from here, and most farmers can't afford to take that much time away from crops this time of the season. Not many people take this road, either, which is why I claimed it for the start of our journey."

"What if they've had a minstrel through here?" she asked. Then she remembered Westhaven, and shook her head. "Never mind, even if it was two days ago, we'll still be a novelty, won't we? Even if they have their own musicians. It was that way at the Hungry Bear in my village."

He laughed. "Well, with luck, we'll be the first musicians they've seen in a while. With none, they still won't have had a musician down this way for a few days, and what's more"—his grin grew cocky and self-assured—"he won't have been as good as we are, because he won't have been a Free Bard."

She chuckled and bent her head to keep her eye on her footing.

They walked on in silence; the grass grown over the track muffled their steps, and though their appearance frightened the birds right on the road into silence, farther off in the woods there were plenty of them chirping and singing sleepily in the heat. These woods had none of the brooding, ominous qualities of the ones around Skull Hill, and she began to relax a little. There was nothing at all uncanny that she could sense— and in fact, after all those weeks of throngs of people, and living with people at her elbow all the time, she found the solitude quite comforting.

She was glad of her hat, a wide-brimmed straw affair that she'd bought at the Faire; it was a lot cooler than her leather hat, and let a bit of breeze through to her head when there was any to be had. Though the trees shaded the road a bit, they also sheltered it from what little breeze there was, and the heat beneath the branches was oppressive. Insects buzzed in the knee-high weeds beside the road, a monotonous drone that made her very sleepy. Sweat trickled down her back and the back of her neck; she'd put her hair up under the hat, but she still felt her scalp and neck prickling with heat. At least she was wearing her light breeches; in skirts, even kilted up to her knees, she'd have been fighting her way through the weeds. Grasshoppers sprang away from their track, and an enterprising kestrel followed them for a while. He was quite a sight to see, hovering just ahead of them, then swooping down on a fat 'hopper that they frightened into bumbling flight. He would carry it on ahead and perch, neatly stripping wings and legs, then eating it like a child with a carrot, before coming back for another unfortunate enough to be a little too slow.

"Why Allendale Faire?" she asked, when the silence became too much to bear, and her ears rang from the constant drone of insects.

"It's a decently large local Faire in a town that has quite a few Sires and wealthy merchants living nearby," he replied absently. "We need to start thinking about a place to winter-up; I'm not in favor of making the rounds in winter, personally. And you never have; it's a hard life, although it can be very rewarding if you hit a place where the town prospered during the summer and the people all have real coin to spend."

She thought about trekking through woods like these with snow up to her knees instead of weeds, and shivered. "I'd rather not," she said honestly. "Like I told you when I met you, that isn't the kind of life I would lead by choice. That was one reason why I wanted to join the Guild."

"And your points were well made. So, one of those Sires or the local branches of the Merchants' Guild in or around Allendale might provide a place to spend our winter." He turned his head sideways, and smiled. "You see, most Sires can't afford a permanent House musician—at least the ones out here in the country can't. So they'll take on one that pleases their fancy for the winter months, and turn him loose in the spring. That way they have new entertainment every winter, when there are long, dark hours to while away, yet they don't have the expense of a House retainer and all the gifts necessary to make sure that he stays content and keeps up his repertory." The tone of his voice turned ironic. "The fact is that once a Guild Minstrel has a position, there's nothing requiring him to do anything more. It's his for life unless he chooses to move on, or does something illegal. If he's lazy, he never has to learn another new note; just keep playing the same old songs. So the people who have House Minstrels or Bards encourage them to stir themselves by giving them gifts of money and so forth when they've performed well."

"Gifts for doing the job they're supposed to do in the first place?" she replied, aghast.

"That's the Guild." He shrugged again. "I prefer our way. Honest money, honestly earned."

Still—*A place in a Sire's household, even for just the winter? How is that possible?* "I thought only Guild musicians could take positions with a House," she offered.

He laughed. "Well, that's the way it's supposed to work, but once you're away from the big cities, the fact is that the Sires don't give a fat damn about Guild membership or not. They just want to know if you can sing and play, and if you know some different songs from the last musician they had. And who's going to enforce it? The King? Their Duke? Not likely. The Bardic Guild? With what? There's nothing they can use to enforce the law; out here a Sire is frequently his own law.''

"What about the other Guilds?" she asked. "Aren't they supposed to help enforce the law by refusing to deal with a Sire who breaks it?''

"That's true, but once again, you're out where the Sire is his own law, and the Guildmasters and Craftsmasters are few. If a Craftsman enforces the law by refusing to deal with the Sire, he's cutting his own throat, by refusing to deal with the one person with a significant amount of money in the area. The Sire can always find someone else willing to deal, but will the Craftsman find another market?" He sighed. "The truth is that the Guildmasters of other Crafts might be able to do something—but half the time they don't give a damn about the Bardic Guild. The fact is, the Bardic Guild isn't half as important out of the cities as they think they are. Their real line of enforcement is their connection with the Church, through the Sacred Musicians and Bards, and the Church is pragmatic about what happens outside the cities.''

"Why is it that the Bardic Guild isn't important to the other Guilds?" she asked, hitching her pack a little higher on her back. There was an itchy spot right between her shoulderblades that she ached to be able to scratch. . . .

If she could keep him talking a while, she might get her mind off of the itch.

"Because most of the Crafts don't think of us as being Crafters," he said wryly. "Music isn't something you can eat, or wear, or hold in your hand, and they never think of the ability to play and compose as being nearly as difficult as their own disciplines." He sighed. "And it isn't something that people need, the way they need Smiths or Coopers or Potters. We aren't even rated as highly as a Limner or a Scribe—''

"Until it's the middle of winter, and people are growling at each other because the snow's kept them pent up for a week," she put in. "And even then they don't think of us as the ones who cheered everyone up. Never mind, Master Wren. I'm used to it. In the tavern back home they valued me more as a barmaid and a floor-scrubber than a musician, and they never once noticed how I kept people at their beer long past the time when they'd ordinarily have gone home. They never noticed how many more people started coming in of a night, even from as far away as Beeford. All they remembered was that I lost the one and only fiddling contest I ever had a chance to enter.''

Silence. Then—''I would imagine they're noticing it now,'' he said, when the silence became too oppressive. ''Yes, I expect they are. And they're probably wondering what it is they've done that's driving their custom away.''

Were they? She wondered. Maybe they were. The one thing that Jeoff had always paid attention to was the state of the cashbox. Not even Stara would be able to get around him if there was less in it than there used to be.

But then again—habit died hard, and the villagers of Westhaven were in the habit of staying for more than a couple ales now; the villagers of Beeford were in the habit of coming over to the Bear for a drop in the long summer evenings. Maybe they weren't missing her at all. Surely they thought she was crazed to run off the way that she had. And the old women would be muttering about ''bad blood,'' no doubt, and telling their daughters to pay close attention to the Priest and mind they kept to the stony path of Virtue. Not like that Rune; bastard child and trouble-maker from the start. Likely off making more trouble for honest folk elsewhere. Up to no good, and she'd never make an honest woman of herself. Dreams of glory, thought she was better than all of them—and she'd die like a dog in a ditch, or starve, or sell herself like her whore of a mother.

No doubt. . . .

Talaysen kept an ear out for the sound of a lumber-wagon behind them. The road they followed was cleared of weeds, if still little more than a path through the forest—but this *was* forested country; the towns were small, and the cleared fields few. Many of the villages hereabouts made their livings off the forest itself. Every other village boasted a sawmill, or a Cooper making barrels, or a craftsman hard at work on some object made of wood. The Carpenter's Guild had many members here, and there were plenty of craftsmen unallied with the Guild who traded in furniture and carvings.

Allendale was a half-day away, and Talaysen was both relieved and uneasy that their goal was so nearly in sight. The past two weeks had been something of a revelation for him. He'd been forced to look at himself closely, and he hardly recognized what he saw.

He glanced sideways at his apprentice, who had her hat off and was fanning herself with it. She didn't seem to notice his covert interest, which was just as well. In the first few weeks of the Midsummer Faire, when Rune's arm was still healing, he'd been sorry for her, protective of her, and had no trouble in thinking of her strictly as a student. He'd felt, in fact, rather paternal. She had been badly hurt, and badly frightened; she was terribly vulnerable, and between what she'd told him straight off, and what she'd babbled when she had a little too much belladonna, he had a shrewd idea of all the hurtful things that had been said or done to her as a child. Because of her helplessness, he'd had no difficulty in thinking of her *as* a child. And his heart had gone out to her; she was so like *him* as a child, differences in their backgrounds aside. One unwanted, superfluous child is very like another, when it all comes down to it. He had sought solace in music; so had she. It had been easy to see himself in her, and try to soothe her hurts as his father would never soothe his.

But once she stopped taking the medicines that fogged her thoughts; and even more, once her arm was out of the sling and she began playing again, all that changed. Drastically. Overnight, the child grew up.

He strode through the ankle-high weeds at the walking pace that was second-nature to him now, paying scant attention to the world about him except to listen for odd silences that might signal something or someone hidden beside the road ahead—and the steady clop-clopping of the hooves of draft-horses pulling timber-wagons; this was the right stretch of road for them, which was why the weeds were kept down along here.

Bandits wouldn't bother with a timber-wagon, but he and Rune would make a tempting target. Highwaymen knew the Faire schedule as well as he did, and would be setting up about now to try to take unwary travelers with their pouches of coin on the way to the Faire. They wouldn't be averse to plucking a couple of singing birds like himself and his apprentice if the opportunity presented itself.

And if Talaysen didn't anticipate them. He'd been accused of working magic, he was so adept at anticipating ambushes. Funny, really. Too bad he wasn't truly a mage; he could transform his wayward heart back to the way it had been. . . .

It was as hot today as it had been for the past two weeks, and the dog-days of summer showed no sign of breaking. Now was haying season for the farmers, which meant that every hot, sunny day was a boon to them. Same for the lumberjacks, harvesting and replanting trees in the forest. He was glad for them, for a good season meant more coin for them—and certainly it was easier traveling in weather like this—but a short storm to cool the air would have been welcome at this point.

A short storm . . . Summer thunderstorms were something he particularly enjoyed, even when he was caught out in the open by them. The way the air was fresh, brisk, and sharp with life afterwards—the way everything seemed clearer and brighter when the storm had passed. He wished there was a similar way to clear the miasma in his head about his apprentice.

He'd hoped that being on the road with her would put things back on the student-teacher basis; she didn't have real experience of life on the road, and for all that she was from the country, she'd never spent a night camped under the open sky before she ran away from home. This new way of life should have had her reverting to a kind of dependence that would have reawakened his protective self and pushed the other under for good and all.

But it didn't. She acted as if it had never occurred to her that she should be feeling helpless and out of her depth out here. Instead of submissively following his lead, she held her own with him, insisting on doing her share of everything, however difficult or dirty. When she didn't know how to do something, she didn't make a fuss about it, she simply asked him—then followed his directions, slowly but with confidence. She took to camping as if she was born to it, as if she had Gypsy blood somewhere in her. She never complained any more about the discomforts of the road than he did, and she was better at bartering with the farm-wives to augment their provisions than he was.

Then there was music, God help them both. She was a full partner there, though oddly that was the only place her confidence faltered. She was even challenging him in some areas, musically speaking; she wanted to know *why* some things worked and some didn't, and he was often unable to come up with an explanation. And her fiddling was improving day by day; both because she was getting regular practice and because she'd had a chance to hear some of the best fiddlers in the country at the Faire. Soon she'd be second to none in that area; he was as certain of that as he was of his own ability.

Not that he minded, not in the least! He enjoyed the novelty of having a full partner to the hilt. He liked the challenge of a student of her ability even more. No, that wasn't the problem at all.

This was all very exciting, but he couldn't help but notice that his feelings towards her were changing, more so every day. It was no longer that he was simply attracted to her—nor that he found her stimulating in other areas than the intellectual.

It was far worse than that. He'd noticed back at the last Faire that when they'd sung a love duet, he was putting more feeling into the words than he ever had before. It wasn't acting; it was real. And therein lay the problem.

When they camped after dark, he was pleased to settle the camp with her doing her half of the chores out there in the darkness, even if she didn't do things quite the way he would have. When he woke up in the middle of the night, he found himself looking over at the dark lump rolled in blankets across the fire, and smiled. When he traded sleepy quips over the morning fire, he found himself not only enjoying her company—he found himself unable to imagine life without her.

And that, frankly, frightened him. Frightened him more than anything he'd ever encountered, from bandits to Guild Bards.

He watched her matching him stride-for-stride out of the corner of his eye, and wanted to reach out to take her hand in his. They suited each other, there was no doubt of it; they had from the first moment they'd met. Even Ardis noticed it, and had said as much; she'd told him they were two of a kind, then had given him an odd sort of smile. She'd told him over and over, that his affair with Lyssandra wouldn't work, that they were too different, and she'd been right. By the time her father had broken off the engagement because he'd fled the Guild, they were both relieved that it was over. That little smile said without words that Ardis reckoned that *this* would be different.

Even the way they conversed was similar. Neither of them felt any great need to fill a silence with unnecessary talk, but when they *did* talk, it was always enjoyable, stimulating. He could, with no effort at all, see himself sharing the rest of his life with this young woman.

That frightened him even more.

How could he even *think* something like that? The very idea was appalling! She was younger than he was; *much* younger. He was not exaggerating when he had told Ardis that he was twice her age. He was, and a bit more; on the shady side of thirty-five, to her seventeen or eighteen. How many songs were there about young women cuckolding older lovers? Enough to make him look like a fool if he took up with her. Enough to make *her* look like a woman after only his fame and fortune if she took up with *him*. There was nothing romantic about an old man pairing with a young woman, and much that was the stuff of ribald comedy.

Furthermore, she was his apprentice. That alone should place her out of bounds. He was appalled at himself for even considering it in his all-too-vivid dreams.

He'd always had the greatest contempt for those teachers who took advantage of a youngster's eagerness to please, of their inexperience, to use them. There were plenty of ways to take advantage of an apprentice, from extracting gifts of money from a wealthy parent, to employing them as unpaid servants. But the worst was to take a child, sexually inexperienced but ripe and ready to learn, and twist that readiness and enthusiasm, that willingness to accommodate the Master in every way, and pervert it into the crude slaking of the Master's own desires with no regard for how the child felt, or what such a betrayal would do to it.

And he had seen that, more than once, even in the all-male Guild. If the Church thundered against the ways of a man and a maid, this was the sin the Priests did not even whisper aloud—but that didn't mean it didn't occur. Especially in the hothouse forcing-ground of the Guild. That was one of the many reasons why he'd left in a rage, so long ago. Not that men sought comfort in other men—while he did not share that attraction, he could at least understand it. The Church called a great many things "sins" that were nothing of the sort; this was just another example. No, what drove him into a red rage was that there were Masters who abused their charges in body and spirit, and were never, ever punished for it. The last straw was when two poor young boys had to be sent away to one of the Church healers in a state of hysterical half-madness after one of the most notorious lechers in the Guild seduced them both, then insisted both of them share his bed at the same time. The exact details of what he had asked them to do had been mercifully withheld—but the boys had been pitiful, and he would not blame either of them if they had chosen to seek the cloisters and live out their lives as hermits. In the space of six months, that evil man had changed two carefree, happy children into frightened, whimpering rabbits. He'd broken their music, and it was even odds that it could be mended.

Talaysen still boiled with rage. It was *wrong* to take advantage of the trust that a student put in a teacher he respected—it was worse when that violation of trust included a violation of their young bodies. He'd gone to the Master of the Guild when he'd learned of the incident, demanding that the offending teacher be thrown out of the Guild in disgrace. Insisting that he be turned over to the Justiciars. Quite ready to take a horsewhip to him and flay the skin from his body.

He'd been shaking, physically shaking, from the need to rein in his temper. And the Master of the Guild had simply looked down his nose at him and suggested he was overreacting to a minor incident. "After all," Master Jordain had said scornfully, "they were only unproven boys. Master Larant is a full Bard. His ability is a proven fact. The Guild can do without them; it cannot do without *him*. Besides, if they couldn't handle themselves in a minor situation like that, they probably would not have passed their Journeyman period; they were just too unstable. It's just as well Master Larant weeded them out early. Now his valuable time won't be wasted in teaching boys who would never reach full status.''

He had restrained himself from climbing over the Master's desk and throttling him with his bare hands by the thinnest of margins. He still wasn't certain how he'd done it. He had stalked out of the office, headed straight to his own quarters, packed his things and left that afternoon, seeking shelter with some Gypsies he'd met as a young man and had kept contact with, renouncing the Guild and all that it meant, changing his name, and his entire way of life.

But there it was; he'd seen how pressure of that nature could ruin a young life. How could he put Rune in the untenable position those poor boys had been in? Especially if he'd been misreading her, and what he'd been thinking was flirtation was simple country friendliness.

And there was one other thing; the stigma associated with "female musicians." Rune didn't deserve that, and if they remained obviously student and teacher, all would be well. Or at least, as "well" as it could be if she wore skirts. But he wouldn't ever want her to bear that stigma, which she would, if she were ever associated with him as his lover. Assuming she was willing . . . which might be a major assumption on his part.

Oh, if he wasn't misreading her, if she *was* interested in him as a lover, he could wed her. He'd be only too happy to wed her. . . .

Dear gods, why would she *ever* want to actually wed him? Him, twice her age? She'd be nursing a frail old man while she was still in the prime of her life, bound to him, and cursing herself and him both.

Furthermore, there would always be the assumption by those who knew nothing about music that she'd become his apprentice only *because* she was his lover; that she was gaining her fame by borrowing the shine of his.

No, he told himself, every time his eyes strayed to her, and his thoughts wandered where they shouldn't. *No, and no, and no. It's impossible. I won't have it. It's wrong.*

But that didn't keep his eyes from straying.

Or—his heart.

Rain fell unceasingly down from a flat gray sky, plopping on her rain-cape, her hat, and into the puddles along the road. Rune wondered what on Earth was wrong with Talaysen. Besides the weather, of course. He'd been out of sorts about something from the moment they'd left the Allendale Faire. Not that he showed it—much. He didn't snap, rail about anything, or break into arguments over little nothings. No, he *brooded.*

He answered questions civilly enough, but neither his heart nor his thoughts were involved in the answer.

It could be the weather; there *was* more than enough to brood over in the weather. After weeks of dry, sunny days, their streak of good luck had finally broken, drowning the Allendale Faire in three days of dripping, sullen rain.

But they'd gotten around that; they'd succeeded in finding a cook-tent big enough to give them a bit of performing room, and they'd done reasonably well, monetarily speaking, despite the weather.

The rain had kept away all the wealthy Guildmasters and the three Sires that lived within riding distance, however. Perhaps that was the problem. They'd made no progress towards finding a wintering-over spot, and she sensed that made Talaysen nervous. At the next several large Faires, he had told her soberly, they could expect to encounter Guild musicians, Journeymen looking for permanent places for themselves. And they could encounter toughs hired by the Guild, either to "teach them a lesson" or to keep them from taking hire with one of the Sires for the winter.

One thing was certain, and only one; *she* was just as out-of-sorts as he was, but her mood had nothing to do with the weather or the state of their combined purse. She knew precisely why she was restless and unhappy. Talaysen. If this was love, it was damned uncomfortable. It wasn't lust, or rather, it wasn't lust alone—she was quite familiar with the way *that* felt.

The problem was, Talaysen didn't seem inclined to do anything to relieve her problem, despite all the hints she'd thrown out. And she'd thrown plenty, too. The only thing she hadn't tried was to strip stark naked and creep into his bedroll after he fell asleep.

Drat the man, anyway! Was he made of marble?

She trudged along behind him, watching his back from under her dripping hat-brim. Why didn't he respond to her?

It must be me, she finally decided, her mood of frustration turning to one of depression, as the rain cooled her temper and she started thinking of all the logical reasons why he hadn't been responding. *Obviously, he could have anyone he wanted. Gwyna, for instance. And she's not like me; she's adorable. Me, I'm too tall, too bony, and I can still pass for a boy any time I choose. He just doesn't have any interest in me at all, and I guess I can't blame him.* She sighed. The clouds chose that moment to double the amount of rain they were dropping on the two Bards' heads, so that they were walking in their own road-sized waterfall.

She tallied up her numerous defects, and compared herself with the flower of the Free Bard feminine contingent, and came to the even more depressing conclusion that she not only wasn't in the running, she wasn't even in the race when it came to attracting her Master in any way other than intellectually. And even then—the Free Bards were anything but stupid. Any of the bright lovelies wearing the brotherhood's ribbons could match witticisms with Talaysen and hold her own.

I don't have a prayer. I might as well give up.

Depression turned to despondency; fueled by the miserable weather, she sank deep inside herself and took refuge in composing the lyrics to songs of unrequited love, each one worse and more trite than the one before it. Brother Pell would have had a fit.

She stayed uncharacteristically silent all morning; when they stopped for a brief, soggy lunch, she couldn't even raise her spirits enough to respond when he finally did venture a comment or two. He must have sensed that it would be better to leave her alone, for that was what he did, addressing her only when it was necessary to actually tell her something, and otherwise leaving her to her own version of brooding.

On the fifteenth repeat of rhyming "death" with "breath," she noticed that Talaysen had slowed, and was looking about for something.

"What's the matter?" she asked dully.

"We're going to have to stop somewhere for the night," he said, the worry evident in his voice, although she couldn't see his expression under *his* dripping, drooping hat brim. "I'm trying to find some place with at least a little shelter—however small that may be."

"Oh." She took herself mentally by the scruff of the neck and shook herself. *Being really useful, Rune. Why don't you at least try to contribute something to this effort, hmm?* "What did you have in mind?" she asked.

He shrugged—at least, that was what she guessed the movement under his rain-cape and pack meant. "I'd like a cave, but that's asking for a bit much around here."

She had to agree with him there. This area was sandy and hilly, rather than rocky and hilly. Not a good area for caves—and if they found one, say, under the roots of a tree, it would probably already have a tenant. She was not interested in debating occupancy with bears, badgers or skunks.

"Let's just keep walking," she said, finally. "If we don't find anything by the time the light starts to fade, maybe we can make a lean-to against a fallen tree, or something. . . ."

"Good enough," he replied, sounding just as depressed as she was. "You watch the right-hand side of the track, I'll watch the left."

They trudged on through the downpour without coming to anything that had any promise for long enough that Rune was just about ready to suggest that they *not* stop, that they continue on through the night. But it would be easy to get off the track in weather like this, and once tangled in the underbrush, they might not be able to find their way back to the road until daylight. If there was anything worse than spending a night huddled inside a drippy lean-to wrapped in a rain-cape, it was spending it caught in a wild plum thicket while the rain beat down on you unhindered even by leaves.

Meanwhile, her thoughts ran on in the same depressing circle. Talaysen was tired of her; that was what it was. He was tired of his promise to teach her, tired of her company, and he didn't know how to tell her. He wanted to be rid of her. Not that she blamed him; it would be much easier for him to find that wintering-over place with only himself to worry about. And if that failed, it would be *very* much harder for him to make the winter circuit with an inexperienced girl in tow.

He must be bored with her by now, too. She wasn't very entertaining, she wasn't city-bred, she didn't know anything about the Courts that she hadn't picked up from Tonno—and *that* was precious little.

And he must be disgusted with her as well. The way she'd been shamelessly throwing herself at him—he was used to *ladies,* not tavern-wenches. Ill-mannered and coarse, a country peasant despite her learning. Too ugly even to think about, too.

She felt a lump of self-pity rising in her throat and didn't even try to swallow it down. Too ugly, too tall, too stupid—the litany ran around and around in her thoughts, and made the lump expand until it filled her entire throat and made it hard to swallow. It overflowed into her eyes, and tears joined the rain that was leaking through her hat and running down her face. Her eyes blurred, and she rubbed the back of her cold hand across them. They blurred so much, in fact, that she almost missed the little path and half-ruined gateposts leading away from the road.

Almost.

She sniffed and wiped her eyes again hastily. "Master Wren!" she croaked around the lump in her throat. He stopped, turned. "There!" she said, pointing, and hoping he didn't notice her tear-marred face. She was under no illusions about what she looked like when she cried: awful. Blotchy face and swollen eyes; red nose.

He looked where she pointed. "Huh," he said, sounding surprised. "I don't remember that there before."

"It looks like there might have been a farmhouse there a while back," she said, inanely stating the obvious. "Maybe you didn't notice it because the last time you were through here you weren't looking for a place to shelter in.''

"If there's a single wall standing, it'll be better than what we have now,'' he replied, wearily. "If there's two, we can put something over them. If there's even a corner of roof, I'll send Ardis a donation for her charities the next time we reach a village with a Priest.''

He set off towards the forlorn little gate; she followed. As overgrown as that path looked, there wasn't going to be enough room for them to walk in anything other than single file.

It was worse than it looked; the plants actually seemed to reach out to them, to tangle them, to send out snags to trip them up and thorns to rake across their eyes.

The deeper they went, the worse it got. Finally Rune pulled the knife from her belt, and started to hack at the vegetation with it.

To her surprise, the going improved after that; evidently there was point of bottleneck, and then the growth wasn't nearly so tangled. The bushes stopped reaching for them; the trees stopped fighting them. Within a few moments, they broke free of the undergrowth, into what was left of the clearing that had surrounded the little house.

There was actually something left of the house. More than they had hoped, certainly. Although vines crawled in and out of the windows, the door and shutters were gone entirely, and there was a tree growing right through the roof, there were still walls and a good portion of the roof remaining, perhaps because the back of it had been built into the hill behind it.

They crossed the clearing, stepped over a line of mushrooms ringing the house, and entered. There was enough light coming in for them to see—and hear—that the place was relatively dry, except in the area of the tree. Talaysen got out his tinderbox and made a light with a splinter of wood.

"Dirt floor—at least it isn't mud.'' Rune fumbled out a rushlight and handed it to him; he lit it at his splinter. In the brighter flare of illumination, she saw that the floor was covered with a litter of dead leaves and less identifiable objects, including a scattering of small, roundish objects and some white splatters. Talaysen leaned down to poke one, and came up with a mouse-skull.

He grinned back at Rune, teeth shining whitely from under his hat brim. "At least we won't have to worry about vermin. Provided you don't mind sharing your quarters with an owl.''

"I'd share this place with worse than an owl if it's dry,'' she replied more sharply than she intended. Then she laughed, in a shaky attempt to cover it. "Let's see what we can do about putting together someplace to sleep. *Away* from where the owl is. I can do without getting decorated with castings and mutes."

"Why Rune, we could set a whole new fashion," Talaysen teased, his good humor evidently restored. He stuck the rushlight up on what was left of a rock shelf at the back of the house, and they set about clearing a space to bed down in.

CHAPTER SEVENTEEN

"There," Rune said, setting her makeshift broom of broken branches aside. "That's as clean as it's going to get." She made a face at the piled debris on the other side of the ash tree; there had been too much garbage to simply sweep out the door.

"That's clean enough," Talaysen told her, from where he knelt just under the window, striking his flint and steel together as he had been the entire time she'd been sweeping. He had a knack for fires that she didn't; making a fire from sparks was a lot harder than village-folk (or especially city-folk) realized. "Now if I can just—there!"

He blew frantically at the little pile of dry leaves and shavings in front of him, and was rewarded this time with a glow, and then with a tiny flame. Carefully sheltering it from an errant breeze, he fed it with tiny twigs, then branches, then finally built a real fire with wood scavenged from the cottage's interior about his core-blaze. Just as well, as it was definitely getting darker outside. Hopefully the smoke would go *out* the window, and not decide to fill the cottage. The chimney of this place was choked with birds' nests and other trash.

Rune took a look around, now that she had more light to see by. This hadn't been a big farmhouse; one room, with a tiny loft just under the roof for sleeping. But the inside looked very odd for a place gone to ruin, and she puzzled over it as Talaysen picked up wood, trying to figure it out.

Then she had it: the cottage had been abandoned in a hurry. Nothing had been taken, not even the smallest stool. The wood that Talaysen was collecting had come from wrecked furniture. The doors and windows had been forced—but forced *out*, not in, and the shutters over the windows had been smashed at about the same time. *Something got in here, then smashed its way out. But what could have been strong enough to do that—and nasty enough to keep the owner from coming back for his goods?* She felt a chill finger of fear trace a line down the back of her neck. . . .

But then she shrugged and turned her attention to setting up their "camp." Whatever had done this was long gone, and not likely to return; there was no sign that anything had been living here except the owl.

He handed their nesting cook-pot and kettle to her; she dug out the dried meat and vegetables and the canister of herb tea. It was Talaysen's turn to cook, while she spread out the sleeping rolls and went to get water.

Well, that wouldn't be hard. There was a lot of water available right now.

She stuck the kettle, then the pot, out the window, holding them under the stream of water coming off the eaves. After all the rain they'd been having, the roof was surely clean. As clean as most streams, anyway. The presence of the owl probably kept birds from perching on the roof by day, and there wasn't much else that would matter.

Already it was hard to see across the clearing. She was profoundly grateful that they'd found this bit of shelter when they had. Now they'd be able to have a hot meal, warm and dry their clothing by the fire, check their instruments, maybe even practice a little.

As if he had followed her thoughts, Talaysen looked up from his cooking. "Get my lute out, will you, Rune? I think it's warm and dry enough in here that it won't come to any harm."

She nodded, and took the instrument out of its oiled-leather case, inspecting it carefully for any signs that the rain or damp might have gotten to it. Satisfied that it was untouched, she laid it on his unrolled bedding and did the same with her fiddle.

Like any good musician, she made a detailed examination of both instruments. So detailed, in fact, that by the time she was finished, the food and tea were both ready. She dug into her own portion with a nod of thanks, a little surprised at how hungry she was. The food evaporated from her wooden bowl, and she mopped every last trace of juice up with a piece of tough traveler's bread. The bowl hardly needed to be washed after she was through, and Talaysen's was just as clean.

Once they had finished eating, Talaysen was not to give her any time to brood over the thoughts that had caused her depression today, either. Instead, he insisted that they rehearse a number of songs she was only vaguely familiar with.

Odd, she thought, after the first few. He seemed to have chosen them all for subject-matter rather than style—every single one of them was about young women who were married off to old men and disappointed in the result. In a great many of the songs, they cuckolded their husbands with younger lovers; in the rest, they mourned their fates, shackled for life to a man whose prowess was long in the past. Sometimes the songs were comic, sometimes tragic, but in all of them the women were unhappy.

After about the fifth or sixth of these, she wondered if he was trying to tell her something. After the fifteenth, she was certain of it. And despite the message, she grew more and more cheerful with every chorus.

He *had* noticed how she'd been flinging herself at him! And this wasn't the reaction she'd been thinking he'd had to her. Was the message in these ballads that he was attracted, but thought he was too old to make her happy? It surely seemed likely.

Where did he get an idea like that? He wasn't *that* much older than she was! Girls in Westhaven got married to men his age all the time— usually after they'd worn out their first wives with work and childbearing, and were ready for a pretty young thing to warm their beds at night. Oh, at thirty-mumble, if he had been a fat merchant, or an even fatter Guild Bard, maybe she'd have been repulsed . . . but it would have been the overstuffed condition of his body that would have come between them, not his age.

At first she was too startled by what she thought he was trying to tell her to act on it—then, after a moment of reflection, she decided she'd better not do anything until she'd had a chance to plan her course of attack. She held her peace, and played the dutiful apprentice, keeping her thoughts to herself until they were both too tired to play another note. By then, the fire was burning low, and she was glad to creep into her now-warmed blankets.

But although she intended to ponder all the possible meanings of the practice session, though she did her best to hold off sleep, it overtook her anyway.

There. I think I've gotten my message across. Talaysen put his lute back in its case with a feeling of weary, and slightly bitter, satisfaction. Hopefully now his young apprentice would think about what she was doing, and stop making calf's-eyes at him.

What he was going to do about the way he felt was another matter altogether.

Suffer, mostly.

Eventually, though, he figured that he would be able to convince himself that their relationship of friendship was enough. After all, it was enough with all the other Free Bard women he'd known.

Maybe he could have another brief fling with Nightingale to get the thought of Rune out of his head. Nightingale had yet to find the creature that would capture *her* heart, but she enjoyed an amorous romp as well as anyone.

At least he'd given Rune something to think about. And the next time they met up with one of the gypsy caravans or another gathering of Free Bards, she'd start looking around her for someone her age. That should solve the problem entirely. Once he saw her playing the young fool with all the other young fools, his heart would stop aching for her.

He looked down at her sleeping face for a moment, all soft shadows and fire-kissed angles. *Maybe I shouldn't have been so hard on Raven,* he thought, dispiritedly. *Maybe I should have encouraged him. He was one of her teachers before; he knows her better than I do. They might get on very well together. . . .*

But though the idea of Rune with another was all right in the abstract, once he gave the idea a face, it wrenched his heart so painfully that his breath caught.

Dear God, I am a fool.

He slipped inside his own bedroll, certain that he was going to toss and turn for the rest of the night—

Only to fall asleep so quickly he might have been taken with a spell of slumber.

It was the sound of a harp being played that woke him; he found himself, not lying in his bedroll in the tiny, earthen-floored cottage, but standing on his feet in the middle of a luxuriously green field. Overhead was not a sky filled with rain clouds—not even a sky at all—but a rocky vault studded with tiny, unwinking lights and a great silver globe that shone softly down on the gathering around him.

Before him, not a dozen yards away, was a gathering of bright-clad folk about a silver throne. After a moment of breathlessness and confusion, he concluded that the throne was *solid* silver; for the being that sat upon it was certainly not human. Nor were those gathered about him.

Eyes as amber as a cat's stared at him unblinking from under a pair of upswept brows. Hair the black of a raven's wing was confined about the wide, smooth, marble-pale brow by a band of the same silver as the throne. The band was centered by an emerald the size of Talaysen's thumb. The face was thin, with high, prominent cheekbones and a sensuous mouth, but it was as still and expressionless as a statue. Peeking through the long, straight hair were the pointed ears that told Talaysen his "host" could only be one of the elven races.

There were elvenkin who were friends and allies to humans. There were more who were not. At the moment, he had no idea which these were, though the odds on their being the latter got better with every passing moment.

The man was clothed in a tunic of emerald-green silk, with huge, flowing sleeves, confined about the waist with a wide silver belt and decorated with silver embroidery. His legs were encased in green trews of the same silk, and his feet in soft, green leather boots. His hands, resting quietly on the arms of his throne, were decorated with massive silver rings, wrought in the forms of beasts and birds.

A young man sat at his feet, clad identically, but without the coronet, and playing softly on a harp. Those about the throne were likewise garbed in silks, of fanciful cut and jewel-bright colors. Some wore so little as to be the next thing to naked; others were garbed in robes with such long trains and flowing sleeves that he wondered how they walked without tripping themselves. Their hairstyles differed as widely as their dress, from a short cap like a second skin of brilliant auburn, to tresses that flowed down the back in an elaborate arrangement of braids and tied locks, to puddle on the floor at the owner's feet, in a liquid fall of silver-white. All of them bore the elven-king's pointed ears and strange eyes, his pale flesh and upswept brows. Some of them were also decorated with tiny quasi-living creations of magic; dragon-belts that moved with the wearer, faerie-lights entwined in the hair.

Talaysen was no fool, and he knew very well that the elves' reputation for being touchy creatures was well-founded. And if these considered themselves to be the enemies of men, they would be all the touchier. Still—they hadn't killed him out of hand. They might want something from him. He went to one knee immediately, bowing his head. As he did so, he saw that his lute was lying on the turf beside him, still in its case.

"You ventured into our holding, mortal," said a clear, dispassionate tenor. He did not have to look up to know that it was the leader who addressed him. "King" was probably the best title to default to; most lords of elvenkin styled themselves "kings."

"Your pardon, Sire," he replied, just as dispassionately. "I pray you will forgive us."

When he said nothing else, the elven-king laughed. "What? No pleas for mercy, no assertions that you didn't *know*?"

"No, Sire," he replied carefully, choosing his words as he would choose weapons, for they were all the weapon that he had. "I admit that I saw the signs, and I admit that I was too careless to think about what they signified." And he had seen the signs; the vegetation that tried to prevent them from entering the clearing until Rune drew her Iron knife;

the Fairie Ring of mushrooms encircling the house. The ash tree growing right through the middle, and the condition of the house itself. . . .

"The mortal who built his house at our very door was a fool, and an arrogant one," the elven-king replied to his thought, his words heavy with lazy menace. "He thought that his God and his Church would defend him against us; that his Iron weapons were all that he needed besides his faith. He knew this was our land, that he built his home against one of our doors. He thought to keep us penned that way. We destroyed him." A faint sigh of silk told him that the king had shifted his position slightly. He still did not look up. "But you were weary, and careless with cold and troubles," the king said. His tone changed, silken and sweet. "You had no real intention to trespass."

Now he looked up; the elf lounged in his throne in a pose of complete relaxation that did not fool Talaysen a bit. All the Bard need do would be to make a single move towards a weapon of any kind at all, and he would be dead before the motion had been completed. If the king didn't strike him down with magic, the courtiers would, with the weapons they doubtless had hidden on their persons. The softest and most languid of them were likely the warriors.

"No, Sire," he replied. "We had no intention of trespass, though we *were* careless. It was an honest mistake."

"Still—" The elf regarded him with half-closed eyes that did not hide a cold glitter. "Letting you go would set a bad example."

He felt his hands moving towards his instrument; he tried to stop them, but his body was no longer his to control. He picked up his lute, and stripped the case from it, then tuned it.

"I think we shall resolve your problems and ours with a single stroke," the elf said, sitting up on the throne and steepling his hands in front of his chin. "I think we shall keep you here, as our servant, to pay for your carelessness. We have minstrels, but we have no Bards. You will do nicely." He waved his hand languidly. "You may play for us now."

Rune awoke to a thrill of alarm, a feeling that there was something wrong. She sat straight up in her bed—and a faint scrape of movement made her look, not towards the door, but to the back of the cottage, where it was built into the hillside.

She was just in time to see the glitter of an amber eye, the flash of a pointed ear, and the soles of Talaysen's boots vanishing into the hillside as he stumbled through a crack in the rock wall at the rear of the cottage. Then the "door" in the hill snapped shut.

Leaving her alone, staring at the perfectly blank rock wall.

That broke her paralysis. She sprang to her feet and rushed the wall, screaming at the top of her lungs, kicking it, pounding it with hands and feet until she was exhausted and dropped to the ground, panting.

Elves. That was what she'd seen. Elves. And they had taken Talaysen. She had seen the signs and she hadn't paid any attention. She should have known—

The mushrooms, the ash-tree—the bushes that tried to keep us out—

They were all there; the Fairie-circle, the guardian ash, the tree-warriors—all of them in the songs she'd learned, all of them plain for any fool to see, if the fool happened to be thinking.

Too late to weep and wail about it now. There must be something she could do—

There had to be a way to open that door from this side. She felt all over the wall, pressing and turning every rocky projection in hopes of finding a catch to release it, or a trigger to make it open.

Nothing.

It must be a magic door.

She pulled out her knife, knowing the elves' legendary aversion to iron and steel, and picked at anything she found, hoping to force the door open the way she had forced the trees to let them by. But the magic in the stone was sterner stuff than the magic in the trees, and although the wall trembled once or twice beneath her hand, it still refused to yield.

Thinking that the ash tree might be something more than just a tree, she first threatened it with her dagger, then stabbed it. But the tree was just a tree, and nothing happened at all, other than a shower of droplets that rained down on her through the hole in the roof as the branches shook.

Elves . . . elves . . . what do I know about elves? God, there has to be a way to get at them, to get Talaysen out! What do I have to use against them?

Not much. And not a lot of information about them. Nothing more than was in a half-dozen songs or so. She paced the floor, her eyes stinging with tears that she scrubbed away, refusing to give in, trying to think. What did she know that could be used against them?

The Gypsies deal with them all the time—

How did the Gypsies manage to work with them? She'd heard the Gypsies spoken of as "elf-touched" time and time again . . . as if they had somehow won some of their abilities from the secretive race. What could the Gypsies have that gave them such power over the elvenkin?

Gypsies, elves—

She stopped, in mid-stride, balancing on one foot, as she realized the secret. It was in one of the songs the Gypsy called Nightingale had taught her.

Music. They can be ruled by music. They can't resist it. That's what the song implied, anyway.

She dashed to her packs and fumbled out her fiddle. Elves traditionally used the harp, but the fiddle was *her* instrument of choice, and she wasn't going to take a chance with anything other than her best weapon. She tuned the lovely instrument with fingers that shook; placed it under her chin, and stood up slowly to face the rock wall.

Then she began to play.

She played every Gypsy song she knew; improvised on the themes, then played them all over again. The wailing melodies sang out over the sound of the storm getting worse overhead. She ignored the distant growl of thunder, and the occasional flicker of lightning against the rock in front of her. She concentrated all of her being on the music, the hidden door, and how much she wanted that door to open.

Let me in. Let me in. Let me in to be with him. Let me in so I can get him free!

She narrowed her eyes to concentrate better. She thought she felt something—or rather, *heard* something, only it was as if she had an extra ear somewhere deep inside, that was listening to something echo her playing.

Echo? No, it wasn't an echo, this was a different melody. Not by much—but different enough that *she* noticed it. Was she somehow hearing the music-key to the spell holding the door closed, resonating to the tune she was playing?

She didn't stop to think about it; obeying her instinctive feelings, she left the melody-line she was playing and strove to follow the one she heard with that inner ear. She felt a tingle along her arms, the same tingle she had felt when Gwyna had been transformed back to her proper form.

Not quite a match . . . she tried harder, speeded up a little, trying to anticipate the next notes. Closer . . . closer . . .

As she suddenly snapped into synch with that ghostly melody, the door in the wall cracked open—then gaped wide.

She found herself in a tunnel that led deep into the hillside, a tunnel that was floored with darkness, and had walls and a ceiling of swirling, colored mist. If she had doubted before, this was the end of doubts; only elves would build something like this.

The door remained open behind her. She could only hope it would stay that way and not snap shut to block her exit.

If she got a chance to make one.

She clutched her fiddle in her hand and ran lightly down the tunnel; it twisted and turned like a rabbit's run, but at length she saw light at the end. More than that, she heard music, and with her ears, not whatever she'd used to listen before. Music she knew; Talaysen's lute. But not his voice; he was not singing, and that lack shouted wrongness at her. There was a stiffness to his playing as if he was being constrained by something, forced to play against his will.

She ran harder, and burst through a veil of bright-colored mist at the very end of the tunnel. She stumbled onto a field of grass as smooth and close-clipped as a carpet, under a sky of stone bejeweled with tiny, artificial stars and a featureless moon of silver. Small wonder the songs spoke of elven "halls"; for all that they aped the outdoors, this was an artifice and would never look like a real greensward.

The elves gathered beneath that artificial moon in the decorous figures of a pavane stopped and turned to stare in blank surprise at her. Talaysen stood between them and her—and his expression was of surprise warring with fear.

She knew she daren't give them a moment to get over their surprise; if they did, they'd attack her, and if they attacked her, they'd kill her. The songs made *that* perfectly clear as well.

She grasped for the only weapon she had.

So you want to dance, do you?

She shoved the fiddle under her chin, set bow to strings, and played. A wild reel, a dance-tune that never failed to bring humans to their feet, and called the "Faerie Reel." She hoped there was more in the name than just the clever title—

There was. Or else the elves *were* as vulnerable to music as Gypsy legend suggested. They seized partners by the hands and began flinging themselves through the figures of the dance, just as wildly as she played, as if they couldn't help themselves.

She didn't give them a respite, either, when that tune had been played through three full sets; she moved smoothly from that piece into another, then another. Each piece was repeated for three sets; she had a guess from some of what the Gypsy songs said that "three" was a magic number for binding and unloosing, and she wanted to bind them to their dancing, keeping them occupied and unable to attack.

She played for them as fiercely as she had for the Ghost, *willing* them to dance, faster and faster, until their eyes grew blank, and their limbs faltered. Finally some of them actually began dropping from exhaustion, fainting in the figures of the dance, unable to get up again—

One dropped; then two, then a half dozen. The rest staggered in the steps, stumbling over the fallen ones as if they could not stop unless they were as unconscious as the ones on the ground seemed to be. Another pair fainted into each other's arms, and the elven-king whirled, his face set in a mask of un-thought.

Then she changed her tune. Literally.

She brought the tune home and paused, for just a heartbeat. The elves' eyes all turned toward her again, most of them blank with weariness or pleading for her to stop. The elven-king, stronger than the rest, staggered towards her a step or two. She set bow to the strings again, and saw the flicker of fear in *their* eyes—

And she launched into the Gypsy laments.

Before she had finished the first, the weariest of the elves were weeping. As she had suspected, the Gypsy songs in particular held some kind of strange power over the elves, a power they themselves had no defense against. By the time she had completed the last sorrowing lament that Nightingale had taught her, even the elf with the coronet was in tears, helpless, caught in the throes of grief that Rune didn't understand even though she had evoked it.

She took her bow from her strings. Now there was no sound but soft sobbing.

They're mine. No matter what they try, they're too tired and too wrought up to move fast. I can play them into the ground, if I have to. I think. Provided my arms hold out. . . .

Elves, she couldn't help but notice resentfully, looked beautiful even when weeping. Their eyes and cheeks didn't redden; their noses didn't swell up. They simply sobbed, musically, perfect crystal tears dropping from their clear amber eyes to trickle like raindrops down their cheeks.

She looked for the one with the coronet; he was climbing slowly to his feet, tears in his eyes, but his chin and mouth set with anger. She strode quickly across the greensward to get past Talaysen as the elven-king brought himself under control, and by the time he was able to look squarely at her, she was between him and her Master, with her bow poised over the strings again, and her face set in an expression of determination she hoped he could read.

"*No!*" he shouted, throwing out a hand, fear blazing from his eyes.

She removed her bow a scant inch from the strings, challenge in hers.

"No—" he said, in a calmer voice. "Please. Play no more. Your magic is too strong for us, mortal. We have no defense against it."

About him, his people were recovering; some of them, anyway. The ones who could control themselves, or who had not fainted with exhaustion earlier, were helping those who were still lying on the velvety green grass; trying to wake them from their faint, helping them to their feet.

Rune said nothing; she only watched the elven-king steadily. He glanced at his courtiers and warriors, and his pale face grew paler still.

"You are powerful, for all that you are a green girl," he said bitterly, turning a face full of carefully suppressed anger back to her. "I knew that the man was powerful, and I confined him carefully, wrapping his music in bonds he could not break so that he could not work against us. But you! You, I had not expected. You have destroyed my defenses; you have brought my people to their knees. No!" he said again, as she inadvertently lowered her bow a trifle. "No, I—beg you. Do not play again! Elves do not weep readily; many more tears, and my people may go mad with grief!"

"All right," she replied steadily, speaking aloud for the first time in this encounter, controlling her voice as Talaysen had taught her, though her knees trembled with fear and her stomach was one ice-cold knot of panic. "Maybe I won't. If you give me what I want."

"What?" the elven-king replied swiftly. "Ask and you shall have it. Gold, jewels, the treasures of the Earth, objects of enchantment—"

"Him," she interrupted, before he could continue the litany, and perhaps distract her long enough to work against both of them. "I want my lover back again."

Then she bit her lip in vexation. *Damn. Damn, damn, damn.* She had *meant* to say "Master," but her heart and her nerves conspired to betray her.

"Lover?" the elven-king said, one eyebrow rising in disbelief as he looked from Talaysen to her and back to Talaysen. "Lover? You—and he? What falsehood is this?" But then he furrowed his brows, and peered at her, as if he was trying to look into her heart. "Lover, no—" he said slowly, "but beloved, yes. I had not thought of this, either. Small wonder your music had such power against me, with all the strength of your heart behind it."

"You can't keep him," she said swiftly, trying to regain the ground she had lost with her inadvertent slip of the tongue. "If you can see our thoughts, then you know I am not lying to you. If you cage a songbird, it won't sing; if you keep a falcon mewed up forever, it will die. Do the same to my Master, and he'll die just as surely as that falcon will.

He gave up everything for freedom—take it from him, and you take away everything that makes him a Bard. He'll waste away, and leave you with nothing. And I will *never* forgive you. You'll have to kill me to rid yourself of me, and the cost will be higher than you may want to pay, believe me.''

The elven-king's eyes narrowed. ''There's truth in that,'' he said slowly. ''Truth in everything you have said thus far. But you, mortal girl—you're made of sterner, more flexible stuff. *You* would not pine away like a linnet in a cage. Tell me, would you trade your freedom for his?''

''Yes,'' she said, just as Talaysen cried out behind her, ''No!''

The elf considered them both for a moment longer, then shook his head. ''No,'' he said, anger filling his voice. ''No, it must be both of you or neither. Cage the one, and the other will come to free it. Keep you both, and you will have my kingdom in ruins within the span of a single moon. You are too powerful to hold, too dangerous to keep, both of you. Go!''

He flung his arm up, pointing at the tunnel behind her. But Rune wasn't finished yet; the treachery of elves was as legendary as their power and secretiveness. She dropped the bow to the strings and played a single, grief-filled phrase.

''Stop!'' The elven-king cried over it, tears springing into his eyes, hands clapped futilely over his ears. ''What more do you want of us?''

She lifted the bow from the strings. ''Your pledge,'' she replied steadily. ''Your pledge of our safety.''

She saw the flash of rage that overcame him for a moment, and knew that she had been right. The elven-king *had* planned to ambush them as soon as their backs were turned, and probably kill them. He had lost a great deal of pride to her and her music; only destroying them would gain it back.

''Swear,'' she insisted.

''By the Moon our Mother, the blood of the stars, and the honor of the Clan,'' Talaysen whispered.

''Swear by the Moon our Mother, the blood of the stars, and the honor of the Clan that you will set us free, you will not hinder our leaving; you will not curse us, nor set magic nor weapons against us. Swear it!'' she warned, as the rage the elven-king held in check built in his eyes and threatened to overwhelm his self-control. ''Swear it, or I'll play till my arms fall off! I played all one night before, I can do it again!''

He repeated it between gritted teeth, word for word. She slowly lowered her arms, and tucked fiddle and bow under one of them, never betraying by a single wince how both arms hurt.

She turned just as slowly, and finally faced Talaysen, just as fearful of what she might see in his eyes as of all the power the elven-king could raise against them.

He smiled, weakly; his face a mask that covered warring emotions that flickered behind his eyes. But he picked up his lute and case, and offered her his arm, as if she was his lady. She took it gravely, and they strolled out of that place of danger as outwardly calm as if they strolled down the aisles of a Faire.

But once they reached the cottage, the rock door slammed shut right on their heels, and she began throwing gear into her pack, taking time only to wrap her fiddle in her bedding and stow it in the very bottom for safety. He joined her.

"Are you thinking what I'm thinking?" he said, over the steady *boom* of thunder from overhead. The fire was almost out, but they didn't need it to see; lightning flashing continuously gave them plenty of light to see by.

"I think so," she shouted, stuffing the last of her gear into her pack, with her tiny harp cushioned inside her clothing to keep *it* safe. "I don't trust him, no matter what he swore by. He'll find a way to get revenge on us. We'd better get out of here."

"This may *be* his revenge!" Talaysen said grimly, packing up his own things and slinging them on his back, throwing his rain-cape over all, then pointing to the storm outside the windows. "He didn't swear not to set the weather on us. As long as he doesn't touch us directly, he hasn't violated his pledge. A storm, lightning—those aren't strictly weapons."

She swore. "Elves," she spat. "They should be Churchmen. Or lawyers. Let's get out of here! A moving target is harder to hit!"

Talaysen was in perfect agreement with her, apparently; he strode right out into the teeth of the storm, and she was right behind him.

The trees didn't stop them this time; evidently the prohibition against using magic held the grasping branches off. But the storm was incredible; lightning striking continuously all about them. Rain lashed them, pounding them with hammers of water, sluicing over their rain-capes until they waded ankle-deep on the path. Talaysen insisted, shouting in her ear to be heard over the storm, that they walk down in the streambed next to the road; it was full of rushing water that soaked them to their knees, but with the rain lashing them from every angle it didn't much matter, they were wet anyway. And when lightning struck the roadway, not once, but repeatedly, she saw the sense of his orders. The streambed was deep enough that not even their heads were above the roadway. Lightning always sought the highest point; they had to make certain that point wasn't them.

But the streambed turned away from the roadway eventually, and ran back into the trees. Now the question was: follow the road, and take their chances with the lightning, or follow the streambed and hope it led somewhere besides into the wilderness?

Talaysen wavered; she made up his mind for him, pushing past him and following the streambed under the trees. People always built their homes beside water; with luck, they'd come across something in a day or two.

With no luck, at least they wouldn't be turned into Bard-shaped cinders. And they could retrace their path if they had to, until they met up with the road again.

The terrain was getting rockier; when she could see through the curtains of water, the streambed looked as if it had been carved through what looked like good, solid stone. And the banks were getting higher. If they couldn't find a house, maybe they could find a cave.

If they couldn't find either, maybe they could just walk out the storm.

It was awfully hard to think with rain beating her skull, and water tugging at her ankles, forcing her constantly off balance. She was so cold she couldn't remember being warm.

The thunder and lightning raged above their heads, but none of it was getting down to the ground anymore, not even the strikes that split whole trees in half. And the very worst of it seemed to be behind them, although the rain pounded them unabated. Her head was going to be sore when they were out of this. . . .

Maybe they were getting out of the elven-king's territory. How far could magic reach?

She found out, as there was a sudden slackening in the rain, a moment when the lightning and thunder stopped. Both she and Talaysen looked up as one, but Rune was not looking up with hope.

She felt only a shudder of fear. This did not have the feeling of a capitulation. It had the feeling of a summoning. The elven-king was bringing one final weapon to bear upon them.

That was when they saw the wall of wind and water rushing down on them, walking across the trees and bending them to the earth as it came. Not like a whirlwind—like a moving waterfall, a barrier of water too solid to see through.

Talaysen was nearer to shelter; he flung himself down in a gully carved into the side of the streambed. She looked about frantically for something big enough to hold her.

Too late.

The wind struck her, staggering her—she flailed her arms to keep her balance, then in a flash of lightning, saw what looked like half a tree heading straight for her—

Pain, and blackness.

Talaysen saw the tree limb, as thick around as he was, hit Rune and drop her like a stone into the water, pinning her in the stream beneath its weight.

He might have cried out; it didn't matter. In the next instant he had fought through the downpour and was clawing at the thing, trying to get it off her, as the wind screamed around him and battered him with other debris. She'd been knocked over a boulder, so at least her head was out of the water—but that was all that fortune had granted her. She was unconscious; she had a pulse, but it was weak and slow.

And he couldn't budge the limb.

Frantic now, he forced himself to calm, to think. Half-remembered hunter's lessons sprang to mind, and he recalled shifting a dead horse off another boy's leg with the help of a lever—

He searched until he found another piece of limb long and stout enough; wedged it under the one pinning Rune, and used another boulder for a fulcrum. There should have been two people doing this—he'd had the help of the huntsman before—

Heave. Kick a bit of flotsam under the limb to brace it. His arms screamed with pain. *Heave.* Another wedge of wood. His back joined the protest. *Heave*—

Finally, sweating and shaking, he had it balanced above her. It wouldn't hold for long; he'd have to be fast.

He let go of the lever, grabbed her ankle, and pulled.

He got her out from under the limb just as it came crunching back down, smashing to splinters one of the bits of wood he'd used to brace it up.

The wind died, and the rain was slackening, as if, with Rune's injury, the elven-king was satisfied. But the lightning continued, which now was a blessing; at least he had something to see by.

He bent down and heaved Rune, pack and all, over his shoulders, as if she was a sack of meal. Fear made a metallic taste in his mouth, but lent him strength he didn't know he had and mercifully blanked the pain of his over-burdened, aging body.

He looked about, frantically, for a bit of shelter, anything. Somehow he had to get her out of the rain, get her warm again. Her skin was as cold as the stones he'd pried her out of—if he couldn't get her warm, she might die—

Lightning flickered, just as his eyes passed over what he'd thought was a dark boulder.

Is that—

He staggered towards it, overbalanced by the burden he carried, and by the press of the rushing water against his legs. Lightning played across the sky overhead—he got another look at the dark blot in the stream wall. No, it wasn't a boulder. And it was bigger than he thought—

He climbed up onto the bank, peered at it in another flash of lightning—and nearly wept with relief. It was. It was a cave. A small one, but if it wasn't too shallow, it should hold them both with no difficulty. Pure luck had formed it from boulders caught in the roots of a tree so big two men couldn't have spanned the trunk with their arms.

And a pair of bright eyes looked out of it at him.

He didn't care. Whatever it was, it would have to share its shelter tonight. The eyes weren't far enough apart for a bear, and that was all he cared about.

Somehow he got himself up into the cave; somehow he dragged Rune up with him. Erratic lightning showed him what it was in the cave with him; an entire family of otters. They stared at him fearlessly, but made no aggressive moves towards him. He ignored them and began pawing through the packs for something warm and dry to put on her.

He encountered the instruments first. His lute—intact. Hers was cracked, but might be repaired later. Her penny-whistle was intact, and the tiny harp he'd given her. The bodhran drum was punctured; his larger harp needed new strings—

All this in mental asides as he pawed through the packs, pulling out soaked clothing and discarding it to the side.

Finally he reached the bottom of the packs. And in the very bottom, their bedding; somehow dry. Her fiddle wrapped in the middle of it, safe.

There wasn't much time, and he didn't hesitate; every moment she stayed chilled was more of a threat. He stripped her skin-bare and bundled her into both sets of bedding. Then he stripped himself and eased in with her, wrapping her in his arms and willing the heat of his body into her.

For a long time, nothing happened. The storm died to the same dull rain they'd coped with for the length of the Faire; the lightning faded away, leaving them in the dark. Rune breathed, but shallowly, and her body didn't warm in the least. Her breathing didn't change. She wasn't waking; she wasn't falling into normal sleep. If he couldn't get her warm—

Lady of the Gypsies, help me! You are the queen of the forests and wilds—help us both!

Finally he heard faint snuffling sounds, and felt the pressure of tiny feet on his leg and knee.

The otters' curiosity had overcome their fear.

They sniffed around the bundle of humans and blankets, poking their noses into his ear and sneezing into his face once. It would have been funny if he hadn't been sick with worry for Rune. She wasn't warming. She was hardly breathing—

One of the otters yawned; another. Before he realized what was happening, they were curling up *on* him, on Rune, everywhere there was a hollow in the blankets, there was an otter curling up into a lithe—warm!—ball and flowing over the sides of the hollows.

As they settled, he began to warm up from the heat of their six bodies. And as he warmed, so, at last, did Rune. Her breathing eased, and finally she sighed, moved a little—the otters chittered sleepily in complaint—and settled into his arms, truly asleep.

He tried to stay awake, but in a few moments, exhaustion and warmth stole his consciousness away, and he joined her and their strange bedcompanions in dreams.

He woke once, just after dawn, when the otters stirred out of sleep and left them. But by then, they were not only warm, they were a bit *too* warm, and he bade the beasts a sleepy, but thankful, good-bye. One of the adults—the female, he thought—looked back at him and made a friendly chitter as if she understood him. Then she, too, was gone, leaving the cave to the humans.

Rune woke with an ache in her head, a leg thrown over hers, and arms about her. Behind her, someone breathed into her ear.

What happened? She closed her eyes, trying to remember. They weren't in the cottage they'd found; that much was for certain. . . .

Then she remembered. The elves, her one-sided fight with music and magic, then the flight through the storm. After that was a blur, but she must have gotten hurt, somehow—

She wormed one arm out of the blankets, reached up to touch the place on her head that hurt worst, and found a lump too tender to bear any pressure at all, with a bit of a gash across the middle of it.

That was when she realized that she wasn't wearing so much as a stitch. And neither was Talaysen.

He murmured in his sleep, and held her closer. His hands moved in half-aware patterns, fitfully caressing her breasts, her stomach. . . .

And there was something quite warm and insistent poking her in the small of the back.

She held very still, afraid that if she moved, he'd stop. Despite the ache in her head, her body tingled all over, and she had to fight herself to keep from squirming around in his arms and—

Suddenly he froze, one hand on her breast, the other—somewhat lower.

He woke up. And now he's going to go all proper on me.

"If you stop," she said conversationally, "I am going to be very angry with you. I thought you taught me to always finish a tune you've started."

Please, God. Please, whoever's listening. Don't let him go all formal now. . . .

"I—I—uh—" He seemed unable to form any kind of a reply.

"Besides," she continued, trying to think around the pain in her skull, "I've been trying to get you into this position for weeks."

"Rune!" he yelped. "I'm your *teacher*! I can't—"

"You can't what? What difference does being my Master make? You've only got one apprentice, you can't be accused of favoring me over anyone else. You haven't been trying to seduce *me*, I've been trying to waylay *you*. There's a difference." *There,* she thought with a certain satisfaction. *That takes care of that particular argument.* "It's not as if you're taking unfair advantage of your position."

"But—the pressure—my position—"

"I like the pressure," she replied thoughtfully, "though I'd prefer to change the position—" And she started to squirm around to face him. He choked.

"That's not what I meant!" he said, and then it was too late; they were face-to-face, cozily wound in blankets, and he couldn't pretend he didn't understand her. She could read his expression quite clearly from here. She smiled into his eyes; he blushed.

"I know that's not what you meant," she told him. "I just don't see any 'pressure' on me to drag you into my bed except the pressure of wanting you."

"But—"

"And if you're going to tell me something *stupid*, like you're too old for me, well you can just forget that entirely." She kissed his nose, and he blushed even redder. "I wouldn't drink wine that was a month old, I wouldn't play a brand new fiddle, and I wouldn't hope for fruit from a sapling tree."

"But—"

"I *also* wouldn't go to an apprentice in *any* Craft for anything important. I'd go to a Master."

"But—"

She blinked at him, willing the pain in her head to go away. "You're not going to try and tell me that you've been celibate all these years, are you? If you are, then Gwyna was lying. Or you are. And much as I'd hate to accuse my Master of telling falsehoods, I'd believe Gwyna on this subject more than I'd believe you."

His mouth moved, but no words emerged. She decided he looked silly, gasping like a fish, and saved his dignity by stopping it with a kiss.

He disengaged just long enough to say, "I yield to your superior logic—" And then the time for talk was over, and the time for a different sort of communication finally arrived.

CHAPTER EIGHTEEN

"You *are* going to marry me, aren't you?" Talaysen asked plaintively, picking his now-dry clothing off the rocks beside the stream and packing it away. There was no sign of last night's storm; even most of the debris had been washed downstream. And as if in apology, the day had turned bright and sunny around noon. Rune had caught a fish, using some of their soggy bread for bait; he'd managed to get a fire going, so they could cook it. The rest of the day they'd spent in laying out everything that had gotten wet to dry, and figuring out just how badly Rune had gotten hurt.

She'd gotten off fairly easily, as it turned out. She had gotten a bad knock on the head, but nothing a lot of valerian couldn't help. They were now a day behind, of course, but that was better than being lightning victims, or confined in the elven-king's hall.

Rune looked over at Talaysen's anxious face, and grinned wickedly, despite the black eye and bruises the tree limb had gifted her with. "Isn't it supposed to be *me* that's asking that?" she mocked. "You sound like one of the deflowered village maidens in a really awful Bardic Guild ballad."

He flushed. "I'm serious. I—you—we— We can't just go on like this. You're going to get harassed enough if we're legally wed! If we aren't—"

She looked at him with an expression of exasperation, and carefully folded one of her shirts before answering. "Is that the only reason? To make an 'honest woman' out of me? To protect me from disgrace?"

"No!" he blurted, and flushed again. "I mean—I—"

"Ah." She put the shirt back into her pack. "That's just as well, since protecting a nameless bastard from disgrace is pretty much like protecting a thief from temptation. Why don't you just tell me why you're so set on this, and let me think about your reasons."

For a moment, he sat back on his heels and stared at her helplessly. For all that he was a Bard, and supposed to be able to work magic with words, he felt suddenly bereft of any talent with his tongue whatsoever. How could he tell her—

She waited patiently, favoring her left side a little. He marshaled his thoughts. Tried to remember what he always told others when they were tongue-tied, when the gift seemed to desert them.

Begin at the beginning. . . .

So he did.

She listened. Once or twice, she nodded. It got easier as he went along; easier to find the words, though they didn't come out of his mouth with any less effort. He'd lived for so long without telling people how he felt—how he *really* felt, the deep feelings that it was generally better not to reveal—that each confession felt as if he was trying to lift another one of those trees. Only this time, the back he was lifting it from was his own. The logical reasons: why it was better not to give the Guild another target; how being legally married would actually cut down on petty jealousy within the Bards; how it might keep petty officials of the Church not only from harassing *them,* but from harassing other Free Bard couples who chose to perform as a pair.

The reasons with no logic at all, and these were harder to get out: that he not only loved her, he needed her presence, that she made him feel more alive; his secret daydreams of spending the rest of his days with her; how she brought out the best in everything for him.

The reasons that hurt to confess: how he was afraid that without some form of formal tie binding them, one day she'd tire of him and leave him without warning; how he felt as if her refusal to formally wed him was a kind of rejection of *him,* as if she were saying she didn't feel he was worth the apparent sacrifice of her independence.

Finally he came to the end; he had long since finished his packing, and he sat with idle hands clenched on stones to either side of him.

She let out her breath in a sigh. "Have you thought about this?" she asked. "I mean, have you really thought it through? Things like—how are the other Free Bards going to react to a wife? You *think* that it will cut down on petty jealousy—why? I think it might just make things worse. A lover—that would be no problem, but a wife? Wouldn't they see me as some kind of interloper? I'm the newest Free Bard; how did I get you to wed me? Wouldn't they think I'm likely to try interfering with you and the rest of them?"

"I can't read minds," he said, slowly. "But I truly don't think there'd be any problem. I know every one of the Free Bards personally, and I just don't think the kinds of problems you're worried about would even occur. Marriage might make things easier, actually; I can't be everywhere at once, and sometimes I've wished there were two of me. And there are things the females haven't always felt comfortable in bringing to me—they tell Gwyna a lot of the time, but that really isn't the best solution. With you there—my legal partner—there's a partnership implied with marriage that there isn't with a lover. Stability; they aren't going to tell you something then discover the next time we met that there's someone else with me, and wonder what that means to their particular problem." He relaxed a little as she nodded.

"All right—I can see that. But we should try to anticipate problems and head them off before they *become* problems. For instance: divided authority. Someone trying to work us against each other. If you give me authority, it should be only as your other set of ears. All right?" She waited for his nod of agreement before continuing.

"What about children?" she said, surprising him completely.

"What about them?" he replied without thinking.

"I want them. Do you? Have you thought about what it would take to raise them as Free Bards?" She held up her hand to forestall his protest that it would not be fair to *her* to saddle her with children she might well have to raise alone. *"Don't* tell me that you're old, you'll die and leave me to raise them alone. I don't believe that for a minute, and neither do you."

He snapped his mouth shut on the words.

"Well?" she said, rubbing her head to relieve the ache in it. "Is there a way to have children and still be Free Bards?"

"We could settle somewhere, for a while," he suggested tentatively.

She shook her head, and winced. "No. No, I don't think that would work. You have to be visible, and that means traveling. If we lived in a big city, we'd have to leave the children alone while we busked—no matter how good we were, we would still be taking whatever jobs the Guild Minstrels didn't want, and that's pretty precarious living for a family. And the Guild would be only too happy to flaunt their riches in the face of your poverty—then come by and offer you your old position if you just gave all the Free Bard nonsense up."

She watched him shrewdly to see if he'd guess the rest of *that* story. "And of course, that would mean either giving you up, or persuading you to turn yourself into a good little Bard-wife and give up *your* music." He shook his head. "What a recipe for animosity! You know them better than I thought you did."

She snorted. "Just figured that if there was a way to make people jealous of each other, and drive a wedge between them, they'd know it. I imagine there's a lot of that going on in the Guild."

He pondered her original question for a moment, and emptied his mind, waiting to see if an answer would float into the emptiness. He watched the dance of the sunlight on the sparkling waters, flexing and stretching his fingers, and as always, waiting for the tell-tale twinges of weather-soreness. His father had suffered terribly from it—

But then his father had also shamelessly overindulged himself in rich food and wine, and seldom stirred from his study and office. That might have had something to do with it.

"There's another way," he said suddenly, as the image of a Gypsy wagon did, indeed, float into his mind. "We could join a caravan of Gypsy families; get our own wagon, travel with them, and raise children with theirs. If there are older children, adolescents, they watch the younger ones, and if there aren't there's always someone with a task that can be done at the encampment that minds the children for everyone else."

She raised an eyebrow skeptically. "Mind you, this is all nasty tale-telling from evil-mouthed, small-minded villagers, but—I've never heard anything about Gypsy parents except that they were terrible. Selling their children, forcing them to work, maiming them and putting them out to beg—"

"Have you ever actually *seen* any of that with your own eyes?" he asked. She shook her head, carefully. "It's not true, any of it. They know how to prevent having children, so they never have more than they can feed—if something *does* happen to one or both parents, every family in the caravan is willing to take on an extra mouth. The children are tended carefully, the encampment is always guarded by dogs that would take on a wolf-pack for their sakes, and the children loved by everyone in the caravan. They grow up to be pretty wonderful adults. Well, look at Gwyna, Raven and Erdric."

She gave a dry chuckle. "Sounds too good to be true."

"Oh, there're exceptions," he admitted. "There are families other Gypsies refuse to travel with—there are families that are hard on their children and a general nuisance to the rest of the adults. Any child that doesn't learn how to get out of the way of a drunk or a serious situation is going to be on the receiving end of a cuff. You must admit, though, that can happen anywhere. Mostly, Gypsy children are the healthiest and happiest I've ever seen. The drawback is that they won't learn reading, writing, or the Holy Book—the Gypsies don't hold with any of the three."

"Reading and writing we can teach them ourselves," Rune countered. "And the Holy Book—they should read it when they're old enough to understand that what they're reading is as much what the Church wants you to believe as it is Holy Words.'' She thought that proposition over for a long moment. ''That would work,'' she concluded, finally. ''Having a wagon to live in eliminates one of the biggest *expenses* of living in a town or city, too.''

''What, the rent?'' He grinned. She'd already told him about her job at Amber's, and he knew very well they could always find something comparable if they ever cared to settle in one place for long.

''No,'' she countered. ''The damned tithe and tax. If they can't catch you, they can't collect it. And if you leave before they catch you—''

''Point taken,'' he admitted. ''Though, I'll warn you, I do pay tax; I've been paying both our shares. If you want decent government, you have to be prepared to pay for it.''

He saw a shadow of something—some remembered pain—pass across her face. ''Point taken,'' she said, quietly. ''Tonno—felt the same way as you, and lectured me about it often enough. But the tithe serves no damned purpose at all. If it got into the hands of Priests like your cousin, that would be different. Most of the time, though, it ends up in the hands of men that are no better than thieves.''

He snorted, and tried not to think too hard about most of his dealings with the Church—those that hadn't involved Ardis seeking out someone specific for him to speak to. ''I've known thieves with more honor— and Ardis would be the first to agree with you. But we weren't talking about Ardis.''

''No, we weren't.'' She leaned forward, intently. ''Talaysen, what do you intend to *do* with the Free Bards?''

''Do?'' Was she really asking what he thought she was asking? ''What exactly do you mean?''

''What I said,'' she replied. ''What are you going to *do* with them? Oh, it was enough to form them, to keep the Bardic Guild from getting rid of them when there were only a handful of you, I'm sure. But there are nearly fifty of you now—not counting the ones that didn't come to the Midsummer Faire. And there are more joining every year! They think of you not only as the founder, but as the leader—now what are you going to lead them to? Or is this just going to be a kind of Gypsy Clan with no other purpose than to live and play music?''

Of all of the Free Bards, Rune was the only one that had asked him that question, the question he had been asking himself for about three years.

''There are a lot of things I would like to do,'' he said, slowly, ''but all of them involve having more power than we do now. That's why

I've gotten the rest involved in trying to ingratiate ourselves with the Sires and Guildmasters outside the big cities.''

''So that when you come to demand a change, there will be someone backing you.'' She nodded enthusiastically. ''What's the change?''

''Mostly, we—I—want to see some of the privileges and monopolies taken away from the Bardic Guild,'' he replied. ''I want them put on a completely equal footing with us. I don't want to set up the Free Bards in place of the Guild, but I want *any* musician to be free to take *any* place that's been offered him. I want the Sires able to hire and fire members of the Guild the same way they can hire and fire Free Bards and traveling minstrels. And there are some abuses of power within the Guild that I want looked into.''

She sat back on her heels, and smiled. ''That'll do,'' she replied. ''That's enough for anyone's lifetime. Let your successor worry about the next step.''

''Are you going to marry me now?'' he asked, trying to sound plaintive, and actually sounding testy. She laughed.

''Since you ask me so romantically, I think so,'' she said, tossing a shirt at him that he had forgotten. ''But don't think that you can go back to being aloof until the bonds are set.'' She bared her teeth at him, in a playful little snarl that was oddly erotic. He restrained himself from doing what he would have liked to do. For one thing, he wanted a more comfortable bed than the boulders of the stream-bank, sun-warmed though they were. . . .

''I don't know why I shouldn't,'' he replied provokingly. ''After all, you've been hurt, your head probably aches and I'm sure you couldn't *possibly* be interested in—''

She pounced on him, and proved that she could, most *definitely* be interested in—

And he found that the rocks weren't as bad as he had thought.

Rune would have laughed at her lover, if she hadn't been so certain that she would badly hurt his feelings by doing so. Now that they were lovers, *she* was perfectly content. But *he* was heading them into Brughten, despite the fact that there was no Faire there and the pickings would be slim, because he wanted to find a Priest to marry them. Immediately. Incredible.

Well, there was a Priest and a Church, and the town was at least on the road. It wasn't the road they had left; this one they'd struck after following the stream for a couple of days rather than backtrack over the elven-king's territory. And they might be able to get lodging and food at one of the town's two inns. . . .

Talaysen left her at the marketplace in the center of the town, and she was grateful for a chance to find some fresh supplies. The storm had washed away or ruined most of their food, and they had been living off the land thanks to the fish in the stream and her scant knowledge of forest edibles. That had been mostly limited to the fact that cattail roots could be eaten raw, knowing what watercress looked like, and recognition of some bramble-bushes with fruit on them.

Their money hadn't washed away, but it was hard to get a squirrel to part with a load of nuts in exchange for a copper penny.

She had just about completed her final purchase, when she turned and caught sight of Talaysen striding towards her through the light crowd. Most people wouldn't have noticed, and he was being quite carefully courteous to the other shoppers as he made his way past and around them—but she saw the set jaw, and the stiff way that he held his head, and knew he was furious.

"What's wrong?" she whispered, as he reached her side. He shook his head.

"Not here," he said quietly, and she heard the anger in his voice. "Are you done?"

"Just a moment." She turned back to the old farm-wife and quickly counted out the money for another bag of traveler's bread without stopping to bargain any further. The old woman blinked in surprise, but took the coins—it wasn't *that* much in excess of what the real price should have been—and gave her the coarse string bag full of rounds of bread in exchange.

"All right," she said, tying the bread to her belt until she got a chance to put it in her pack. "Let's go."

He led her straight out of town, setting a pace that was so fast she had to really stretch her legs to keep up with him, until he finally slowed when they were well out of sight of the last of the buildings. She tugged at his arm, forcing him to slow still further. "All right!" she exclaimed, catching sight of the rage on his face, now that he was no longer having to wear a polite mask. "What happened?"

"I was told by the Priest," he said, tightly, "that we were vagabonds and tramps. He told me that trash such as you and I weren't fit to even set foot on sacred ground, much less participate in the sacrament of marriage. He further told me that if we didn't want him to call the Sire's watch to have us *both* pilloried, even though you weren't even there, that we'd better take ourselves out of town." He took a deep breath, and let it out in a long sigh. "There was a great deal more that he said, and I won't repeat it."

The look on his face alarmed her. "You didn't do anything to him—"

"Oh, I *wanted* to throw him into the duck pond on the green," Talaysen replied, and the rage slowly eased out of him. "But I didn't. I did something that was a lot worse." He began to smile, then, and the more he thought about whatever it was that he'd done, the more he smiled.

She had a horrified feeling that he had done something that really *would* get them pilloried, and her face must have reflected that, because he tossed back his head and laughed.

"Oh, don't worry. I didn't do anything *physical*. But it will be a very long time before he insults another traveling musician." He waited, the smile still on his face, for her to ask the obvious question.

"Well, what *did* you do?" she asked impatiently, obliging him.

"I informed him that he had just insulted Master Bard Gwydain—and I proved who I was with this." He reached into his pocket and extracted the medallion of Guild membership that she had only seen on satin ribbons about the necks of the Guild Masters at the trials. This medallion was tarnished, and it no longer hung from a bright, purple satin ribbon, but there was no mistaking it for the genuine article.

A Master's medallion. The Priest must have been just about ready to have a cat.

He handed it to her; she turned it over, and there was his name engraved on it. She gave it back to him without a word.

"I don't think it ever occurred to him to question the fact that I had this," Talaysen continued, with satisfaction. "I mean, I *could* have stolen it—but the fact that I had puffed myself up like the proud, young, foolish peacock I used to be probably convinced him that it, and I, were genuine. He started gaping like a stranded fish. Then he went quite purple and tried to apologize."

"And?" she prompted.

"Well, I was so angry I didn't even want to be in the same town with him," Talaysen said, with a glance of apology to her. "I informed him that if he heard a song one day about a Priest so vain and so full of pride that he fell into a manure-pit because he wouldn't listen to a poor man's warning, he would be sure and recognize the description of the Priest if he looked into a mirror. Then I told him that I wouldn't be wedded by him or in his chapel if the High King himself commanded it, I shoved him away, and I left him on the floor, flapping his sleeves at me and still babbling some sort of incoherent nonsense."

"I wouldn't be wedded by a toad like that if it meant I'd *never* be wedded," she said firmly. "And if that's the attitude of their Priest, we'd better tell the rest of the Free Bards that Brughten is probably not a good place to stop. The Priest generally sets the tone for the whole village, and if this one hates minstrels, he could make a lot of trouble for our folk."

"I'm sorry, though—" he said, still looking guilty. "I never meant to deprive you of your wedding."

"Our wedding. And I really don't *care,* my love—" It gave her such a thrill to be able to say the words "my love," that she beamed at him, and he relaxed a bit. "I told you before. Amber showed me a lot of things; one of them was that there are plenty of people who have the 'proper' appearance who aren't fit to clean a stable, and more who that fat Priest would pillory, who have the best, truest hearts in the world." She touched his hand, and he caught hers in his. A delightful shiver ran down her back. "I don't care. You love me, I love you, and if a ceremony means that much to you, we'll get one of your Gypsy friends to wed us. It will be just as valid and binding, and *more* meaningful than anything *that* fat lout could have done."

She looked up at his green, green eyes, now shadowed, and started to say something more—when a dark cloud behind his head, just at the tree line, caught her eye. And instead of continuing her reassurance, she said, "What's more, we have a bit more to worry about than one stupid Priest. Look there—"

She freed her hand to point, and he turned. And swore. The cloud crept a little more into view.

"How long have we got until that storm hits us?" she asked, motioning to him to turn his back to her so she could free his rain-cape from the back of his pack, then doing the same so he could get hers and stow the bread away so *it* wouldn't get soaked.

"As quickly as that blew up?" He handed her the cape with a shake of his head. "I don't know. A couple of hours, perhaps? Would you rather turn back?"

"Not for a moment," she declared. "I'd rather have rain. I'd rather be *soaked* than take shelter in a place that has people in it like that Priest. Let's see how far we can get before it hits us. If we spot a place to take shelter along the way—"

"No deserted farmhouses!" he exclaimed.

She laughed. *After all, if it hadn't been for that farmhouse, he'd still be avoiding me like a skittish virgin mare!* "No," she promised. "No deserted farmhouses. Only ones with farmers, wives, and a dozen children to plague us and make us wish we were back with the elves!''

Just as the storm was close enough for them to feel the cold breath of it on their backs, Talaysen spotted a wooden shrine by the roadside. Those shrines usually marked the dwelling of a hedge-Priest or a hermit; a member of one of the religious Orders that called for a great deal of solitary meditation and prayer. Rune had seen it too, but after Talaysen's earlier experience, she hadn't been certain she ought to mention it.

But Talaysen headed right up the tiny path from the shrine into the deeper woods, and she followed. This time, at least, the trees weren't reaching out to snag them. In fact, the path was quite neatly kept, if relatively untraveled. Thunder growled—to their right, now, rather than behind them—and lightning flickered above and to the right of them as the woods darkened and the clouds rolled in overhead.

She caught a glimpse of the black, rain-swollen bellies of the clouds, and a breath of cold wind snaked through the trees. *This is going to be another bad one—*

Talaysen had gotten a bit ahead of her, but abruptly stopped. She just about ran into him; she peeked around him to see what had made him halt, and stared straight into the face of one of the biggest mastiffs she had ever seen in her life. The dog was absolutely enormous; a huge brindle, with a black mask and ears—and more teeth than she really wanted to see at such a close range.

She froze. Talaysen had already gone absolutely still.

There was another dog behind the first, this one tawny-and-black; if anything, it looked even bigger. The first dog sniffed Talaysen over carefully while the second stood guard; when it got to his boots, Rune quietly slipped his knife from the sheathe and pressed it into his hand, then drew her own. Knives weren't much against a dog the size of a small pony, but if the creature took it into its head to attack, knives were better than bare hands.

The dog raised its head, turned, and barked three times, as its companion watched them to make certain they didn't move. It waited a moment, then barked again, the same pattern, but this time there was no denying the impatience in its voice.

"All right, all right, I'm coming!" a voice from the path beyond the dogs called, sounding a little out of breath. "What on Earth can you two have—oh.''

A brown-robed man, gray-brown hair cut in the bowl-shaped style favored by some of the Orders, and a few years older than Talaysen, came around the turning in the path that had blocked him from their view.. He stared at them for a moment, as if he hadn't expected to see anything like them, and stopped at the second dog's rump. "You great loon!" he scolded affectionately, and the first mastiff lowered its head and wagged his tail. "It's just a couple of musicians! I would have thought you'd cornered an entire pack of bandits from all the noise you were making!"

The dog wagged its tail and panted, grinning. Talaysen relaxed, marginally..

"Oh, come *off*, you louts!" the robed man said, hauling at the second dog's tail until it turned around, and repeating the process with the first one.. "Go on, be off with you!. Back home! Idiots!"

The dogs whuffed and licked his hands, then obediently padded up the path out of sight.. The robed man turned to them, and held out his hand (after first wiping it on his robe) to Talaysen.. "I'm Father Bened," he said, shaking the hand that Talaysen offered in turn vigorously. "We'll save other introductions for the cottage—" He looked up as a particularly spectacular bolt of lightning arced over their heads.. "If you'll just follow me, I think we might just out-race the rain!" Without any further ado, he picked up the skirts of his robes and ran in the same direction the dogs had taken without any regard for dignity. Talaysen wasn't far behind him, and Rune was right at Talaysen's heels. They all made the shelter of the cottage barely in time; just as they reached the door, the first, fat drops began falling. By the time Rune got inside and got her pack and gear off, the storm was sending down sheets of water and thumb-sized hailstones into the bargain. She pushed forward into the room so that the Priest could get at the door, but things seemed to be a confusion of firelight, shadows, and human and canine bodies.

"There!" Father Bened slammed the door shut on the storm outside and took Rune's pack away from her, stowing it in a little closet next to the door, beside Talaysen's. "Now, do come in, push those ill-mannered hounds over, and find yourself a bit of room. I'm afraid they take up most of the space until they lie down. Down, you overgrown curs!" The last was to the dogs, who paid no attention to him whatsoever, being much too interested in sniffing the newcomers over for a second time, in case they had missed some nuance on the first round of sniffs.

After a great deal of tugging on the dogs' collars and exasperated commands which the beasts largely ignored, Father Bened got the mastiffs lying down in what was evidently their proper place; curled up in the chimney corner on one side of the hearth. Together they took up about as much space as a bed, so it wasn't too surprising that the Father didn't have much in the way of furniture, at least in this room. Just three chairs and a table, and cupboards built into the wall.

Father Bened busied himself at one of those cupboards, bringing out a large cheese, half a loaf of bread, and a knife. He followed that with three plates and knives, and a basket of pears. Very plainly he was setting out supper for all three of them.

Talaysen coughed, and Father Bened looked over at him, startled. "Excuse, Father," the Bard said, "but you don't—"

"But I *do,* son," the Priest said, with a look of reproach. "Indeed I do! You've arrived on my doorstep, on the wings of a storm—what am I to do, sit here and eat my dinner and offer you nothing? I am not so poor a son of the Church as all that! Or so niggardly a host, either!"

While he was speaking, he was still bringing things down out of the cupboards; a couple of bottles of good cider, three mugs, and in a bowl, a beautiful comb of honey that was so rich and golden it made Rune's mouth water just to look at it.

"There!" he said in satisfaction. "Not at all bad, I don't think. The bread and honey are mine, the cheese is local—I trade honey for it. I can trade the honey for nearly everything that my local friends don't give me. Here, let me toast you some cheese—there is only one toasting-fork. I fear. I'm not much used to getting visitors—"

There didn't seem to be anything they could do to stop him, so Rune made herself useful by pouring cider, while Talaysen cut the bread and cheese. The dogs looked up hopefully at the proceedings, and Rune finally asked if they needed to be fed as well.

"The greedy louts would gladly eat anything that hits the floor, and look for more," Father Bened said, as he laid a second slab of toasted cheese, just beginning to melt, on a slice of bread. "I've fed them, but they'll try to convince you otherwise. I could feed them a dozen times a day, until their eyes were popping out, and they'd still try to tell you they were starving."

"What on Earth do you feed them?" Talaysen asked, staring at the dogs as if fascinated. "And where did you get them? They're stag-hounds, aren't they? I thought only Sires raised stag-hounds."

Father Bened ducked his head a little, and looked guilty. "Well—the truth is, they aren't mine, really. They belong to a—ah—a friend. I—ah—keep them for him. He comes by every few days with meat and bones for them; the rest of the time I feed them fish or whatever rabbits I can—ah—that happen to die."

Rune began to get a glimmering of what was going on. It was a good thing no one had ever questioned the good Father; he was a terrible liar.

"And if the meat your friend brings them is deer, it's just really lucky that he found the dead carcass before it was too gone to be of use, hmm?" she said. Father Bened flushed even redder.

"Father Bened," she said with amusement, "I do believe that you're a poacher! And so is this 'friend' of yours!"

"A poacher? Well, now I wouldn't go that far—" he said indignantly. "Sire Thessalay claims more forest land hereabouts than he has any right to! I've petitioned the Sires and the barons through the Church I don't know how many times to have someone come out and have a look, but no one ever seems to read my letters. My friend and I are simply—doing the work of the Church. Feeding the hungry, clothing the naked—"

"With venison, cony, and buckskin and fur," Talaysen supplied. "I take it that a lot of the small-holders out here go hungry in the winter, else?"

The Father nodded soberly. "When the Sire claimed the forest lands, he also laid claim to lands that had been used for grazing and for pig-herding. Many of the small-holders lost half their means of support. You're Free Bards, aren't you?" At Talaysen's nod, he continued. "I thought you might be. A year ago last winter one of your lot stayed with me for a bit. A good man; called himself 'Starling' if I mind me right. I told him a little about our problem; he went out with my friend a few times to augment food supplies."

"I know him," Talaysen replied. "From a small-holder family himself."

"I thought as much." Father Bened shrugged, and laid out the third slice of cheese, then wasted no time in digging into his portion. Rune picked up the bread and nibbled gingerly; the cheese was still quite hot, and would burn her mouth if she wasn't careful. It tasted like goat-cheese; it was easier to raise goats on marginal land than cattle, especially if your grazing lands had been taken from you.

"I'm city-bred, myself," the Father continued. "When I was a young-ster, the Church was very special to me, and I grew up with this vision of what it must be like—full of men and women who'd gotten rid of what was bad in them, and had their hearts set on God. Always felt as if the Church was calling me; went straight into Orders as soon as I could."

He sighed. Talaysen nodded sympathetically. "I think the same thing happened to you that happened to my cousin Ardis."

"If she had a crisis of conscience, yes," Father Bened replied sadly. "That was when I found out that the Church was just like anyplace else; just as many bad folk as good, and plenty that were indifferent. Since I hadn't declared for an Order yet, I traveled a little to see if it was simply that I'd encountered an unusual situation. I came to the conclusion that I hadn't, and I almost left the Church.''

"Ardis decided to fight from within," Talaysen told him. "She got assigned to the Justiciars.''

"I decided the same, but to work from below, not above,'' Father Bened replied. "There were more of the bad and indifferent kind when you were in the city, in the big cloisters attached to the cathedrals, or so it seemed to me. So I got myself assigned to the Order of Saint Clive; it's a mendicant order that tends to wayside shrines. I thought that once I was out in the country, I'd be able to do more good.''

"Why?" Rune asked. "It seems to me if you were city-bred you'd have a hard time of it out in the wilds. You must have spent all your time trying to keep yourself fed and out of the weather—''

"I didn't think of that," he admitted, and laughed. "And it was a good thing for me that God takes care of innocent fools. My Prior took pity on me and assigned me here; this cottage was already built, and my predecessor had been well taken care of by the locals. I simply settled in and took up where he'd left off.''

"What do you think of the Priest in Brughten?" Talaysen asked carefully. Father Bened's face darkened.

"Father Bened can only say that his Brother in the Church could be a little more charitable," he replied carefully. "But I am told that there is a poacher of rabbits who roams these woods that has called him a thief who preys on widows and orphans, a liar, and a toady to anyone with a title or a fat purse. And the poacher has heard that he goes so far as to deny the sacraments to those he feels are too lowly to afford much of an offering.''

"I'd say the poacher is very perceptive," Talaysen replied, then described his encounter with the Brughten Priest, though not the part where he revealed himself to be Gwydain. Father Bened listened sympathetically, and shook his head at the end.

"I can only say that such behavior is what I have come to expect of him," the Priest said. "But at least I can offer a remedy to your problem. Friends, if all you wanted was to be wed—well, I have the authority. I don't have even a chapel, but if this room will suit you—''

"A marsh would suit me better than a cathedral right now," Rune said firmly. "And that fat fool in Brughten may have joy of his. This room will be fine.''

Father Bened beamed at her, at Talaysen, and even at the dogs, who thumped their tails on the floor, looked hopefully for a morsel of cheese, and panted.

"Wonderful!" he exclaimed. "Do you know, you'll be my first wedding? How exciting! Here, finish your dinner, and let me hunt up my book of offices—" He crammed the last of his bread and cheese into his mouth, and jumped up from his chair to rummage through one of the cupboards until he came to a little leather-covered book. "I should have some contracts in here, too, if the beetles haven't gotten to them—" he mumbled, mostly to himself, it seemed. "Ah! Here they are!"

He emerged with a handful of papers, looked them over, and found the one he wanted. It had been nibbled around the edges, but was otherwise intact. He placed it on the table next to the cider, and leafed through the book.

"Here it is. Wedding." He looked up. "I'm supposed to give you a great long lecture at this point about the sanctity of marriage, and the commitment it means to each of you, but you both strike me as very sensible people. I don't think you need a lecture from *me*, who doesn't know a *thing* about women. And I don't expect you're doing this because you don't have anything else to do tonight. So, we'll skip the lecture, shall we, and go right into the business?"

"Certainly," Talaysen said, and took Rune's hand. She nodded and smiled at Father Bened, who smiled back, and began.

"Well, did that suit you?" Talaysen asked, as they spread their blankets in Father Bened's hardly used spare room. There was no furniture, the light was from one of their own candles, and the only sounds were the snores of Father Bened's mastiffs in the other room and the spattering of rain on the roof.

"Practical, short, to the point, and yes, it suited me," Rune replied, carefully spreading their blankets to make one larger bed. It practically filled the entire room. "There's a duly signed sheet of parchment in your pack that says we're married, and the next town we go through, we'll drop the Church copy off at the clerk's office." She stood up and surveyed her work. "Now, are *you* happy?"

Talaysen sighed. "If I told you how happy I was, you probably wouldn't believe it—"

Rune turned, smiled, and moved closer to him, until there was less than the width of a hair between them. "So why don't you show me?" she breathed.

He did.

It was a long time before they slept.

CHAPTER NINETEEN

"I cannot *believe* this!" Talaysen fumed, testing the bonds about his wrists and giving the effort up after a few moments. A good thing, too; since they were roped together at the wrists, his efforts had been wrenching Rune's shoulders out of their sockets. "First the damn Guild gets all free-lance musicians barred from the last three Faires—and now *this*—"

Rune didn't say anything, which was just as well. There wasn't much she could say—and certainly none of it would have made their guards vanish, eased his temper, or gotten them free of their bonds.

There were three major Faires up here in the north of the kingdom, all within a week of each other: the Wool Faire at Naneford, the Cattle Faire at Overton, and the Faire of Saint Jewel at Hyne's Crossing. Talaysen had planned to make all of them, for all three of them were good places to make contacts for wintering-over.

All three were held within the cathedral grounds inside each city— and at all three, when Talaysen and Rune had tried to gain entrance, they had been turned back by guards at the gates. Church guards, even though the Faires were supposed to be secular undertakings.

Each guard looked down his nose at them as he explained why they had been barred. There were to be no musicians allowed within except those with Guild badges. That was the beginning and the end of it. The Guild had petitioned the City Council and the Church, and they had so ruled; the Council on the grounds that licensing money was being lost, the Church on the grounds that musicians encouraged revelry and revelry encouraged licentiousness. If Rune and Talaysen wished to play in the streets of the city, or within one of the inns, they could purchase a busking permit and do so, but only Guild musicians and their apprentices would be playing inside the Faire. They found out later that there was *no* "free" entertainment in the Faires this year; anyone who wished to hear music could pay up a copper to listen to apprentices perform within a Guild tent, or a silver to hear Journeymen. That was the entertainment by day—anyone who sought music after dark could part with *three* silvers to listen to a single Master at night. There were no dancers in the "streets" or otherwise. In fact, there was nothing within the Faire grounds but commerce and Church rituals. Rune would not have been overly surprised to learn that the Guild had even succeeded in banning shepherds from playing to their herds within the Faire bounds.

It was Rune's private opinion that there would be so many complaints that this particular experiment would be doomed after this year, and Talaysen agreed—but that didn't help them now.

Talaysen had been angry at the first Faire, furious at the second, and incoherent with rage at the third. Rune had actually thought that he might brain the third gate-guard—who besides his Church-hireling uniform had worn Guild colors and had been particularly nasty—with his own two hands. But he had managed to get control of his temper, and had walked away without doing the man any damage.

But by then, of course, their coin-reserve was seriously low, and their efforts to find an inn that did not already have a resident musician had been completely without result. So rather than risk a worse depletion of their reserves, they headed out into the countryside, where, with judicious use of fish-hook and rabbit snare, they could at least extend their supplies.

In a few days they had gotten as far as Sire Brador Jofferey's lands. And that was where they ran into a trouble they had never anticipated.

Sire Brador, it seemed, was involved in a border dispute with his neighbor, Sire Harlan Dettol. By the time they entered Sire Brador's lands, the dispute had devolved into warfare. Under the circumstances, strangers were automatically suspect. A company of Sire Brador's men-at-arms had surrounded them as they camped—and Rune thanked God that they had not put out any rabbit snares!—and took them prisoner with hardly more than a dozen words exchanged.

A thin and nervous-looking man guarded them now, as they sat, wrists bound behind their backs and feet hobbled, in the shade of an enormous oak. *At least they gave us that much,* Rune thought wearily; they could have been left in the full sun easily enough. The Sire's men were not very happy about the way things were going; she had picked that up from listening to some of the conversations going on around them. Exchanging of insults and stealing or wrecking anything on the disputed land was one thing—but so far six men had been killed in this little enterprise, and the common soldiers were, Rune thought, justifiably upset. They had signed on with the Sire to be guards and deal with bandits—and to harass their neighboring Sire now and again. No one had told them they were going to go to war over a silly piece of land.

Another man-at-arms approached on heavy feet, walking towards them like a clumsy young bull, and the nervous fellow perked up. Rune reckoned that their captivity was at an end—or that, at least, they were going somewhere else.

Good. There's pebbles digging into my behind.

"The cap'n 'll see the prisoners now," the burly fellow told their guard, who heaved a visible sigh of relief and wandered off without any warning at all. That left the burly man to stare at them doubtfully, as if he wasn't quite certain what to do with them.

"You got t' get t'yer feet," he said, tentatively. "You got t' come with me."

Talaysen heaved a sigh of pure exasperation. "That's going to be a bit difficult on both counts," he replied angrily. "We can't *get* to our feet, because you've got us tied back to back. And we can't *walk* because you've got us hobbled like a couple of horses. Now unless you're going to do something about that, we're going to be sitting right here until Harvest."

The man scratched his beard and looked even more uncertain. "I don't got no authority to do nothin' about that," he said. "I just was told I gotta bring you t' the cap'n. So you gotta get t'yer feet."

Talaysen groaned. Rune sighed. This would be funny if it weren't so stupid. And if they weren't trussed up like a couple pigs on the way to market. It might get distinctly *un*funny, if their guard decided that the application of his boot to their bodies would get them standing up . . . she contemplated her knees, rather than antagonize him by staring at him.

She looked up at the sound of footsteps approaching; yet another man-at-arms neared, this one in a tunic and breeches that were of slightly better quality and showing less wear than the other man's.

"Never mind, Hollis," said the newcomer. "I decided to come have a look at them myself." He surveyed them with an air of vacant boredom. "Well, what do you spies have to say for yourselves?"

"*Spies?*" Talaysen barked in sheer outrage. "Spies? Where in God's Sacred Name did you get *that* idea?"

Rune fixed the "captain," if that was what he was, with an icy glare. "Since when do spies camp openly beside a road, and carry musical instruments?" she growled. "Dear God, the only weapons we have are a couple of dull knives! What were we supposed to do with *those,* dig our way into your castle? *That* would only take ten or twenty years, I'm sure!"

The captain looked surprised, as if he hadn't expected either of them

to talk back to him. *If all he's caught so far are poor, frightened farmers,
I suppose no one has.*

He blinked at them doubtfully. "Well," he said at last, "if you aren't
spies, then you're conscripts." As Talaysen stared at him in complete
silence, he continued, looking them over as if they were a pair of sheep.
"You—with the gray hair—you're a bit long in the tooth, but the boy
there—"

"I'm not a boy," Rune replied crisply. "I'm a woman, and I'm *his*
wife. And you can go ahead and conscript me, if you want, but having
me around isn't going to make your men any easier to handle. And
they're going to be even harder to handle after I castrate the first man
who lays a hand on me."

The captain blanched, but recovered. "Well, if you're in disguise as
a boy, then you're obviously a spy after all—"

"It's not a disguise," Talaysen said between clenched teeth. "It's
simply easier for *my wife* to travel in breeches. It's not her fault you
can't tell a woman in breeches from a boy. I'm sure you'll find half the
women in this area working the fields in breeches. Are you going to
arrest them for spying, too?" The captain bit his lip. "You must be
spies," he continued stubbornly. "Otherwise why were you out there on
the road? You're not peddlers, and the Faires are over. Nobody travels
that road this time of year."

"We're *musicians,*" Rune said, as if she was speaking to a very
simple child. "We are carrying *musical instruments*. We *play and sing*.
We were going to Kardown Faire and your road was the only way to
get there—"

"How do I know you're really musicians?" he said, suspiciously.
"Spies could be carrying musical instruments, too." He smiled at his
own cleverness.

Talaysen cursed under his breath; Rune caught several references to
the fact that brothers and sisters should not marry, and more to the
inadvisability of intercourse with sheep, for this man was surely the
lamentable offspring of such an encounter.

"Why don't you untie us and give us our instruments, and we'll *prove*
we're musicians?" she said. "Spies wouldn't know how to play, now,
would they?"

"I—suppose not," the captain replied, obviously groping after an
objection to her logic, and unable to find one. "But I don't know—"

Obviously, she thought; but she smiled charmingly. "Just think, you'll
get a free show, as well. We're really quite good. We've played before

Dukes and Barons. If you don't trust both of us, just cut *me* loose and let me play.''

Not quite a lie. I'm sure there were plenty of Dukes and Barons who were passing by at Kingsford when we were playing.

''What are you up to?'' Talaysen hissed, as she continued to keep her mouth stretched in that ingenuous smile.

''I have an idea,'' she muttered back out of the corner of her mouth. And as the captain continued to ponder, she laughed. ''Oh come now, you aren't afraid of one little woman, are you?''

That did it. He drew his dagger and cut first the hobbles at her ankles, then the bonds at her wrists. She got up slowly, her backside aching, her shoulders screaming, her hands tingling with unpleasant pins-and-needles sensations.

She *did* have an idea. If she could work some of the same magic on this stupid lout that she'd worked on the elves, she *might* be able to get him to turn them loose. She'd noticed lately that when they really *needed* money, she'd been able to coax it from normally unresponsive crowds— as long as she followed that strange little inner melody she'd heard when she had played for the elven-king. It was always a variation on whatever she happened to be playing; one just a little different from the original. The moment she matched with it, whatever she needed to have happen would occur. She was slowly evolving a theory about it; how it wasn't so much that the melody itself was important, it was that the melody was how she ''heard'' and controlled magic. Somehow she was tapping magic through music.

But she couldn't explain that to Talaysen. Or rather, she couldn't explain it right now. Later, maybe. If this really worked.

The captain poked their packs with his toe as she stood there rubbing her wrists. ''Which one is yours?'' he asked, without any real interest.

''That one, there,'' she told him. ''Why don't you hand me that fiddle—that's right, that one. A spy would *never* be able to learn to play this, it takes years—''

''A spy could learn to play a couple of tunes on it,'' the captain said, in a sudden burst of completely unexpected thought. ''That's all a spy would need.''

He looked at her triumphantly. She sighed, took the instrument from him before he dropped it, and took it out of its case to tune it. ''A spy could learn a couple of tunes,'' she agreed. ''But a spy wouldn't know them all. Pick one. Pick anything. I couldn't possibly know what you were going to pick to learn to play it in advance, so if I know it, then I'm not a spy. All right?''

She saw Talaysen wince out of the corner of her eye, and she didn't blame him. No fiddler could know every tune; she was taking a terrible risk with this—

But it was a calculated risk, taken out of experience. If he'd been a bright man, she wouldn't have tried this; he might purposefully pick something really obscure, hoping to baffle her.

But he wasn't bright; he was, in fact, the very opposite. So he did what any stupid man would do; he blurted the first thing that came into his mind. Which was, as she had gambled, "Shepherd's Hey"; one of the half-dozen fiddle-tunes every fiddler wishes he would never have to play again, and which someone in every audience asks for.

She played it, thinking very hard about getting him to release them, and listening with that inner ear for the first notes of the magic. . . .

He started tapping his toe halfway through the first repetition; a good sign, but not quite what she was looking for. But his eyes unfocused a bit, which meant she might be getting through to him—

Or that he was so dense he could be entranced, like a sheep, by perfectly ordinary music.

Three times through. Three times was what had worked with the elves; three times had coaxed pennies from otherwise tight fists.

Two repetitions—into the third—and—

There. Just an echo, a faint sigh of melody, but it was there. She was afraid to play the tune again, though; repeating it a fourth time might break the magic.

"Pick something else," she called out to him, breaking into his reverie.

He stared at her with his mouth hanging open for a moment, then stammered, " 'Foxhunter.' "

Another one of the tunes she had learned to hate while she was still at the Hungry Bear. She sighed; if her feelings got in the way of the music, this might turn out to be a bad idea instead of a good one. But the magic was still with her, and stronger as she brought the "Hey" around into the first notes of "Foxhunter." His eyes glazed over again, and she began to get the sense of the inner melody, stronger, and just a little off the variant she played. She strove to bring them closer, but hadn't quite—not before she'd played "Foxhunter" three times as well.

But this was a subtle, slippery magic that she was trying to work. She had to get inside him somehow, and control the way he thought about them; this called for something quieter. Maybe that was why she hadn't quite managed to touch the magic-tune yet. . . .

This time she didn't ask him to pick something. She slowed the final bars of "Foxhunter," dragged them out and sent the tune into a minor key, and turned the lively jig into something else entirely different; a mournful rendition of "Captive Heart."

That did it! The hidden melody strengthened suddenly; grew so clear, in fact, that she glanced at Talaysen and was unsurprised to see a look of concentration on his face, as if he could hear it too.

Once, twice—and on the third repetition, something dropped into place, and her tune and the magic one united, just as the sun touched the horizon.

She played it to the end, then took her bow from the strings and waited to see what, if anything, the result of her playing was going to be.

The captain shook himself, as if he was waking from a long sleep. "I must—how—I think—" He shook himself again, then drew his knife and cut Talaysen's bonds, offering him a hand to pull the Master to his feet. "I don't know what I was thinking of," the captain said, vaguely. "Thinking two minstrels like you were spies. Stupid, of course. These past couple of weeks, they've been hard on us. We're looking for spies behind every bush, it seems."

"No harm done, captain," Talaysen said heartily, as Rune put up her fiddle as quickly as she could, and slung her pack on her back. She dragged his over to his feet, and he followed her example, still talking. "No harm done at all. Good thinking, really, after all, how could you know? I'm sure your Sire is very pleased to have a captain like you."

When Talaysen stopped for a moment to get his pack in place, Rune took over, pulling on his elbow to get him moving towards the edge of camp and the road. "Of course, how could you know? But we obviously *are* musicians and you don't need to detain us, now, do you? Of course not. We'll just be on our way. Thank you. No, you needn't send anyone after us, we'll be fine—we know exactly where we need to go, we'll be off your Sire's land before you know it—"

She got Talaysen moving and waved good-bye; Talaysen let her take the lead and wisely kept quiet. The other men-at-arms, seeing that their captain was letting the former captives go, were content to leave things the way they were. One or two of them even waved back as Rune and Talaysen made all the speed they could without (hopefully) seeming to do so.

It wasn't until they were on the open road again that Rune heaved a sigh of relief, and slowed her pace.

"All right, confess," Talaysen said, moving up beside her and speaking quietly out of the corner of his mouth. "I saw what happened, and I *thought* I heard something—"

"How much do you know about magic?" Rune asked, interrupting him, and gazing anxiously at the darkening sky.

"Not much, only the little Ardis tells me, and what's in songs, of course." He hitched his pack a little higher on his shoulders. "You're telling me that you're a mage?"

She shook her head slightly, then realized he might not be able to see the gesture in the gathering gloom. "I'm not—I mean, I don't know if I am or not. I know what happened with the elves, but I thought that was just because the elves were easier to affect with music than humans. Now—I don't know. I hear something when I'm doing—whatever it is. And this time I think you heard it too."

"Ardis told me every mage has his own way of sensing magic," Talaysen said thoughtfully. "Some see it as a web of light, some as color-patterns, some feel it, some taste or smell it. Maybe a mage who was also a musician would hear it as music—"

He faltered, and she added what she thought he was going to say. "But you heard it too. Didn't you? You heard what I was trying to follow."

"I heard something," he replied, carefully. "Whether it was the same thing you heard or not, I don't know."

"Well, whatever is going on—when I really need something to happen, I think about it, *hard,* and listen inside for a melody at the same time. When I find it, I try to match it, but since it's a variation on what I've playing, it takes a little bit of time to do that, to figure out what the pattern is going to be. And it seems like I have to play things in repeats of three to get it to work. It's the moment that I match with that variation that I seem to be able to influence people."

"But what about with the elves?" he asked. "You weren't doing any variations then—"

"I don't know, I'm only guessing," she replied, looking to the west through the trees, and wondering how long they had before the sun set. "But what I was playing was all Gypsy music or music already associated with the elves, like the 'Faerie Reel.' Maybe they're more susceptible to music, or maybe the music itself was already the right tune to be magic. Next Midsummer Faire we are going to have to talk to your cousin about all this—I don't like doing things and not knowing how or why they work. Or what they might do if they don't work the way I think they will."

She was looking at him now, peering through the blue twilight, and not at the road, so she missed spotting the trouble ahead. Her first inkling of a problem was when Talaysen's head snapped up, and he cursed under his breath.

"We'll do that. If we're not languishing in a dungeon," Talaysen groaned. "If this isn't the worst run of luck I've ever had—if I hadn't already been expecting the worst—"

She turned her head—and echoed his groan of disgust. Just ahead of them was a roadblock. Manned by armed soldiers with a banner flapping above them in Sire Harlan's black-and-white stripes.

"Well, there's no point in trying to avoid them; they'll only chase us," Talaysen sighed, as the soldiers stirred, proving that they'd been sighted too. "God help us. Here we go again."

"This time, let's see if we can't get them to let us prove we're minstrels right off," Rune said, thinking quickly. "I'll try and work magic on them again. And since you heard what I was trying to follow, *you* join me on this one. Maybe with both of us working on them, we can do better than just get them to let us go."

"All right," Talaysen replied quietly, for they were just close enough to the barricade that a sharp-eared man might hear what they were saying. "Follow my lead."

He raised his arm and waved, smiling. "Ho there!" he called. "We are certainly glad to see *you!*"

Looks of astonishment on every face told Rune that he'd certainly managed to confuse them.

"You—sir, are you the captain?" he continued, pointing at one of the men who seemed to be in charge. At the other's wary nod, Talaysen's smile broadened. "Thank goodness! We have a lot to tell you about. . . ."

"Ten pennies and quite a little stock of provisions, *and* an escort to the border," Talaysen said in satisfaction, patting the pouch at his belt. "Not bad, for what started out a disaster. Maybe our luck is turning."

"Maybe we're turning it ourselves," Rune countered, but lazily. She was not going to argue about results, however they came about.

A good night's sleep in the Sire's camp had helped matters. They'd done so well that they'd become honored guests by the time they were through playing, instead of captives. And while Sire Harlan was not interested in taking on a musician until his little feud with his neighbor had been settled, he *did* know about the banning of non-Guild minstrels from the previous three Faires. When they had played for him personally, he spent quite some time talking with them afterwards, over a cup of wine. He had assured them that a similar attempt at Kardown had been blocked.

"Did you hear the rest of the story about the Faires?" Talaysen asked. "I asked Captain Nours about it, and got an earful."

She shook her head. "No, I wasn't close enough to listen, and that terribly earnest cousin of the Sire was pouring his life-story into my ear."

"That's what you get for being sympathetic," he chuckled, and kicked at a rock to keep from stepping on it. "It wasn't just the Bardic Guild. *All* the Guilds got together and barred non-Guild participants. Sire Harlan's captain is also a wood-carver, and he's heard that if they try the same again next year, the non-Guild crafts-people have threatened to hold their own Faires—*outside* the gates, and just off the road. Which means no Church tax or city tax on sellers, as well as an open Faire."

She widened her eyes. "Can they do that?" she asked.

"I don't know why not," he replied. "One of the farmers has agreed to let them use his fallow fields for free for the first year. That may be how the Kingsford Faire started; I seem to recall something like that— the Church putting a ban on entertainment or levying an extra use-tax. I can tell you that most common folk would rather go to an open Faire, given a choice. Anyway, he asked me to spread that bit of news as well, so that the small crafters are ready, come next year."

She nodded, stowing the information away in her memory. That was another thing the Free Bards did that she hadn't known; they passed news wherever they went. Often it was news that those in power would prefer others didn't know. Ordinary minstrels might or might not impart news as the whim and the generosity of their audience moved them; Bardic Guild musicians never did.

So in a way we are spies, she reflected. *Only not in a way that sheep-brained captain would ever recognize.*

"Aren't we going to meet Gwyna at Kardown?" she asked, suddenly, squinting into the sunlight, and taking off her hat to fan herself with it.

"That was the plan," he replied. "Why?"

"Oh, nothing—" she replied vaguely. She hadn't thought about the coming encounter, until the association of "news" brought it to mind.

She and Talaysen *were* news, so far as the Free Bards were concerned. When they had parted from the Free Bards, she and Talaysen had been Master and Apprentice. Now their relationship was something altogether different. Gwyna planned a course of travel that put her in and out of contact with a good half of the Free Bards over the year, not to mention all the gypsy Clans. *She* would be the one telling everyone she met of Master Wren's change of status, and if she didn't approve . . .

Rune realized then that she wanted not only Gwyna to approve, but all the rest of the Free Bards, including people she didn't even know yet. And not just for her own sake. If there was divisiveness in the Free Bards, trouble with Talaysen's leadership, the things she and Talaysen had talked about would never come to pass. The group might even fall apart.

We will never make a difference if that happens, she thought worriedly, and then realized with a start that for the first time in her life she was thinking of herself as a part of a group. Worrying about "we," where "we" meant people she'd never met as well as those she knew and liked.

It was a curious feeling, having been a loner most of her life, to suddenly find herself a part of something.

If Gwyna didn't approve of what had happened between her and Talaysen—

Then she mentally took herself by the scruff of the neck and shook herself. *Of course she'll approve,* she scolded. *She was practically throwing us into bed together before we all broke up. I'm running from shadows that aren't even there. The fact that we're married shouldn't make any kind of a difference to her. She told me herself that Talaysen spent too much time alone.*

She noticed that Talaysen was watching her with a concerned frown, and smiled at him. "It's all right, no disasters. Just thinking things through," she said cheerfully. "Tell me something, do you think we were working magic last night, or not?"

He hesitated a moment, taking the time to wipe some of the dust from his face with his scarf. "I never thought of myself as a mage, or anything like one," he said, finally. "Even though everything I've ever *really* wanted I've gotten. Now that I think about it, that is rather odd; I don't know of anyone who always gets what he wants or needs. I always thought it was plain fool luck, but maybe it wasn't just extraordinary good luck. Maybe it was magic all along."

"Your cousin's a mage," she pointed out. "I'd always been told that sort of thing runs in families. That's the way it is in ballads, anyway."

"That might explain it." He paused a moment, and Rune had an idea that he was gathering his thoughts. "Last night I told you that I heard the melody you were trying to match the first time we were caught. You wanted me to see if I could actually match it myself when we were wooing Sire Harlan's men, and I said I'd try, and we didn't have a chance to talk about what I did in private. Well, I heard the melody, just like before, and I tried to match it. Easier on a lute than a fiddle, by the way.''

She nodded. ''And you did it; I felt you snap into the melody at the end of the first time through, and the tune got stronger as we played it. Which was probably why they asked us to stay and play for them, why the men gave us supplies, and why the Sire gave us money and an escort.''

''I think it's also why the Sire talked to us personally,'' he said. She raised an eyebrow in surprise, and he nodded. ''When we played for his men, he was listening just beyond the fire. I didn't *see* him, but somehow I knew he was there, and I knew we needed his goodwill. I saw you were doing all right with the men, so I turned my attention to him. I hoped I could get him to help us out; the captain was pretty reluctant to exceed his authority.'' He frowned, as if thinking of something unpleasant.

''I'd say it worked,'' she replied, wondering why he was frowning.

''That's the trouble, it *did,* and too well.'' His frown deepened, and he tucked his scarf around his neck again. ''He talked to us very like equals, he gave us money and an escort. He shouldn't have done any of those things, it's just not in the character of most Sires to welcome strangers into their camps and treat them like old friends. What I did somehow made him act completely differently—''

''Maybe not,'' she countered. ''He was camped out there with his men, after all, and he's obviously liked as well as respected. Maybe he would have done all that anyway. Maybe he's used to treating underlings well; maybe he just likes music.''

''Maybe, but it's not likely.'' He shook his head. ''But that's not the point. The problem here isn't what he did, it's that *I made him do it.* I made him do those things just as surely as if I'd held a knife to his throat and ordered him to tell us the same things. Even though it kept us out of trouble, I don't like the implications. Being able to change the way people think and react is—well, it's frightening.''

She started to object, then shut her mouth, thinking about it. It *was* frightening, and she found many reasons why what she was doing was wrong. ''Can Ardis do that?'' she asked.

He nodded. ''That, and other things. Healing, for one. Mostly she doesn't use her magic. I think she told me that she uses it only when— after very careful consideration—she thinks it's just and fair to do so, and not simply convenient.''

How would I feel about somebody coming in and changing my thinking around? she wondered. "Was it just and fair of us to keep those men-at-arms from throwing us in a dungeon, or conscripting us?" she countered. "I certainly think it was! They wouldn't listen to reason or logic, and I was running out of patience."

He grinned. "I'd have to say yes and you know it," he mocked. "That's a cheating question."

"Would it have been just and fair to get that Priest to marry us?" she continued.

"Now that is a good question." He mulled that over for a bit. "I would have to say no. Even though he was being an officious, uncharitable, vain and foolish man."

"Why not?" she asked, wanting to hear his reasoning.

"It would not have been just and fair to change his mind, because we were only inconvenienced. On the other hand, if those men-at-arms had jailed or conscripted us, we would undoubtedly have been harmed." He smiled feebly. "I don't do well in damp dungeons. And I wouldn't know one end of a sword from the other. In the former, I'd probably become ill rather quickly, and as a conscript I'd probably become *dead* just as quickly."

"Obviously the same goes for the elven-king," she replied, thoughtfully.

He nodded. "Elves aren't predictable. He might have kept us a while, or killed us when he tired of us. Now, whether or not we should have used this power of ours to change the minds of people at those Faires to let us in—I don't know."

"It's not worth debating," she told him, as a jay overhead called raucous agreement. "We couldn't have done anything to help ourselves or others at the last three Faires because the people we needed to influence directly were not going to come out to listen to us."

"True, but we could have started a riot," he said, so soberly that she knew he was not joking. "All we'd have needed to do would be stand outside the Church gates and sing rabble-rousing songs with that power behind them. People were annoyed enough already, especially the ones being turned away. We could quite easily have started a riot without anyone suspecting we were to blame."

The morning seemed suddenly cold, and she shivered. She'd never seen a riot. She didn't want to see one. People could be killed in riots; children often were trampled and either killed outright or maimed for life. "We don't do that," she said forcefully. "We don't *ever* do that."

"I agree," he replied, just as forcefully. "It would have to be something worlds away more serious than what we encountered to make starting a riot justified."

She paused to collect her thoughts. "You do realize that we're talking about this as if it's real, and not the product of some really good luck and our imaginations, don't you?"

"I don't have any doubt that it's real," he told her. "We've managed to change things three times with this—whatever it is. When something happens three times, it's not a coincidence, it's real."

It's more times than that, she thought wryly, remembering how she had coaxed money from unresponsive audiences. And then she sobered, thinking about what she'd done in a new light.

Had that been "fair and just"? After all, she hadn't done anything important to them, had she? They wouldn't have parted with their coins if they hadn't had them to spend. Would they?

Yes, but— She had still changed their thoughts, the most private thing a person could have. The poorest person in the world, the man accused of heresy and thrown into the Church's dungeons, a cripple who couldn't move arms or legs—they could still claim their thoughts as their own, and in that much they were wealthy and free.

But what she and Talaysen did could change that. Not in any large way, but it was still a change. And for what? Convenience, again. The convenience, perhaps, of not working quite so hard. . . .

Never mind that finding that elusive thread of magic-song and matching it was harder work than simply playing well. She had to assume that one day it might become easy. What then? Wouldn't it be a temptation to simply sit back and play indifferently, knowing that she would be well-paid no matter how she played?

She thought of all the cold days in the winter, busking on a corner in Nolton, and had to admit that it would have been more than a temptation. If she'd known about this, she'd have done it. And she'd have probably teased her audiences into buying hot cider and sausage rolls from her vendor friends as well, whether the listeners were hungry or not.

No. That was wrong. Absolutely wrong. It was a cheat, and it made her music into a lie.

"We don't use it to make audiences like us, either," she said into the silence, with more force than she intended. "They either appreciate us on their own or not at all."

He raised an eyebrow at her outburst but agreed immediately. "What do we have, then? Not for the sake of convenience, not when there are other ways to deal with a situation, only when it's fair and just?"

She nodded and sighed. "You know, I hate to admit this, but it sounds as if we're saying we can't use it to help ourselves at all."

He laughed. "Oh, partially. We can't use it unless we're really being threatened, shall we say? Or it's for something that truly needs to be done."

"That sounds good." She glanced at him, and couldn't help grinning. "Now, does threat of *hunger* count?"

"I don't—"

"Or how about if I wait until you're hungry to ask that question?" she said, and chuckled.

He only shook his head. "Women," he said, as if that explained everything, and then changed the subject.

Just like a man, she thought with amusement, and let him.

CHAPTER TWENTY

The Kardown Faire lasted only three days; it wasn't a very large Faire, but because it was a wool-market Faire, it tended to be a wealthy one. They found Gwyna waiting for them at the bare excuse for a gate in the sketchy fence surrounding the Faire on the town common; she had already found a good camping site, screened on three sides by bushes and trees, and claimed it for all three of them. Rune was happy to see her; a real friendly face, a known face, was a luxury she'd missed without realizing it.

Three days were just enough time for them to recoup some of their losses—and barely time for Gwyna to finish telling them the news of her adventures, and those of the other Free Bards she'd met with. Rune noticed something a little odd about Gwyna's behavior from the first, though it was nothing having to do with either her or Talaysen. Gwyna would keep glancing about nervously when she thought she was alone, and no longer bantered with strangers. And whenever she saw someone in a long robe, she became very, very quiet.

They had stayed together as a trio during the entire Faire; Gwyna had been delighted to hear of the wedding (much to Rune's relief). But that wasn't why they stayed as a group; their primary consideration was that Gwyna no longer seemed quite so fearlessly self-reliant, which accounted for the odd behavior Rune had noticed. Her misadventure with the mage-Priest had shaken her more than she would admit to anyone, even Rune. But Rune saw it in the way she constantly looked over her shoulder for trouble, even when there was no reason to, and in her troubled dreams at night. Gypsy Robin had gotten a bad shock, and she hadn't recovered from it yet.

She'd parted with Master Stork about a week after the Midsummer Faire, and it looked to Rune as if she hadn't had a steady night of sleep since. Talaysen told her he thought Gwyna must be sleeping with one eye open, and Rune figured he was probably right.

Gwyna played at being lighthearted, still, but her jesting often fell flat, her spirits were dampened, and she seemed to be certain that there was danger lurking just out of sight, especially at night. Not that Rune blamed her. But she was carrying more knives now, and openly; something that had the potential for serious problems if she felt herself threatened. If someone propositioned her in a way she thought was dangerous, in her state of heightened nerves, she might well draw on him—and use what she drew.

At the end of the third day, Gwyna went off to bring back water for their little camp, leaving Rune cleaning vegetables and Talaysen setting the fire, alone together for the first time that day. She decided to broach what had been on her mind since she'd seen the state Gwyna was in.

"Is it going to be any harder to find a wintering-over spot for a trio than it is for a duet?" she asked.

He looked up from the fire. "No, I don't think so," he said. "Are you thinking what I'm thinking?"

Rune nodded. "We can't let her go out there by herself until she gets over her nerves. She'll either wear herself out, or hurt someone."

"Or herself." He sat back on his heels. "I hadn't wanted to ask you, because it means—well—" He blushed. "We won't have our privacy."

"Lecher," she said, and grinned. "Oh, we can have our privacy. We just ask her to take a long walk. Seriously, though, we ought to invite her."

"You ought to invite her to what?" Gwyna asked lightly, as she rounded the corner of the half-shelter they'd erected, coming into their little protective circle of trees.

"We thought you ought to come with us for a while," Talaysen said. "We'd like your company. We've missed you."

"And?" Gwyna replied, setting down the canvas bucket in the hole they'd dug to hold it. "You're not inviting me because of my sparkling conversation, and you two have got quite enough companionship on your own, thanks."

"You look awful," Rune said frankly. "I told Wren that I thought it was because you're trying to stay up all night on guard. And we could use a third to split the watches with. It's hard enough sleeping at night with two; you never get a full night's sleep going watch-on-watch, and if you both fall asleep, well, you take your chances. Three can keep watches and still have time for a decent night's sleep."

"True," Gwyna replied thoughtfully, twining a strand of her hair around one finger. "There's a lot of unrest out in the countryside. I know there's been more feuds lately. They say it's because the High King is getting old and he's not keeping the Twenty Kings in line."

"What difference does that—" Rune began, then made the connection herself. "Oh. The Twenty Kings are busy trying to compete to be High King and ignoring the Barons and Dukes. And they're playing their own power games, and ignoring the Sires."

"Who are now free to take up their feuds again," Talaysen finished. "It all comes down to the bottom, eventually. That means us, who end up having to deal with bandits on the road; bandits who are there because the Sires aren't hunting them down." He grimaced. "The Church *should* be taking a hand here, but they won't."

"Other things come down to the common folk, too," Gwyna said. "I haven't seen any more bandits, but that's because I don't travel the main roads. Some of the others have run into trouble, though, and it seems to me to be more this year than last." She sat in thought for a while, her skirts spread in a colorful puddle around her. "I'll tell you what; I'll stick with you until the first snow. If you haven't found a wintering-up place for all three of us by then, we'll go thirds on a wagon and join one of my Family caravans. Will that suit you?"

Talaysen nodded and Rune heaved a silent sigh of relief. Gwyna could be so touchy when she thought someone was trying to protect her, but this time she *needed* protection. She was a lot younger than she looked, sounded, or acted. Gypsy children tended to grow up very quickly, but that didn't mean she was as mature as she appeared. A shock like she'd gotten could unseat the reason of someone Talaysen's age. Gwyna needed time to find her balance again.

"That solves our problem pretty neatly," Rune offered with absolute truth. "After getting shut out of three Faires, we were wondering if we were going to have even a chance at finding a winter position. So, if we don't"— she shrugged—"then we don't and we've got an alternate plan."

"Well good, then," Gwyna replied, relaxing. "Glad to be able to help. And don't worry about my getting underfoot too much. I'll find lots of reasons to take long walks, and some of them may even be genuine!" She winked, and Rune blushed, glad that the sunset color hid the red flush of her cheeks. "Are we leaving tomorrow morning early or late?"

"Late," Talaysen said. "All the heavy wagons and the herds are moving out at dawn, and I'd rather wait until they're well on their way. It's easier for us to pass them on the road than it is to get around the tangle when they leave." He grimaced. "And the drivers are a little less—"

The unusual sound of the clopping of hooves coming towards their campsite made him look up from his fire. "Who or what could that be?"

Rune shrugged, and looked over to Gwyna, who also shrugged. *Odd. It's plainly someone with beasts. What can he want with us?*

A weathered old man, a horse-trader by the harness-bits attached to his jacket, came around the corner of the half-shelter. He led a pair of sturdy pony-mules of the kind that the Gypsies used to pull their wagons and carry their goods, and stopped just as he reached conversational distance. The beasts stopped obediently behind him, and one nuzzled him and blew into his hair.

"Be you a minstrel called Rune?" he asked, looking directly at her.

Rune nodded in surprise.

"Can ye name me yer ma and yer village?" the old man continued.

"My mother is Stara, who last worked in the Hungry Bear Inn; that's in my old village of Westhaven," she replied politely. This had the sound of someone trying to identify her for some reason. Possibly a letter from Amber? But why send it via a horse-trader?

"An' who would ye say's yer best friend there?" the man persisted, though just as politely as she.

"That's an easy one," she said. "I only had one good friend when I left: Jib, the horse-boy."

"Then ye be the Rune I be lookin' fer." The man doffed his hat, and grinned. "Yon Jib's the lad I took on as m'partner this spring, an' damn if he ain't done better nor any on' us had reason t' think. He sen's ye these liddle lads, by way'o thanks, he says." He proffered the lead-reins, and Rune rose to take them, stunned with surprise. "He says ye's a right 'nuff lass, an' ye know how t' take care of a beast—I mind ye got a gyppo there by ye, though—" he nodded towards Gwyna, who nodded back. "There ain't none born can take care 'f a horse like a gyppo, so's ye make sure'n lissen t' the lady, eh?"

"I'll do that," Rune promised solemnly, too stunned to say anything else. "These are Vargians, right?"

"Aye," the man replied. "An' good lads, too. I wouldna let 'em go t' none but a gyppo or a friend or friend a'the lad. He's a good lad, Jib is."

"That he is," Rune replied faintly. This was a little too much to take in all at once. "One of the best in the world."

"Aye, well, I seen ye an' yer man an' yer fren' here at Faire, an' ye got all th' right friends," the man told her, so serious in his frankness that she couldn't even think of him as being rude. "Free Bards, eh? Free Bards an' gyppos, ye're the best folks on th' road. So, I'll tell Jib I caught up wi' ye, an' give his presents, an' I'll tell 'im ye're doin' right well. He'll be happy fer ye."

He turned to go, and Rune stopped him for a moment with one hand on his leather sleeve. "How is he, really?" she asked anxiously. "Is he all right? Is he happy?"

The man smiled, slowly, like the sun coming out from behind a cloud. "I reckon," he chuckled. "Oh, I reckon he'd say he's all right, though since he's set on weddin' m' girl an' I know her temper, I dunno how all right he'll stay! Still—they'll be settlin' down, I 'spect. Her mam had same temper, an' we never kilt each other enough so's ye'd notice. Like as not ye'll catch 'em both at Midsummer next year."

And with that, he put his hat carefully back on his head, and walked back down the road in the darkness, leaving Rune staring after him with the mules' reins still in her hands.

"Well, that solves one big problem," Gwyna said, breaking the silence. "And I know where we can get a wagon cheap, if you're willing to stay over a day while we get it refitted. I know I've got a third share's worth of coin. How about you two?"

"Oh, we have it," Talaysen replied, as Rune broke out of her stunned state, and came over to the fire for a couple pieces of wood for tethers and some rope for hobbles. "And draft beasts are always the expensive part of fitting up a wagon, am I right?"

Gwyna nodded, then rose and came over to look at the new acquisitions. She patted them down expertly, running her hands over their legs, checking their feet, then opening their mouths to have as good a look as she could with only firelight to aid her.

"A little old for a horse-mule, but middle-aged for ones out of a pony," she said, giving them both a final pat, and turning to help Rune stake them out to graze. "Especially for this breed; just like Rune said, they're Vargians. They'll live thirty useful years and probably die in harness, and they can eat very nearly anything a goat can eat. Hard to tell without pushing them, but their wind seems sound; I know their legs are, and he hasn't been doctoring them to make them look good." The same one that had blown into the old man's hair nuzzled her. "They're gentle enough even for you to handle, Master Wren!" She laughed, as if at some private joke, and Talaysen flushed.

"Here, let me see what they're called." She nudged the mule's head around so she could read the letters stamped on his halter in the flickering firelight. "This lad is Socks, evidently. And"—she squinted at the second halter—"the other is Tam. Good, short names, easy to yell." She left the mules, who applied themselves to grass with stolid single-mindedness. "I like your choice of friends, Lady Lark," she concluded. "It's nice to have friends who know when you might need a mule!"

*   *   *

The mules were a gift that impinged perilously on "too good to be true," and Talaysen pummeled his brain ceaselessly to reassure himself that neither he nor Rune had worked any of their "magic" to get them.

Finally, he slept, conscience appeased. They had not been anywhere near the animal-sellers. There had been no way that the old man could have heard them sing and been inadvertently magicked into giving them a pair of beasts. The mules were, therefore, exactly what they appeared to be: repayment of Rune's generosity to her old friend. When Rune had explained what she'd done, Gwyna had questioned her about the amount of money she'd sent the boy, and Gwyna had nodded knowingly.

"That's the right-size return on a gift like that," she had pronounced, when Rune worried aloud that she had bankrupted the boy. "Truly. He didn't send you horses, nor young mules; he didn't include any harness but the halters. If his year's been as good as the old man says, that's about right, and he'll still have profit."

Rune had been even more concerned how the old man had found them, since there was no way—she had thought—for Jib to find out where she was. She'd been afraid the gift might have been some machination of the Guild in disguise. But Gwyna and Talaysen had both been able to put her mind at ease on that score.

It was the Gypsies, of course. Rune had sent her gift with them; they, in turn, knew all the news of the Free Bards and would have known as soon as Rune had joined them. When Jib wanted to find her, he would likely have turned to the Gypsies who had brought him the money in the first place. Sooner or later he would have found someone who'd been at Midsummer, and who would have known the general direction of the Free Bards' travels, and by extension, what Faires Rune and Talaysen were planning on going to. Then it was just a matter for the old man of planning *his* selling trip to try intercepting them at one or more of those Faires.

With everyone's fears eased, all three of them slept soundly. In fact, it was the rattle of the mules' halters the next morning that awoke them, as the beasts tried in vain to reach grass outside the circles they'd eaten bare.

Rune took them down to the well to water them, while Talaysen and Gwyna set off in search of a wagon.

Many Gypsies settled in Kardown, for it was on the edge of the treeless, rolling plains of the Arden Downs. The soil was thin and rocky; too hard to farm, but it made excellent pasturage, and most of the folk hereabouts depended on the sheep that were grazed out there. Most households had a little flock, and the most prosperous had herds of several hundred. There was always work for someone good with animals, and when Gypsies chose to settle, they often became hired shepherds. Such a life enabled them to assuage their urge to wander in the summer, but gave them a snug little home to retire to when the winter winds roared and the sheep were brought back into the fold.

Because of that, there were often Gypsy wagons for sale here. Gwyna, obviously a Gypsy and fluent in their secret language, was able to make contact with one of the resident families as soon as they reached the marketplace.

From there it was a matter of tracking down who had wagons for sale, who had wagons they were keeping but might be induced to part with, and where they were.

They had looked at three, so far. The first two were much too small; fit only for two, or one and a fair amount of trade goods. The third was a little too old and rickety; Gwyna clucked her tongue over it and told its owner that he'd waited a bit long to sell it; he'd have to spend a lot of time fixing it up now, before it was road-worthy again. The owner agreed, and said with a sigh that he'd not been truly certain he wanted to settle until this summer. . . .

They traded road stories for a bit, then moved on to the fourth and last.

"This lad will take a bit of persuading, I think," Gwyna said as they approached the cottage. "He came off the road because his wife wanted to settle a bit, though he didn't. That means the wife will be on our side; if she can get him to part with the wagon, it means she'll not have to fret about him taking the bit in his teeth, packing them all up, and rolling out without so much as a 'do you think we should,' or a word of warning."

Thus armed, Talaysen set about charming the lady of the house while Gwyna tackled the man. He was very young to have come off the road; a half-dozen children playing in the yard told Talaysen why the wife had wanted to settle. Two children in a wagon weren't bad, but a mob like this would strain the seams of even the largest wagons he'd seen.

He couldn't hear what Gwyna was telling the man, a very handsome Gypsy with long, immaculately kept black locks and a drooping mustache of which he seemed very proud. He didn't make much of an effort to overhear, either. She was giving the young man some advice from a woman's point of view, he thought. The Gypsies believed in the right of a woman to make her own decisions, and she was probably telling him that if he decided to pack up and take to the road again, he might well find himself doing so alone.

Whatever it was she told him, it had the desired effect. He agreed—reluctantly, but agreed—to show them the wagon and sell it if it was what they wanted.

He kept it in a shed in the rear of his cottage, and unlike the wagon that had been kept out in the garden, it was easy to see that the owner of *this* rig had been serious about his desire to return to the road one day. The bright red and yellow paint was fresh and shiny; every bit of bright-work, from the twin lamps at the front to the single lamp over the window at the rear, was polished until it gleamed like gold. The leather of the seat had been kept oiled, and the wheels were in perfect repair, not a spoke missing.

Right away, Talaysen knew that it was the *kind* of wagon they needed; this was a two-beast rig, and provided the pony-mules could pull it, they would have the strength of both at their service. With a one-beast rig, the mule not in harness would have to be tethered to the rear. It was possible to switch them off to keep them fresh, but a dreadful nuisance to harness and unharness in the middle of the day.

But when the young man pushed the rig out, Talaysen knew that without a shadow of a doubt—if the mules were up to it—this was exactly what they'd been looking for.

It slept four; two in one bed at the rear, and two in narrow single bunks along the sides that doubled as seating. There was ample storage for twice what they carried; the harness was coiled neatly in the box built beneath the right-hand bunk. There was even a tiny "kitchen" arrangement that could be used in foul weather, and a charcoal stove to keep it warm in the winter.

"Can the little mules pull it?" he asked Gwyna and her fellow Gypsy. She looked over at the man. "Vargians," she said.

He nodded. "No problem. It's built light, lighter than it looks." He showed them, by pushing it forward by himself. "I had Vargians. The harness is already rigged for them." Then he sighed and made mournful eyes at his wife, who did her best to hide her smile of triumph. "Looks like the Lady meant this rig for you. I'd best resign myself to being off the road till the little ones are marriage-high."

Gwyna then began some spirited bargaining, that ended with them shaking hands and most of Talaysen's money joining hers. The wife looked even happier at that, which made him guess that *she* had some plans for the unexpected windfall.

"Bring the mules here, and I'll harness her and you can drive her over," the man said, looking less resigned and more content by the moment. That eased Talaysen's mind quite a bit; he would never have willingly deprived someone of a cherished dream, however impractical it was.

They returned to camp and Gwyna took charge of the mules, leaving Talaysen and Rune to divide the chores of breaking camp. There wasn't much to do, since they'd be reloading everything into the wagon; and shortly after they were finished, burying the little garbage they'd produced in the fire-pit, covering it with the ashes, and putting the frame of the half-shelter over it all, Gwyna appeared, driving the wagon up the road, with the mules moving briskly and looking altogether content to be in harness.

It was a matter of moments to load the wagon and stow everything. Talaysen was amazed at how pleased and proprietary he felt. "Now what?" he asked Gwyna.

"Now we drive back to town, leave the wagon at a stable for safe-keeping, and go up to the market to buy what we need. Oil for cooking, oil for the lamps, harness-mending kit, salt and fodder for the mules—" She looked over at Rune.

"Hmm. Flour, salt, honey; some vegetables that keep well. Spices. A couple of pots and a frying pan." Rune's brow wrinkled as she thought. "Featherbeds, if we're going to winter over in there. Charcoal for the stove. A bit of milk. Cider. Oh, a fresh-water keg, there doesn't seem to be one. Currycomb, brush and hoof-pick. I think that's it."

"That sounds about right," Gwyna agreed. "If I can get some eggs, I'd like to."

Talaysen grinned, completely at sea in this barrage of domesticity, and perfectly content—

"A chicken," he said, suddenly. "Bacon. The bacon will keep fairly well. Sausage and cheese." He tried to remember what the family horses had needed. "Oh, blankets for both mules; they'll need them in the winter."

"Good." Gwyna nodded. "Now, the big question; have we enough money for all that?"

They put their heads and their resources together, and decided that they did—if they skipped the bacon and chicken, and bargained well.

"Split up?" Rune asked.

Gwyna shook her head. "Better stay together. Master Wren, try and look pinch-pursed and disapproving, as if everything we're buying is a luxury."

He set his face obediently in a scowl, and she chuckled. "That'll do. Rune, we'll take turns. When we get into a sticky spot, the other one will jump in and say 'He's cheating you,' or something like that."

"Good, and look like the vendor's a thief."

"Exactly." Gwyna surveyed the marketplace. "Well, shall we attack?"

The market wasn't as large as some, but it was held every day, rather than just one day a week. Talaysen found his part altogether easy, and watched the women bargain with the stall-keepers like a couple of seasoned housewives. At the vegetable stall, Rune leaned over and pointed out the discolored places caused by insects that might hide soft-spots or larvae, and gave the poor man a glare as if he'd put them there himself. He capitulated immediately. The cheese-maker was a fellow Gypsy, and so came in only for some good-natured bantering. The miller was condescending, and the women bent their entire attention on him, and to both his and Talaysen's amazement, actually *caught* him cheating, with sacks with gravel weighting the bottom. When they threatened to expose him there and then, he *gave* them their flour. They then went back to the cheese-maker and betrayed his secret. Gwyna grinned nastily as they went on to the charcoal-maker.

"He won't be able to get away with that anymore," she said. "I suspect the only reason he's gotten by this long is because he only pulls that trick on strangers. But short measure's against the law, and he knows it. He could be pilloried for that." She looked well content. "Once we get the charcoal, we'll have everything we need, I think."

It was at just that moment that Talaysen felt ghostly fingers on his pouch. He reached back, quick as a striking snake, and caught a wrist. A bony wrist; he pulled on it, hauling the owner forward before he could bolt.

The owner made not a sound as Talaysen dragged him—for it was a "he"—around to the front of them.

"What—?" Rune said in surprise, then nodded. "So. Someone who didn't do well at the Faire, hmm?"

"Caught a light-fingers?" Gwyna asked mildly. She crossed her arms and stared at the boy, who dropped his gaze to his bare, dirty feet. "You should know better than to try that game with a Gypsy, sirrah. We *invented* that game."

The thief was a lot older than Talaysen had expected; roughly Rune's or Gwyna's age. Undersized, though, for his age; he didn't top Gwyna by more than an inch. The bones under Talaysen's hand were sharp; the bones of the face prominent. Three-quarters starved and filthy, with an expression of sullen resignation, he made no effort whatsoever to escape.

Talaysen shook him a little. "Have you anything to say for yourself before I turn you over to the constables?" he asked. There was a flash of fear in the boy's face as he looked up, but then he dropped his eyes again and simply shook his head.

"He doesn't look much like a thief, does he?" Rune mused. "At least, not a good thief. I thought they tended to look a bit more prosperous."

Gwyna tilted her head to one side, and considered the boy. "You're right, he doesn't. He looks to me like someone who's desperate enough to try anything, including picking a pocket, but he doesn't look much like a real thief."

Talaysen thought privately that what the boy looked like was *bad*—blood and bone. But he held his peace; though no stranger would know it, Gwyna had already warmed to this rag-man.

"I don't think you should turn him over to anyone," Rune continued. The boy looked up, quickly, surprise then apprehension flashing over his face, before he dropped his eyes again. Talaysen sighed.

"I don't think we should turn him over to anyone, either," Gwyna put in. She reached over and shook the boy's shoulder. "Here, you—if we feed you and give you a chance to clean up, will you promise not to run off until we've talked to you?"

He looked up again, and the expression of bewildered gratitude made Talaysen abruptly revise his opinion. That was not the expression of a bad youngster—it was more along the lines of a beaten dog who has just been patted instead of whipped. Maybe there was something worth looking into with this boy after all.

The boy nodded violently, and Talaysen released the hold he had on the boy's wrist. The youngster rubbed it a little, but made no move to escape, even though he probably could have gotten away in the crowd.

"Here," Gwyna said, shoving her load of packages at him. He took them, automatically, his eyes widening with surprise as he staggered beneath the weight. "Make yourself useful and carry these for me. Come along."

The boy followed her with complete docility. Or perhaps he was just stunned. If he was about Gwyna's age, he might not be too eager to run away at this point. Older men than he had been stunned by Gwyna on a fairly regular basis.

Talaysen smiled a little; there was a method to Gwyna's seeming foolishness. With that much burdening him, he couldn't run—unless he dropped the entire load, he was effectively hobbled. And if he dropped the packages, they'd know he was going to run.

They finished their purchases and returned to the wagon. The youngster handed his packages up to Rune to be stowed away, and looked—longingly, Talaysen thought—at the pony-mules.

Gwyna looked the boy up and down, critically. "You'll never fit Master Wren's clothes, nor mine," she said. "Rune, do you have a pair of breeches and a shirt I can borrow? His clothing won't be fit to wear without a lot of cleaning, and maybe not then."

"If you don't mind that they're not that far from the rag-bin themselves," Rune replied, doubtfully.

Gwyna snorted. "It's better than what he's wearing now."

Talaysen thought he detected a flush—of embarrassment?—under the layer of dirt coating the young man's face.

He still hasn't spoken a word . . . I wonder why?

With clean clothes in one hand and the boy in the other, Gwyna marched him off to the stream that had been serving for their bathing pool. He'd either bathe, or Gwyna would hold him down and wash him herself. Talaysen knew that look. He wouldn't have bet on the Master of the Bardic Guild against Gwyna when she wore that look.

And maybe this young man will give her something to think about besides her fear. For a little while, anyway.

Despite Gwyna's determination, Talaysen wasn't entirely certain that they'd see the lad again. On the other hand, he hadn't been acting as if he was going to run off. So Talaysen led the horses and wagon to their old campsite and waited for Gwyna to reappear, with her charge, or without him.

She returned with him—and cleaned up, he looked a great deal better than Talaysen had expected. Some of the sullenness proved to be nothing more than dirt.

"Here, lad," the Bard said. "We've got time to eat before we go, I think." He cut the boy a chunk of bread and cheese, and poured him a mug of water, presenting him with both as soon as the pair reached the wagon.

The boy didn't snatch at the food as Talaysen would have expected from his starved appearance. Instead he took it politely, with a little bow, and ate it slowly and carefully rather than bolting it. Which was something of a relief; in Talaysen's experience, food bolted by someone in the boy's condition tended to come right back up again.

"All right," Talaysen said, as the young man finished the last crumb of his meal. "The ladies here seem to have taken a liking to you. I suspect they want me to invite you to come along with us for a bit. On the other hand, you did try to lift my purse. So what do you have to say for yourself?"

"I'm s-s-s-sorry, s-s-s-sir," the young man stammered. "I was s-s-s-starving. I d-d-d-didn't kn-kn-know wh-wh-what else t-t-t-t-to d-d-do."

The stutter, severe as it was, seemed to be something habitual rather than feigned or out of fear. The youngster was obviously forcing the words out, and having a hard time of it. He was red with effort and embarrassment by the time he'd completed the simple sentence.

Talaysen wanted to ask him more, but he was at a loss of how to get any information from the youngster without a similar struggle. Then he noticed that the lad's attention wasn't on him, but on something in the wagon.

He turned to see what it was—but the only thing in sight was Gwyna's three-octave harp, the one she could only play while seated. She rarely took it out unless they were somewhere that it wouldn't be moved much. She'd been about to cover it for the trip in its oiled-canvas case, but during the packing it had been wedged between the side bunk and their packs for safekeeping.

"Do you play, lad?" Talaysen asked. The young man nodded vigorously. Without prompting, Gwyna climbed up into the wagon and handed the harp down.

He sat right down on a stone with it cradled in his arms; placed it reverently on the ground, and began to play.

Talaysen had heard many Masters play in his time, but this young man was as good on the harp as Rune was on her fiddle. And this was an original composition; it had to be. Talaysen knew most of the harp repertory, and this piece wasn't in it.

So, the boy could compose as well as play. . . .

The young man's face relaxed as he lost himself in the music, and his expression took on the other-worldly quality seen in statues of angels. In repose he was as gently attractive as he had been sullenly unattractive when Talaysen caught him.

Talaysen felt something else, as well; the undercurrent of melody he associated with magic. The young man made no effort to match it, but it harmonized with what he was playing, and Talaysen found himself being lulled into a meditative trance. *Perhaps he hasn't learned to match it because he doesn't know he can—but the power is there, and so is the heart.*

Oh yes, the power was there indeed. He shook off the lulling effect of the music to glance over at Rune—just in time to intercept *her* glance at him. He inclined his head toward the young man; she nodded.

She hears it too.

Insofar as music went, this boy was a Bard in everything but name.

Now who is he, where is he from, and how in heaven's name did he get that *way?*

CHAPTER TWENTY-ONE

Talaysen reflected that it was a good thing that the wagon slept four. They looked to have acquired a second "apprentice."

After hearing the young man play, there was no way that Talaysen was going to let him wander off on his own again. Even if he hadn't been determined in that direction, the ladies were. So they packed everything down for travel, and he and the boy went into the back while Gwyna handled the reins and Rune watched and learned.

"Remember, speak slowly," he told the lad—no, not "the lad." The youngster had a name. Jonny Brede. He was going to have to remember that. A personable lad; thin and wiry, with a heart-shaped face and an unruly tangle of wavy brown hair. His eyes were the most attractive feature he had, probably because he tried to do most of his speaking with them rather than expose himself to ridicule. That stutter—the youngster must have gotten a lot of cruel teasing over it. "Speak very slowly. Take your time. I'm in no hurry, and neither are you, so take all the time you need."

Strange, lying here at ease on a bed, instead of trudging down the dusty road. Very strange, but obviously much more comfortable. Though he knew why he hadn't done this long ago, and it had nothing to do with money. He knew very little about the care of horses and nothing about harnessing or driving—all of his knowledge was of riding and hunting. That didn't serve to tell him what to do with these stout little draft-beasts. How often should they be rested, for instance? And how on Earth did one manage two sets of reins? What did one do if they didn't *want* to get between the shafts of the wagon?

Rune and Gwyna took up the bench seat in front, with their backs to the interior, although they could hear everything he and Jonny said. Rune evidently knew enough about mules from her days at the inn that she was a logical candidate for secondary driver. He and Jonny took their ease back in the wagon itself.

"Tell me the earliest thing you remember," he said, staring at the bottom of a cupboard just over his head. Like the rest of the interior of the wagon, it was of brown wood polished to a high gloss.

Jonny shook his head, his hands knotting and un-knotting in his lap.

"Don't you remember being very small?" Talaysen prompted. "Do you recall schoolmates? Siblings? Tutors or Priests? A birthday party, perhaps?"

Jonny shook his head even harder. "N-n-no," he replied. "N-n-nothing like that. Jus—just being sick, for a long, l-long time, and m-m-my M-M-Master."

"Start with that, then," Talaysen told him. "Slowly. Don't force the words out. Think of speech as a song; you wouldn't rush the cadence."

"I was r-r-real sick," Jonny said thoughtfully. "Fever; I w-w-was hot all the time. I was seeing things t-t-too. Men f-f-f-fighting, buildings b-b-burning. P-p-people yelling." He bit his lip. "Th-th-then I was at K-K-Kingsford, and M-M-Master was taking care of me."

"Master who?"

"M-M-Master D-D-Darian," the young man replied promptly.

Interesting. That was a name Talaysen knew, largely because Master Darian's arrival had caused such a fuss. *Master Darian wasn't rightly at Kingsford at all; he was from the Guild in Birnam. He should have gone there to retire, not to our kingdom.* Talaysen remembered the minor stir that had caused; Master Darian, half-senile, demanding to be allowed to lodge in the great Guildhall at Kingsford, claiming outrageous things. That his life was in danger, that there were assassins looking for him. How had that ended up? There had been something about a usurper—

Yes, he had it now. There had been a palace uprising, with the King of Birnam deposed by his brother, and a lot of the usual civil unrest that followed such a coup. Darian had been one of the King's Bards—a position that did not normally make one a target for assassins. The Guild had decided that old Master Darian might have seen a thing a two that had proved too much for his mind, and voted to permit him to stay instead of forcing him back to a place where he was afraid to go.

Had there been a boy with him, an apprentice? Talaysen couldn't remember—

Wait, there had been, and the boy had been sick with a marsh-fever. That was it. And that was another reason why the Guild had decided to let the Master stay. By the time they'd reached Kingsford, the boy had been in a bad way. It seemed too cruel even to the normally callous Guild Bards to turn them out for the boy to die on the road.

Hmm. If he'd been at Kingsford, one of the mages might have healed him of it. Ardis would know.

He made a mental note to write to her and ask.

"So, you were ill, and when you finally got well, you were in Kingsford. What then?"

"M-M-Master Darian took care of m-m-me, and when he got sick, I t-t-took care of him." The chin came up, and the big brown eyes looked defiantly into his. "Th-th-they said he was m-m-mad. He w-w-wasn't. He j-j-just had trouble remembering."

Yes, and that was why they had permitted him to keep the "apprentice" even though the boy probably wasn't learning anything from the old man. He took care of his Master, and that had freed up a servant to run attendance on other Masters. As long as he didn't get in the way, the rest of the members of the Guild ignored him. Talaysen recalled now thinking that he ought to do something about the boy himself; teach him, perhaps. But then other things had gotten in the way, and he'd forgotten all about it by the time he left the Guild in a rage.

"Th-th-they left us alone until M-M-Master died. Th-th-then they said I had t-t-t-to l-l-l-leave." The stutter got worse as he grew more distressed.

"Why?" Talaysen asked.

"B-b-because I d-d-didn't have a M-M-Master any-m-m-more," he said, his eyes dark with anguish. "And th-th-they s-s-s-said it w-w-wasn't w-w-worth w-w-wasting t-t-time on a ha-ha-halfwit."

Talaysen's fists clenched and he forced himself to relax them. *The bastards. The lazy bastards. A stutter is curable—and even if it wasn't, most people don't stutter when they sing, and they knew it! But this poor child had no one to speak for him, and he was a foreigner. So out he went.*

"Jonny, you are *not* a halfwit," he said quietly, but forcefully. "Whoever told you that was an idiot. The Guild Masters were too lazy to train you, and too foolish to see your worth, so they got rid of you and told you that to keep you from trying to get your rights." He thought quickly about all he knew of Guild law. "You came to Kingsford as an acknowledged apprentice. You had a right to another Master when yours died. You could have gone to any other Guild in Kingsford and gotten help to enforce that right—but the Bardic Guild Masters told you that you were a halfwit to prevent you from claiming that right."

"Th-th-they did?" Jonny's eyes cleared a little.

"I would bet fair coin on it. It's *just* the kind of thing they would do." He kept a tight hold on his temper; this was all in the past. Nothing could be done about it now—except to rectify what the Guild had done himself.

"B-b-but they s-s-said I c-c-couldn't s-s-sing, or wr-wr-write m-m-music—" he objected. "And I *c-c-c-can't*."

"Jonny, when did anyone ever *teach* you to do those things?" Talaysen asked gently. "Those are skills, not things that you absorb just by being around Bards. Ask Rune; she'll tell you."

"Two years," Rune replied, leaning back into the wagon so she could be heard. "It took me two years to learn those things, and several different Masters."

"You see?" Talaysen's lips tightened. "Now if you really want to know what I think was going on—it's simple. The Bardic Guild is full of lazy, self-centered fools. They saw you had no Master, you weren't important to anyone, and in fact, no one in this country even knew you were here. So they decided you were too much trouble and sent you out the door."

Jonny nodded, slowly, his own hands clenched at his sides, knotted into tight little white-knuckled fists.

"Then what did you do?" Talaysen prompted. "After you left?"

"I w-w-worked. At wh-wh-whatever I c-c-could. Wh-wh-when the Faire came, I w-w-worked the Faire. Animals, m-m-mostly. Animals l-l-like me."

Talaysen could well imagine how the inarticulate lad had sought refuge in caring for creatures who didn't demand speech of him.

"How did you get from Kingsford to the Kardown Faire?" he asked.

"H-h-hiring fairs," the lad said simply. "G-g-got j-jobs all over. Had a j-j-job with a herder b-b-brought me here, b-b-but he sold his g-g-goats, and he d-d-didn't need me, and the m-m-man that b-b-bought them had his own h-h-h-herders."

Hiring fairs. That made sense. Hiring fairs were held in the spring and the fall, mostly for the benefit of farmers looking for hands or servants. Sometimes other folk would come looking for skilled or un-skilled laborers—and Talaysen had heard of fairs that even had mercenaries for hire. The problem was, the unskilled labor jobs seldom lasted more than a season, as Jonny had undoubtedly learned. "So, that got you to the Downs. When?"

"Ab-b-b-bout two w-w-weeks ag-g-go," he said, sighing heavily. "Was all right d-d-during Faire, b-b-but there wasn't nothing f-f-for me after."

Gwyna laughed without humor. "True, when the Kardown Faire is over, the town pretty much dries up, unless you're an experienced hand with sheep. Shepherd's classed as skilled labor, not unskilled, and the only person that might be trusted to come on without experience is a Gypsy.''

"And I take it you've always applied as unskilled?" Talaysen asked the young man. "And you've never learned a trade?"

He shook his head dumbly.

"G-g-got n-n-no one," he whispered. "And n-n-nothing. N-n-no g-g-good for anything. I w-w-was h-h-hungry, and I s-s-saw you b-b-buying th-th-things. I th-th-thought you w-w-wouldn't m-m-miss a c-c-copper or t-t-two.''

"You play the harp the way you just did, and you say *that*?" Talaysen replied indignantly. The young man's mouth opened and closed as he tried to say something; Talaysen held up a hand, silencing him.

"You listen to me," he said fiercely. "You're among friends now. The Guild Bards may be fools, but the Free Bards aren't. I don't ever want to hear you say that you aren't good for anything. Not ever again. Is that understood?''

The young man had scooted back on the bunk as far as the limited space would permit when Talaysen began the tirade. With wide eyes, he nodded his agreement.

Both Gwyna and Rune had turned around, and their eyes carried a message to him that was child's play to read. Not that he minded, since he'd already made his decision about this young man.

"All right," Talaysen said, as much to them as to Jonny. "You're a Free Bard now. We'll undertake to do for you what the Guild *should* have. You, in turn, will have to abide by our rules. No theft, no troublemaking, no law-breaking. Treat us the way you would treat your family. When we play together, it's share and share alike, no holding anything back for yourself. Abide by those and we'll teach you everything we know, take you with us, with chores and profits shared alike. Will that do?''

For a moment, Talaysen feared the young man might burst into tears. But instead, he pulled himself up, looked each of them straight in the eyes, and said, with only a trace of a stammer, "Y-yes, sir. That w-will do. Y-you have my w-word on it.''

"He'll need an instrument," Gwyna said from the front bench, her attention seeming to be entirely on the team. "He can use my harp until we get him his own—unless I find one I like better.''

This time Talaysen distinctly saw him blink away tears before replying. "Th-thank you," he said. "Very much.''

"I'll teach you lute, since we have two," Talaysen continued. "In fact, if it won't bother the drivers, I can begin now.''

"It won't bother the drivers," Rune assured him. "And we're making splendid time. We'll be just outside Abbeydown at sunset; that's about two hours from now, which is more than enough time for a first lute lesson." She turned and grinned, and wriggled her fingers. "As I should know. Go ahead and use mine."

The young man looked completely overwhelmed, and paralyzed with indecision, unable to think of what to say or do next. Talaysen solved his problem for him, stripping Rune's lute of its case and putting it into his hands.

"Now," he said, positioning Jonny's fingers. "This is an A-major chord. . . ."

Three more days brought them to Ralenvale, and the Saint Brisa Faire. Technically, this was the first of the Harvest Faires that took place during the autumn months, since it featured all of the traditional Harvest Faire activities. There were competitions in vegetables, livestock and farm activities like tossing hay; contests in baking, preserving and handicrafts. There were races for anything that ran, from humans to ungelded stallions. Most of the trade here dealt with farm livestock, from chickens to enormous draft horses. The nobly born Sires—unless they thought of themselves as "gentlemen farmers"—seldom attended Saint Brisa's, but their stewards and seneschals did. It was barely possible that the quartet could find their wintering-over position through them.

Since this was the end of summer, few people wished to call it a "Harvest Faire." Winter was too close now, and no one wanted to be reminded of that. To reinforce that, there was a tradition that if anyone had the poor taste to refer to Saint Brisa's as a Harvest Faire, winter would arrive six weeks early.

Talaysen had no idea if that was true or not; *he* was looking forward to it as a chance to meet up with some of Gwyna's kin. Most especially he wanted to speak with Peregrine, a Gypsy horse-trader who had a reputation as a mage, and was reputed to deal regularly with elves.

Because they were here every year in such numbers, the Gypsies had their own traditional camp for this Faire; outside the Faire palisade, and on one side of a spring-fed pool. The other side was where most folk watered their beasts, but it was said that the spring was haunted—some said by the spirit of a jilted shepherd—and no one would camp there except the Gypsies and their Free Bard friends.

There was already a substantial group in place when they drove their new wagon up the trail towards the camp. Enthusiastic greetings met them when their identity was established, and Gypsies swarmed towards them.

But when Gwyna stood up on the wagon-seat, and announced to the entire camp that Rune and Talaysen were *vanderie*—in the Gypsy tongue, wedded—the greetings turned into an impromptu wedding celebration. In fact, for one moment Talaysen was afraid they'd all demand that the pair wed *again,* just so the entire gathering could witness it.

Talaysen was just glad that they no longer had to worry about setting up a camp, for they would have had no chance to do so. A swirl of adolescents descended on the surprised pony-mules, and had them unharnessed, rubbed down, and picketed with the rest of the camp-beasts before the poor mules knew what had happened. The wagon was parked in the outermost circle, pulled there by a dozen Gypsy men amid the cheers of the rest. And the entire party was carried off to the great fire in the center of the camp, where food and drink of every description was pressed upon them. As soon as they settled into seats around the fire, more Gypsies broke out instruments and struck up a dancing tune.

Even Jonny found himself seized upon and greeted with the same wild enthusiasm as the others, for all that he was a stranger to them. Talaysen was afraid at first that he might bolt for the wagon to hide, or even worse, just run away. But he didn't; he stayed, and even though Talaysen saw his eyes were wide with surprise tinged with apprehension, he managed a tremulous smile.

The Gypsies—particularly the girls—were chattering at him like so many magpies; half in their own language, and half in the common tongue, most of it completely unintelligible. Talaysen thought about interfering, then hung back, waiting to see how Jonny would handle it. The young man was going to have to learn to deal with crowds of strangers some time; far better that it be a friendly crowd.

Jonny let the group carry him along; let them press food and drink into his hands, and sat where they put him, still with that shy little smile that was slowly, slowly warming. He didn't speak—not surprising, since he was still painfully embarrassed by his stutter—but he let his eyes speak for him, and for the Gypsies, that was enough.

He'll do, Talaysen decided, and turned his attention to his own greeting-party, as they tried to press enough food and drink on him for five men.

Later, when the party had quieted down, Talaysen excused himself from the circle of musicians that had claimed him, and went wandering over the camp. Peregrine *was* here; he'd found out that much. But he hadn't appeared at the fire or at the dancing as darkness fell. Then again, Talaysen hadn't expected him; although he was a superb dancer, Peregrine seldom displayed his talent to such a large circle.

There was no point in *looking* for Peregrine; he'd learned long ago that Peregrine would permit himself to be found when Peregrine was ready. So it didn't much surprise him to find the Gypsy appear discretely at his elbow as he exchanged greetings with the clan chief.

"How goes your journeying, my brother?" Peregrine asked, when the amenities had been attended to and he turned to greet the Gypsy who some claimed was a mage. The Gypsy looked much the same as always; ageless, lean face, muscular body of a born fighter or dancer, bright black eyes, and long, flowing black hair without a single strand of gray.

Talaysen raised an eyebrow. *Something is going on here. Peregrine has never called me "brother" before—only "old friend."* "Strangely," he supplied.

"How, strangely?" the Gypsy asked, leading him to a pair of stools in the relative privacy of the shadow of his wagon. He took one; Talaysen settled on the other. From here they could see most of the camp, but because of the shadow, most of the camp could not see them.

"I have heard a new music," he replied, following the Gypsy way of circling around a subject for a while before plunging in. No Gypsy ever came straight to the point on any serious subject. If he had come out and asked Peregrine about magic, the Gypsy would assume he wanted to talk about something else entirely. Small wonder those who did not know them found the Gypsies infuriating to speak to.

"Music of what sort?" Peregrine returned, patient as a falcon waiting-on, as they moved their stools to get a better view of the camp.

"Music that is not heard by the ears," Talaysen stated calmly. "Music that sings to the thoughts, unheard, and sometimes unnoticed. Music that follows its own melody, and not that of the musician."

Peregrine was very quiet for a moment. "Music that causes things to happen, perhaps. Or so it seems. Music that the musician must match his own song to."

"Yes." Talaysen offered only that one word answer. Peregrine sat in silence again; in silence offering bread and sausage, in silence pouring wine. It was Talaysen's turn to be patient. While the offering of food and drink was a kind of ritual of hospitality with most Gypsies, he sensed that this time it represented something more. An offering of fellowship, perhaps. . . .

"I have waited for you to come into your power, my brother," he said, when the food was accepted and eaten, and the wine drunk. "That was the meaning of my greeting. I have long known that you and a

handful of others among the Free Bards were among the *drukkera-rejek*—
the mages of music—as I am. The sign of the power is without mistaking
to one trained—as is the sign that a mage has come into his power. And
now—there is much that I must tell you, and little time to do it in.''

Talaysen's pulse quickened.

"So this *is* magic that I have touched—" Talaysen would have said
more, but Peregrine hushed him, and the Bard subsided into silence.

"It is magic, indeed; it is the magic that the Bards and the elves both
use. And there is one here who would speak to you.'' Peregrine waved
his hand in an unobtrusive signal, and a shrouded shadow detached itself
from the back of the wagon to approach them, and resolve itself into a
two-legged creature enveloped from head to toe in a hooded cape. Talaysen had not seen anyone there, nor had he noticed anyone move there
while he and Peregrine were speaking. He restrained himself from starting with surprise only with great effort.

The figure pulled back the hood of its cape to show that it was male—
and elven.

Now Talaysen started, his hand going briefly to the hilt of his knife
before dropping away.

He trusted Peregrine; the Gypsy had apparently invited the elf here.
And besides, if the elf truly wanted Talaysen dead, the knife would be
of little use against him. Striking him down where he sat would be
child's play for an elven mage.

"Stars light your path," he said, instead. The solemn elven mouth
lifted in a slight smile, and the elf moved a few steps closer.

"I see you have courtesy when you choose, mortal.'' The elf came
within arm's length of them, then examined Talaysen as if the darkness
and dim firelight was more than enough for him to see by.

Maybe it is. Elves were popularly supposed to have enhanced senses
of hearing and sight.

"I have courtesy when I am not constrained against my will, and
when I am an invited guest instead of being considered a superior type
of pet," he replied boldly. "We mortals have a saying 'like begets like.'
That holds true with manners as well as livestock.'' Peregrine bit off a
bark of a laugh, and the elf nodded, his smile now ironic.

"I warned you not to match wits with a full Bard," the Gypsy
mocked. "And this one most of all. Not just because of his training as
a Bard, which makes of words a weapon. Talaysen dares to speak only
the truth—which makes his speech bite all the sharper when he chooses
to make it so." Peregrine's feral smile gleamed whitely in the darkness.
"He has fangs, this one."

"I would not care to match either wits or magic against this one, new and raw as he is to his power," the elf replied, with complete seriousness not at all affected by the gypsy's derisive speech. Then he turned back to Talaysen. "Listen, for I bear word for you from *our* High King. He knows what occurred, and you need not anticipate reprisals. To Master Wren, he says, 'Think not to be caged, for that has been forbidden.' To Lady Lark, he says, 'Courage is rewarded.' And he sends these tokens—"

The elf held out a pair of slender silver bracelets that gleamed in the firelight, with a liquid sheen, so perfect it looked like the still surface of a pond. "Place these upon your wrists; they shall close, never to be removed, but fear not. They are meant to mark you as mortals with the High King's favor." Now the elf smiled, a wry smile that mimicked Peregrine's. "There shall be no more dances with lightning."

Peregrine laughed at that, in a way that made Talaysen think that he'd heard at least part of the story. The elf raised an eyebrow at him, knowingly.

Talaysen reached out gingerly and took the cool silver bracelets, sliding one over his hand. And as promised, once around his wrist it shrank to fit comfortably, the metal band becoming just a fraction thicker in the process. His stomach felt a little queasy, watching it—this was the first time he'd ever seen magic close at hand, magic that affected the material world. There would be no removing this "token" without first removing his hand.

"Thank you," he said to the elf, and meant it. "We have enemies enough without angering the Fair Ones."

"Oh, you angered only a greedy hothead with no thought but his own pleasure," the elf replied off-handedly. "He got his own desert, and that speedily. That it was delivered by a mere mortal simply humiliated him beyond bearing. There were those in his own court who thought he had gone too far when he took you, and were certain of it when he set the storm upon you. The High King has cooled his temper, I promise you."

"Still, I thank you," Talaysen replied. Then added with a rueful grin, "Is it now safe to cross a Faerie Ring, even by accident?"

The elf laughed aloud. "Safe enough, e'en by accident," he said. "With polite invitations tendered to you once you are within it to play for a brief evening. Your fame has traveled from Hill to Hill, and I think you should expect such invitations in the future. There will be many who wish to see the mortal Bards that could subdue King Meraiel. And more who will wish to hear your side of the tale."

And with no warning and only those parting words, he swirled his cloak about his shoulders and stepped into the shadows, to melt into them and vanish completely. As Talaysen had not seen him arrive, so he had no idea how the elf left—although he *thought* he heard a faint whisper of music as the shadows swallowed him.

Peregrine sighed, and shook his head. "Melodramatic, as ever," he commented. "Trust an elf to make a great show of simple leave-taking."

Talaysen chuckled, and relaxed a bit more. "Was that what you wished to show me and speak to me about?" he asked. "I must admit, that alone was worth being here for." He glanced over his shoulder at the now-empty shadows at the tail of the wagon. "I haven't said anything to the others, but the fact is, I've been uneasy about camping outside of settled lands ever since that particular incident occurred. This little trinket"—he tapped the bracelet—"takes a tremendous load off my mind."

Peregrine sobered. "In part, but only in part. I must speak to you of magic; of the usage and taming. Some of what I tell you, you may not understand for years—but it is all important, and I must ask you to pay close attention and grave it deeply in your excellent memory. If all goes as we wish, I may be able to continue to teach you for years to come. But if Fate rules against us, this may be all the instruction you will ever receive. I would give you as much as you can hold, planning for that."

Talaysen nodded, and quickly put himself into the little half-trance he used when he memorized lyrics in a foreign tongue. Everything he heard would be remembered, regardless of whether or not he understood it.

"Good." Peregrine took a deep breath, and held his hands out. A soft blue glow played over them, and Talaysen heard a faint, flute-like song, somewhere deep inside of him. "This is the way of the inner path, the hidden power. The way of magic. And now—it begins. . . ."

Rune watched Gwyna out of the corner of her eye, and grinned. There was *no* doubt about it; Gypsy Robin was well and truly smitten with their new charge, even though she might not know it yet.

She didn't act a great deal differently; in fact, it wasn't likely that anyone else noticed. But she paid no attention to anyone else in the camp, and when over the course of the evening several young men came up to her and whispered invitations in her ear, she declined them all with a shake of the head. That was not normal. Gwyna had a reputation as a lusty lover that rivaled any of the male Free Bards, and Rune had never heard of her declining all invitations for dalliance before. And especially not when several of those she declined had been her lovers in the past.

But she didn't leave the firelit circle with anyone, not even for an hour. And she stayed with Jonny, who smiled much and said little.

He was doing very well, now that he had begun to relax. The Gypsies paid no heed to his stutter, which was putting him at ease. He had begun to laugh at the jokes, and look up from his knees occasionally.

Gwyna was praising his melodic ability just now, which made him blush. Over the past two days, he had set melodies to several of Robin's lyrics that were easily the equal of any of the younger Free Bards' efforts. "Oh, but it's true," she said, to his mumbled disclaimer. "The words come easily to me, but melody? Never. You have the hardest part, Jonny."

"B-but I c-cannot find w-words," he replied earnestly. "I am j-just n-not cle-cle-cle-cle—cle-cle-cle—cle—oh d-d-*damn!*" His face twisted up, and Rune started to get to her feet, afraid that such a blatant exposure of his stutter would send him fleeing to solitude.

But he stayed, as the silence deepened, and the Gypsies held their breaths, sensing how precarious his moment of courage was. He stared at his fists which were balled up on his knees, and Rune hoped that it was not because he was about to go silent again.

Finally he looked up from his clenched fists, and managed a feeble smile. "D-d-damn it," he repeated. "S-s-stupid s-s-stutter. Cle-cle-cle— I s-s-sound l-l-like a *k-k-kestrel.*"

A relieved laugh answered his feeble joke, and Giorgio, one of the largest of the clan, slapped him lightly on the back, with a care to his thin body and small stature. "Then you have named yourself, my friend!" he boomed. " 'Master Kestrel' you shall be! And never disparage the kestrel, for he is bolder for his size than even the goshawk, brave enough to take on enemies that would make a meal of him if they could, brave enough even to attack the human who comes too near his nest!"

Giorgio raised his mug of wine. "To Master Kestrel!" he shouted.

The rest followed his lead. "To Master Kestrel!" they replied, Rune shouting just as loudly as the rest. And when she had drained her mug in the toast, and looked again, Jonny's eyes were shining, and he no longer stared at his hands.

Later, Gwyna even coaxed him out of his seat to dance with her. By then, Gwyna's other suitors had noticed her interest in the young musician, and had turned their attentions elsewhere. Rune couldn't help wondering at that point if Gwyna herself realized what had happened to her. She finally decided that the Gypsy probably hadn't recognized the symptoms of a condition she had caused so often in others. Gwyna had been heart-whole until now, enjoying her companions the way she enjoyed a round of good music or a dance. The oldest game of man and maid had been a sport to her, and nothing more.

I don't think it's a sport anymore, Rune thought, with amusement. *I wonder how long it's going to take her to notice that her outlook's changed in the past few days.*

The music, dance, and tale-spinning continued on long into the night, until the stars had swung halfway around in their nightly dance, and the moon had set. At moonset, the Gypsies and Free Bards began to trickle away to tents and wagons; singly, in pairs, and in family groups with sleeping children draped like sacks over their parents' backs. Just as Rune started to yawn and wonder where Talaysen was, he appeared at her side and sat down beside her.

"Where have you been?" she asked—curiously, rather than with any hint of accusation. "You said you were going to talk to Peregrine, and then no one knew where you were. I thought the Earth had swallowed you up."

"It almost did," he replied, rubbing his temple with one hand, as if his head ached.

She saw a gleam of silver in the firelight, and caught at the wrist of that hand. He was wearing a silver bracelet that fit so closely to his wrist that it might have been fitted to him, yet which had no visible catch. "Where did you get that? From Peregrine?" she asked, fascinated by the trinket. "It's really lovely—but I thought you didn't wear jewelry."

"I usually don't. Here." He slipped an identical bracelet over her hand before she could pull away, and she muffled an exclamation as it shrank before her eyes to fit her wrist just as tightly as Talaysen's fit his.

He put his lips to her ear. "A gift from the High King of the Elves. His messenger says that it marks us as under his protection."

She blinked, as a thousand possible meanings for "protection" occurred to her. "Is that good, or bad?" she whispered back. "I don't think I'm interested in another visit under a Hill like the last one."

"According to the messenger, these are supposed to keep visits like that within polite boundaries. By invitation, and of reasonable duration." She lifted an eyebrow at Talaysen, and he shrugged. "Peregrine said that the messenger's word was good, and he's been dealing with elves for longer than we have. I'd be inclined to trust his judgment."

"All right," she replied, still dubious, but willing to take his word for it. "So what else have you been doing, besides collecting bits of jewelry that are likely to get us condemned by the Church as elf-loving heretics?"

He chuckled, and put his arms around her, drawing her close to him so that her back nestled against his chest and they could both watch the dancing. "Nothing much, really. Just learning things that would get us condemned by the Church as renegade mages."

She restrained herself from jumping to her feet with a startled exclamation. "I hope you're going to explain that," she said carefully. "Since I assume it has something to do with that music we've both been playing with."

"Peregrine is a mage. It seems that we are, too. He told me that he'd identified the fact that we've 'come into our power' by something he saw when we showed up at camp. Then he gave me a very quick course in the Bardic use of magic, most of which I haven't sorted out yet." He sighed and his breath stirred her hair. "It's all in my head, though. I expect we'll get it figured out a bit at a time."

"I think I'm relieved," she replied, after a moment to ponder it all and turn the implications over in her mind. "I don't think it's a good idea to go wandering all over the countryside, playing about with magic without even knowing the first thing about it."

"That's almost exactly what Peregrine said, word for word," Talaysen chuckled. "He gave me quite a little lecture on—"

The bracelet tightened painfully around Rune's wrist, and she gasped. Her first thought was that the elven-made object was trying to cut her hand off—but then, it released the pressure on her wrist just as quickly as it had clamped down.

And Talaysen released *her*. He sat up quickly, and scanned the area outside the fire.

"There's someone out there, someone using offensive magic," he said, in a low, urgent voice. "Peregrine told me that these bracelets, being magic, would react to magic."

"Offensive magic?" she repeated. "But what is it? I don't see anything going on—how do we know it's being used against us, or even against the camp?"

He hushed her, absently. "We don't," he said unhelpfully. "But Peregrine will know. We might not be seeing anything because whoever it is may be using something to watch us, or to try and identify someone. Peregrine has all kinds of tricks and traps around this camp—and whoever it is will trip one of them sooner or—"

A cry of anguish from behind them interrupted him, and Rune turned just in time to see a pillar of flame, twice the height of a man, rise up from the shore of the pond.

A moment later she realized that it wasn't a pillar of flame—it was a man, standing bolt upright, transfixed in agony, burning like a pitch-covered torch.

She turned away, her stomach heaving, just in time to hear Peregrine shouting in the Gypsy tongue, of which she only knew a few words.

She couldn't make out what he was saying, but the warning was clear enough. She flattened herself to the ground, instinctively. And just in time, for an arrow sang out of the darkness, buzzing wasp-like past her ear, and *thock*ing into the wood of a wagon just where Jonny had been sitting a moment before. Two more followed it, both obviously aimed at Jonny, before the Gypsies got over their shock and counterattacked.

She had no weapons to hand, and no idea of where the enemy was, so Rune stayed right where she was, as angry Gypsies, men and women both, boiled out of the camp. They headed for the place where the arrows had come from, ignoring the man who was still burning.

He had fallen and was no longer moving; the Gypsies parted about the grisly bonfire as if his presence was inconsequential. They spread out over the area around the pond with torches in one hand and knives at the ready.

But after an agonizingly long time, it still didn't look as if they were finding anything. Rune got slowly to her feet, and made her way over to where Jonny and Gwyna had taken shelter behind a log-seat.

"Are you all right?" she asked Jonny, who nodded, his eyes wide and blank with fear.

"How about you?" she said to Gwyna.

The Gypsy sat up slowly, her mouth set in a grim line. "I've been better, but I'm not hurt," she replied. "What in the name of the Lady was that?"

"I don't know," Rune told her—as movement caught her eye and she saw Peregrine striding towards her, something shiny clutched in one hand, and a long knife in the other. "But I have the feeling we're about to find out. And that we won't like it when we do."

Peregrine sat back against the wooden wall of the wagon, his face impassive. "This was no accident."

Rune snorted, and gave Peregrine one of her most effective glares. "Why heavens, Peregrine, I thought assassins with magic amulets *always* hung around outside of farm Faires, looking for random targets!"

The Gypsy met her look with one of unruffled calm.

"All right," Gwyna said irritably. "We know it wasn't an accident. And I don't think anyone's going to doubt that Jonny was the target. Now *why*? Who's behind this, and why are they picking on a simple musician, a lad with a stutter, who wasn't even a good thief?"

Talaysen shook his head and sighed. All five of them were huddled inside Peregrine's wagon, one of the largest Rune had ever seen, so big it had to be pulled by a team of four horses. The windows had been blocked with wooden shutters, and the only way at them was through the door at the front, guarded by Peregrine's fierce lurcher-hounds.

And still Rune kept feeling her neck crawl, as if there was someone creeping up behind her.

Jonny shivered inside one of Peregrine's blankets, a glass of hot brandy inside of him, his eyes telling them what his tongue couldn't. That he was frightened—that was easy to understand. They were *all* frightened. But Jonny was terrified, so petrified with fear that he balanced on a very thin rope of sanity, with an abyss on either side of him.

Peregrine watched Jonny with an unfathomable expression, and the rest of them watched Peregrine, as the silence thickened. Finally the Gypsy cleared his throat, making them all jump nervously.

"The secret to all of this is—him," he said, stabbing a finger at Jonny. "This is not the first such attack, is it, boy?"

Jonny started, and shrank back—but as Peregrine stared at him, he shook his head, slowly.

"And it will not be the last. Two of the men got away. They will return." Rune didn't know why Peregrine was so certain of that, but it didn't seem wise to argue with him.

"So—young Kestrel. It comes down to you. *You* are the target of men who are very expensive to hire. And you say that you do not know the reason." Peregrine rubbed his upper lip thoughtfully. "Yet there must be one, and before we can decide what to do about this, we must discover it."

Gwyna obviously could stand no more of this. "Well?" she demanded, waspishly. "Are you going to stop playing the great mage and *tell* us how we're going to do this?"

Peregrine turned his luminous black eyes on her, and she shrank back. "I am," he said slowly. "But it is a path that will require courage and cooperation from one who has no reason to trust me."

He turned his gaze back to Jonny. "That one is you," he said. "Are you willing to place your mind and soul in my hands? Tell me, Kestrel, are you as brave as your namesake? Are you willing to face your past— a past so fearful that you no longer remember it?"

Jonny stared at him, and Rune wondered if Peregrine had snapped that last link he had with a sane world.

CHAPTER TWENTY-TWO

Talaysen touched Jonny's forehead, and his closed eyelids didn't even flutter. He held the young man's wrist for a moment, and found a pulse; slow, but steady. He had seen Ardis work this spell before, but never for this effect; for her, the sleep-trance was an end, not a means. He wondered if Ardis knew of this application: to search the patient's memory, even finding things he had forced himself to forget. "I think he's ready," he said to Peregrine. "As ready as he's ever likely to be."

"Oh, he is ready," the Gypsy replied. "What he may not be prepared for is his own fear. I hope in the days you have been with him that you have taught him trust to go with that fear, else all is lost." Peregrine leaned forward and tapped the young man's forehead three times, right between the eyes. "Kestrel," he rumbled, "do you hear me?"

"I hear you," Jonny whispered—without so much as a hint of a stammer. Out of the corner of his eye, Talaysen saw both Gwyna and Rune start with surprise.

"You will answer my questions. The one you know as Master Wren will also ask you questions, and you must answer him, as well. Do you trust him?" Peregrine's brow furrowed as he waited for an answer.

"I do," Jonny said, his voice a bit stronger.

"Good. You have placed your trust well. He and I will not do anything to harm you; and we will keep you *safe* from harm. We will be with you, even though you cannot see us. You will believe this."

"I believe this," Jonny affirmed.

Peregrine gestured curtly. "Ask," he said. "You know more of this than I, and you know more of the world that spawns those who hire assassins than any gypsy. I would not know what questions are meaningful and what without meaning."

Talaysen leaned into the tiny circle of light cast on Jonny's face by the lantern Peregrine had used to place him in a trance. "Jonny—Kestrel—do you hear me?"

"Yes," the young man sighed.

"I want you to remember the first day you came to Kingsford, to the Guild Hall. Can you remember that?"

"Yes." Jonny's forehead wrinkled, and his voice took on the petulant quality of a sick child. "I'm cold. My head hurts. My eyes hurt. Master Darian says I'm going to get better but I don't, and I feel awful—"

"He relives this," Peregrine said with a bit of surprise. "This is useful, but it can be dangerous, if he believes himself trapped in his past. Have a care, Master Wren."

Talaysen swallowed, and wet his dry lips. "Jonny, can you remember farther back? Go back in time, go back to before you entered Kingsford. Can you remember before you were sick?"

Abruptly the young man began to scream.

Peregrine moved as quickly as a ferret, clamping his right hand over the young man's forehead, and his left on Jonny's wrist. The screaming stopped, as if cut off.

"Who are you?" Peregrine said, with no inflection in his voice whatsoever.

Who are you? Talaysen thought, bewildered. *What kind of a question is that?*

"I—I *can't*—" Jonny bucked and twisted in Peregrine's grip; the mage held fast, and repeated the question, with more force. The young musician wept in terror—Talaysen had heard that sort of weeping before, from the boys that had been ruined by their Guild Masters. . . .

Peregrine had no more pity than they had, but his harshness was for a far better cause. *"Who are you?"*

"Ah—" Jonny panted, like a frightened bird. "I—I—ah—Sional! I'm Sional! I have to run, please, let me go! Master Darian! Master Darian! They're killing my father! Help me! *Ahhhhhhhhh—"*

"Sleep—" Peregrine snapped, and abruptly the young man went limp. The mage sat back on the bunk, and wiped sweat from his brow. He looked to Talaysen as if he had been running for a league. He was silent for a moment, staring at the young musician as if he had never seen him before.

"So." Peregrine took a sip of water from the mug safely stored in a holder mounted on the wall just above him. "So, we know this 'Jonny Brede' is nothing of the kind, and that his true name is Sional, and that someone wished his father dead. Do you know of any Sionals? Especially ones who would have run to a Guild Bard for help?"

Talaysen shook his head. Rune and Gwyna both shrugged. Peregrine scratched his head and his eyes unfocused for a moment. "Well, whoever he is, he is important—and long ago, someone killed his father. I think we must find out who and what this father was.''

"Are you going to hurt him?" Gwyna asked in a small voice.

Peregrine shook his head. "I can promise nothing. I can only say I will try not to hurt him. The alternative is to find out nothing—and one day there will be nothing to warn him of the assassin in the dark. I think this the lesser of two bad choices.''

Gwyna nodded, unhappily. Peregrine touched Jonny's—Sional's—forehead again. "Sional, do you hear me?"

"I—hear you," said a small, young, and very frightened voice. It sounded nothing like Jonny; it sounded like a young child of about twelve.

"How old was he, when he came to you at the Guild?" Peregrine asked Talaysen. The Bard furrowed his brow and tried to remember what the nondescript child had looked like on the few occasions he had seen the boy. The memory was fuzzy, at best, and the child had been quite ordinary.

"Twelve? Thirteen?" He shook his head. "He can't have been much younger than that, or I'd have noticed. Thirteen is just about as young as apprentices are allowed to be in Bardic Guild. Children younger than that are just that—children. They aren't ready for the kind of intensive study we give them. Their bodies and minds aren't suited for sitting in one place for hours at a time.''

"Good. That gives me a safer place to start." He raised his voice again. "Sional—you are ten years old. It is your birthday. You are waking up in the morning.''

Abruptly all the tenseness poured out of Sional's body, and a happy smile transformed his face.

"Good, a safe time, and a happy one," Peregrine muttered. "Sional, what is to happen today?"

"Today I get my first horse!" Sional's voice really *did* sound like a ten-year-old's, and Talaysen started in surprise. "It's my birthday present from father, a *real* horse, not a pony! Victor and I get to go to the Palace stables and pick it out, too! Victor's going to teach me trick riding! Then Master Darian will give me the present from mother that he's been saving for me; it's a harp, a big harp, with lots more strings than my little harp!"

"Why isn't your mother giving it to you?" Peregrine asked, curiosity creeping into his voice.

"She's dead," Sional said, matter-of-factly. "She died when we moved to this place. That was a long time ago, though. I hardly remem-

ber her at all. Just the way she sang—'' His voice faltered a moment.
"She was a wonderful musician and Master Darian says that if she hadn't
been a woman and a princess she'd have been a Bard and—''

"Stop." Peregrine glanced over at Talaysen, with one eyebrow raised.
Talaysen didn't have to ask what he was thinking.

*A princess? Is that real—or just a child's fantasy and an old teacher's
flattery?*

"Sional, who is your father?" Peregrine asked, slowly and carefully.

"The King." Once again, the voice was completely matter-of-fact. "I
have to call him My Lord Father; Master Darian calls him Your Majesty.
Everybody else has to call him Your Royal Highness. But I don't see
him very often."

"Stop." Peregrine was sweating again. "Sional, where do you live?"

"In the Dowager's Palace."

"No, I mean what land do you live in?"

"Oh, that. Birnam. It's the red place on the map. The green one next
to it is Leband, the blue one is Falwane, the yellow one is—''

"Stop." Now Talaysen was sweating.

"Do realize what we have here?" he whispered. "This is the Crown
Prince of Birnam—no—the *King* of Birnam!" He groped for Rune's
hand and held it.

"Tell me!" the Gypsy demanded. "Tell me what you know of this!"

"I have to think," Talaysen replied, shivering despite the heat of the
wagon. Dear God, what a cockatrice they had hatched! Their foundling
was the rightful King of Birnam—and small wonder there were assassins
seeking him. The current King was not likely to tolerate any rivals to
his power.

"About six years ago, I think it was, the King of Birnam was over-
thrown by his brother. Mind you, the only reason *I* know about this is
was because I was on the Guild Council at the time, and we were dealing
with that entire business of Master Darian. The old man came to us with
a boy he called his apprentice, claiming sanctuary with our branch of
the Guild because he was supposedly in danger as a supporter of the
former King."

"So your understanding is likely to be accurate, if sketchy?" Peregrine
asked.

He nodded. "We did do some checking with the Guild in Birnam.
The way I heard it, the brother slipped his men into the palace by night,
murdered the King and all his supporters, and by dawn there was a new
King on the throne and all the bloodstains had been politely cleaned
away."

Peregrine snorted. "How—tidy of them."

Talaysen shrugged. "At that point, I imagine that there was nothing anyone could do. Darian swore to the Guild that he'd escaped death at the hands of the assassins as one of the old King's retainers—and he swore that both the King and his only child were dead. Obviously *that* wasn't true."

"Obviously," Peregrine said, with heavy irony. "Well, our Kestrel has turned into a most peculiar cuckoo. What are we to do with him? It is plain that his uncle knows that he is alive, and where he is, or we would not have ki' rs at our wagons."

"Can't we hide him?" Gwyna asked, but her voice betrayed her own doubt.

Peregrine confirmed that doubt with a shake of his head. "Not possible," he said. "The amulet I found upon the man my trap took was one of seeking. No matter how or where we hid him in this land, they could find him with another such. He himself has confirmed that there have been attempts to slay him before this."

Talaysen remained silent, as Gwyna and Peregrine discussed other possibilities; concealing the young man with magic, or even asking the elves to take him under one of their Hills. *That* was chancy; what the elves took, they might not want to give back, once they'd heard young Sional play. He had the glimmering of an idea then—

It had occurred to him that there was too much they didn't know, and the only place to learn that information was in Birnam. So why not go *there*?

After all, why would the current King ever look for Sional in his own kingdom? The assassins could comb all of Rayden, from border to border—but if the object of their search was in the last place they expected him—

"We don't know nearly enough," he said, into an opportune silence. "We don't know if this is an idea of the King's, or if it's something one of his advisors thought was best. We don't even know if this is something set in motion long ago and forgotten. This King may be a tyrant—there may already be a movement in place to topple him that only lacks a focus. It seems to me that Jonny—I mean, Sional—ought at least to find these things out. Until he does, no matter where he goes or how he runs, he'll be running away from something, not *to* something."

Peregrine raised his eyebrows thoughtfully. "A good point, my brother," he acknowledged. "And there are things about the young man now that the assassins cannot know. Unless I miss my guess, they have associated him with you, but only at a distance, and as a chance-met set of friends. They would be looking for a group of three men and a woman—not two couples. Rune has been in breeches most of the time, yes?''

Rune shrugged. ''It's habit mostly,'' she said, ''But yes. And most men don't look twice at me in breeches, they assume I'm a boy.''

''So now you wear skirts, and become most extravagantly feminine. Master Wren, we shall dye your hair as black as mine, but with magery, so that the dye neither grows out, nor washes out.'' Peregrine grinned. ''And if I ever wished to be a rich man, I would sell the working of *that* spell, eh? It is a pity it only is effective on one who is already a mage.''

''So we'll have two *young* gypsy couples traveling together. Good.'' Talaysen played that over in his head, and found no flaw with it. ''Most wagons look alike to outsiders. Once we're on the road, there'll be no telling us from dozens of others without one of those amulets. Those have to be expensive; I'm sure not every hired killer has one.''

''And if you leave by darkness tomorrow, we can make certain you are not followed,'' Peregrine told him. ''Now, what of the Kestrel? Do I wake him with his memories, or no?''

''With them,'' Gwyna put in quickly. Peregrine turned to stare at her. ''If I was in his place, that's what I would want,'' she said defensively. ''While he still thinks he's Jonny Brede, he doesn't know why these people want to kill him. As Sional, he *will*. It seems to me that makes them less frightening.''

Talaysen nodded. ''I agree with her. Fear is worse when you don't know what it is you're afraid of. Right now these people are simply faceless, irrational attackers from a nightmare. Once he has his memories and identity as Sional back, they aren't faceless anymore, and they have a reason for what they're doing.''

Peregrine nodded slowly. ''Very well. Let me see if I *can* do this. He has built him a very stout wall between himself and those memories. It may take some doing to breech it.''

When they showed no sign of moving, he coughed delicately. ''I have no need of you now, and this were better done in private.''

They took the hint, and left, crawling over the driver's seat and the lurcher-hounds draped over and on top of it, and down to the ground again.

''Now what?'' Gwyna asked.

''We go back to our wagon and sleep,'' Talaysen told her and Rune both. Rune nodded; Gwyna looked rebellious. ''Look, we can't help

Peregrine and we're all tired. We *need* sleep. We already know the worst, and nothing we do or don't do in the next few hours is going to change it. So?"

"So we sleep," Gwyna sighed. "Though personally, I don't think I'm going to be able to do anything but stare into the dark."

Gwyna had been wrong, of course; despite their tension, all three of them fell deeply asleep once they reached the safety of their beds. And thanks to their Gypsy friends, their beds were as safe as possible in an open camp. The wagon had been moved from the outer to the inner circle, and a half-dozen fierce lurchers had been tied about it to keep away intruders. The wagon itself was stoutly built enough to withstand a siege once the doors and shutters were closed. Talaysen thought it a pity to shut out the cool night air, but better stuffy air than unexpected knives and arrows.

When he woke, it was near noon by the sun coming through the little smoke-hole over the charcoal stove, and the fourth bunk had a clothed and wakeful occupant.

It was Kestrel—and yet it wasn't Jonny Brede. Talaysen couldn't put his finger on the differences, but they were there; in the way the young man held himself, in the direct way he met Talaysen's gaze.

"Sional?" he said, tentatively.

The young man nodded, solemnly. "B-better stick to K-Kestrel, though," he replied, his stammer improved, but still very much a part of his speech. "Th-that's not a n-name we ought to b-be using much."

"Point taken." He sat up and scrutinized the young man carefully. He looked much older in an indefinable way—*now* he looked his real age; when he had been "Jonny," he had looked several years younger. Interesting.

"P-Peregrine t-told me what you want to d-do," the young man continued. "I th-think you're r-right; I th-think w-we ought to at l-least f-find out wh-what my uncle th-thinks he's d-doing. Th-there's j-just one thing—he s-said y-you w-were maybe th-thinking of f-finding a r-r-rebellion. W-well m-maybe I'm a p-prince, b-but I don't kn-know anything ab-bout b-being a K-King."

Talaysen's estimation of the young man rose several notches. Whatever Master Darian had taught him—whatever he had learned himself in his years of rootless wandering—this was the wisest conclusion he could possibly have come to. "That's very astute of you, Kestrel," he said. "I'm not being patronizing; you're very right. If there is a movement afoot to depose your uncle, we are going to have to investigate it very carefully. They may only be interested in putting a puppet on the throne.''

"And r-right now th-that's all I'd b-be,'' Kestrel replied without bitterness. "Th-there's some other th-things you should kn-know. My f-father. He w-wasn't a n-nice man. He p-put m-me and m-mother away in the D-Dowager P-Palace, and j-just tr-trotted us out on s-special oc-casions. Th-that's why she d-d-died. Sh-she c-caught s-something, and he d-didn't bother sending a d-doctor until it was t-too l-late.''

"So—what are you getting at?'' Talaysen asked.

"I d-don't kn-know, really,'' Kestrel said frankly. "J-just that I d-don't f-feel like g-going after my uncle f-for r-revenge, I g-guess. I hardly ever s-saw my f-father. I m-mean, I kn-knew who h-he w-was, and he g-gave m-me p-presents wh-when it s-suited him, b-but th-that was all. I s-saw him d-die by accident. B-but it w-was j-just s-someone I kn-knew d-dying, n-not m-my *father*. R-revenge w-would b-be p-pretty s-stupid.''

He shrugged, and Talaysen read in that gesture that the young man was confused on any number of subjects, but that on this one he was certain: he was not interested in heroic vendettas.

"Most young men your age with your background would be champing at the bit, hardly able to wait to get their uncle at the point of a sword and give the big speech about 'You, scum, killed my noble, sainted Father! Now you die by the son's blade!' I was all ready to try and calm you down—''

"M-most p-princes h-haven't s-spent th-the last f-four y-years s-sweeping f-floors and t-tending g-goats,'' Kestrel interrupted, with that disarming matter-of-factness. "I d-don't know, I'm p-pretty c-confused. I j-just w-want t-to s-see what's g-g-going on. And I *really* w-want p-people t-to *stop* t-trying t-to *k-kill* me!''

"Fine,'' Talaysen replied. "We'll take it from there, and see where it leads.''

"Good,'' Kestrel replied, nodding vigorously.

The young man's reaction gave Talaysen a great deal of food for thought, as they waited for darkness to fall so that they could sneak away. That reaction was, as he had told Sional, not what he had expected. It was a great deal more practical than he had anticipated.

It *might* be wise to see if there was a rebellion brewing; the rebels might be able to protect Sional better than they could. But then again— they might already have their figurehead for revolt, and they might not welcome the intrusion of the "rightful King'' into their plans.

There was a possibility that they could stage Sional's "death'' convincingly, enough to get the hounds called off. That was another plan to be discussed and plotted out.

Gwyna slowly coaxed a few more of his memories out of him over the course of the day. Talaysen slowly built a picture up in his mind of the boy Sional had been, some eight years ago.

A lonely boy; packed away in what was apparently a drafty, damp "palace" in constant need of repair, with a single, half-deaf servant and his tutor, Master Darian. That surprised him; Guild Bards—and Darian *had* been a Guild Bard, his credentials were impeccable—were not normally employed as tutors for boys, not even when they were princes. Although he could not be certain, Talaysen framed the notion that Master Darian had been a great friend and admirer of the unhappy Queen, and had volunteered his services in the capacity of tutor when the lady died.

The obvious romantic notion—that Darian was really Sional's father, and that Queen and prince had been mewed up out of sight because of the scandal—Talaysen discarded after only a few moments of consideration. *If* it had been true, the King would have gotten rid of the erring spouse and unfortunate offspring—either directly, or discreetly. There were a dozen routes he could have taken, and a dozen princesses who would have brought a great deal of advantage to Birnam as new brides. No, it seemed that Master Darian's relationship with the Queen was the same as Tonno's with Rune: friend and mentor.

So why had the Queen been put away?

Most likely was that the King disliked her intensely, but that she was too circumspect to give him a reason to be rid of her.

But then, why had the prince been discarded with her? In the hopes that he, too, would die, and leave his father free to seek a spouse more to his taste, with the urgency of the succession giving him a reason to urge the wife he *wanted* on his Councilors?

It wouldn't have been the first time that particular ploy had been used, particularly not when the first wife was one chosen for the King by his own father.

Sional, as he had said, had seen very little of his father. He had been in the Crown Palace completely by accident the night that his father had been murdered.

It would have been comic if the circumstances had not been so dire. He had discovered on a previous visit that there was a greenhouse full of fruit-trees that were forced to bloom and bear out of season. He got very little in the way of luxurious food; it seemed that he, Darian, and the servant were brought whatever was left from meals at the Crown Palace after the servants had taken their shares. He *never* saw out-of-season fruit, and boy-like, had decided to filch himself a treat. The greenhouse was just under the King's private chambers, and the way into it—if you were an adventurous child—was through the air vents in the glassed-over roof.

Not only had it been a marvelous adventure, it had been an unrivaled opportunity to spy on his mysterious and aloof father. Double the guilty pleasure for a single act.

Even better had been to discover that his father was not alone. Master Darian had described the goings-on between men and women in a singularly detached fashion that had left him wondering why anyone bothered. *Now* he saw why they bothered—and he stayed and stayed—

So he had been looking in the windows when the assassins surprised his father—and the lady—in bed, just about ready to finish their evening's exertions. The men sent to kill the King had not been expert, and in a panic at the lady's screams, they had also butchered her.

Terror-stricken, sick, and in shock, he had run straight to Master Darian, his only friend and protector.

Poor old man, Talaysen thought pityingly. *No wonder we thought him half-mad. How did he do it? How did he smuggle a child out of a place crawling with killers, get the boy away, and smuggle him out of the country? He was no hero—he wasn't even young. He was an old, tired man with his best days behind him. One day I am going to have to write a song about him. Bravery and intelligence like that are all too rare . . . and we never even recognized them while he was alive.*

Sional must have been in shock for some time, shock that made him terribly vulnerable to illness. Small wonder he took marsh fever crossing the fens at the Birnam-Rayden border. But that must have been a blessing to Master Darian, for during the boy's illness, he managed to convince him that he was someone else entirely—the boy named "Jonny Brede." And that made it easier to hide him.

The rest, Talaysen knew—except for one small detail. The reason *why* Jonny Brede had been unable to hold a job, anywhere.

The killers, the mysterious murderers, who would appear out of nowhere and try to take his life.

They'd made their first attempt right after Master Darian had died. He'd had three close calls, not counting the attempt last night, and on numerous occasions he had learned they were looking for him just in time to flee. Small wonder he'd been starving. The place Talaysen had offered must have seemed God-given—for surely if he moved about every few days, no mysterious killer was going to be able to find him!

Talaysen could hardly imagine the hellish life the boy must have endured. Having no friends for more than a few months, constantly hungry, cold, lonely—with people out of a nightmare one step behind him, and never knowing the reason why.

Now he knew one difference in Kestrel's demeanor: relief. Now Sional *knew* why the killers were after him. There was a logical reason. He no longer lived in an irrational nightmare.

Now he lives in a rational one.

Somehow, that made him angrier than anything else. Talaysen made himself a small promise. If and when they found Sional's uncle in a position of vulnerability, *he* was going to give the man a little taste of what he'd been dealing out to Sional all these years. Just a little.

But it would be a very sharp taste. . . .

They moved out by night, with Gypsies spread all over the downs on either side of the road to make sure they weren't spied upon, in company with three other wagons of the same general shape and size. The other three turned back at moonrise; Gwyna kept the ponies moving on, to the north. Across the downs and past the fens on the other side was the border with Birnam. It could be crossed two ways—by the causeway, or, if you were desperate, through the fens on paths only the marsh-dwellers knew. Talaysen guessed that the latter was the way Master Darian and Sional must have arrived. *They* would take the causeway. There was no reason not to—and every reason to be as open as possible.

Birnam itself could cause them any number of problems. None of them, other than Sional, had ever been there. The few Gypsies who had could give no real details about the place, and in any event, they hadn't been much past the border area. The fens were too tedious to cross, and in bad seasons, the causeway flooded. Once you crossed the fens, Birnam had no large faires; most commerce took place at weekly Markets instead. Goods moved through the auspices of the Trader's Guild. The Free Bards were not yet numerous enough to expand outside this kingdom, so Talaysen had no idea of what the lot of the traveling musician was like within Birnam.

Not terribly helpful, he thought sleepily, taking his turn at the reins while Gwyna dozed inside. Somehow young Kestrel was sound asleep—but perhaps, like a soldier, the young man had learned to take sleep when and where he could get it.

He and Rune were to drive while the moon was up, giving the mules light enough to see the road. Since it was a straight track across the downs, bounded on either side by hedgerows, there was small chance they'd get lost. The worst that could happen would be that the mules would stop, pull the wagon over to the side of the road, and proceed to gorge themselves or sleep in their harness until someone woke up and got them back on the job.

Even if something frightened them, they likely wouldn't bolt—or so Gwyna claimed, saying that was the reason the Gypsies preferred mules over horses as draft animals. She claimed that when startled, they would probably stand stock still and wait for whatever it was that frightened them to show itself to be either aggressive and dangerous, or not a threat after all.

"And if they *do* bolt," she'd told him, "Let them have their heads. If they run, they've either been hurt badly by something you can't see, or they've seen something they already know is dangerous. They probably have a better idea of what's safe to do when there's real danger than you do. Let them follow their instincts."

As if he could do anything else! If they took it into their stolid heads to run off, he wasn't even sure he'd be able to hang onto the reins.

Rune climbed out of the back to sit beside him on the driver's bench. After a moment, she began massaging his shoulders, and he sighed with pleasure.

"I've been thinking," she said. "About magic."

"So have I," he replied. "I know we don't know everything. I know *Peregrine* doesn't know everything, however much he likes to pretend that he does."

"Exactly." She nodded her head vigorously. He glanced out of the corner of his eye at her, and smiled.

"Can I say something gauche and male?" he asked. "I think you look wonderful. The dress, your hair down, no leather hat hiding your face—"

"Oh, that's gauche and male, all right," she grinned. "But I like the compliment. I have to admit, sometimes I get a little tired of breeches and loose tunics. A pretty dress—well—Gwyna will probably tell you I was preening like a popinjay when we were going through the outfits the other women offered me and picking out the new clothing."

He cautiously took his attention from the road for a moment to steal a kiss. She stole one back.

"Now, about magic—" she said. He sighed.

There was no getting her mind off business when she was determined. "All right. About magic."

"For every offense in *everything* else, there's always a defense. I can't believe that there's no defenses against this seeking-talisman those killers are using.'' She braced herself against the swaying of the wagon over an uneven stretch of road, and waited for his response.

"I've been thinking the same thing," he said. "That was why I managed to talk Peregrine out of the one he took from the dead man. I was hoping we could find a way to fool it if we studied it long enough."

He transferred the reins cautiously to his left hand, and fished the talisman out of his breeches pocket. "Here," he said, handing it to her, and taking proper control of the reins again.

She examined it as best she could by the illumination of the three-quarter moon. It wasn't very impressive by either sun or moonlight; there wasn't much there but a small copper disk with a thin lens of glass cemented over it, suspended from a copper chain. She peered at it.

"Is there something under that glass?" she asked.

She had better eyes than he did. "Peregrine says it's a single strand of hair. He says that places where magic is used more openly tend to be very careful about things like nail-clippings and hair. We'd probably better assume that Birnam is one of those places. They'd probably been keeping every strand of hair he lost since he was a baby, and when they knew he was alive, they started making talismans to find him."

Talaysen had no idea how the thing had been made, but the fact that it had survived the fire intact was remarkable enough. It didn't look at all damaged, in spite of the fact that it had been the actual focus of Peregrine's defenses, the point from which the fire sprang. A distinct disadvantage of having a magical object; unless you also had a magical defense—which Peregrine called a Shield—your object could actually call an offensive spell to it, simply by existing.

Once they'd figured out how to outwit this thing, Talaysen planned to sink it in a deep well.

"Does it still work?" she asked.

"Try it for yourself," he told her. "Hold it in your hand and tell yourself that you want to find Sional."

She obeyed—and frowned. "It still works, all right. Nasty thing." She rubbed the hand that had been holding it against her skirt, although there was nothing physically there to rub off. Talaysen had done exactly the same thing after Peregrine had shown him the trick of working it.

"I haven't been able to figure out *how* it works," he confessed. "Though I have to admit, I haven't done as much with it as I might have if it didn't feel so—slimy."

She agreed, grimacing distastefully. "Still—I grew up working in an inn. I emptied chamber pots, cleaned up after sick drunks, mucked out the stables. It won't be the first time I've had to do something nasty, and so far, this doesn't make me feel any worse than one of those jobs. I'll see what I can do with it.''

She was quiet for a very long time, her brow furrowed, her eyes half-closed. After a while he began to ''hear,'' with that strange inner ear, little snatches of melody and dissonance.

When she finally spoke, he wasn't ready for it, and he jumped, startled.

''Sorry,'' she apologized. ''I guess I should have moved or something first.''

''It's all right,'' he assured her. ''I was sort of dozing anyway, and I shouldn't have been. Have you gotten anything figured out?''

''Well, I think I know why Peregrine said nothing could be done about it,'' she replied thoughtfully. ''This doesn't work like *our* magic—in fact, I'd be willing to believe that it wasn't made by a *human* at all.''

''Huh.'' That made sense. Especially if you were doing something that you didn't want countered. There were pockets of strange races scattered all over the Twenty Kingdoms; it wouldn't be unheard of to find other races that worked magic. And unless you found another mage of the same race, your odds against countering what had been done might be high.

''That could be why it feels—and sounds—so unpleasant,'' he offered. ''It's not operating by laws of melody that we understand, or even feel comfortable with. I've been told that there are some things living off by themselves in the swamps in the south that can make you sick by humming at you.''

She nodded vigorously. ''You know, that's really what's going on here; it isn't that it really feels *bad*, it's that it makes *you* feel bad. I had a chance to talk to a Mintak about music once; he said he couldn't stand human sopranos and a lot of human instruments because they were too shrill for him. And I couldn't hear half of the notes of a Mintak folk-song he sang for me.''

He bent his head down so he could scratch the bridge of his nose. One of the mules looked back at him, annoyed at getting a rein-signal it didn't understand.

''Maybe what we need to do is figure out the logic, the pattern in it—then and try and disrupt or block that pattern with something we can stand?'' he offered.

''I don't know,'' she replied, dubiously. ''That could be like trying to catch a Mintak with a minnow-net. Or a minnow in a snare. But I suppose that's the best we can do right now. You want to try?''

He took the charm with distaste. "I don't *want* to, but I will. Besides, maybe some of this stuff Peregrine stuck in my head will help."

"Maybe," she replied. "It couldn't hurt, anyway, as long as you remember we aren't playing by human rules anymore."

"I don't think I could forget," he said, and bent with grim determination to his task.

CHAPTER TWENTY-THREE

Rune's stomach heaved. "You know," she said conversationally to Kestrel, as they neared the border-post at the edge of the fens, "if I didn't like you so much, I think I'd have left you back in the mud with that copper charm and saved myself this.."

Heat pressed her down and humidity made her head ache. The ever-present reek of the marsh permeated everything. Gnats and midges buzzed in annoying clouds around her head, but thanks to the thick, sticky herb-juice the Gypsies had given them, neither landed nor bit. But the juice itself had a bitter, unpleasant smell, and that added to her misery. The sun glared down through a thick heat-haze, making the road shimmer and dance.

After much trial and error, she and Talaysen had worked out the counter to the magic of the talisman. Comprised of notes they felt more than heard, it only made them *slightly* ill to work. Just enough that Rune refused to eat anything this morning, since they were going to have to cross the border before noon. She hadn't wanted anything in her stomach, and right now she was chewing a sprig of mint in the vain hope that it would settle her rebellious insides.

Sional grimaced. "I'd d-do it m-myself, but I'm not g-good enough yet." He held out his hands and shrugged. "I w-wish I w-was."

"Oh, don't worry about it," she replied, closing her eyes to subdue another surge of nausea. "Besides, if I'd dumped you in the mud, Robin would have gone back after you, and then we'd have gotten to smell fen-stink until we cleaned you up."

As she opened her eyes, she saw him flush and turn away, and smiled in spite of her roiling stomach. Robin was in love with Kestrel, and he was returning her feelings with interest. How long it would last, she had no idea.

Nor did she know whether it would survive the kinds of pressures put on a would-be King. . . .

Worry about that if we get there, she told herself firmly. *We have enough trouble to handle right now.*

One problem they did not have to worry about was whether Sional would be recognized from a physical description. Anyone looking for Jonny Brede as he had last appeared would never see him in this young man. Regular meals and hauling the wagon out of soft spots in the road through the fens had put a lot of muscle on him, and the sun had tanned him as dark as any Gypsy. In clothing given by some of the younger men and his long hair tied back in a tail, he didn't look much like Jonny Brede, and even less like a prince.

The border-station grew from a dot at the end of the long, straight causeway, to a tiny blob of brown, to a doll's house with doll-guards, to something her eyes would accept as a building. This flat expanse of fen was disorienting to someone used to forested hills. There were no trees, no points of reference—just an endless sea of man-high grass stretching in either direction. Forever, as far as eyes could determine.

The border-guards had plenty of time to see them coming and take up their stations in a leisurely manner. No surprise inspections at *this* post, assuming anyone ever bothered inspecting at all. And if there should ever be hostilities between Rayden and Birnam, it was improbable that anyone would ever try to bring an army along this way.

She would not have been at all surprised to see that the guards were slack and slovenly, but in fact, they were the very opposite. Brisk, business-like, they did a brief inspection of the wagon and the occupants and sent them on their way. In fact, there were only two jarring notes.

The first was that they were plainly looking for someone. The serjeant in charge consulted a piece of paper and kept glancing from it to them, as if comparing them with a set of notes.

The second was that one of the men did not come out at all. Rune caught a glimpse of him in the doorway; he was not wearing a uniform of Birnam's soldiers, and she thought she saw a glimpse of copper in his hand—and that was when she thought she heard a bit of that unsettling drone that came from the seeking-charm. She increased the humming that rattled her teeth unpleasantly and made her stomach churn, and concentrated very hard on creating a barrier between Kestrel and the rest of the world.

Finally the inspection was over, and the man she'd seen moved to the door again, just long enough to shake his head at the serjeant. She didn't get a good look at him, but she thought he had a face that was so ordinary that the fact in itself was remarkable. And it occurred to her that if *she* was creating a disguise, that was precisely how she would go about doing so.

It wasn't until after they were out of sight of the guard-house that she stopped her humming and dropped her magical defenses. By then, they were nearing the end of the causeway, and in the distance there was a haze of green that marked the blessed presence of trees.

Gwyna fanned herself with her hat, her hair curling from the heat and damp. "Blessed Lady, no wonder no one comes this way," she said faintly. "It's *fall,* for heaven's sake! Doesn't it ever cool off in there?"

"All that shallow water holds heat very well, Robin," Talaysen said from his place on the driver's bench. "The damp air makes it seem worse than it is. Just be glad we had that juice Vixen made up to rub on us, or we'd have been eaten alive by insects, and the mules with us."

"I want a bath," Rune said, sick to death of feeling sticky and hot. "I want a bath, and fresh food, and I *don't* want to have to hum that Shielding spell again. Or at least, not for a while."

Kestrel, silent until now, roused at that. "D-did you s-see the s-s-sorcerer? The one in the guardhouse?"

"I did," she replied grimly. "And he was looking for you. For us. He didn't catch that we were what he was looking for, though."

"We hope," Talaysen replied pessimistically.

Kestrel shook his head. "He d-didn't. Th-they w-wouldn't have l-let us by. Th-they'd have k-killed us."

"True, oh doubting Wren," Gwyna said. "They haven't hesitated for a moment, before this, even when Kestrel was nothing more than a harmless boy. They would have had no reason to hesitate now, and *every* reason to cut all four of us down. After all, who'd miss a few Gypsies?"

Talaysen's shoulders relaxed. "You're right," he admitted. "I probably worry too much. I think of all the sneaking things I might try, then assume someone else would do the same things I would. But there's no reason for them to let us into Birnam to kill us, when they could kill us with impunity anywhere."

"Well, the first hurdle is passed," Rune told him. "We're in Birnam. Now what?"

"Now we find a good place to camp and people who are willing to talk, in that order," Talaysen told them all, turning for a moment to meet their eyes, each in turn. "And remember: this is the enemy's home ground. We have to be much cleverer than he is. Quiet, elusive, and completely harmless as far as anyone can tell. We have to keep the enemy's eyes sliding right past us."

"And m-most of all," Kestrel added unexpectedly. "W-we have t-to find out wh-what he's up to. And *why.*"

"Exactly," Rune said. "Exactly. And maybe the why is more important than the what."

Kestrel met her eyes, and nodded.

But a week later they were no nearer to the answer to either question. They camped for the night in the shelter of an arm of a greater forest that stretched the length of Birnam, and set up a camp complete with a very welcome fire. Now that they were out of the marsh, it got cold at night, and the days of frost weren't far off. Rune sat and stared at the flames beside Talaysen, waiting for Kestrel and Robin to settle down too.

"If I were looking for a place to foment rebellion, I'd throw up my hands in despair," Talaysen said, as he leaned back against the tree trunk behind him. "These people are so contented it sounds like a tale. I find it all very hard to believe, except that the evidence is right before my eyes. The King can't have paid *everyone* off to pretend to contentment!"

Sional nodded, reluctantly. Rune held her peace. Both of the men had done their level best to find trouble; they had found nothing at all. No trouble, no discontent, just a placid, contented countryside. This was grazing land, full of sheep and dairy cattle, though it was not the hilly, stony ground of the downs they had left in Rayden. These hills were rich, covered with a lush grass that cattle thrived on; not only cattle, but every other grazing animal. And the people were as fat and contented as their cattle.

"I wish we could find someone to talk to that we knew we could trust," Talaysen said fretfully. "I don't like it. These people are like sheep; they're so happy with King Rolend that it makes no sense. *Everyone* has at least a little grievance against those in power!"

Rune fingered the elven-bracelet on her arm, then stopped and stared at it as an idea slowly formed in her mind. "Maybe we can find someone—at least, someone who's neutral. That is, if you're willing to trust the word of an elf."

Talaysen sat straight up, his laziness vanishing. "An *elf*? Where would we find an elf?"

"We call one," she told him, staring into his eyes from across the fire. "All four of us, together. I think that if we work as a group we're strong enough to manage it."

Talaysen licked his lips nervously; the other two watched her with speculation. "Wh-what did you have in m-mind?" Sional asked.

"There's a song we do, with the name of 'Elf-Call,' and now that I know about this magic we can do with music, I wonder just how close to the truth the title is," she said speculatively. "Especially since that friend of Peregrine's gave us these—"

She held up her wrist. Was it her imagination, or did the silver seem to shine with an especially brilliant gleam?

"So what do you intend us to do?" Talaysen asked, with one eyebrow raised.

"Well, we're in a forest, and there might be a Hill of elves around here," she replied, thinking as she spoke. "If we sang 'Elf-Call,' and thought about how we'd like someone to come talk to us—well, maybe someone would."

"We'd better hedge that in," Talaysen said grimly. "Put conditions around it, before we get ourselves in trouble. We'd better limit our 'wish' to elves nearby, and to elves who don't have anything particular they want to do tonight. I *don't* want to get another King angry with me!"

"Uhm—right." Neither did she, actually. One such experience was enough for a lifetime. "All right, how many conditions do we have?"

"Four, one for each of us," Gwyna supplied. "An elf who actually *knows* the answers to the questions we have, one who is willing to talk to humans, one who is nearby, and who would probably be amused by our ingenuity and audacity." She stood up. "Shall I get the instruments?"

Rune nodded. "Do that. I'll help."

"I'll ready the circle," Talaysen offered. "Kestrel, would you make sure we have enough wood for the fire? And food; we're all going to be hungry after this."

Sional nodded without speaking; while his stammer was much better, and improving daily, he preferred not to speak, if he could avoid it. Rune couldn't help wondering what that would do to his effectiveness as a leader.

Well, maybe they'll think he's just very wise, too wise to waste words.

She and Gwyna brought out the harp, Talaysen's round-drum, Gwyna's lute and Rune's fiddle. "Elf-Call" required a strong, hypnotic rhythm pattern, quite as complex as any of the instrumental parts. Talaysen was by far and away the best drummer of the four of them.

While Sional piled wood between his place in the circle and Gwyna's, she and Robin set up the instruments and tuned them. Talaysen positioned their cushions so that they would all be comfortable enough to concentrate, and so that each of them was precisely at a compass point. Talaysen had north; Rune east. Robin was in the south and Kestrel beside her in the west. Male faced female across the fire. This, they had worked out, was the best way to perform Bardic magic in a group. Much of what they were doing now was in the nature of experiment; in some things they had completely outstripped everything Peregrine had taught Master Wren, and in others, they had barely scratched the surface of those teachings.

They settled into their places, each taking up his instrument as if it was a weapon—

At least, that was the way Rune felt.

"I'll take the condition of 'friendly,' " she said. "That may be the hardest to find."

"Ah, 'nearby' for me," Gwyna decided. "I'm not as good as the rest of you are at this. That's going to be the easiest to concentrate on."

" 'Knowledge.' " Kestrel chose with as few words as possible.

"That leaves me with 'willing,' the compliment to 'friendly,' and probably just as difficult a condition to fill," Talaysen finished. "All right are we ready? In tune? One run-through to get the fingers working and the mind set, then we start concentrating. Remember, *listen* for the under-song, and match it. And on four—"

"Mortals. So ponderous."

The voice behind Rune was full of humor and amusement, but it startled her heart right out of her body; she jumped a good foot, and dragged her bow across her strings with a most unmusical squawk.

With a full-throated laugh, their visitor stepped between her and Talaysen into the circle of firelight, stole a cushion from the pile behind her back and dropped gracefully down onto it. If all she had seen was his costume, she'd have known him for elven; no human could have stitched those fanciful silken feathers of scarlet and gold, a tunic in the likeness of a phoenix. But the sharply pointed ears gave his race away as well, and the distinctly unhuman cast of his features as he turned to smile at her.

"You really should have learned by now that you've trained your *wills*," he scolded gently. "For creatures sensitive to magic, you need only be thinking about your needs and channeling the magic with the *thought* of the music. For mortals, perhaps, as earth-bound as you are, you will need a formal ceremony, or the music sung aloud. But not for us. Now, what is it that I can answer for you? In return, of course, you will come to the Hill to play for our dancing tonight."

"Of course," Talaysen said with grave courtesy. Rune couldn't speak; she was still trying to get her heart to take its proper place in her chest. "Thank you for responding to us."

"Oh, how could I not?" the elf laughed. "You are legend, after all! The mortals favored by the High King—you do realize, don't you, that one day you'll have to perform for *him*? And the favor he will ask for his protection might be a weighty one. Or—not. He has his whims, does the High King."

His smile was a bit malicious, but Talaysen simply shrugged. "Nothing comes without a price," he said philosophically. "But what we would ask of you is so little that you may consider it inconsequential."

"And that is?" The elf crossed his legs tailor-fashion, propped one elbow on his knee, and rested his chin on his hand.

"We want to know what the people of this land think of their King—and what they thought of the last one—"

"What, this lad's father?" At Kestrel's start, he laughed again. "Don't trouble your head, child, your secret is safe with us. While King Rolend has the wisdom to welcome us and leave us in peace, we never meddle in mortal politics. So, you wish the tale of King Rolend and his wicked brother, King Charlis, hmm?"

"Wicked brother?" Talaysen raised an eyebrow. "Is that an elven judgment, or the judgment of history as written by the victor?"

The fire popped and crackled, flaring up briefly, and reflecting from their visitor's eyes. "Both, actually." The elf sobered. "I hope the boy there has no great illusions about the quality of his parent—"

Kestrel shook his head. "H-hardly knew him."

"Good. Your father should never have been given power, and that is *our* judgment. He was ill-suited to it, being spoiled and accustomed to having his will in all things. I take it you have been asking discreet questions of the fat herds out there?" The elf nodded towards the road and the dairy farms beyond. "And they have been full of praise for King Rolend? They are right to be. Under his brother, they and their lands groaned beneath taxes so ruinous that their children went to bed hungry one night out of three—and that *here,* in the richest land in the Kingdom. And what did the wicked King Charlis spend their money on?"

He looked at Rune, who shrugged. "Armies?" she hazarded, shifting her position a little.

"They might have forgiven armies. No, he spent it on his own amusement. On exotic pleasure-slaves, on foods from far beyond his borders; on magical toys and rare beasts for his menagerie. On extravagant entertainments for himself and his court—caging the gardens under a great tent and heating it until the trees bloomed in midwinter, flooding the walled court with water and staging a battle of ships." The elf shook his head, and his long hair rippled with the motion. "He neglected his

Queen, who did not share his exotic tastes, and his son, who was an inconvenience. That neglect killed his Queen, and cost him the regard of that son. Oh, a few loved him. The Bardic Guild, whom he showered with gifts and gold. The men of the Church, whom he gave license to pursue anything not human as unholy and anathema—which meant ourselves, of course. The select courtiers he favored, and the Dukes and Sires, who he left to themselves, so that they could feud and rule their lands and people as they chose, and make riot of the countryside. But no one else."

"But King R-Rolend?" Kestrel asked. As far as Rune could tell, he wasn't the least upset by the unflattering description of his father.

"Ah, now that is interesting." The elf tapped the bridge of his nose with a long, graceful finger. "He is mixed, like most mortals; some bad, but most good. He remitted many of the taxes when he stole the throne, and spent what was left in the treasury restoring the lands. The *honest* Churchmen, whom he raised up after casting a-down the corrupt and proud, favor him and his policy of tolerance to those not human. His people love him, and love his son, who is so like the father that one must look for gray hairs to determine which is which." The elf smiled sardonically, and cast a glance at the bracelets Rune and Talaysen wore. "He has received certain—considerations—from my people. The courtiers no longer receiving rich gifts do not favor him. The corrupt men of the Church curse his name and lineage. The Sires, who must now bend to the laws of the land, grumble among themselves. And the Bardic Guild is—very quiet, lest he recall where so much of the kingdom's coin vanished. From time to time men gather and speak of a 'rightful King,' and talk of rebellion, but nothing comes of it."

"No one is as perfect as you claim King Rolend is," Talaysen said dryly.

"Did I say he was perfect?" The elf shrugged, and his wing-like eyebrows flew up towards his scalp. "He is mortal. No mortal is perfect. He hears the rumors of a 'rightful King,' and he fears, of course. He has had men put to death for simply whispering such words. With every year, he grows less flexible, less forgiving, harder. Power brings him temptations, and he does not always withstand them. But as Kings go, there have been worse, and these people give praise to their Sacrificed God daily for the one they have."

He stood up from his cushion, so smoothly Rune hardly knew he was doing so until he was looking down at them. "Have I given you all that you desire?"

Talaysen looked over at Kestrel, who nodded, slowly.

"Well, then. I have answered your invitation, now you must answer mine."

"Willingly," Talaysen said, getting to his feet. Rune and the others did the same, gathering up their instruments. She cast a nervous glance at the wagon and mules; the elf followed her glance and thoughts with the lightning-quick understanding of his kind.

"Never fear for your goods and beasts," he said—he didn't *quite* mock. "They will be guarded. The fire will be tended. Now, to the Hill, and the feast, and the dancing!"

Certainly. And allow me to get my little dig in at you and yours, my friend. "Gladly," she said sweetly, as they followed him into the forest. "And we promise to *stop* when you are weary."

His teeth gleaming back at her in a vulpine smile were all the answer he gave.

The King's private study seemed full of lurking shadows tonight, not all of them born of firelight. Some of them were born of unpleasant memory.

Why did I ever take the throne?

Rolend's temple throbbed, and nothing the Healer-Priests did for him would make the pain stop. One of them had the audacity to tell him that he was doing it to himself. He slumped over his desk and buried his head in his hands.

He was doing it to himself. Whatever the hell that was supposed to mean.

The question of why he had taken the crown was rhetorical, of course; he'd usurped the throne to keep his brother from looting the country to the point where the people would rise up and slaughter anyone with a drop of noble blood in his veins. And *that* had been nearer than anyone but he and a few choice advisors even guessed.

Shadows danced on the wall, shadows that mimed the conflict of men and their dreams. He had hoped to capture Prince Sional; the boy had been young, young enough, he had hoped, to be trained. Young enough even to come to understand what his uncle had done, and why, and forgive him one day?

Perhaps. Perhaps not. It didn't matter. The boy's tutor had taken him and fled. For years he had forgotten the child—had hoped, when he thought of him at all, that the boy had died. But then the rumors had started—that the old man had fled to the Bardic Guild in Rayden, that he had the boy with him. There was no telling what hate-filled lies he'd brought the child up on; the Bardic Guild hated him because there were no more rich plums falling into their laps from the Crown. Doubtless the Guild in Rayden had seen to it that the boy learned only to hate and fear his uncle, and to dream of the day when _he_ would take back the throne. Doubtless they had filled his head with idle ballads of foul usurpers and the noble heroes who threw them down.

Doubtless they had made him grateful to them for sheltering him— encouraged him to trust in _their_ word, and the words of those who waited for his return.

Doubtless he was now a handsome young puppet for their playing; everything a King should _look_ like, but nothing of substance. And certainly no more in his head but the insubstantial sugar-fluff of vanity and dreams.

The Bardic Guild was very, very good at creating the semblance of dreams.

Those Churchmen he trusted had warned him of this. When he heard their prophecies fulfilled, he acted. He dared be nothing less than ruthless, so he called upon the wizened, unhuman folk of the fens, the ones his people termed "goblins," and gave them Sional's hair, bidding them make him seeking-charms. And when the charms came back, wrapped in leaves, he gave them to his agents and told them to kill. His conscience had troubled him, but he had soothed it with visions of _who_ would use the boy for their own ends, if they found him. He would not give them that focus.

He had slept better, then, except for the times when he agonized about ordering the death of a mere child—he had been sure, despite the three times that the boy had escaped, that eventually they would find him and dispose of him. He had been utterly certain of that—until tonight.

Tonight the last of his agents had sent him word. One of their number was dead, killed by magic. The boy was gone. No one knew where, or how. The entire area had been combed and recombed, and not a trace of him could be found. The Gypsies he had last been with professed to know nothing of him, and had closed ranks against King Rolend's agents. There were forty or more of _them_, and only three of the agents; the men had wisely deemed it time to retreat.

My hold on the throne is shaky enough. Once my enemies find out the boy lives—and they will—they'll track him down. He may even come to them. Even if he's still innocent—even if by some miracle the Guild did not fill him full of hate for me, they will when they find him. And they'll use him. A boy of eighteen has no chance against them.

He groaned aloud, and then looked up as footsteps from the royal suite warned him of someone's approach from the private rooms. He had no fear that it might be an enemy; his guards were loyal and alert, and the only way into the suite besides this door was through a window. But he hoped that it wasn't his wife; she was as dear to him as his right hand, but he did not want to be soothed at the moment.

"Father?" His son hesitated on the threshold, just within the reach of the firelight, and Rolend sighed with relief. Victor was welcome; he wouldn't try to pretend that troubles would just go away if he ignored them. And he wouldn't try to *soothe* his father. "Father, I heard you—ah—"

"It's my head again, Victor," he replied. "It doesn't matter; I was going to call for you anyway."

"Ah." The young man—twenty, and mature for his age—walked on cat-quiet feet into his father's study, then settled into a chair beside Rolend's desk. Looking into his son's face was like looking into a time-reversing mirror. The same frank brown eyes under heavy brows, now knitted with concern—the same long nose, the same thin lips and rounded jaw. "Bad news, I take it?"

"They've lost him." No further explanation was needed; Rolend had kept his son advised of everything from the day he'd taken the crown. That accounted for his maturity, perhaps. Sometimes Rolend felt a pang of guilt for having robbed the boy of a carefree childhood, but at least if something happened to *him*, Victor would have the knowledge, the wits, and the skill to keep himself and his mother alive.

"Oh." Victor's expression darkened with unhappiness. "Father—"

"Speak your piece." Victor was about to say something he thought Rolend wouldn't like, but the King had never forbidden his son to speak his mind before and he wasn't about to start now.

"Father, I can't be sorry. I think you were wrong to try and—" The young man hesitated, choosing his words with care. "To try to—get rid of him—in the first place. He has never done anything to give you a moment of lost sleep—never even tried to come home! Why should he try to conspire against you now?"

Rolend sighed, and tried once more to make the boy see the whole truth of the situation. He didn't blame Victor for the way he felt; the boy remembered his cousin quite clearly, and when Victor thought of the assassins his father had sent out to Rayden, he probably pictured himself in Sional's place. "Even if he were as innocent as a babe, son, he's still a danger to me. As long as he lives, he can be used against me. And the hard fact is, he's not the cousin who you taught to ride and the one you gave your old pony to. He's probably been fed hate and bitter words with every meal, and he's probably looking forward to spitting you like a skewered capon, right beside me."

Victor shook his head stubbornly. "I can't believe that, father. Master Darian loved Queen Felice, and he *hated* Uncle Charlis for what he did to her. *He's* the one that took Sion, and he took him into *Rayden*, not to the Guild here! You *know* that no branch of the Guild really gives a clipped coin for what happens to another, so long as nothing happens to them! I can't believe that Master Darian would bring Sion up to be as twisted as you think."

"It doesn't matter, son," Rolend sighed. "It really doesn't matter. Once the Church and the Guild here find out he's alive, they'll have him. And once the Church mages have him—the dark ones, anyway—they'll strip his mind bare and put what *they* want in there."

Now Victor fell silent, and nodded. Reluctantly, but in agreement. He'd seen at first hand what a dark mage could do to someone's mind, when they'd taken back what had once been a faithful guard from those who had captured him. No matter what had been in there before, when the dark mage was done, there was nothing left of the original but the shell.

"I don't like it," he said, finally. "But I can't think what else you could do."

"Do you think *I* like it?" Rolend burst out. He lurched up out of his chair and began to pace in front of the fire. "I've ordered a murder—I ordered the murder of a *child*. I sent those agents out when the boy was fourteen—perhaps fifteen! But what else am I to do?" He sat down again, heavily; buried his face in his hands, and confessed to his son what he would not have told another living man, not even his Priest. "I hate what I've done, and I hate myself for ordering it. And sometimes I think that perhaps this is my punishment from God for trying to murder a child. Maybe I deserve to find myself facing Sional across a blade. But what else could I have done?"

"I don't know, Father," Victor whispered. "I don't know."

Rune took her turn at the reins, with everyone else closeted inside the wagon. The capital city of Kingstone loomed ahead of them, a huge place that had long ago spilled out past its walls. She wondered what was going on in Kestrel's mind right now. They were near the end of their goal, and still he had not decided what he wanted to do—

Well, if he has, he hasn't told us.

The elf hadn't lied, or even exaggerated. The people of Birnam were content with King Rolend on the throne, and were secure in the belief that his son would be just as good a ruler as his father.

Nor had the elf made any mistake in the quality of King Rolend's enemies. He had them, but they were all too often the kind of men— and a few women—who made Rune's skin crawl. Selfish, greedy, venial, power-hungry . . . there were some honest folk among them, people who felt that the "rightful King" should be on the throne. Frequently they voiced a legitimate concern: could a man who had ordered the murder of his own brother, for whatever reason, however good, remain uncorrupted himself? How long would it be before he found other reasons to order the deaths of those who opposed him—and how long would it be before merely disagreeing with him became "opposing" him?

Power corrupted; power made it easy to see what you wanted as something that was morally "right." Power made it easy to find excuses. Had King Rolend already fallen victim to the seductive magic that Power sang?

Those who voiced those questions hoped for the "lost prince" to return as someone who had not yet fallen victim to that seductive song. Rune couldn't help noticing that they used the same words in describing this mythical Sional as the Priests used in describing the Sacrificed God. . . .

But behind all these well-meaning and earnest folk, these dreamers and mystics, there were always the others. The powerful who had lost the power they craved, the Priests who had been toppled from thrones of their own, the pampered and indulged who had fallen from grace.

If they found Sional they'd make him over into *exactly* the image the others craved. The pure innocent.

The pure innocent fool, who'll say whatever they tell him to say. . . .

But there was one possible way that Sional could win back his throne without becoming a puppet. To take it the same way that his uncle had. Except that instead of soldiers, he'd have Bardic magic on his side. Magic that might even make it possible to avoid killing King Rolend and the cousin he vaguely remembered.

And if that was what he truly wanted—well, Rune would back him, and she suspected that Talaysen would, too. They'd had some long, late-night discussions about good government, about the seduction of power. Discussions that reminded her poignantly of the ones she'd had with Tonno.

They'd slipped into more than a dozen meetings of these purported enemies of the King, most of which were held on Church grounds, which somehow hadn't surprised her much. She and Talaysen had gotten fairly adept at rooting out who the malcontents were, convincing them to reveal what they knew with a focused thought and a few hummed phrases of music. They were even more adept at going to the meeting-places cloaked, and persuading the guards with their magic that they were trusted conspirators. Once or twice, they'd even put guards to sleep that way. This magic, though it left them weary, still represented a lot of power, and it was very tempting to use it for more than defense. And it was in one of those discussions of power that Rune had realized with a little shock how easy it was to just *use* it. Power was as seductive as anything else, and now she could see why others had succumbed to the lure of it, even in the Church. How close had she and the others come to that kind of attitude, where the end was more important than the means, and all that mattered was that the end be *theirs*?

That was when they'd had other discussions, about the kind of people who were behind the uneasy stirrings of unrest. Unspoken agreement had been reached about the use of magic, then, and the late-night sorties into the camps of the conspirators ended.

She knew that Talaysen was worried. However well-meaning Sion was, how could he stay out of the hands of those people for long once he revealed who and what he was? And if he somehow managed to, against all odds, how long would he be able to *hold* his throne? How long could he play their game without getting caught at it?

She sighed, and the mules flicked back their ears at the sound.

They'd turn against him eventually—unless he managed to play the Church against the nobles, and vice versa—and use the Guild to keep both sides stirred up.

She shook her head, and rubbed her temple. Her head ached from all the unresolved problems. A man as old as Rolend, and as experienced, could probably do just that. In fact, there were some signs that he had begun to play that very game, now that his country was stable and prosperous. Several of the little cabals they had visited had been very suspicious of outsiders, and not as agents from the King, but as agents from one of the *other* groups. That must surely be Rolend's work, at least in part.

But could Sional play that kind of game?

I don't know. Talaysen could—but Sional—he's no older than I am. And I don't think I could, not for long.

And there was one final concern—insignificant so far as the fate of a kingdom was concerned, but one that was tearing her heart in two.

Gwyna.

Gypsy Robin had fallen in love with Kestrel, and he with her. And now, the nearer they came to the palace and the throne, the more Gwyna looked at Kestrel and saw Prince Sional.

Prince Sional, who could not possibly marry even with a commoner, much less with a Gypsy.

Gwyna grieved—characteristically, in silence, hiding her grief behind a smile and a quick wit. But she mourned Kestrel's loss already. Rune felt it, and she could do nothing, for there was nothing she *could* do. Their worlds could not be reconciled. If Prince Sional took his throne, Kestrel died.

If Prince Sional failed in his attempt to take his throne, Kestrel died.

But if Kestrel was to live, *something* must be done about the assassins. And what *that* solution was, Rune had no idea.

It wasn't possible that the King would believe that Sional didn't want the throne. And even if he did, he must know that the moment his enemies discovered Sional's existence, they'd try to use him.

So even if Prince Sional gave up his throne, sooner or later, Kestrel would die.

If Talaysen had any plans on that score, he hadn't confided them to her.

So they had their answers now—but they weren't any help. And Rune couldn't keep herself from feeling that she was driving their little wagon into a maze with no escape.

CHAPTER TWENTY-FOUR

The wagon seemed the safest place to stay, all things considered. Rune found a travelers' inn that would let them pull their wagon in behind the stable for a fee. It was clean, shaded and secluded back there; evidently there were often travelers staying in their own conveyances, and the inn had set up this little yard for them. A little more money produced fodder and water for the mules, and gave them use of the inn bathhouse. While the others got their baths, she fetched some hot food from the inn's kitchen; they were all tired of their own limited cooking abilities. They returned about the same time she did, and she went for her wash.

By the time she got back, it was obvious from the tense atmosphere in the wagon that Kestrel was about to make a decision, and had been waiting for her to return. He and Gwyna sat on one bunk, not touching, and Talaysen sat facing them. The food was hardly touched, Gwyna was sitting very still and her face had no color at all, and Talaysen had not bothered to light the lamps.

Rune climbed into the wagon, lit the lamp beside the door herself and shut the door behind her. Kestrel cleared his throat self-consciously, and Gwyna jumped.

"I—I d-d-don't want the d-d-d-d-damn th-throne," he said, thickly. "I w-wouldn't b-be ha-ha-half the K-King m-my uncle is. I'm a g-good m-musician. I'd be a *ho-horrible* K-King!"

Gwyna made a curious little sound, half laugh, half sob. Talaysen let out the breath he'd been holding in, and Rune sat down on the bunk with a *thud*.

"I can't tell you how glad I am that you've decided that," Talaysen said, wiping his brow with the back of his hand. "I agree with you. But that just gives us another problem. How the hell are we going to keep you alive?" He reached for his mug of cider and took a long drink. Rune picked up a barely warm meat pie to nibble on. Their problems weren't over yet; in fact, as Talaysen had pointed out, they'd just begun.

"C-can't we k-keep d-doing what w-we have b-been?" Kestrel asked, after a moment of forlorn hesitation.

Rune and Talaysen both shook their heads, and Rune spoke first. "Sooner or later he's going to find another kind of seeking-charm, and give the *new* ones to his agents. We won't know how to counter them, and they'll find you again. And while we're waiting for that to happen, some of these other lunatics we've seen are going to realize you really are alive, and come looking for you themselves. Then what?"

She put the pie down; her appetite was entirely gone.

Sional set his mouth stubbornly and raised his chin. "I t-tell them t-to g-go t-to hell."

"And when they find a mage to change your mind for you?" Talaysen asked, gently. "Oh, don't shake your head, Kestrel. They've got mages, especially Church mages. And ask Gwyna how powerful some of them are. She spent several days as a bird—a real bird, with feathers—and for anyone who can turn a woman into a bird, taking over your mind would be a mere exercise." He closed his eyes for a moment. "What we've begun to learn—it's nothing compared to what happened to Gwyna. I think that one day, we *will* be powerful enough to protect you from all of them. Rune, especially; I've never heard of anyone facing down elves the way she did. But we aren't that strong yet."

"I—I d-d-d—" He paused, and flushed. "I h-have to t-talk t-to my uncle," he said, his eyes meeting first Rune's, then Gwyna's. "I d-don't kn-know what else t-t-to s-say. H-he w-wasn't always l-like th-this. M-m-maybe if I t-talk t-to him, he'll und-d-derstand. And l-leave m-me al-l-lone. Th-that's th-the only th-thing I c-can th-think of." His face twisted up, and he looked about to cry. "R-Robin, I l-l-l-"

She caught his hands in hers. "I know that," she replied. "I do, I know that. I love you. And if there's *any* way I can make you safe—"

"How are we going to get you to him?" Rune asked. "That's the first question—"

"I c-c-an remember th-the p-palace, g-g-good enough to d-draw a m-map," he said. "If Master Wr-wren c-can d-do what P-P-Peregrine d-did to m-make m-me remember—"

"I can," Talaysen said slowly. "Then what?"

"I f-find a w-way to t-talk t-to my uncle alone," Sion repeated. "In h-his b-bedroom, m-maybe. If I c-can t-talk t-to him alone, h-he'll *have* to believe me!"

"First problem," Rune pointed out. "Getting into the palace."

"You can leave that to me," Talaysen told her. "I've slipped into a fair number of buildings in my time. The easiest way in is as a servant, openly, since servants are invisible to those they serve."

"Next problem—what if your uncle won't believe you?" Gwyna was still pale, and she didn't look as if she liked this plan at all.

"Magic," Rune said. "At least we can keep him convinced long enough for us to get out of here and somewhere safer. After that—well, our influence is going to wear off after a while."

"I say we can fake Kestrel's death once we're well away," Talaysen said unexpectedly. "I faked my own, I ought to be able to do his!"

Slowly Gwyna's color came back, and she nodded. "That should work," she said, and grinned a little—a feeble grin, but it was there, and real. "If it makes him safe from his uncle and those greedy fools, that's the best solution of all."

Rune sighed with relief. *Good sense to the rescue,* she thought. "The only question I can see is, the fake won't hold forever—it didn't for Master Wren. Then what? We're right back at the beginning!"

Talaysen chuckled, much to her surprise, and evidently to Kestrel and Robin's as well, from the incredulous looks they gave him.

"Kestrel wasn't a famous Bardic Guild Master who refused to quit making music," he said. "That was my own fault. If I'd had the sense to become a carpenter or something, they'd never have found me again. Kestrel, on the other hand, is *not* going to go find himself another position as a prince, and no one but us knows he really *is* a Bard."

"All right," Rune said. "I can accept that. So now the question is— how to we get into the palace? Everything we want to do hinges on that. If we can't get in and convince Rolend long enough to give us that breathing space to fake a death, we can't make all this work."

"I've been thinking for the past week or so," Talaysen said slowly. "Trying to come up with a plan that would work whether Kestrel wanted the crown or not—and I think I've got one."

He couldn't possibly have said anything that would have had a better chance of capturing their attention. As one, they leaned forward to listen.

Talaysen nodded, as if he was satisfied. "Remember what I said about servants being invisible? Think about that—then remember what Rune and I can do to fog peoples' thoughts and confuse them. Combine those two factors, and I think we can get in ourselves, find a way into the private quarters, for all of us, and once we have that, we have everything. Now—here is what we do, to start. Or rather, what Rune and I do. . . ."

Rune scrubbed pots with a will, her hands deep in lukewarm, soapy water, and kept her head down with her hair straggling into her eyes. She hummed as she worked, concentrating on *not being noticed*. The girl whose clothes she had stolen was her same height and general build, but she looked *nothing* like the Bard—and while she could use magic to keep people from looking too closely at her, if she worked too hard at bespelling people now, she'd have no energy reserves for dealing with King Rolend later. The kitchen suffered from lack of light, though, which was to her advantage. Talaysen and the other two looked a great deal more like their own counterparts, but she was the weakest link here; there simply weren't too many women with Rune's inches.

Too bad she didn't have another job, Rune thought, with an idle corner of her mind, as she chipped away at some burnt-on porridge that had been left there since this morning. *When I left the Bear, I thought I'd left this behind me too. Ick. I hate pot-scrubbing.*

The stone-walled kitchen, too small for the number of people crowded into it, was ill-lit, with only two lanterns for the whole room, cramped and hot; in the inevitable confusion of dinner preparation it had been fairly simple for them to slip into the root-cellar to hide, then to lure individuals away and knock them out with a song of sleep. Their victims would be found in the cellar sometime tomorrow, but the chances of their being discovered before then was fairly remote—Talaysen had waited until the last foray after roots and onions was over before sending them to dreams. There was no reason for anyone to go down there now, and raw roots weren't high on anyone's list of edibles to steal. King Rolend's expert handling of his people extended to his kitchens and servants—they were all well-fed, and if they stole anything to munch on, it would be a bit of meat or a pastry, not a raw onion.

The pot-scrubbers ate first, even before the courtiers and high servants that the meal had been prepared for, so the only time anyone said anything to Rune and her fellow cleaners, it was about the dirty dishes. Other than that, they were left alone.

She freed a hand long enough to wipe sweat from her forehead and the back of her neck. The other three had taken the place of other cleaners and sweepers. Gwyna was two stations over, in charge of pewter mugs and utensils; Talaysen and Sional had been in charge of carrying garbage out to the compost-heaps. Now they waited, brooms in hand, for the signal that the nobles were finished eating. That was when they and the other cleaners would trot up the steps into the dining-hall—

That is, that's what they would do if they really *were* sweepers.

The lowest of the low, the invisibles. Dull-witted, just bright enough to clean up after others, not bright enough to be any danger to anyone. That was the kind of servant Talaysen had been looking for to impersonate. Someone no one in his right mind would ever suspect.

It wouldn't be long now. The great ovens were closed; the last of the pastry courses had been sent out. Servants were trickling out of the kitchen, in the opposite direction of the stair *they* were going to take; heading for the barn-like servants' hall and their own dinner. A gong sounded above, as Rune watched them out of the corner of her eye. That was the signal that dinner was over, and no one was lingering over food or wanted something else. The cooks gathered up the last of their utensils and dropped them in the nearest dishtub. The cleaners could now begin their job—

The chief cook and all her helpers swept out of the room, chattering and complaining, which left no one to oversee the kitchen itself. The drudges on dishwashing duty were normally half-wits at best, like Maeve; dull creatures that would do anything they'd been set at until the last dish was washed, or until they were stopped and set on something new. They wouldn't notice when Gwyna and Rune left.

Talaysen and Sional hung back from the rest of the sweepers; like the drudges, the sweepers weren't the brightest of folk. Probably no one would notice that they were missing until noses were counted—and then it would be assumed that the missing men were either off drinking filched wine, or tupping the missing drudges. When servants were missing, their superiors generally assumed "improper conduct" rather than anything sinister, and the lowlier the servant, the more likely that was. That was why Talaysen had chosen the ones he had; the ones thought to be shift-less, ne'er-do-wells. When he and Rune had made their earlier foray into the kitchens, there'd been trouble with those two men over laziness and slacking. For the kitchen steward, it would simply seem a repetition of the same, with the tall simpleton drawn into the group to make up a foursome.

Gwyna and Rune dropped what they'd been working on back into the dishtubs and joined the men. As they had figured, the other drudges didn't even look up from their work.

"Follow me," Talaysen whispered, propping his broom in an out-of-the-way corner full of shadows where it might not be seen for a while. Kestrel did the same. Rune wiped her hands on her apron, grateful that the King's concern for his servants extended to keeping them bathed and clean. Some of the drudges she'd seen in inn kitchens would have given them away by the reek of their stolen clothing, and there weren't any fleas to torment the conspirators with unexpected biting at precisely the wrong moment.

They followed Talaysen up a back stair—not quietly, but yawning and letting their feet scuff against the stairsteps, talking among themselves as if they had just finished dinner and were heading for bed. Talaysen first, followed by Kestrel—then Robin and Rune together, as if they were two best friends, whispering and giggling behind Kestrel's back. This part of the staircase was well and brightly lit, and it would have been impossible to slip past the guard posted at the entrance to the second floor—so they weren't even going to try. Instead, they were going to be as obvious as possible.

The guard on the landing of the second floor—the floor with the royal suite on it—nodded to each of the men, and winked slyly at the women. Rune giggled and hid her face behind her hand as if she was shy. Robin gave him a saucy wink right back, and wrinkled her nose at him.

He gave her a pinch as she went by; she squealed and slapped playfully at his hand—but once again, the King's care for choosing his servants came to the fore. He made no effort to follow them, and no effort to back up his flirtation except a verbal one.

"Saucy wench like you needs a man t' keep her warm o'nights," the guard said, with a grin, but without leaving his post. "Tell ye what, ye be tired of an empty bed, or cold around about midnight, ye come lookin' for Lerson, eh? By then I be off."

"I might," Gwyna replied smartly, not betraying by so much as a blink that the guard had just told them something they hadn't known—when the change of guard was. "Then again, I might *not!*"

"Ah," Lerson growled playfully, faking a swat at her with his halberd. "Get along with ye!"

She scampered up the stairs behind Rune, who'd waited for her. They giggled together all the way up to the next landing—which was unguarded—where they opened and closed the door twice, to make it seem as if they'd gone to their quarters.

But instead of leaving the stairs at the servants' floor, they continued quietly, carefully, to the top, and the seldom-used storage rooms for old furniture.

Talaysen had been here before them, in the guise of a dim-witted fellow assigned to carrying up barrels of summer clothing, and he had made certain that the door at the top of the stairs was well-oiled. Nevertheless, Rune held her breath as he opened it, they all filed through it, and he closed it behind them without a betraying creak.

The darkness in this hall was total, and the air was thick with dust. She suppressed a sneeze.

This part of the plan was pivotal. She waited as Talaysen felt his way past them; then took Gwyna's hand at his whispered command. Gwyna held Kestrel's hand, and Kestrel had hold of Talaysen. Careful questioning of palace servants on Talaysen's last visit had told him of the existence of a spiral stairway that went straight from the Royal Suite to the attics, with no doorways out onto any other floors. It was guarded—but by only one man. It came out in a linen closet at the end of the hall, and had been built so that bedding and furniture could be lowered down the hollow center of the stairs by means of a block and tackle. That had been Talaysen's second job here—lowering *down* the boxes of warming-pans and featherbeds for winter. With no landings in between, the stairs could be made as narrow as feasible and still be used by men to guide the burden up or down. There was, however, no railing. And the stairs were bound to be just as dark as these attics.

Talaysen found the door and opened it, a little at a time. It *did* creak, and Rune just hoped that the guard at the bottom would attribute the tiny squeaks as Talaysen moved it, bit by bit, to mice.

She tried not to think of the drop that awaited her if she missed her step, and waited until it was her turn to follow Gwyna into the stairway. She felt her way along the wall, and inched her foot over the doorframe. *There.* Her hand encountered the rough brickwork of the inside of the staircase, and her foot found the first step. And the abyss beyond it.

She pulled her foot back, and began the agonizingly slow progress down.

There was no way of telling time in the thick, stuffy darkness. She thought she heard Gwyna breathing just ahead of her, and the occasional scuff of a toe against the stone of the stair, but that was all. She couldn't have seen her hand if it was right in front of her face, rather than feeling the wall. She counted twenty steps—thirty—began to wonder if there was going to be an end to them. Maybe this was all a dream—or worse yet, maybe they were all really dead, killed protecting Kestrel, and this was their own private little hell, to descend this staircase forever and ever and never come to the bottom of it—

But before she managed to give herself a case of the horrors, her questing foot found only a flat surface, and she bumped into Gwyna.

Talaysen held his breath for a moment, and pressed his ear against the crack that marked the door into the linen closet. He heard nothing. *Good.*

The King never expected any serious threat from above—so the guard on this stair was really one of the guards that patrolled the hallway beyond. And if what he had been told—under the influence of a "trust me" spell on another of the guards—was true, the guard stationed here was more in case someone broke in through one of the windows. He never checked in with anyone, from the moment he went on station, to the moment he turned his watch over to the next guard.

Talaysen eased the door open, slowly—*this* one, thank God, had been better taken care of than the one above. It opened with scarcely a squeak. *Now* there was light; outlining the door at the other end of the closet. He motioned to the others to stay where they were, and eased himself up to kneel beside it, pressing his ear against the gap between door and frame.

There—there were the steps, slow, and steady, of the guard. He began to hum under his breath, timing his magic so that the guard would begin to feel sleepy just about when he reached the door to the linen closet.

The footsteps receded—then neared, and began to falter a little. He heard a yawn, quickly stifled, then another.

He hummed a little louder, concentrating with all his might. He would have to overcome the will of a stubborn, trained man—one who *knew* his duty was to stay awake, and would fight the magic, although he didn't know what he was fighting.

Another yawn; a stumble. A gasp—

The sound of a heavy body falling against the wall beside the door, and sliding to the floor.

He flung open the door, quickly, squinting against light that was painful after the darkness of the stairway. A man in guard-uniform sprawled untidily on the dark wooden floor, his brow creased as if he was still trying to fight off the effects of the spell. With a quick gesture, Talaysen summoned Kestrel, and together they pulled the guard into the closet.

In a few moments, as the women sent him deeper into sleep, they had stripped him of weapons, bound and gagged him, and muffled him in a pile of sheets and comforters. Talaysen took his sword; while he wasn't an expert, he knew the use of one. Kestrel, who hadn't held a sword since childhood, seized the knife. With a quick glance up and down the hall to be certain they were unobserved, they stole out and headed for the King's private study at the end of the suite—the one place they knew they had a chance of catching the King alone. That had been the last bit of information they'd gotten on their scouting foray. No one entered that room without Rolend's express permission, not even servants—and Rolend always went there directly after dinner.

It was a rather ordinary room, when they finally found it. Talaysen had been expecting something much grander; this place looked to have been a kind of heated storage closet before Rolend had taken it over. A single lantern burned on the desk; the rest of the light came from a cheerful blaze in the tiny fireplace. There were no windows; the walls were lined with bookshelves, and the only furniture was a scratched and dented desk, and three comfortable-looking chairs. It was an odd-shaped room as well, with a little niche behind the door, just large enough for all four of them to squeeze into without having the door hit them in the faces when it opened. Which was exactly what they did.

Rune tapped his shoulder once they were in place, with Kestrel, as the youngest and most agile, at the front of the group. He leaned over so that she could put her lips right up against his ear and whisper.

"It would be just our luck that he decided to go straight to bed, wouldn't it?" she said.

Silently he begged God and the Gypsy's Lady that Rune wouldn't prove to be a prophet.

They huddled there long enough for him, at least, to start feeling stiff and cramped, and more than long enough for him to begin to think about all the possible things that could go wrong with the plan. . . .

Footsteps.

They stiffened as one, and he held his breath, listening. Someone *was* coming this way; someone with the slow, heavy gait of the middle-aged—someone wearing men's boots—

Someone who saw no need to carry a candle; someone who knew there would be light and a fire waiting in here.

The door opened; closed again. Before them was the back of a large, powerful man. Kestrel struck, like his falcon-namesake.

Sheer youth and desperation gave him the reflexes to overwhelm a man who had fought for most of his life; he had a knife across his uncle's throat in a heartbeat, and Talaysen was right behind him. As the older man whirled, his first instinct to throw his attacker off, he found himself facing the point of one of his guard's swords in the hands of someone he didn't recognize.

"I wouldn't shout if I were you," Talaysen whispered quietly. "Between us, Sional and I can take out your throat before you could utter a single sound."

The man's eyes widened at Sional's name, and the blood drained from his face, leaving it pasty and white. His eyes went dead, and Talaysen sensed that he expected to die in the next few moments.

That, and the family resemblance to Sional, convinced him that they had the right man. That had been a possibility he hadn't mentioned to anyone—that someone else might be caught in their little trap.

"So, King Rolend, what have you got to say for yourself?" he continued, cruelly—*knowing* that he was being cruel, but with the memory of

Kestrel's own frightened face in the back of his mind. "And what do you have to say to your nephew?"

The man was brave, he had to give him that much. As Sional relaxed his grip a little, and Talaysen transferred the tip of his sword to the base of Rolend's throat and backed him up against the desk so that Sional could come to stand beside him, Rolend didn't beg, didn't plead. His eyes went to Sional, then back to Talaysen.

"Who are you with?" he said, harshly. "Whose pay are you in?"

Talaysen shook his head slightly. "That wasn't what I expected to hear," he chided. "You've been sending killers after this young man for years. Don't you think an explanation is in order?"

"Before I die, you mean?" Rolend drew himself up with as much dignity as a man with a sword at his throat could muster. "I did what I thought I had to do for the good of the country."

"For the good of the country—or for your own good?" Rune asked, challengingly, coming up behind Talaysen, her own knife in her hand. "They're not the same, and don't try to pretend they are."

The King's eyes widened in surprise, and he opened his mouth, as if to shout—

But nothing came out, and Talaysen heard Gwyna humming behind him. "Robin's got him silenced," Rune said, not taking her eyes off Rolend. She raised her chin with that defiant look Talaysen recognized from the past. "You can whisper if you want, King, but it won't do you any good to call for help."

His eyes were now as round as coins, and his lips formed a single word.

"Magic—"

"Y-y-you ought to kn-know, Uncle," Kestrel said bitterly. "Y-you s-set it on m-m-me enough!"

He moved closer, and strangely, Talaysen saw tears in his eyes.

"Wh-why, uncle?" he whispered in anguish. "Wh-why? I n-n-never d-d-did anything t-to you! V-V-Victor w-w-was th-the only f-f-friend I h-had, b-besides M-Master D-Darian!"

The young man's obvious anguish got through to Rolend as nothing else had. "I thought—I thought—you'd hate me—"

Rune was humming, and Talaysen recognized the "trust me" spell. So far the plan they'd made had fallen in place—to find Rolend alone, and somehow convince him, with the aid of magic if need be—to leave Kestrel in peace. But would it work? He sensed the King fighting the spell—and a man with a strong will could get himself clear of it.

Then a gleam of silver on the King's wrist suddenly caught his attention, and he remembered that the elf they had spoken with had mentioned something about the non-humans of Birnam now being under a sort of royal protection.

He held up his wrist to show the elven bracelet there, and once again, the King's eyes went round in surprise. The surprise at seeing the elven token made his resistance falter. "You asked me whose pay I was in," he said fiercely. "No—*not* the elves. And not the Church's, nor the Bardic Guild, nor the men you cast down out of power. And Sional is *not* here as my puppet! We—*we* are here beside him because he is our friend, for no more reason than that."

"We are under the protection of the High King of the elves," Rune said, breaking off her humming, and showing her own elven token. "Think on that a moment—think what that might mean if you harmed us—and *listen* to your nephew."

"I d-d-don't want th-the d-d-damned th-throne!" Sional hissed. "I d-d-don't w-want the c-c-crown! M-my F-Father w-w-was a d-d-damned f-f-*fool*, and y-y-you're a h-h-hundred *times* th-th-the King he w-w-was! W-w-will you c-c-call off y-your hounds? I j-just w-w-want t-t-to b-be left *alone*!"

"I can't do that—" the King faltered. "You know I can't. I can't let you go free—the moment someone discovers that you're alive—"

He's weakening. We have him off-balance, and he's weakening.

"Wait—" Talaysen said, and held up the bracelet again. "Remember this. Remember that we are mages. We could have killed you; we didn't. If we say we know of a way to take Sional out of the game completely, will you believe us and at least listen?"

The King nodded, slowly, and Talaysen took a chance and lowered the sword. Rolend sagged back against his desk, then made his way to the chair behind it, and collapsed into its embrace.

"L-listen to me, Uncle," Sional said. "I'm n-not a r-ruler. D-d-do you th-think for a m-minute that p-people w-would r-r-respect a m-man wh-who s-sounds l-like I d-d-do?" He laughed, a sound with no humor in it. "N-not even a Ch-church m-mage c-could m-make p-people b-believe I'm anyth-thing other th-than a s-s-simpleton!"

"Well—" Rolend looked uncertain.

"I've b-b-been a b-beggar, a th-thief, a sh-shit-s-s-sweeper. Th-think *those* are g-g-good qu-qualific-c-cations f-f-for a K-King?"

"I—"

Rune was humming again; since Kestrel seemed to have the situation well in hand, stutter and all, Talaysen joined her. The King had stopped resisting the spell—now if they could just get it to take—

"B-but I've s-s-seen wh-what y-you've d-d-done. I've b-b-been one of th-the p-p-people. Th-they'd r-rather a g-g-good ruler th-than a fool. T-tomorrow m-morning, y-you and I c-c-can g-g-go stand on F-Father's d-d-damned b-balcony and I'll r-r-renounce th-the throne." He took a deep breath. "As I am. S-s-stutter and all. S-s-so p-p-people c-can s-see I'm n-n-not s-s-some g-g-gilded p-prince out of a b-b-b-ballad."

The King was capitulating; Talaysen felt it. So did Sional. "L-let me g-g-go g-get V-V-Victor," he urged. "We c-c-can *all* t-t-talk about it. Even Aunt Fe-Fe-Fe—"

"No—please," Rolend said, closing his eyes and putting his hand to his head. "Not your Aunt Felice. She'll raise half the palace, and then she'll take you off and have you married to one of her ladies-in-waiting before the sun rose. Go get Victor; he's in the Rose Room." He looked each of the Bards in the eyes, in turn. "You're right. We should talk. Perhaps—"

Talaysen saw hope dawning in the King's eyes slowly, and the relief of seeing the end of a burden in sight.

"—perhaps we can make this work—"

Talaysen watched from the steps of the balcony over the Audience Square, standing with the other servants from the King's retinue, with one arm around Rune and one at Gwyna's waist. Sional was doing very well, though he doubted that anyone else was under that impression. The abdication ceremony took three times as long as expected, because of Sional's stutter. Enough witnesses were found to swear that this *was* the lost Prince to have convinced most people—and one of Rolend's mages clinched it by casting a spell over the young man that proved that hair known to have been Sional's had been his. As he had promised, he never changed from his rough working-man's garments, and if anyone had any notions of a romantic hero, he managed to crush them all.

Surely before he was through, a good portion of the people watching— and criers had gone through the city at dawn to ensure that the square was full—were going to be convinced he was a halfwit.

But how long will Rolend believe that he's no danger? That was the one doubt that kept nagging at him. While they remained, all would be well—but the spell they'd worked would fade in time—and then what? How long could they hope to keep Sional safe? Despite his earlier assurances, it was not easy to fake a death; would they have time to set up Kestrel's demise convincingly enough?

There were few cheers as Sional completed the ceremony, swearing on the holiest relics that could be found that neither he nor any of his progeny would ever return to claim the throne from Rolend and his heirs. But as Rolend and the Priest in charge of the ceremony turned to lead the way off the balcony, he stopped those few cheers with an upraised hand.

This wasn't in the plan! What was the boy up to?

"I kn-know that th-there are s-still p-people who w-won't believe m-my sw-sworn w-word," he said clearly, now looking down on the folk below, suddenly transformed from the bumpkin to something else entirely, despite the stutter. "S-s-so I'm g-going to m-make c-certain that n-no one c-can ever use m-me or m-mine ag-gainst my uncle."

He turned, ran down the stairs to the assembled servants, caught Gwyna's hand, and drew her up the stairs to the front of the balcony where everyone could see her. She looked around in confusion, not certain what he had in mind.

Rune squeezed Talaysen's hand in excitement, and he hugged her back. Was the boy about to do what he *thought*?

There were gasps from the people below, as they saw her in all her Gypsy finery. Gasps of outrage, mostly. Bad enough to have this bumpkin-prince on the royal balcony, but a Gypsy?

They were about to get an even bigger shock.

"G-Gwyna Kravelen, Free B-Bard, will you m-marry me?" he asked, his voice carrying clearly to the edge of the square.

The silence could have been cut and eaten.

"I—oh—I—" she stammered just as badly as *he* had, and Rune giggled.

"I'll t-take that for a yes," he said, and looked over her head at the Priest who had conducted the abdication ceremony. "Y-you've w-w-witnessed it, Father," he continued, and kissed her.

At that, Victor could no longer restrain himself. He was already half delirious at having his cousin back—and discovering that Sional *didn't* hate them. Now he lost every shred of dignity.

He gave a wild whoop of joy, threw his hat into the air, where it sailed up and landed on the roof—and threw his arms around the both of them.

Then the cheers began.

CHAPTER TWENTY-FIVE

"So, who's the happiest man in Birnam today?" Rune asked Talaysen, as they showered the mob of mixed Gypsy and servant children under the balcony with candy to keep them out of mischief.

"Kestrel?" Talaysen hazarded. She shook her head, and pitched sweets to some of the littlest who weren't getting any.

"Almost, but not quite," she told him. "He will be when he gets Robin out of here, but the celebrating is wearing thin. Weddings are really for women, anyway." She giggled. "I think the happiest *person,* not only in Birnam but in all of Alanda, is the Queen. She not only got to plan an entire wedding, she got to play mother to the groom *and* the bride!"

"The King?" Talaysen guessed. "No—probably not. When he offered to host this wedding he never guessed that every Gypsy within three kingdoms was going to descend on him." They both laughed, though Rune couldn't help but think he deserved at least that much anxiety, after all those years of pain that he'd given Kestrel. But there would be bills coming to the Palace for pilfered goods and stolen livestock for the next month at least. And stodgy little Birnam would never be the same again. They'd been invaded by an army of folk who had no ties but to the road, no responsibilities but to each other, and they had been set on their ears by the experience.

"It isn't me," the Bard said, after a moment.

"Really?" She raised an eyebrow at him. "You got what *you* wanted. Free Bards have exactly the same privileges as Guild Bards in Birnam—"

He nodded, and sighed. "But to get that, I had to agree to be Laurel Bard to the throne."

That had been to keep the Bardic Guild out of making mischief with the King's enemies. Now there would be an information network every-where—the Free Bards and the Gypsies who remained—that the Church, the Guild, and the disgruntled Sires couldn't touch or even trace.

She *tsked* at him, and threw another handful of candy. "Poor Master Wren. Property, the title of Sire—I know people who'd kill for that—"

"I had that all and gave it up," he reminded her. "Never mind. We can go scandalize Birnam some more, and build a Free Bard school in the manor—how does that sound?"

"Good," she told him contentedly. "But you still haven't answered my question."

"I give up," he said, and popped a candy in her mouth.

"Victor," she said, tucking it into her cheek.

"Why Victor?" That answer had clearly surprised him.

"First—he got his cousin back. Second—his mother got to have a wedding, and *he* didn't have to get married. She'll probably leave him alone for a few more months. Third—the King isn't a child-killing ogre anymore, and I don't think he's in any danger of making that grave a moral decision again—and last, but by no means least—Prince Victor has been *very* popular with our Gypsy friends." She laughed at the look on his face. "He's their favorite *gejo* at the moment. He has gotten *quite* an education, I promise you! Frankly, I'm surprised he can walk of a morning!"

"So that's why he's—" Talaysen broke off what he was going to say, much to her disappointment. "Look—here comes the wagon!"

A brand new and beautifully painted wagon, the King's wedding gift to the happy couple, driven by Raven and drawn by two glossy black mares, clattered across the cobblestones of the courtyard. Nightingale balanced on the top, scattering coppers to all sides, which had the effect of sending the children out of harm's way, shrieking with delight.

Raven pulled them up smartly, and just below the balcony, the great doors flew open. Kestrel and Robin, dressed head-to-toe in the Gypsy finery in which—to the utter scandal of the court—they had been wedded, ran hand-in-hand out onto the cobblestones. Raven jumped down off the driver's bench as Nightingale slid from the top. Raven handed Gwyna up, holding her long enough for a hearty kiss, then turned the reins over to Kestrel.

Kestrel jumped up onto the driver's bench and took his place beside Gwyna. He had proved to be a good driver, with Raven to tutor him, and the mares responded to his touch on the reins promptly. As he got the spirited mares turned, the thunder of hooves rang out from the entrance to the courtyard.

A flood of of Gypsy riders poured in, each one trying to outdo the other in stunt-riding.

They swirled around the wagon, and as Kestrel cracked the whip above the horses' heads, they surrounded it, whooping at the tops of their lungs.

And just as the entire equipage started to pull out, escort and all, another rider appeared at the far side of the courtyard, from the direction of the royal stables.

He let out a wild war-cry that caught even the Gypsies' attention, and plunged towards them.

"Is that—*Victor*?" Talaysen said, incredulously.

It was. Dressed—not quite in wild Gypsy regalia, but certainly in the brightest gear his closet had to offer. He spurred his horse towards the wedding cortege with another wild cry, circled the group three times, and cried, "Come *on*! The road won't wait forever!"

He pounded off towards the courtyard gate, the clear leader of the pack, with the rest of the mob streaming along behind him, wagon in their midst.

The stunned silence that filled the courtyard was more eloquent than words. Finally Talaysen shook his head.

"Poor Birnam," he sighed. "Poor, stiff-necked Birnam. We've unmade their King, turned their Princes into Gypsies, their lands into a haven for ne'er-do-well vagabonds, elves, and Free Bards, and stolen the power from their Bardic Guild. What's left?"

"Oh," she said, thinking of a little secret she had just shared with Gwyna. *He'll find out about it in a month or two. I think he'll like being a father*. "I'll think of something. Trust me."

"And you'll probably manage to surprise me as much as we've surprised Birnam," he chuckled.

She just smiled, and waved to the vanishing Gypsies.